UNIDENTIFIED FUNNY OBJECTS 9

EDITED BY ALEX SHVARTSMAN

PUBLISHED BY:

UFO Publishing

1685 E 15th St.

Brooklyn, NY 11229

www.ufopub.com

Trade paperback ISBN: 978-1-951064-03-7

Cover art: Tomasz Maronski

Typesetting & interior design: Alex Shvartsman

Graphics design: Jay O'Connell

Logo design: Martin Dare

Copyeditor: Elektra Hammond

Associate editors: Frank Dutkiewicz, James A. Miller, Tarryn Thomas

Visit us on the web
www.ufopub.com

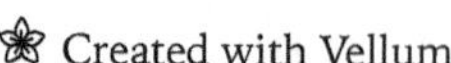 Created with Vellum

CONTENTS

FOREWORD

Alex Shvartsman

The Unidentified Funny Objects series is back with another volume packed with original stories that span the range from funny to unidentifiable and—if I did my job right—are often both.

From overworked fairies distributing swords of destiny to the unwilling, to alien yeti slackers, to North Pole elves figuring out what to do after Santa kicks the bucket, there's no shortage of amusing and unusual ideas in the twenty-one stories collected herein.

For over a decade now this series has featured the best contemporary writers of humorous speculative fiction in the field, as well as introducing exciting newcomers. Many of those newcomers have since gone on to become best-selling and award-winning authors in their own right. It won't surprise me one bit if some of the neo-pros you meet in this volume will follow in those same footsteps.

Happy reading!

THE HERO OF SMALL THINGS

Amanda Saville

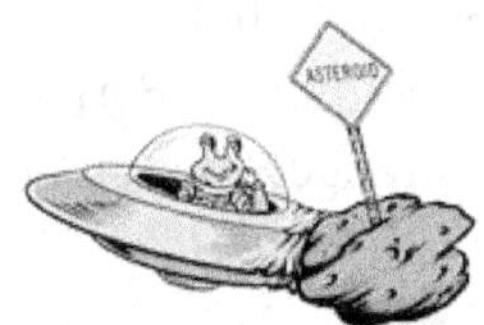

Destiny came to me one evening as an arm rising out of my tea, brandishing a sword.

I really should've been more surprised. It's not every day a whole-ass flippin' broadsword pops out of your Earl Grey, but I had just finished a long workweek and had saved up just enough energy to sit on the couch and stare at the wall. The best I could muster at that moment was a flinch and an "Oh no. Now what?"

The arm could've belonged to a child, just small enough to fit in my cup and clad in gauzy, shimmery fabric, probably spun out of moonbeams or babies' dreams or the feeling you get when you look at pictures of kittens. The sword could've come straight off a sword-and-sorcery movie set, with a red scabbard and a glittering jeweled hilt that easily cost more than my annual income. It was a sword built for heroes, magical quests, riddles at bridges, and maybe a daring rescue or two for flavor.

I've done exactly one heroic thing in my life, and that was rescuing my cat, Mr. Sparkleboots. He, by the way, had done the sensible thing and left the living room when the sword appeared.

The arm waggled the sword in my direction, impatient. "Hello?" I ventured. Yes, I spoke to my tea. My evening had flown completely off the rails, but I wasn't about to make it worse by being rude.

My tea bubbled in a huff, and a voice rose from its depths, high-pitched and singsong. It sounded like it could belong to a princess frolicking in the woods if it wasn't so indignant. "Are you going to take this sword or not?"

My mind flailed for an answer. "Sorry, I'm not in the habit of accepting swords from strangers, let alone one swimming in my tea."

The arm considered a moment. "Is that what I'm in?"

"Earl Grey to be precise."

My tea burbled, almost sighing. "Oh, bother. I should be in a proper lake or a fountain or something. Okay. Not to worry, I will explain everything, even if I have to do it from a … teacup." The voice took on the sort of gravity I associate with graduation ceremonies. "Child of nobility, take up this sword given unto you by destiny, and fulfill your role as savior."

Only some professional residue left over from work kept me from bursting out laughing. "I'm pretty sure you've got the wrong … cup?"

My tea fell silent, and the arm shifted, as if its owner was wrangling something one-handed. "Dana Collins … apartment … summer solstice … no, this is the correct place and time. This sword is yours. Use it to save the world."

"Hang on. First off, there's not a drop of noble blood in me, and even if there was it's not like it would magically make me competent. Second off, outside of *The Princess Bride* and using wrapping paper tubes as lightsabers, I don't know the first thing about using a sword. Third, save the friggin' world?"

"Of course!" my tea replied. "It's your destiny. You are bound to do great things."

I suppressed a shudder and shook my head. "Oh, no. No.

Nope, sorry. The last time someone said that it cost me three years of my life and a lot of college debt. Magic or not, I'm not going down that path again."

"But the world needs you! You're supposed to take the sword!" My tea was frothing.

"And what exactly am I supposed to do with it? Kill a dictator? Defeat a hundred-foot marshmallow man? Maim climate change? Slay hunger?"

My tea stilled. "I'm … not exactly sure to be honest. Your assignment only says 'savior,' and I know those are particularly rare, so I have to assume you're destined for something no less than world saving. You would have to get in contact with dispatch for the details and … well … they're not the easiest to get ahold of."

Great. "Look—what's your name?"

The hand holding the sword cocked like a question mark. "You may call me Nim."

"Okay. Look, Nim, I'm flattered someone out there thinks I'm not wasted potential, but to be honest, I don't want big expectations laid on my shoulders. Besides, I've read enough books to know when someone shows up claiming you're the Chosen One your life is about to get much worse. Now, would you please leave me alone?"

The tea fizzed in preparation for another protest, then stilled. "Of course. How silly of me. You require time to consider your destiny before you accept it. A slight delay shouldn't affect my metrics. I will return."

I thought that was the end of it when my cup held only tea once again. As much as I love Earl Grey, I wasn't gonna drink it after a sword and an arm had been floating in it. I went to the kitchen to dump it out, and set to work on battling the mountain of dishes in my sink. My mind was drifting to hospital beds and neglected paintbrushes and disappointed faces when that same sword burst out of my sink, spraying me with dishwater.

"Are you freaking kidding me?" I said. Mr. Sparkleboots, who was attempting to forget the whole affair with a nap on one of the chairs, offered his own opinions alongside mine.

"Have you reconsidered and prepared yourself for destiny?" Nim asked, her tone reminiscent of my mother's when I overslept.

Suds and ghosts of breakfasts past spattered my shirt. "You've been gone all of five minutes," I said, wiping off a cereal remnant. "What happened to 'later'?"

"Technically it is later. Sil just cut our allotted time in half. I have no time for formalities, I have to finish this delivery."

Nim's arm was bigger now, closer to an adult than a child. That probably meant she grew to fit whatever she was coming out of, with a horrifying follow-up thought. "Wait. You appear out of anything watery, don't you? Sinks? Bathtubs? ... toilets?"

Her arm reared backwards in shock. "Stars and strings, what do you think I am, a voyeur? Never mind. My numbers are dropping the longer you delay."

"I told you, I don't want it."

"It's supposed to go to you." There was a tightness in her voice that reminded me of a strained rubber band. I knew that tone all too well. "If you don't take it I can't mark this delivery as complete, and if I can't finish in time I'll get docked performance points, and then—"

"Hang on, hang on. This is all sounding—can you come out of there? I feel really strange talking to your arm, and you've got to be getting tired."

Nim's arm trembled with the weight of the sword. "I am perfectly fine where I am."

"Liar. Come on. We can talk better face-to-face."

Her arm sagged. "Oh, very well."

A moment later, and Nim stood in my kitchen, remarkably dry and reminiscent of a box of crayons melted on a book of fairy tales, all multicolored diaphanous robes and sparkling eyes and ultramarine hair hanging in loops and curls. She held herself pin straight as she clutched the sword. I exchanged a glance with Mr. Sparkleboots, who gave me a dubious side eye.

"Do you want to sit down?" I asked, indicating a spare chair.

Nim squared her shoulders. "No, thank you. I would like to finish this delivery and be on my way."

"Yeah, about that. You're telling me if I don't take this sword, you're going to have a bad performance review?"

Her lip trembled, then set again. "An 'advisory meeting to investigate and correct flaws to avoid dismissal.'"

I rubbed my temples. I didn't want Nim getting filleted by her management on my account, especially when she looked ready to shatter in my kitchen, but I still didn't want that damn sword. Every time I looked at it, old voices materialized in my head.

Don't worry, we have Dana in our group, we're sure to get an A!

I would normally advise against such a heavy course load, but your grades are exemplary. I'm sure you can handle it.

We really need you on this project. It's only for a few weeks, and you're so good at your job. You can juggle both, right?

Dana's the best, she's always ready to lend a hand.

I pushed the voices away. "Can't you explain to, your … manager? Supervisor? Can't you explain to whoever you answer to that I'm passing on this?"

"Sil?" Nim swayed where she stood. "Oh no, I couldn't. You don't understand what she's like. Every fate not delivered perfectly is a failure. She reduces completion goals and punishes us when we don't deliver under time. She—" Nim stumbled backwards, the sword clanging against the counter and jostling my tea boxes.

I reached out to steady her. "Okay. You're sitting. Now." Sword debate could wait. The last thing I needed was to explain to an EMT why someone probably made of rainbows had passed out in my kitchen.

The ethereal fairy creature sat at my kitchen table, setting the sword on the floor beside her as casually as a purse. Mr. Sparkleboots grumbled a little at our unexpected guest, turning over and making a show of napping. "This is so shameful," Nim said, "I have so many fates to deliver and I'm just sitting here! I can hear them piling up. I can hear Sil yelling already …"

"It won't kill you to rest for a few minutes," I said, flipping the switch on my kettle. "You look like hell."

Nim's shoulders sagged. "I can't remember the last time I had a break. Must be decades now. There's never the time. I think we're supposed to get breaks, but it's all efficiency and meeting number goals and maximizing production. There's always the chance we'll get to move up into management if we do well enough. Then you get actual time off, so they say."

"Geez, I thought mandatory overtime was bad. That sounds pretty shitty."

Nim shrugged. "This is the job I'm destined to do. There's nothing else out there for me."

"Come on, I can't believe that."

"It's the truth!" She accepted a cup from me, peppermint tea in my Jackson Pollock mug. "This is what I've trained to do ever since I was a spark. Who am I to question fate? Which brings me back to—"

"Nope, not going there right now. You're off the clock."

Nim balled her fists into pastel-riot hair. "You don't understand. I don't have a choice. I have to do this."

"No, I get it," I said, an edge creeping into my voice unbidden. "I understand what it's like for someone to give you a label. Mine was 'smart.' My teachers decided who I was before I had a chance to figure it out for myself. I really liked to draw, but that didn't matter. 'You're so good with numbers.' 'Don't you want to have a real job when you grow up?' 'An artist? You'll be a burden on your parents.' 'But you have so much potential!'

Eventually I stopped saying anything. After all, they were the adults.

"So I did everything I was told and more. By university I was losing weight. I couldn't sleep. I passed out leaving advanced biochemistry and woke up in a hospital bed. And you know what I was worried about? Whether or not I'd still be able to turn in my homework on time."

Recognition resonated in Nim's eyes. Maybe at some point she'd found herself unconscious in a birdbath, exhaustion her only crime. "That must have been hard on you."

"It sure as hell made me reprioritize things. I had been saying 'yes' to everyone my entire life. It took me a long time to figure out how to say 'no.' I'm saying 'no' here. I'm fed up with everyone telling me what to do with myself." I took a breath, forcing out old feelings. "Sorry, I shouldn't be unloading on you like this. You're just the messenger, and you've got your own shit to deal with."

Nim stared into her tea. "No, it's alright. I've never had the chance to think about it from the recipient's side. There's always so many deliveries." She closed her eyes. "I can't keep up with it. It's like I'm drowning."

"Maybe you should quit, then."

"What? Oh no, I couldn't. There's so much—and then what would—where would I go—what would everyone think?"

I thought of the disappointment in my parents' eyes when I told them I was quitting school. How hard it was to find a job that paid enough to keep me in soup and cat kibble. It sucked, but it was better than unraveling. "You have to think about what's best for you, not what everyone else thinks."

For a moment I wondered if she might actually consider it. Then she stood up. "No, I can't. It's best if I just keep my head down and do my job. I have to go. I need to report in—"

Nim's cup seemed to explode as a hand holding an accounts

ledger emerged, followed by another melted crayon fairy creature, all cotton-candy pinks and ink-stain reds.

Nim cringed. "Sil!"

Nim's supervisor stared at her, an eight-foot-tall tower in the middle of my little kitchen. Even Mr. Sparkleboots decided to avoid getting involved, opting to hide under a chair and snarl instead.

"Here you are," Sil said. "We have a backup of fates as long as the Styx and it's not getting any shorter. Care to explain to me why you are having tea and cookies with your recipient instead of working?"

"I'm sorry," Nim stammered. "She wouldn't accept the fate right away, and I've tried to explain it's her destiny, but she has a good reason not to, and—"

"Enough. I don't have time to hear the excuses of a mere courier. Your job is to deliver, not to debate philosophy. Never in my centuries have I seen such a lazy worker. Absolutely no consideration for the job you were born to do."

"But I'm so tired—"

"If we don't get back on schedule do you know what will happen? Fines. Loss of credibility. My superiors will come down on my head. You don't want that, do you?"

"Well, no, I—"

"I didn't think so." Sil's voice took on a honeyed quality that set my teeth on edge. "But we can salvage this. Potentially. If you finish this delivery, come back, and *focus*, perhaps we can sort out the backlog. I expect in a couple of years we'll have this all sorted out."

Nim's gaze flicked to me, even as she twisted her hands into knots. Then, they stilled. "No."

Sil's eyebrows raised. "No?"

"I can't do this anymore. If I'm so lazy, find someone else to do the job."

I'm not sure who was more shocked, me or Sil. "You don't get to choose your job," Sil said. "This is your role in life."

"It doesn't have to be! I … quit!"

Sil looked like she would erupt into a pillar of pink flame, her nails elongating into claws. "You are coming back with me right now or—"

I'd heard enough. I placed myself between Nim and Sil. "No. Hell no. Hell no to all of this. She said no." I might as well have sprung from the ground covered in dirt, the way Sil looked at me.

"So, you're the anomaly." She sneered, and for a moment I felt reduced to a data point. "Pity I can't reprimand you as well. Regulations and all. If you had simply accepted your fate in the first place we wouldn't have this problem."

I folded my arms, hoping it would give me enough backbone to do this. Saying "no" to a fairy creature was one thing. Actively courting a fight with an irate fairy creature with neon-pink claws was another. I shoved down the urge to run. "Not everyone wants to put up with what they're 'supposed' to do. The world needs to be saved a hundred times over, and you expect it to all fall down to me?"

Sil scoffed and batted away my protest. "Oh, come now, you're exaggerating." She glared at Nim. "Did you tell her that?"

Nim shifted. "All my assignment said was 'savior.'"

"I suppose I should expect this. Logistics is full of incompetents." Sil turned to me. "Not saving the world, per se, just defeating a tyrant. You mortals do that every week, don't you?"

Seriously? "Oh sure, and then we stop an asteroid before breakfast. That's giving us way too much credit. Hell, getting a group of people to save a sliver of the world is hard enough. I'd rather focus on things I can actually achieve."

I caught a glimpse of Mr. Sparkleboots under the chair, ears flat against his head, snarling in the face of Madam Fairy Middle Management. He was so much more now than the scrawny, dirty, mewling ball of grime and fluff I had rescued from a dumpster. My brain shifted. *Things I can achieve. Small things. Like saving a cat. Or helping someone leave a shitty job.*

The sword had been pushed half-under the table in the commotion. I reached down and grasped the sword's surprisingly light hilt. There was no tingling of fate-magic, no voice in my head telling me I was now bound to the sword, but I wasn't taking any chances. I thought as hard as I could at it. *Look, you. I'm not committing to anything, but I need you now to pull this off. The moment I catch you trying to toy with my life I'm throwing you in the nearest lake. Got it?* There was no response, so I figured it was okay with those terms.

Thinking of bluffing swordsmen and intimidation through sheer gumption, I withdrew the blade and pointed it at Sil, striking a pose I hoped she wouldn't realize I'd pulled from a movie. "So. Funny thing I just noticed. You said I'm supposed to defeat a tyrant, right?"

Sil stared down the blade, turning an interesting shade of purple. "What? You can't possibly—"

"Why not? You didn't specify who, and I think you're acting pretty damn tyrannical." I smiled a challenge. "Care to test my fate?"

She sputtered and stammered with all the energy of a broken tea kettle, shrinking before my eyes. "This is outrageous! I have never been so insulted in all my life! You know nothing about meeting numbers or employee management. Me? A tyrant? If we weren't so behind I would teach you a lesson here and now, regulations be damned!" She glared at Nim. "Is this some kind of a joke? You'd let her interpret her fate that way?"

Nim stood beside me, straighter. "I'm only a courier. I deliver fates, I don't debate philosophy."

I wiggled the blade, expectant. "Well?"

I couldn't tell if Sil wanted to strangle Nim or run as far away as possible. She settled for giving Nim a withering glare.

"Don't bother coming back. There won't be a job waiting for you. Let's see how long you last fateless." She vanished in a puff of dust, the lingering scent of rotten lemons on the air.

It took me a moment to realize she was gone. I dropped my arm, careful to not let the blade smash into anything. "Damn, I didn't expect that to work."

"She backed down," Nim murmured, slumping into a chair. "She never backs down." Her brow furrowed. "Can I be fired if I've already quit?"

"Does it matter?" I asked as I struggled to wrangle the sword back into its sheath. Having had precisely thirty seconds of sword experience, it was harder than it looked.

"Thank you," Nim said, turning away. "I should've been able to do that by myself."

I shook my head. "It's hard as hell to say 'no' sometimes."

"I suppose so." Nim stiffened. "Stars and strings, what did I just do? I … quit? I quit. I quit! I quit? Oh no, I quit … and I didn't even file paperwork!"

I looked at Mr. Sparkleboots, who had emerged to survey the damage. He had no kitty wisdom for how to handle a panicking fairy creature beyond a slow blink I interpreted as "Not my problem, dude."

I put the sword on the table and turned to face her, placing myself in the days after my hospital stay, fighting past the smell of antiseptic and the chasm of reckoning my life. What did past-me do? "Don't focus on that right now. This feels like a lot, but try to look forward. You're getting out. That takes a lot of guts."

Nim hid her head in her hands, her shoulders shaking. "But no one's ever done this before. I don't know what I'm going to do. I've never done anything but deliver fates."

"That doesn't mean it's the only thing you can do," I said. "Haven't you ever heard of transferrable skills? You clearly can figure your way around. You know a thing or two about logistics. You're damned persistent. You can do a lot with that. Give yourself a little more credit." A thought came to mind. "You're not one of those fairy types who turns to dust or sunbeams if you stay here more than a day, are you?"

Nim glared at me. "You presume I'm made of spun sugar? I'll have you know I've endured icy water and boiling fire to complete my deliveries."

I smiled. "Okay, so why not try staying here and finding a job on this side of the teacup? You could even crash here for a bit, at least until you've got your feet back under you."

"What? Oh, no, I couldn't. Not after the nuisance I've been."

I shrugged. "I've had worse roommates. Besides, I feel a little responsible for all of this."

Nim's jaw worked. "I don't know what to say. No one's ever done anything like that for me before. How would I repay you?"

"Let's start with sharing chores, and we can figure out the rest later. If nothing else, you'll be a better conversationalist than Mr. Sparkleboots."

Mr. Sparkleboots responded with a blink and an ear twitch.

"Don't worry, he'll warm up to you. Eventually."

Nim stared at the cup where Sil had emerged, fiddling with a fold of her rainbow dress. "Staying here, finding a new job ... it's terrifying. But maybe a little thrilling too. Sil said I was fate-less. Maybe I could make my own fate."

My thoughts drifted back to my room, to the sketchbooks I never had the heart to throw away, the pencils, the paints. Why hadn't I picked them back up after I quit school? Work kept me really busy, of course. No. That's an easy excuse. I could face down a supernatural middle manager, but I was too scared to go back to the thing I loved? Bullshit. Quitting my job now would be an ass move, especially if I was going to have a roommate that needed support for a bit, but I could find time to draw again. The thought made my stomach wriggle and roil. I guess sometimes you have to be brave to say "yes," too.

"So, now there's just this," I said, holding up the sword. "I didn't really just accept some world-saving fate, did I?"

Nim frowned. "I don't know. It could be you just fulfilled it. But maybe not. I wonder, if you're given a fate, and you refuse it, was that what was supposed to happen all along?"

I cringed. "Oh no, no circular philosophical questions, they make my head hurt. I guess there are worse things than having a cool sword, though. I bet it'll cut a mean loaf of bread."

Nim's mouth dropped open. "You're not seriously suggesting using an instrument of fate to make sandwiches, are you?"

I smiled at my new roommate. "Why not? It's mine now. I'm going to do whatever the hell I want with it."

Amanda Saville lives in North Carolina with her partner, a small herd of plants, and her yarn stash. She does science during the day, and at night she spins stories from collections of multicolored threads, peculiar sights, and the occasional misheard word. Her fiction has been previously published in *Mermaids Monthly* and elsewhere. Find her on Twitter @acsaville.

CHAI NOON

Esther Friesner

The lanky stranger pushed his chair away from the saloon poker table and tilted the brim of his black ten-gallon hat a little farther down over his eyebrows. "'Fraid this game's getting a mite too rich for my blood, ma'am," he said, smiling fit to charm the birds out of the trees.

The young woman across the table gave him the slightest of smiles in return. His wiles were wasted on her, not least because there were neither birds nor trees on the world dubbed Minyiun Ten. As if to confirm this, from outside the saloon came the unnerving shriek of a rodandelion, one of a variety of mobile, carnivorous plants that made a walk in the park on this planet *not* a walk in any sort of park lacking the qualifier *Jurassic*.

"What's the hurry, cowboy?" she asked lightly. "I know I've been on a winning streak, but you don't see any of *these* gents wanting to cut and run, do you?" The four other men at the table all chuckled.

"Well, ma'am, seems to me like they're old friends of yours. Might be they don't want to do nothin' that'd hurt your feelings. Me, I'm just driftin' through this town, lookin' for a little human company. Can't say I found it. I ain't hardly exchanged more'n ten, fifteen words with any of y'all since I sat in, so I've got no reason to stay."

"You came to this game for *conversation?*" The big-bellied fellow to the lady's left guffawed as he shuffled the cards for the next hand. "I don't think that's *all* you were hoping for when you came in here and saw our Goldie, now was it?"

Quick as a startled lizard, the stranger's grin turned threatening. The line of his jaw hardened. "Nope."

"You really expect us to believe—?"

"Yep."

"Are you pulling my—?"

"Nope." And then: "Next words outa your mouth better say you're sorry for not takin' me at my word, mister." The stranger touched the breast pocket of his checkered shirt ever so delicately. The small oblong shape inside began to hum, low and menacing, and a couple of tiny red lights winked on, easily seen through the fabric.

"Hey, hey, all right, calm down, nothing personal!" The fat man set down the deck and spread his hands in a peacemaking gesture. "You just want to *talk* to a fine-looking gal like our Goldie, right? Make yourself a nice recollection to take with you when you're back out on the trail? Sure, we savvy. Here, take my seat, talk up a storm." He got up and offered his chair with a bow worthy of a swanky headwaiter.

"Keep your seat … friend." The stranger rose from his own chair. "It ain't like I'll be staying, unless—" His gaze passed over the faces of the other players. "—the conversation's gonna pick up soon?"

"That's all you want?" The dealer reoccupied his place. "I think we can provide." He went back to shuffling the deck.

"Maybe," said the player at the drifter's left elbow.

"Maybe?" the drifter echoed.

"Well, you ain't seen fit to share *your* name with us, stranger."

"Hush up now, Micah," said the dealer. "He'll share his name when he's ready. Meanwhile he's been willing enough to share his money." He winked at the drifter. "I'll tell you this, mister, hereabouts it's considered a privilege to go up against Miz Goldie in a friendly game of Hadassah hold 'em. Fact is, we got us a tradition about that. Ain't I right, boys?"

The other men nodded energetically and chorused in agreement: *"Tradition!"*

The fat man gave them an approving look. "Yeah, we say the man who can take the pot three times straight when Goldie's in the game gets to drink free for the week. How's that for a conversation starter *and* a memory, eh? The rest of us pay the winner's way."

"*I* pay his way," Goldie corrected him.

"Tempting, but three straight wins is a mighty tall order, especially now I've seen how *you* play, ma'am." The stranger's lips curved up slightly. "The only bet I'll make now is that you don't have to buy the drinks much, if ever."

"You got that right." The dealer let loose another belly laugh. The rest of the players joined in. "That's what'll make your memory so … memorable. *If* you've got the *chutzpah* to get back into the game and the luck to win."

Goldie giggled behind her towering stacks of chips. "Don't pay any mind to what Abner says, stranger. He runs the *Forward Upward*, our local newspaper; he tells lies for a living. I'm just a simple country girl looking for a little entertainment on a planet where there's not much of that. There's no big tradition about playing against me, neither; just an agreement that a measly *two* straight wins gets you *one* night of free drinks. So, what do you say? Try your luck with one last hand before you go. I promise we'll get a real conversation going, too."

"More'n chit-chat?" the stranger said, his interest piqued. "I'll be movin' on to other worlds soon—boss-lady's orders— and I hoped to learn more 'bout this'n 'fore I left."

"You work for a woman?" It was Goldie's turn to show keen interest.

"Yep."

"Care to tell us more, friend?" the newspaperman asked so attentively that the ghost of a centuries-vanished pad and pen hovered in the air before him.

A single "Nope" from the drifter banished *that* phantom fossil in a nanosecond.

"Let the man be, Abner," Goldie said. "He wants a conversation, not an interview." She rested her elbows on the table, interlaced her fingers, and leaned in. "I'll do my best to oblige you with that, Mister—?" Her voice trailed off, waiting for him to fill in the blank with his name.

"You can call me Lem, ma'am."

"Huh," said Abner. "My great-grandpa was called Lemuel. Not a handle you hear much, these days. Family name?"

"You might say that."

"Well then, Lemuel," said Goldie, "you have my guarantee that whether you win or lose, you'll come away from this table having learned a lot about Minyiun Ten. Mostly about why I hate the place, but that'll still be educational for you."

"'Educational'? Yeah, that's our Goldie." The weasel-faced specimen to Lem's right snickered. "Bet she could teach a man *lots* of—"

The knife *thunked* into the tabletop so quickly, it seemed to have come out of thin air. Weasel-face yelped. His blood was staining the green baize, but only from the tiniest of cuts where the expertly aimed blade had nicked the side of his thumb.

"What was that you were saying, Jebediah?" Goldie asked sweetly.

"Nothin', Miz Goldie, nothin' at all, sorry, nope, thanks fer askin', nothin'." He sucked his wound quietly, eyes bright with terrified respect.

"Dog my cats." The stranger clicked his tongue in quiet

admiration. "You sure are a dab hand with that frog-sticker, ma'am."

"Not everybody can afford a nifty little zap-dealer like you've got there, mister." She indicated his shirt pocket where the two red lights were still glowing, although not as fiercely as before.

"That's true, ma'am. A man's gotta tote a weapon with a deal of firepower when he's ridin' the range on his own, wouldn't you agree? It might not kill a man, but it'll sure 'nuff give him second thoughts." He tapped his pocket again and the red lights went out. "I'd still like to know where a sugar lump like you picked up a skill like that." He nodded at the knife, its bloodied point still embedded in the table.

Goldie shrugged her shoulders expressively. "I'm a quick study. When life teaches me a lesson, I take notes. Sit yourself down again and I might let you copy 'em," she said with a sassy wink. "Oh, and pass that … *frog-sticker* back here, if you don't mind."

The drifter complied. "Well, now, if you can master that bit o' cutlery-chuckin' so easy, you must've been a little firecracker when it came to gettin' you some reg'lar schoolin'."

"'Schooling'?" She laughed the word away. "I got enough of *that* stuff by the time I was ten."

"You quit on book-learnin' that young?" The stranger leaned forward, his eyes narrowing.

"Eh. I stuck it out long enough to pick up my diploma."

"How come, if you didn't fancy it?" He looked at her even more intently.

"I've got no use for it, but some folks are suckers for that kinda thing. A diploma could be my ticket out of this dump someday."

"That so?" Now the stranger was back in his seat, counting out fresh bills onto the table, gesturing for more chips so he could rejoin the game. "How d'you figure?"

Goldie leaned her chin on one hand while the fat man dealt

the cards. "I was born on this planet because my father got shipped here by his company, but I don't mean to die here. You see, Lem, I'm what my folks'd call a prize package."

"Heh. I'm not sayin' they're wrong, ma'am, but ain't that something 'most all good parents'd say about their little girls?"

"Oh, I'm not talking about my *parents*." Goldie fidgeted with her knife. "I mean my folks; my people. You know, the *tribe*?" Seeing his blank look, she specified. "Jews, honey."

"Well, you don't say." The stranger's grin grew wider.

Goldie's offhand attitude vanished. Her scowl was dark and menacing as a twister. "No, *you* don't say." The knife twirled until it was a blur between her fingers. "You *don't* say 'Funny, you don't look Jewish.' You *don't* make any of the ugly jokes. And if I hear one damn sentence out of you that includes the word 'space-laser'—"

The steel flashed across the table a second time, lodging itself in the block of cheese set there to keep the poker players fed.

The stranger's grin vanished. He looked immediately penitent. "Yes'm. No'm. Never crossed my mind."

"Let's keep it that way." Goldie retrieved her little toy, pinched the edge clean, and delicately popped the tidbit of cheese into her mouth before tucking the blade back out of sight. "Now, are we playing poker or what?"

The game proceeded smartly, with Goldie keeping up a friendly patter about the many ways Minyiun Ten was one hell of a great world to be *from*, and the sooner, the better. At one point, she nodded at the neighboring table where a tattered and dusty figure slumped senseless, one hand still clutching a glass, the other arm hugging a half-empty bottle.

"See that sorry souse there?" she said with an arch smile. "He's on the road most folks here take if they want to escape this world. But not me! I'm going to do it *smart*."

As conversations went, it was fairly one-sided, Lem only

contributing a question or two about Goldie's upbringing, family, and occupations other than poker. For the most part he kept his eyes on his cards, although sometimes he squinted hard at her over the top of his hand. The outcome of the game was nothing new: he lost, she won, except now there was no more talk of him leaving. He stayed and played while she talked on and on.

"You really are a caution, Miss Goldie," said a dapper fellow who had the seat to Goldie's right. "I'd like to say it's always a pleasure losing to a fine-looking young lady like you, but my line of work doesn't care for losing at all."

Goldie was amused. "You make it sound like you're a starforce general, Mr. Leonidas, when we all know you're a traveling salesman."

Mr. Leonidas stroked his thin moustache with a fingertip and arched one eyebrow rakishly. "Thank you for not saying I'm *just* a salesman, kind lady. You are as gracious as you are lovely."

She laughed off the compliment. "You're a salesman and a good one, but you can leave off trying to sell *me* a load of soft soap."

"Tsk. I see that my calling is far too humble for your tastes, fair damsel." He put on an expression of ham-it-up sorrow.

"Ha! Interstellar drummers lead such fabulous lives, the rest of us mud-bound folks die of envy whenever we think of all the worlds you've seen!"

"You know, you *could* share my travels, my dear," the salesman said in a wheedling voice. "I have offered you honorable matrimony many times."

"And I have counter-offered a conditional yes just as many times," Goldie replied. "Or have you conveniently forgotten that?" It was obvious this exchange was a bit of a game to her, and she was enjoying it.

Mr. Leonidas looked genuinely pained. "But I don't understand, dear girl: why can't we marry without me converting to your faith?"

"Why do I need to defend my stance as if I'd set some unreasonable obstacle in your path, sir?" Goldie countered. "I'm willing to give any decent man a bit of leeway when it comes to courting me, but some conditions are firm: I will not marry outside of my religion."

The salesman's eyebrows rose. "Begging your pardon, Miss Goldie, but *why*? I must say that I've encountered more than a few ladies and gents of the Hebrew persuasion who've been more than amenable to finding a mate outside of the … *tribe*, did you call it?"

Goldie drew herself up straight and proud. "I'm sure you have." She shifted a bit in her seat so that her back was slightly turned to him. "And now you've met one who isn't … *amenable*, did you call it?"

"I suppose your parents are behind this," the salesman said sadly. "I can only hope that one day you'll find it in your better interests to recall that you're a fully grown woman and assert your independence."

Goldie's face went cold. You could almost hear a mounting rumble of thunder. "Yes, my parents *would* have it so, sir, but how *dare* you presume I'm just parroting them? I know my own mind!"

A flood of apologies spilled from the salesman's lips. Then he added, "All right, I'll allow it's your choice, but I can't say I see why you're so set on this. Might make it hard for you to find a feller, is all I mean. I'm widely traveled and, with all due respect, I haven't found your people to be exactly thick on the ground anywhere."

The lady shrugged. "Never have been. So what? It hasn't held us back from finding one another, even in the new Dizasporal."

"Diaspora." The lanky stranger spoke softly. "I think the word you're after's diaspora, ma'am."

Goldie's eyes widened as she stared at the drifter. "Are *you* also—?" she began.

He chuckled. "Couldn't honestly say so, though some more liberal folks might. But I've spent more'n enough time with Jewish folk to've picked up a thing or two."

With Goldie's focus taken from him, the salesman turned testy. "Damn—*darned* if I see the sense in your decision, little lady. I've sat at this table with you days aplenty to know just how much you want to get off this mudball and see some livelier worlds. I can give you that! I make a good living, I'm a go-getter, I've got a tidy sum set by, and I mean to earn even more in the years to come. I can give you everything you want and then some!"

"Everything but meeting my requirement," Goldie retorted. "Now it's my turn to ask *you*: Why? Why won't you become one of us? Scared of—?" She pantomimed a pair of snipping scissors.

Mr. Leonidas turned crimson, but denied this with a shake of his head.

"Then what *is* your reason? I'll understand if you say you've got a hard bond to your own faith, but if that were so, why court *me*? Why not find one of your own persuasion? I'm sure they're a lot—" Her lips twisted into a wry smile. "—*thicker on the ground* than my kin."

"Well, what d'you say to that, Leonidas?" the fat man asked, leaning in. "You'd rather be married to the Good Book than to this sugarplum?" His laughter boomed through the saloon.

"Er … nope." Mr. Leonidas rubbed the back of his head and was suddenly fascinated by the ceiling. "You see, Miss Goldie, it's like this: when I first left home I sort of maybe in a way might've made a little something like, um, a promise to my dear old white-haired mother that I'd pretty much or nearly so always stick to—"

Goldie laughed. "My, my, Mr. Leonidas, *what* a sentence! Don't worry: I won't question *your* independence just because you want to truckle to your mama's ord—I mean, honor her wishes. Well!" She flounced back in her chair. "Now we've settled matters between us, I *strongly* suggest we return to our game."

Her thwarted swain muttered something under his breath. Goldie's eyes flashed. "What was that, Mr. Leonidas? 'Old maid' did you say?" The hidden knife was suddenly in evidence once more. She used it to slice herself a fresh sliver of cheese, but her gaze at the offending salesman was steelier than the blade. "How kind of you to fret over my fate. No need. You see, our people may be scattered, but all the more reason for us to maintain ways of making connections." She lowered her lashes demurely, as if she were more adept at wielding a lace fan than a keen knife. "I needn't ask if you're a betting man, so I'll just offer you a wager straight out: in less than thirty days by this world's rotation I'll bet you that I'll be well married and on my way to a glorious future somewhere far, far from here."

The salesman considered this. "How much?"

A sum was named and accepted. It was hefty enough to attract the rapacious attention of the other poker players, with the exception of Lem and Abner, the newspaperman. This being reality, and thus devoid of ghostly pens and pads, the latter took a Brainbit NoteScribe™ from his waistcoat pocket and secured the terms of the wager along with the details, personal and financial, of the participants. As he entered the last dab of data, he smiled at the drifter and said, "Can't blame you for not wanting a piece of this, friend. I think I recognize your sort: no more roots'n a billiard ball. You'll likely be long gone, not bound to return to this world when this wager comes to be settled up."

"Nope." The stranger shook his head slowly. "Not that at all. It's more what you might call a question of, uh, ethics."

"What, you promised your mama you wouldn't gamble?"

Abner cast a sardonic eye over the poker table and the few chips remaining in the drifter's possession. "'Cause if that's so, you're not exactly doing a consistent job of keeping your word."

"Nope," the stranger repeated. "It's on account of how I already know how this is gonna play out."

"That so?" One of Abner's brows rose. "How do you figure that?"

"'Cuz I'm the one who's gonna say the word that guarantees the outcome. Fact is—" He raised one finger as if pointing at something fascinating on the ceiling. The first joint was glowing icy blue. "—I'm about to say that word long about now."

With that, Lem stuck the glowing fingertip in his ear and said in a clear, precise voice, "Sheila Maisel."

"*Who* the hell—?" the editor demanded, as the rest of the poker party stared dumbfounded at the stranger. Before he could answer, their astonishment was brought up short by the sound of a high-pitched whine from just outside the saloon, an abrupt flash of white brilliance typical of top-tier transportation devices, and a gust of frigid air that thrust the swinging doors apart as a short, sturdy woman strode through. She was dressed much like the drifter, from boots to hat-brim, except her headgear was dusty rose with a lace band. Her entrance sent the whole saloon into a loud mutter of speculation. Even the drunk at the next table belched in a questioning tone.

"Good day to you," the woman said affably as Lem ceded his seat to her. "Do pardon the interruption. I promise not to take up too much of your valuable time. Or mine."

The men rose and executed a variety of awkward bows to the newcomer. Abner took it upon himself to be spokesman for the group.

"Howdy, Miz Maisel. You're mighty welcome here."

"Miz who?" The newcomer tilted her head in puzzlement. "No, no; my name is Roth. My boy there—" She indicated the drifter. "—has a bit of a stumbling block when it comes to Yiddish."

"Then what *was* he say—?" Micah began, only to be cut off by Abner.

"Well, whatever your name or business here, Miz Roth, you're still welcome. Can we offer you some refreshment?"

The woman's plump cheeks dimpled. "I wouldn't say no to a nosh." As Abner hurried to consult the barman about providing something nourishing for this unexpected guest, she added: "It's been a long day and I must say, I'm not looking forward to this part of it."

A murmur of puzzlement circled the table, excepting only Lem, who stood yardstick-straight and solemn beside the woman's chair.

A look of concern creased Goldie's brow. "Pardon me, ma'am, but are you Lemuel's boss-lady? Because if you didn't want him gambling, I've got to say that it wasn't his fault, entirely. He looked kinda lonesome when he came in here, so the boys and I invited him to play and he was just too polite to turn us down. Please don't fire him over this!"

"Well, aren't you the nicest little thing." The woman's laugh rivaled Abner's for heartiness. "No, child, I'm not about to ditch one of my best workers; not when he came here following my orders. Oh, but where are my manners?" She tapped an unseen device in her shirt pocket, but instead of the telltale red glow of a zap-dealer, the motion triggered the mid-air image of an antique calling card with the name *Shayna Roth* in solitary glory, surrounded by ornate curlicues. "And you must be Goldie, the Mandelbaums' girl."

"How did you—?" Goldie's shocked response was interrupted as the newspaper editor stepped in to set a laden plate and a glass of beer before Miz Roth.

"Eat hearty, ma'am," Abner said jovially. "You won't find a better mess of pickled pigs' feet on this planet."

"Sorry, mister." Shayna pushed the plate away. "I'm a stranger to these parts." Seeing Abner's embarrassment, she said, "No harm done; you couldn't know. I'll just have some of this lovely cheese."

Lem's hand shot out to grab her wrist as she reached for the cheese plate. "You don't want to be eatin' that, ma'am," he said.

"And why not?"

"It's all in my report."

So saying, he dropped to one knee and removed his nose.

Everyone in the saloon gasped, but that was small potato knishes next to their reaction when Miz Roth plucked a slim object from an inner coat pocket, removed what looked like an ordinary cotton swab from its sanitary wrapper, and dipped it deep into the drifter's gaping nasal cavity. She drew it out, dripping luminous green goo, and popped it into her mouth like the all-day sucker from hell.

The resulting ruckus of saloon patrons and employees stampeding from the premises, retching noisily in the sawdust, or hitting the floor in a dead faint, took some time to die down. The only bystander who offered no reaction was the by-sprawling sot, who merely grunted and hugged his bottle all the more closely.

When relative peace returned, the population of the poker table had dwindled to Abner, Goldie, and Mr. Leonidas. Micah was cowering behind the bar, and weasel-faced Jebediah had fled nearly as fast as an actual weasel.

Shayna shifted the stick in her mouth from side to side, the action making her look rather bovine. Lem tapped his nose back into place and spoke softly: "See what I mean, Miz Roth?"

"So I do, Lem." She removed the stick and studied the now-bare tip. "What a shame. I had such high hopes for this one. So many of these youngsters look good when they're just a data set, but reality—" She sighed. "Reality's another story." She looked at Goldie, her eyes filled with regret. "I'm sorry, my dear

Miss Mandelbaum, but Lem used quite the right term for you when he summoned me. You are indeed a Sheila Mais—tsk, his mispronunciation seems to be catching— I mean a *schlimazel*. A misfortune magnet, if you will. Although in your case, bad luck didn't just *happen* to you; you made it for yourself."

"What are you talking about?" Goldie demanded. "How do you know my name when I've never laid eyes on you in my life?"

"Oh goodness, I know you have a dreadfully low opinion of education, but can't you *read* my—?" The older woman glanced up at the image of her calling card, still shimmering above the table. "Oops," she said, abashed. "Please forgive me; it's an old software fail, incomplete image glitch, happens all the time. I simply *must* get around to updating it, but meanwhile—" She took the databox from her pocket and rapped it sharply against the table. The hovering projection flickered, flared, and suddenly displayed its full message:

Shayna Roth

Matchmaker

Brides Groomed

Grooms Bridled

Satisfaction Guaranteed

(No refunds)

Goldie was horrified. "Matchma—? You mean you're the *shadchen* my parents hired? The one arranging my marriage to what's-his-name Finkelstein?"

Shayna sighed again. "Joshua Finkelstein."

"*Josh* Finkelstein?" Mr. Leonidas was visibly impressed. "The heir to the Finkelstein slivovitz fortune?" He glowered at Goldie. "You knew you were going to marry him when you set up that bet! You were going to be rolling in shekels, but you just couldn't resist playing us for suckers, could you?"

Before Goldie could reply, Shayna headed her off at the verbal pass. "Whatever she said or did to you, mister, it doesn't much matter now: the match is off." The shadchen turned to her employee and patted him on the back. "His report really does say it all: a disdain for education, a problematic affinity for gambling, a tendency toward *un*toward flirtatiousness, and worst of all—" She pointed to the cheese plate. "—using a *fleischechdig* knife on dairy? Fine by some, but not the Finkelsteins."

"Fleischa-whuh?" Mr. Leonidas was at a loss.

"An implement to be used on meat," Shayna explained. "*Only* meat. Or in this case, a blade that drew human blood, which is a whole 'nother level of *trayf*." She noted the salesman's even more bewildered look and repeated: "Trayf. Not kosher. Ritually unclean. Big, big nope for some of us Jews. In this case, the family of Miss Mandelbaum's formerly intended spouse."

"But *why*?" Goldie began to panic. "Why disqualify me, just like that? Do not forsake me, oh my shadchen! I can change. I *will* change! Won't you let me have a second chance? Look, Yom Kippur is coming. If the Day of Atonement can give me a clean slate, can't you? And I'll *keep* it clean, I swear! I'll follow all the laws of *kashruth*! I'll quit gambling!" (Her remaining poker playmates smothered their chuckles. Poorly.) "I'll even take night courses and—" She took a deep, shuddering breath. "—read improving literature. But please, *please* don't tell the Finkel—"

"There, there, *ketsaleh*." Shayna cut off Goldie's plea as kindly as she could. "You're young and pretty. You still have possibilities, and I'll do what I can to find you another nice boy. Maybe not as nice as Joshie Finkelstein—" She patted the desperate girl's hand with maternal tenderness. "—but even the best chef can't make matzoh balls from sawdust."

Goldie's eyes hardened with cold rage. She jerked away from the matchmaker so sharply that she stumbled backward and nearly fell. Lem caught and steadied her. "There now, Miz

Goldie," he said in a soothing voice. "This ain't the end of the world, you know."

"Shut up!" Goldie snapped, turning on him. "This is all your fault! You ruined my life, worming your way into the game just so you could spy on me, snitch on me, you—you—"

Eyes flaring and teeth clenched in fury, she seized Lem's collar with one hand and darted the other into his shirt pocket. In an instant she had the little zap-dealer jammed into the side of his neck. She glared defiantly at Shayna Roth.

"Now you listen to me, lady," she snarled. "Here's what you're going to do: you're going to get on the same comm system this varmint used to fetch you here and you'll get in touch with the Finkelsteins. *Now.* You tell them I'm *so* good for their boy Josh that maybe he's not good enough for me, and you're going to tie up every last loose end about the marriage contract so tight that not even a greased-up lawyer could slither out of it. Savvy?"

The matchmaker remained unnervingly calm. "And if I don't?"

"Then I'm dealing your boy Lem the dead man's hand, no matter what happens to me after." Goldie's tough mask began to fracture a bit around the edges and she blinked furiously, struggling against tears. "I can't stand wasting another minute of my life in this hellhole, praying for you or some other shadchen to find me a fresh offworld marriage prospect. I want Joshua Finkelstein, and I'm not going to wait one day longer to get him!" She took a sharp breath and regained her self-control. "So, what'll it be?"

"Go ahead, girlie." Shayna Roth steepled her fingers. "Deal."

"*Deal?*" Goldie stared. "You don't care if I *kill* him?"

"Meh. An empty threat. Zap-dealers can't kill."

"Sure, not *humans.* But for him, one shot right *here*—" She pressed the device harder to the drifter's neck. "—and your robot sidekick is history. Can't be restored or rebooted or *anything.* Fried beyond repair. I know! My father's company *makes* robots. Maybe you're not someone who's emotionally attached to your mecha*mensch,* but I bet you're pretty damn fond of your finances. Buying a new model this realistic would cost you—"

"He's not a robot."

"Oh?" Goldie gave a short, brittle laugh. "He's a human who just happens to have a pop-off nose and a glowing green brain you can poke with a—?"

"Pfft!" The matchmaker dismissed Goldie's words with a wave of her hand. "The proof is in the zapping. What are you waiting for?" She leaned forward. "I call."

"Miz Roth, take it back, I'm begging you," Abner cried. "I've played cards with that gal long enough to know you *never* call her bl—" There was a brief buzz, a blue flash, and an acrid smell spiked through the air of the saloon. "—uff."

Silence held the room. Goldie stood rigid as a fence post, gaping at the hand that held a now-defunct zap-dealer.

All eyes in the saloon fixed themselves on the drifter.

He grinned, not a mark on him. "Hope the recoil didn't sting your hand too bad, Miz Goldie," he said. Then he pushed back the brim of his hat so that his forehead was completely visible. A one-eyed hound dog could see the three golden Hebrew letters glowing there, though it probably wouldn't know their meaning.

Goldie was not a one-eyed hound dog.

"Uhhh—so when you said to call you *Lem,* it wasn't short for *Lemuel,* was it." This was not offered as a question.

"No'm," came the reply. "Short for *Golem*uel. On account of how I'm a mighty man of clay given unnatural life thanks to someone scribin' these three letters right here." He pointed at his forehead. "They spell *emet,* and that means—"

"—*truth,*" Goldie finished for him. "So, that's why the zap-dealer couldn't hurt you, less'n I used it to blast off that first letter and turn *emet* to *met*."

"Yes'm, and *met*'d mean—"

"—*death*," Goldie anticipated him a second time. "I'm—I'm powerful glad it didn't come to that, Lem. I got reckless, and—and stupid. I'm sorry for what I put you through."

The golem laughed and slapped his thigh. "Well, how about that, Miz Roth? She knows about my brand. She reads Hebrew. Looks like she *is* educated after all. And she's got a good heart." He sidled up to his boss-lady and murmured, "Think you could give her a second chance? I got no hard feelings for what she just tried. The little lady lost her head, is all."

Goldie was seized with wild hope. She threw herself on her knees beside the matchmaker's chair. "Forgive me!" she cried, wringing her hands. "I know I was wrong to take your golem hostage, but I was desperate! He's your trusted advance scout, isn't he? Well, can't you trust him now? *He* thinks you should reconsider. Look, I'm not asking for much, just a couple of weeks. Send him back to judge me then, and I guarantee he'll turn in the best report the Finkelsteins could ever—"

"Nope." The matchmaker stood up, stepped around the prostrate girl, and sashayed out of the saloon without another word.

Goldie scrambled to her feet and rushed after her. "Shayna! Shayna! Come back, Shayna!" she cried, but there was no sign of the shadchen. All that remained in the dusty street was the fading afterimage of light from the transportation device that had snatched her away.

Somewhere far away on the wastelands, a lone coyveyote raised a mournful howl. This was cut short by the brutal *snap* of a hungry rodandelion's jaws.

The environmental irony was too much for Goldie, who collapsed in a huddled heap on the plank sidewalk. She buried her face in her clasped arms and wailed loud enough to be mistaken for a coyveyote herself.

A strong hand fell on her shoulder. "Aw now, ma'am, don't carry on like that."

She snuffled against her updrawn knees. "Leave me be, Lem. I ticked off your shadchen boss-lady, my folks won't ante up for another one, and unless I chuck everything I believe in and marry Mr. Leonidas—which I won't!—I'm going to dry up and blow away right here on Minyiun Ten. There's nothing you can do about any of that."

"Oh, I think there is. For starters, I'm not Lem."

Goldie raised her head. She recognized the shabby garments of the sot who'd spent the whole poker game and its aftermath in a boozy stupor at the neighboring table. In this case, clothes *didn't* make the man. The rest of his appearance showed none of the signs of a recent bout with the bottle. The clean-cut lad in *shikker*'s clothing spoke without slurring his words. His eyes were bright and clear, his face unflushed. When he squatted beside her on the sidewalk she noted that his breath was honey-sweet, and his overall scent was far from distillery, close to divine. Her head reeled. Either he held an amazing speed record for hangover recovery or—

Or what?

"Who *are* you?" she demanded.

"Just a man who admires a gal with spirit, strong-minded, someone who knows what she wants and isn't afraid to fight for it," he replied. "But what's more important, Miz Goldie, you've got character. Limits. Moral boundaries. You're proud of ou—your faith, and you'll protect and defend it, not abandon it for convenience's sake."

"You—you heard what I told Mr. Leonidas?"

"I heard nigh onto everything, ma'am. I hope you won't hold it against me. I admit I was spying on you, like that golem fella."

"Why? Who are you working for? Another shadchen?"

"No'm, just for myself. We Jews scattered out here in the stars need shadchens to make matches, not to make up our minds for us. So yes, I spied on you, but I promise I won't snitch about it." He had a charming smile.

Goldie couldn't help smiling back. The cloud of doom hanging over her began to thin away. "Who would you go snitching to, anyway?" she asked coyly.

"My parents. 'Course that matchmaker told 'em about you already, but so what? Mom and Dad won't buck at something I've set my heart on having." He offered her his hand. "The name's Josh Finkelstein, ma'am. But you can call me your groom-to-be … but only if that's what *you'd* fancy?"

From behind the saloon's swinging doors, Lem and the remainder of Goldie's poker buddies watched the happy couple embrace. The jilted Mr. Leonidas sighed dolefully.

"There, there, pardner," Lem said, patting the salesman on the back. "Let's get back to the table. I don't have to leave just yet. Best way I know to forget a gal is by sitting down to a friendly game of cards."

"Good idea," Abner put in. "And with our Goldie out of the game, at least the rest of us have a chance of winning." He gave Lem a companionable nudge. "Especially against this hard-luck fella here."

"Sure, you do," Lem said amiably. Behind the smooth clay of his brow the golem's radiant cerebral goop discreetly shifted modes from *Good-Natured Pigeon (Poker)* to *Winner Take All (Poker/Arm-Wrestling/Real Estate)*. "Sure, you do."

NEBULA AWARD WINNER Esther Friesner is the author of over 40 novels and more than 200 short stories. She is also a poet, a playwright, and the editor of several anthologies. The best known of these is the Chicks in Chainmail series that she created and edits for Baen Books. In addition to sf, fantasy, and a bit of horror, she is also the author of the Princesses of Myth series of Young Adult novels from Random House.

Esther is married, a mother of two, grandmother of two, harbors cats, and lives in Connecticut. She has a fondness for bittersweet chocolate, graphic novels, manga, travel, and jewelry. There is no truth to the rumor that her family motto is "Oooooh, SHINY!"

Her superpower is the ability to winnow her bookshelves without whining about it. Much.

IF PAGES COULD BLUSH

Kyle A. Massa

The evening had been going so well for Augustus Fluff —until he realized a book was loose in the library.

He'd already swept the Science Fiction section, plus Essays, Poetry, and Thrillers. All books accounted for, all shelved properly, spines cracked, pages turned. Presently, Fluff stood in the Horror section, reading the roll call from the Master Librarian's ledger.

"*Necronomicon,*" he read, expecting a "here" in return, or perhaps a "present," even a simple grunt of acknowledgement. Instead, all he heard was silence.

The Horror books huddled around him. Hardcovers, paper-backs, thin and thick and all sizes in between; dimensions of five inches by eight, six inches by nine, or more exotic still; old books, new books, books long forgotten, and books yet to exist. All of them gathered around Fluff, laying on their back covers with their pages half-open so they resembled gaping mouths. That was how the books spoke, after all.

Not that any were speaking now. One book scuffled uncomfortably. Another coughed, puffing a plume of dust. The others waited.

"Necronomicon?" Fluff repeated, hoping the book in question was just hard of hearing. "The quicker we get through roll call, the quicker you can settle into your shelves and get some sleep."

Still no answer. All was eerily silent.

Of course, eerily silent was how the Horror books liked it. This was their section, and it showed. The high roof above was painted black with a full moon in the center, half-covered by a wisp of cloud. The ground below was stiff and crunchy, like the frosted grass of a lonely graveyard. There was even a slight stink of corruption, as if a zombie lurked between the shelves.

"Has anyone seen the *Necronomicon?* Anyone friends with it, perhaps?"

"The *Necronomicon* doesn't have friends," scoffed *Strange Case of Dr. Jekyll and Mr. Hyde*, a slim volume with a pristine front cover and a grungy back cover. "That book is evil. And trust me, I know evil."

Fluff winced. "Well, I understand it has callused membranes for a cover and human skin for pages, and there's all manner of eldritch knowledge about the Old Ones hidden within it. But does that make it *evil?*"

"I can't believe you just asked that question," said *The Haunting of Hill House*. It sported yellow and green weeds on its cover, with the titular house peeking over them.

"I can," said *Frankenstein; or, The Modern Prometheus*, a book with a rather plain cover by comparison; just title, author, subtitle. "There's a reason our friend Fluff here is still an Apprentice."

"Always a Renfield, never a Dracula," lamented *Dracula*. Its cover was yellow with red lettering. "Where is the Master Librarian tonight, anyway?"

"Out," Fluff answered. "On a date, I think. When I asked, she whacked me with her umbrella." His right shin still throbbed. Yet the bruise wasn't all she'd left him; on her way out, the Master Librarian had offered a tidbit of wisdom.

"We call this place a library, Fluff," she had said, "but it's more like a zoo. And what does an animal require from its handlers?"

"Regular poop scooping?" he'd guessed.

"Think harder."

"Compassion?"

"Precisely. Now be compassionate and mind the library while I'm gone, would you?"

And so, he did. Which brought him to his present predicament.

"The Master Librarian will return sometime tonight," Fluff assured the Horror books. "Until then, I'm supposed to be in charge."

"Supposed to be," echoed *The Exorcist*. "No offense, Fluff, but a possessed child could do a better job running this library than you. I mean, remember that time you misshelved those books in our section?"

How could he forget? Fluff thought he'd mastered the Master Librarian's unconventional shelving method, organizing books more by tropes and less by tradition. Yet then he'd misshelved some Fantasy books in the Horror section, and the books fixated on his mistake ever since. He almost said as much to *The Exorcist*, but faltered when he read the addendum to the *Necronomicon's* entry on the ledger, written in the Master Librarian's precise cursive:

A book invented by the influential and—I'm putting this nicely here —shockingly racist twentieth-century weird fiction author H.P. Lovecraft. Contains occult lore and evil rituals. Extremely dangerous. Do not let loose under any circumstances. Would read again.

Fluff gulped. He wiped his forehead with his hand, then wiped his hand on his robes.

"Why are you sweating so much?" asked *The Shining*. "Don't tell us the *Necronomicon* is loose or something."

"Oh don't be silly." Fluff forced a chuckle. It was definitely a chuckle and not a laugh, because laughs don't sound so strained. "I'm sure it isn't. But, as a fun thought exercise, let's imagine the *Necronomicon* really *did* escape. So, hypothetically, does anyone know where it might've escaped to? Hypothetically?"

"I can't tell you that," said a voice, "but I can tell you this: the *Necronomicon* was losing its mind."

Fluff turned to find a slender book with a leather cover and yellow threaded lines swirling over it. *The Yellow Wallpaper*.

"Losing its mind?" Fluff asked the book. "How do you mean?"

"Well," said *The Yellow Wallpaper*, "the *Necronomicon* was speaking nonsense earlier today. Do you know what it asked me? It asked me, 'Why is a raven like a writing desk?'"

Fluff pondered the question. "Because you shouldn't eat either of them?"

The Yellow Wallpaper sighed. "No, Apprentice. It's just a demonstration of lunacy, not a legitimate inquiry. I'm telling you, that book was losing it. I should know—madness is one of my primary themes."

Fluff had to admit, this business of ravens and writing desks did seem a bit mad. Unless it was a joke or a riddle or something …

Wait. It *was* a riddle. Fluff had heard it before—or rather, read it. And once Fluff read a sentence, he never forgot it.

"That's a line from *Alice's Adventures in Wonderland* by Lewis Carroll," he said.

"Is it?" *The Yellow Wallpaper* sounded like it would've shrugged, if it had shoulders. "Huh. I've got to get out more."

Fluff's mind was humming now. If the *Necronomicon* was inquiring about a riddle from *Alice in Wonderland*, then …

"It's a clue," Fluff whispered to himself, suddenly feeling like a detective from a book in the Mystery section. A blundering, oftentimes sweaty detective, yes—but a detective nonetheless.

"Thank you, books." Fluff wheeled and dashed away, stumbling over an empty casket in his haste. "Sleep well!" He shut the door, turned the lock, and hurried through the echoing corridors of the library. He had an escaped book to track down.

THE FANTASY SECTION WAS, well, fantastic. Cascading waterfalls tumbled into glimmering pools of misty froth. Rainbows arced beneath a ceiling of blue sky and golden sunlight. Music twittered in the distance, and the air was ripe with the smell of spring flowers.

Unlike other sections of the library, there was no shelving in the Fantasy section. Instead, books soared on the wind, flapping and coasting like birds. Chunky birds, as it were, since Fantasy books tended toward the higher page counts. Also, multi-volume series flocked together. One such flock surrounded Fluff as he entered.

"The Harry Potter series," he exclaimed, "by J.K. Rowling! I'm trying to locate a book. Can you help me?"

"If we feel like it," sneered *Harry Potter and the Order of the Phoenix*, which was a later entry in the series and therefore moodier. "What's the book you're looking for?"

"It's a visitor from the Horror section. Don't worry, though. I'm on the case."

"Now I'm especially worried," scoffed *Harry Potter and the Goblet of Fire*. "We all know Fluff wouldn't be a first pick for the Triwizard Tournament, if you know what I mean. What was your most recent blunder?"

"He forgot to lock the door to the Graphic Novel section," said *Harry Potter and the Half-Blood Prince*. "It took months to track down *Watchmen*." And they laughed, as if this was one of the greatest jokes ever told.

Fluff spoke over the laughter, trying to sound nonchalant.

"This book I'm looking for, it's your average, everyday, normal sort of book. Skin for pages, blood for ink, some lidless eyeballs here and there. You know, your standard hardcover. Has anyone seen it?"

The laughter died. *Harry Potter and the Chamber of Secrets* coughed as if it had swallowed something rancid. "I mean, I have some creepy elements. But *that* ..."

"The *Necronomicon*." *Harry Potter and the Prisoner of Azkaban* whispered the title like a curse. "You're talking about the *Necronomicon*, aren't you? Of all the books to lose, you lost *that* one?"

"I haven't lost it. I've indefinitely misplaced it. Hasn't anyone seen it?"

Harry Potter and the Sorcerer's Stone flapped forward next. "Of course we haven't. Don't you think we'd notice if we saw a book made of human skin?"

"I should hope so. What about *Alice in Wonderland*? Have you seen that book lately?"

"*Alice?*" *Harry Potter and the Deathly Hallows* asked. "We know Alice. Alice is a weirdo, even for a Fantasy book."

"Yes," added another voice. "And now *Alice* is gone."

A book outside the *Harry Potter* series had said that. It was *The Hobbit*.

"Gone?" Fluff moaned. "Where?"

The Grace of Kings sighed. "Shouldn't the Master Librarian's Apprentice know the answer to that question?"

"Yes," Fluff agreed. "He should." It was then that he realized two things: First, that *he* was the Apprentice, and second, that circumstances had just gone from bad to worse. A single book on the loose was problematic enough. But *two*? The Master Librarian might return from her apparent date at any moment. And if she discovered he'd lost two books while she was away, he wouldn't be employed much longer.

"When?" Fluff breathed. "When did *Alice* disappear?"

"Must've been last night, after yesterday's roll call," guessed

Stardust. It fluttered down from above. "We go for early flights together. Only *Alice* didn't join me this morning. I just thought it forgot."

"Last time you saw *Alice*, did it mention anything unusual? Perhaps something to the effect of, 'If I ever went missing, no worries, here's where I'd be?'"

"Nothing like that. All we talked about was *Alice's* love life. I'm part romance, so books come to me for relationship advice."

"Relationships," Fluff said, nodding as though he knew all about them. "And what is *Alice's* relationship status?"

"It's complicated. *Alice* is—"

"Apprentice!" cried *The Bone Clocks*. "Just tell us the truth. Did the *Necronomicon* escape? And what did it do to *Alice*?"

Fluff smiled—or grimaced. It was hard to tell the difference. He folded his hands and glanced about without blinking, like the Master Librarian would often do. "There's no need to worry," he announced (though he was definitely worried). "Everything's fine." (It most certainly was not.) "I don't believe *Alice* is in any sort of danger." (Actually, that's *exactly* what he believed.) "I have the situation under control." (Which was the biggest lie of all.)

More books were gathering now, settling on the green grass of the meadow to listen.

"Attention, everyone!" bellowed *Best Served Cold*. "New theory: The *Necronomicon* ate *Alice,* and now it's loose in our section. In other words, we're all completely fu—!"

"Hey," said *Where the Wild Things Are*. "Watch your language. There are children's books present!"

"Doomed!" wailed *The Fifth Season*. "We're doomed! This is the end!"

"Let's take vengeance on the Apprentice!" suggested *A Storm of Swords*. "He allowed the *Necronomicon* to escape and eat *Alice.* Therefore, we should slay him in return, just like the Freys slew Robb Stark for spurning their marriage betrothal!"

"Nay, no spoilers," chided *A Midsummer Night's Dream*. "But the portly book doth speak truly. Murther him, I say! Murther the saucy boy!"

"But—but—" Fluff sputtered. "Eaten? There's no evidence of that. Books don't even have digestive tracts. And I'm not saucy, I'm ..."

No one was listening. The entire Fantasy section surged forward, pages flapping, covers snapping, and Fluff had no choice but to stumble backward and run, feet flying over fresh-cut grass, legs pumping until they propelled him through the door. He slammed it, locked it, and slumped against it, breathing hard, feeling jolts in his back as the books pounded the other side.

That hadn't gone well. But at least he had another clue. And he knew just the place to get it solved.

FLUFF TRUDGED into the Mystery section. The streets glistened with artificial rainwater, streetlamps shed brightness into the murky night, and all colors dulled to shades of gray.

"Hello?" Fluff called. "Is anyone here?"

"Depends on who's asking." *The Thin Man* peered around a shelf. It had a cigarette tucked between its page-lips.

"You shouldn't be smoking that," Fluff said, knowing the book would never listen to him. "I'm wondering if I could have your help, Mystery books."

"Help, eh?" said *The Hound of the Baskervilles*. "Is there a game afoot?"

"Definitely. Here's the situation ..."

And so, Fluff recounted the story so far to the Mystery books, doing his best to keep the glumness from his voice (with little success).

"Doesn't seem like much of a mystery," murmured *Dark*

Places, when Fluff was finished. "I'd have to agree with the Fantasy books. Seems like the *Necro*-whatever ate *Alice*, and now it's roaming the library, searching for more books to devour."

Fluff rubbed his temples. "Doesn't that frighten you?"

Murder on the Orient Express answered that one. "We're Mystery books," it explained. "If we were afraid of a bit of murder, we wouldn't be what we are."

Fluff wished he could be what *he* was. He was the Master Librarian's Apprentice. But currently, he felt more like a fraud.

"If the *Necronomicon* is truly eating books," Fluff said, "this could be the end of the library itself."

"Then let's talk it out," suggested *The Shadow of the Wind*. "Perhaps we'll uncover a solution."

"Very well." Fluff thought for a moment. Thinking was not one of his strong suits, but it needed to be done. Finally, after thinking several thoughts, he said, "If the *Necronomicon* ate *Alice*, why wasn't there any sign of a struggle? Surely someone would've seen torn pages or ink staining the grass."

The Girl with the Dragon Tattoo tipped back and forth in a gesture probably meant to be a nod. "An intriguing hole in this plot. Go on."

"And," said Fluff, voice rising, finger waving, "why didn't the *Necronomicon* attack any other books? Why did it even bother escaping its section when there were plenty of Horror books around to snack on? And why did it quote the book it was going to eat?"

"Foreshadowing?" suggested *The Da Vinci Code*. But Fluff carried on, oblivious.

"And another thing!" he shouted, relishing the role of demystifying detective. "*Alice* has a 'complicated' relationship status, according to *Stardust*. I don't know exactly what that means, but I'm assuming it doesn't mean single. So, who was *Alice* seeing? And how does that factor in?"

"Questions, yes!" laughed *The Woman in White*. "So many

questions! Keep them coming!"

"What if …?" Yes. Fluff had a theory. A flimsy theory, perhaps, but a theory nonetheless. "And if that's true, they must be …" *Yes.* The more he considered it, the more sound it seemed. "So then I'll find them both in … of course! Why didn't I see it before?"

"See what?" asked *One for the Money*. "You haven't told us whodunnit!"

The Mystery books surged ahead, moving to block Fluff's escape.

"You can't leave until you explain what happened!" cried *Devil in a Blue Dress*. "You wouldn't do that to a room full of Mystery books, would you!?"

Under any other circumstances, Fluff would never. But there was no time to lose. So, he pushed through the crowd of swarming books and tumbled out the door.

THE ROMANCE SECTION WAS EXTRAVAGANT, elegant, and alluring. Velvet curtains adorned the walls and paintings hung between, each depicting couples of all sorts joined at the lips. Unlike the Fantasy section, the Romance books did not fly around. Rather, they preened on their shelves like cats. Scented candles flickered everywhere, creating an aroma that was simultaneously fragrant and overpowering.

"Want to sign a contract?" called *Fifty Shades of Grey*, when Fluff entered. "It's binding … in more ways than one."

Fluff became instantly sweaty. "Aren't you supposed to be in Erotica?"

"Meh, what's the difference? By the way, did you know I'm part of a trilogy?"

"More's the pity," lamented *Jane Eyre*. "Where is the Master Librarian, Fluff?"

"Out," he answered. "Possibly on a date. So, I'm in charge—nominally, at least. Has anyone seen two unfamiliar books in here?"

The Romance books glanced about, puzzled.

"Please, I need your help. If the Master Librarian returns to find these books lost, I'll lose my job." Just the thought made him want to weep.

"What books are we talking about, exactly?" inquired *Love in the Time of Cholera.*

"*Alice in Wonderland* by Lewis Carroll," Fluff answered. "And, umm …" He doubted the Romance books would take the news of the *Necronomicon* as well as the Mystery books had. So, he covered his mouth and made an unintelligible sound, something halfway between mumble and cough.

"What was that?" asked *Pride and Prejudice.* "Speak up, young man!"

"I said I'm looking for *Alice in Wonderland* and …" He made the same sound again, only a little louder.

"You're mumbling, Apprentice," complained *Sea Glass Island.* "Project. Use your diaphragm."

Fluff sighed. "It's the *Necronomicon,* alright? The *Necronomicon* is hiding somewhere in your section."

The room seemed to momentarily darken. Then *Gone with the Wind* said, "Should we panic? I think we should panic."

And so, panic ensued. The frantic, mindless, get-me-the-hell-out-of-here sort. The Romance books made a beeline for the door. Fluff flattened himself against it, and the books pushed him, shoved him, jabbed him with hardcover corners and slapped him with leatherbound flaps. It was the third time he'd been mobbed by books in as many hours. Just his luck.

"Listen, everyone!" Fluff shouted. "You don't understand! They're in love! They're in *love!*"

If there was a word to mesmerize a room full of Romance books, that was it. The panic ceased.

"Wait. Who's in love?" asked *The Fault in Our Stars*.

"*Alice* and the *Necronomicon*," Fluff said. "It's the only explanation that makes sense. They've run away together, as lovers do, and they're seeking refuge in the only place a forbidden love might work: the Romance section. Isn't that right?" He raised his voice for those last three words, projecting as loudly as possible. "You can come out now. I know you're in here."

There was a moment's pause. Then the crowd of Romance books parted, whispering as they did. A pair of books fluttered through the gap. One was bound in green leather, pages yellowing from age. The other had a grayish cover, shriveled and shrunken, with lidless eyeballs swiveling in every direction. It left a trail of blood behind it.

"He's right," confirmed the latter. Its voice clicked and rattled like bare branches stirred by the wind on a winter's night. "He's right about everything. We met when Fluff misshelved *Alice* in my section, and ever since we've been in love. We came here to tie the knot."

"The proverbial knot," *Alice in Wonderland* clarified. "Not to be confused with a shoelace knot, a sailor's knot, the Gordian Knot, or the homophones for 'knot,' which are 'not,' 'nought,' or 'naught,' depending on your accent—any of which might confuse."

"See?" The *Necronomicon* opened its cover and hugged *Alice* in a bookish embrace. "There's nobody like my *Alice*."

The Princess Bride shuffled forward. "Why didn't you tell anyone? Why did you hide your love?"

"We were worried you would shun us," *Alice* explained, "what with *Necky's* reputation."

"And we thought you might panic if you knew I was present," the *Necronomicon* added, "like you did a few moments ago."

The Romance books exchanged furtive glances, all of them clearly embarrassed.

Fluff raised his hands. "Look, books. There's something I must say … only I don't know how to say it."

"I do," said *The Age of Innocence*. "You can't let them marry, can you? You're the Master Librarian's Apprentice. You're tasked with keeping us books shelved and organized. These two must return to their proper sections, and they can never reunite again. That's what you have to say, isn't it?"

"That's … that's exactly it, yes." Fluff hung his head, eyes downcast. "Though I wish it wasn't."

"You can't!" screamed *Alice*. "*Necky* and I are meant to be together! We're lovers from opposite sides of the looking glass. We're star-crossed!"

"Thou hadst better watch it," said *The Most Excellent and Lamentable Tragedie of Romeo and Juliet*. "That's my line."

Fluff sighed. "I don't want to separate you. You seem so happy together. But it's my job."

Or was it? The Master Librarian's advice twanged in his head, contradicting itself like mismatching chords.

"We put each book in its proper place," she'd always said. "That's the librarian's task."

Yet only a few hours ago, her parting question to Fluff had been, "What does an animal require from its handlers?" And he'd answered, "Compassion."

So, what was most compassionate? When he posed it that way, the choice was simple.

Fluff shook his head. "You know what? Never mind."

"What?" said *Alice*.

"What?" said the *Necronomicon*.

"What?" said *The Notebook*, because everyone seemed to be saying it.

"I said never mind. Forget the whole thing. Be in love. I won't stop you."

"But what will the Master Librarian think?" said *Outlander*.

Fluff grimaced. "I suppose I'll find out soon enough. Now go on, my friends. Get married."

And so, a surprisingly coordinated wedding was planned. The star-crossed lovers had an hour to prepare for the ceremony, which would be officiated by the novelization of the 2005 romantic comedy film *Wedding Crashers*. And when it came time to tie the proverbial knot, *Alice* and the *Necronomicon* exchanged beautiful vows. If pages could blush, both books would've turned bright red.

But Fluff missed all of this. Long before the ceremony, he slipped out the rear door of the Romance section, locking it softly behind him.

WHEN FLUFF FINISHED RECOUNTING the tale, the Master Librarian said, "Seems I missed a lot while I was out."

Fluff wasn't sure whether to be terrified or perplexed by that statement, so he settled for plain desperation. "Please don't fire me, Master Librarian."

"Should I?" The Master Librarian studied him with eyes the color of chocolate. She was a tall woman with curly gray hair clipped short, and she exuded confidence like a fire exudes heat. Her clothes were never wrinkled, her shelves were always orderly, and, unlike Fluff, she was never, ever sweaty. "Do you know how many Apprentices I've had?"

"Umm ..." Fluff chewed his lip. "Twenty?"

She glared at him. "How old do you think I am?" Before Fluff could embarrass himself further, the Master Librarian laughed, one single "ha" that sounded like a tome snapping shut. Then she seated herself in the nearest chair and stacked her feet on the table, revealing high-heeled boots. Pink boots, Fluff realized, which matched the color of the umbrella she'd whacked him with earlier. Fluff had never seen her wear anything half so vibrant.

"Seven," she answered. "I've had seven Apprentices, including you. Now, of those seven, how many would've done what you did tonight?"

Fluff winced. "One?"

"Correct. No other Apprentice would ever do something so unusual."

Unusual. That was a nice way of putting it. He'd let the books shelve themselves rather than put them in the proper place. Now *Alice* might learn eldritch ways from the *Necronomicon* and become a horror novel. The *Necronomicon* might receive too much drug influence from *Alice* and resort to opiates. When books fraternized with books of other genres, you never knew what might happen. And Fluff hadn't just allowed it—he'd endorsed it.

He hung his head. "I'll pack my things, then."

"Very good," said the Master Librarian. "Pack your things. You'll be moving into your new quarters soon."

Fluff moped away, wiping a tear from his eye. If he was to be fired, he wished to leave with his dignity intact, and …

He stopped in the doorway. He turned. "New quarters?"

"Yes, new quarters." The Master Librarian nodded. "A perk for my successor."

Fluff's ears heard the words, but his mind refused to believe them. "Your … successor?"

"You're not a parrot, Fluff—you need not repeat everything I say. Did you know I went on a date tonight?"

Of course, he did. He could tell by her footwear, outfit, and general demeanor. But apparently this was supposed to come as a surprise, so instead Fluff answered, "Why Master Librarian, I had no idea."

She pursed her lips. "It was terrible. He smelled of pipe smoke, he chewed with his mouth open, and the last book he read was something by James Patterson."

Fluff gasped. "Really?"

"Truly. But I forgot how good it feels to get out of this place, much as I love it." Her eyes circumnavigated the room, coming to rest on Fluff. "I'm retiring. And you're going to be my successor."

"I... I ..."

I'm speechless. That's what Fluff wanted to say. But when you're truly speechless, wanting and saying are vastly different things. So, after several failed attempts, he settled on three words. The first was, "But." The second was, "Why." The third was, "Me?"

"Because you *care,* Fluff. You proved that to me today. You care about these books more than anyone—perhaps even more than me. You care so much that you prioritized their personal happiness over my shelving system. And that is something I'd *never* do." She rose. "Now chop chop. Pack up your room."

Fluff blinked as if waking from a peculiar dream. "Of course. I'll get right on that."

"Excellent. And Fluff?"

"Yes, Master Librarian?"

For the first time Fluff could remember, the Master Librarian winked at him. "Keep up the good work."

Augustus Fluff dashed away, wearing a disbelieving grin as he went. Him, Master Librarian. The books would never believe it.

KYLE A. MASSA is a comic fantasy author living somewhere in upstate New York with his wife, their daughter, and three wild animals. His published works include several books and short stories. When he's not writing, he enjoys reading, running, and drinking coffee.

THE TIME LOOP DEVICE IS COUNTING DOWN

Beth Goder

ITERATION 1

Nosentam bursts into the common room of the spaceship *Fortuity*, the time loop device clutched in his hand.

"Give me the blueprints you stole," he says, brandishing the device so the crew members can see it's set to an increment of fifteen minutes. "We're going to keep looping until you do what I ask."

He triggers the device, and the countdown starts.

"Who is this jerk?" asks Prazzaline.

"Does he want the super-ship blueprints? Is that what he's talking about?" asks Tull.

Robin is the only one who addresses Nosentam directly. "You know how to turn that thing off, right?"

ITERATION 2

Nosentam does not know how to turn that thing off. Or perhaps the model is defective.

"You got your blueprints," says Robin. "Why are we still looping?"

ITERATION 3

Blueprints forgotten, the four of them crowd around the time loop device.

"Is the button stuck?" asks Robin.

"Maybe if we hit it with a hammer?" says Tull.

Prazzaline just swears.

Tull bangs the device with a hammer for the full fifteen minutes.

ITERATION 10

They've tried burning the device, submerging it in water, nuking it in the food replicator, and shooting it into space.

"This was not my plan," says Nosentam, as the others glare at him.

ITERATION 83

"I cannot play another game of chess," says Robin. It is very frustrating when she's about to checkmate and the loop restarts, and then Tull says, "Oh no, look at that, we must count it as a tie."

Prazzaline says something, but no one can understand her because her mouth is full of sandwich.

"I'll play," says Nosentam, but the others ignore him. They are still pissed about the whole infinite time loop thing.

ITERATION 1005

Tull suggests a game. It's called: "What A Hammer Can't Do."

This is not a great game, but it's not easy to come up with a new game that can be played in fifteen minutes using only items on the spaceship.

"A hammer can't make a sandwich," says Prazzaline, holding a tuna sandwich with mustard and pickles. She's gotten really into eating sandwiches.

"A hammer can't do my taxes," says Tull. "And neither can I."

"A hammer can't make other hammers," says Nosentam. The others have grudgingly accepted him into their group. He has a good sense of humor and knows lots of facts about lizards, and it does seem like he truly didn't mean to get them stuck in time forever.

"A hammer can't destroy the time device," says Robin morosely, ruining the game.

ITERATION 2060

"What if we dismantle it?" asks Tull.

"We tried that fifty iterations ago," says Robin. "Didn't work then. Won't work now."

"We could speed up the ship to get some weird relativity reaction," says Nosentam.

"Physics doesn't work like that," says Robin. "Also, we already tried it."

Prazzaline comes in with a sandwich the size of her head. It's a mystery how it fit in the replicator. Mango with sardines, and a hint of mint. "Y'all have to try this," she says.

ITERATION 4887

Prazzaline has got them all making sandwiches. She says that it's good to have a hobby.

They are having a sandwich party.

Robin eats a sandwich with turkey and tomato.

Tull likes anything with cheese.

Nosentam chooses lettuce, olives, and relish.

Prazzaline's sandwich contains green curry, bananas, and chocolate ice cream.

"Is that really a sandwich?" asks Robin.

"If it goes on bread, it's a sandwich," says Prazzaline. "That's the philosophy of sandwiches."

ITERATION 7890

They've been through so many iterations that they've created their own traditions.

Every ninety iterations, they have a sandwich party.

Every 270 iterations, Tull does the hammer dance (which involves Tull hopping around with the hammer and the others frantically pushing stuff out of the way so he doesn't hurt himself.)

When the sandwich party and the hammer dance intersect, it's all sandwiches and hammers and everyone except for Tull is glad it only lasts fifteen minutes.

ITERATION 7891

"I have a question," says Prazzaline. "Who is the bad guy, here?"

"What do you mean?" asks Tull.

"Well, we got into this situation because of Nosentam and his time loop device. So maybe he's the bad guy. But he was after blueprints which we had stolen, and stealing is not great." Prazzaline looks like she wants to say more, but gets distracted by her sandwich, radish and vinegar on rye.

"It's ethically twisty, for sure," says Robin.

"Oh, no," says Tull. "Does that mean it's all of us? Am I a bad guy?"

"Why did you want the blueprints, anyway?" asks Robin.

It's been so long that Nosentam has almost forgotten. "I wanted to build the coolest ship ever. I thought everyone would have to like me then. I was very sad. I think I just needed a friend."

"Awww, buddy," says Prazzaline.

They all pile in for a group hug, which lasts until the end of the iteration.

ITERATION 9775

"Why are you always eating?" Robin asks Prazzaline.

Prazzaline gulps down a bite of her sandwich, which has green and purple bits sticking out. "Because when the first iteration started, I was very hungry."

"So, you're hungry all the time?" asks Robin.

"It's not so bad," says Prazzaline. "Now I'm always in the mood for a sandwich."

ITERATION 25,600

It's not easy to become a physics expert in fifteen-minute increments, but Nosentam has managed it. He got everyone into this mess, and he's going to get them out of it.

He tries to explain the plan to the others, but all they hear are phrases like "quantum overdrive looping" and "Borgum's theorem but reversed" and "I invented a new thing and I am calling it squiggle physics."

Nosentam does his thing. It involves lots of calculations and looking very serious.

ITERATION 25,601

There are now five copies of the spaceship *Fortuity*.

"Whoops," says Nosentam.

The ships meet up.

The Robins play chess. The Tulls compare hammers. The Prazzalines trade sandwich recipes.

"Where did we go wrong?" asks Nosentam-5.

"Does this mean other versions of us got out of the loop?" asks Nosentam-3.

Nosentam-1 beckons them to a blackboard. "Let's get back to it. The next thing will work."

ITERATION 25,602

The next thing doesn't work.

ITERATION 70,000

But the four-thousandth thing does.

All copies of the *Fortuity* end up back in the correct time spheres. The only mix up is that Tull-3 left his hammer on *Fortuity*-1.

"More hammers for me," says Tull-1, shrugging.

"Tull-3 can buy another hammer at an actual store," says Robin. "We made it out."

The crew of *Fortuity*-1 celebrates with sandwiches.

Fifteen minutes pass. Then thirty. Then, a whole hour.

"I actually feel full," says Prazzaline.

"I wonder what made the time device get stuck in the first place," says Nosentam. "The fail-safe mechanism should have activated."

"It doesn't matter," says Robin. "We're out. Let us never think about it again."

But Nosentam can't stop thinking about it. He's learned a lot about time and physics and the mechanics of space. Surely, he knows enough now not to make another careless mistake with the device. And he's curious how the device will react now that they are flowing in normal time again. "I think I'll just take a look."

As he reaches for the time device, the rest of the crew pile on top of him.

"Don't even think about it, buddy," says Prazzaline.

"Hold down his arms," says Robin.

"Group hug," says Tull happily, his mouth full of sandwich, two hammers tucked under his arms.

BETH GODER WORKS AS AN ARCHIVIST, processing the papers of economists, scientists, and other interesting folks. Her fiction has appeared in venues such as *Escape Pod, Analog, Clarkesworld, Nature,* and Horton's *The Year's Best Science Fiction & Fantasy*. You can find her online at www.bethgoder.com.

CROUCHING SWAN, HIDDEN POLKA

Jim C. Hines

The real reason superheroes take on sidekicks and do team-ups and join leagues is so they'll have someone to talk to.

People love a dark, brooding loner doling out equal helpings of vengeance and justice, but that isolation isn't healthy. As my old Master once said, beware the man who prefers to dance alone.

My solitude was caused by circumstance, not choice, but the years still took a toll.

I practiced an exaggerated Charleston dance step as I crossed the motel parking lot. Tonight's target should be simple enough, but it was never wise to skip the stretch and warm-up before a performance. My movements were automatic, practiced until I could do them in my sleep.

The Troll was a B-List punk with a history of cyberstalking, blackmail, and harassment both online and in person. He was also the go-to dark web tech guru for supervillains in a five-state area.

I gave the old motel a quick once-over as I approached. On the Motel 6 scale, the place was a 2.5 at best, with flickering lights, an old neon sign, and a parking lot that stank of old urine or *really* bad beer.

I stopped at the door to room four and rapped one leather-gloved hand against the flaking wood. "Maintenance."

"Come back later." The speaker had a deeper voice than I'd imagined.

"I'll only be a minute," I pressed. "We got a report of mutant bedbugs in room five. I need to make sure they haven't spread."

I heard whispers inside. According to my anonymous tip, the Troll was meeting with a brother-sister team who wanted to set up a dating site for domestic terrorists.

The door swung open. A wall of muscle in jeans and a stained Dungeons and Dragons T-shirt peered over his glasses at me. "What the fuck kind of exterminator are you supposed to be?"

My costume was mostly black spandex, highlighting a body strengthened by a lifetime of dance. My black hair was braided and tucked beneath a black bandana. A silver mask covered my eyes and nose, leaving only the brown skin of my lower face visible.

Before I could answer, a twenty-something woman sitting at a desk in the room pointed at me. "Wait, I've heard of this guy. You're whatshisname, the Grey Goose!"

I stifled a sigh. "The Night Swan."

She shook her head. "I'm pretty sure it was the Grey Goose. What kind of superhero name is Swan?"

A man perched on the edge of the bed nodded in agreement. "Geese are scarier. Those things will fuck you up."

"They have teeth on their fucking tongues," said the woman. "Saw it on Animal Planet."

The two people debating my name had similar features: strong cheekbones, prominent noses, and jutting jaws. I guessed them to be the entrepreneurs, which made the mountain in front of me ... "Mister Troll?"

The Troll looked me up and down. His gaze lingered on my silver dance belt, then dropped lower. "Are you wearing *slippers?*"

"They're pointe shoes."

"You're a brave man, going out in public with that getup." He reached for my throat.

I pirouetted twice, whirling inside his reach and raising my arms to deflect his grab. On my third spin, I rose to my toes, hopped, and smashed an elbow into his nose. He fell back, bleeding and cursing.

I wasn't a true Master of the Dancing Arts. Hell, I wasn't even the best in the city. But I'd studied under one of the deadliest dancers in the world. I'd learned secrets hidden in dance techniques both ancient and modern. I'd spent years learning to use my dances to focus the mystic power of my body—my chi, my essence, my overeager adrenal glands, whatever you wanted to call it.

The brother and sister came at me. I jumped nimbly to the left, turning my movement into a modified jeté.

A traditional ballet jeté is a leap with one leg flung outward. Mine was similar, but ended with the steel-reinforced toe of my pointe shoe crunching into the brother's sternum. He howled and tumbled onto the bed.

Sister tried to grab me from behind. I spun and caught her arms, then dipped her like I would a partner before pulling her upright and whirling her at the Troll.

He batted her aside like a mosquito and lunged at me, arms outstretched to wrap me in what doubtless would have been a spine-shattering bear hug.

I dropped into the splits, one leg behind me, the other sliding between the Troll's feet. As I landed, I raised my arms into fourth position, channeling my power into my right hand.

The sound of my hand striking the Troll's pelvic region was like a gunshot. His eyes bulged. He let out a tiny squeak, then doubled over and vomited.

I rolled out of the way, came to my feet, and bowed. Not that they were coherent enough to appreciate it.

I took the heavy-duty zip ties from my belt pouch, but before I could secure my captives, a distant rhythm hooked my attention, like bass thrumming through my chest. Distinct, familiar footsteps approached from outside. Metal soles double-tapped the blacktop in perfect time.

My chest, throat, and ass tightened in unison. My emotional fuses exploded, overwhelmed by a combination of fear, longing, anger, and excitement. I wiped my hands on my thighs, forgetting I was wearing gloves.

The door opened. A woman I hadn't seen in six years surveyed the damage.

"Nora." My mouth was dry. The word was barely a croak.

"We have to go. Yuri is coming."

ELEANOR COLE—NORA to those of us who'd known her as a kid—didn't look like a typical dancer. She was short and heavy-set. Blocky, even. She wore green yoga pants and a baggy purple T-shirt with the cartoon logo from Little Leopards Dance Studio, the place she'd founded when she turned eighteen. Purple-framed glasses with oversized round lenses dominated her pale face. Her mousy brown hair was pulled back in a short, severe Dutch braid.

But the instant she moved, she transformed into a goddess. Every movement was smooth as water, precise as clockwork.

"Did you hear me, 'Night Swan'?" Sarcasm coated her final syllables.

I took a slow, calming breath. "Why would Yuri come here?"

"He's looking for Master. Probably to finish what he started six years ago."

Yuri Foster was the third member of our old trio of misfit

orphans. We'd grown up together, trained together, fought together, loved together. Remembering Yuri's betrayal, his battle with Master, and the loss of everything we'd had, was like a knife scraping the inside of my rib cage.

"We can talk to him," I said numbly.

"You don't know what he's become."

"A villain." Wanted in thirteen countries for theft, hijacking, indecency, fraud, assault, and—I hadn't dug up all the details on this one—unlicensed possession of a kangaroo. "He's still Yuri."

"That's right. The same Yuri who broke Master's—shit."

I blinked, confused. "Who broke her *what*?"

She pointed through the open door to the headlights pulling into the parking lot. "He's here. We have to run." She grabbed my hand. "For once, will you please trust me?"

I tugged free. "Yuri won't hurt me."

"Master thought the same thing."

It was as if she'd stomped her tap shoes directly onto my heart. I didn't answer. I just walked out the door.

Yuri Foster had been a prodigy, a better dancer than Nora or me. I hardly recognized him now, as he climbed out of a purple Cadillac with gold rims.

His silver shirt sparkled in the light. The sequins were overlapping circles of mirror-polished steel, armoring him against most weapons. From the heavy movement of his white bell bottoms, I assumed they were lined with Kevlar or something similar. His shoes were silver oxfords.

He'd grown a bushy black moustache, but he flashed that same practical joker smile as he strode toward me. "Stefano!"

I hoped the Troll and his partners were still unconscious. The Night Swan had a secret identity for a reason. "What are you doing here?"

"My master sent me to complete my Trials." The familiar strength and confidence of his words rippled through the air. His voice was like melted butter, smooth and tantalizing. It pulled me back through time to when the three of us had lived and studied together. Back when we'd been friends and so much more. "You're going to help me."

"Help who?" I asked. "Yuri Foster? Or Mirrorball?"

I thought my use of his villain name sounded nicely dramatic, but the moment was ruined when a guy in room six yelled, "Shut the hell up out there!"

Yuri's smile vanished. He angled his body, his hips swaying to unheard music. His left hand found his hip. His right moved diagonally across his body, pointing down, up, down, gathering a knot of kinetic energy.

When he raised his hand again, that energy shot away. The door to room six splintered inward. The window shattered. A woman screamed from inside.

Yuri continued to dance. Another ball of disco power shot through the air. This time, I heard a wet thump and the crack of bone.

"Yuri, stop!" I shifted onto my toes, gathering my own power.

To my surprise, he did. "Tell me where Master is hiding."

I remembered what Nora had said about Yuri finishing what he'd started. "What are you going to do?"

"Master failed us. She promised to teach us, but she left us incomplete. Empty. I know you feel it. I've been following your work, you know. I knew who Night Swan was from the first viral security cam footage. I recognized your body, the way you moved. And I saw the same yearning."

"You can't force her to finish your training."

"I don't need her training. I have a new master. A new family. All I need to do is finish my Trials, and I'll be a full member of the Obsidian Company." He hesitated, then added, "You could come with me."

Master had never been a superhero, but she'd had plenty of enemies, including her long-standing rivalry with the Obsidian

Company's performance-themed villains. Yuri must have gone to them when he left us. "This isn't you, Yuri. I've been watching you, too. Mirrorball isn't a murderer."

"This isn't murder. It's justice." He spat on the pavement. "Master betrayed me. You all did. Nora ratted me out, and you—you were worst of all. You did *nothing*. You just stood by while it all turned to shit."

"Baryshnikov's ball sack," I swore, my own anger rising in response. "You broke into Master's private chambers. We could have faced the Trials together, but you tried to cheat."

"I tried to save you!"

"What are you talking about?"

"You weren't ready for the Trials."

Shock and denial splashed over me. "What are you talking about?"

"I was always the best dancer." He wasn't boasting. We'd all been Master's students and disciples, but as gifted as Nora and I might have been, Yuri's skills had been supernatural. "Master didn't approve of how close the three of us were. She thought you were a distraction, keeping me from reaching my potential. She wanted the Trials to cripple the two of you, leaving me to focus on my training."

"I don't believe you."

He sneered. "Then you're the same coward you've always been. Too weak to see the truth about Master. About Nora. About yourself."

"And about you?" I adjusted my stance into fourth position, one foot in front of the other. "I love you, Yuri. But I can't let you hurt anyone else."

He attacked without a word, using the same technique he'd flung at the motel. I pirouetted out of the way and performed a double-leap, a sauté-sissonne combination that ended in a kick that would have laid him out, but he'd already shifted into the

Hustle, sauntering sideways, then trying to take my balance with a hip bump.

I absorbed the blow and turned it into another spin.

He stepped back and chuckled. "I've missed this."

"Me, too," I admitted. "I've missed *you*."

"That's sweet. But you can't stop me." His posture changed. "I've studied under the best dancers in the world. While you wasted your life playing superhero, I mastered the polka."

He lunged again, his movements merry and unfamiliar. He bounced like a boxer, zigging and zagging, his feet snapping out to strike my shins. I tried to catch his wrist, but he twisted aside and landed another kick to the side of my knee.

I tried a jumping kick, but Yuri sidestepped again and swept my ankle. My back hit the blacktop hard enough to knock the breath from my chest.

When I tried to sit up, he kicked my elbow. "I'm sorry, Stefano."

His next kick struck the nerves in my thigh, numbing my leg. A quick follow-up disabled my arm.

Death by polka. It wasn't the way I'd expected to go out.

His rhythm quickened, but before he could strike, the sound of tap dancing crackled through the air. I saw him spin, saw fury compress his face, and then the world went black.

I JERKED awake in the passenger seat of an old Jeep Wrangler that smelled like Kentucky Fried Chicken. The car jolted again as we hit another pothole. I turned my head to see Nora driving.

"Oh, good," she said. "The dumbass awakens."

I groaned. "What did you hit us with?"

"Modified Maxie Ford combo. I got lucky, caught him off guard, and drove him back long enough to get you out of there. Barely."

"Barely?"

"He recovered as I was pulling away and tried to take us out with an Irish Jig. Knocked off the rear bumper and wrecked my suspension. There's not much left of the motel, either."

Disco ... the polka ... the jig ... "When did he get so strong?"

"He's been traveling the world for his new master, challenging dancers to learn their secrets. He put the Riverdance guy in the hospital for six weeks."

"I loved that guy. It was like watching a superpowered marionette."

Without looking over, she whispered, "I'm glad you're okay."

"Thanks for saving my ass." I sighed. "You were right."

"I know. And I knew you'd ignore me and try to get through to him. I always loved that hopeless optimism, even though it drove me crazy."

My heart sped up. I wanted to reach over and take her hand. "I felt the same way about your overly practical approach to everything." I looked past her, to the streetlights and houses rushing by. "Where are we going?"

"That depends. Are you going to help me stop Mirrorball, or should I drop you off at the 'Swan Cave,' or whatever you call it?"

"The Nest," I muttered. "How do we stop him?"

She didn't answer.

"You want to kill him."

"I don't want to. We have to." Her voice cracked, ever so slightly. "You have to."

"Why me?"

"Because he won't expect it. He knows how you feel about him."

"About both of you." After all the years of training, all the secrecy and power and intensity, it was no surprise we'd fallen in love with each other. Our dances could knock a man unconscious from fifty yards, but for all our power, we were just kids, young and inexperienced and stupid. "You loved him too. And he loved you."

Silence.

I took a moment to try to calm my heartbeat and ease the anxiety digging at the walls of my stomach. "He told me Master was trying to get rid of you and me by pushing us to face the Trials too soon. He wasn't trying to steal Master's secrets for himself. He was trying to protect us."

"Of course he'd say that." She sighed. "Of course you'd believe him. You always took his side."

It was like fireworks exploding in my head, turning my vision red. "I didn't take anyone's side! Maybe if you hadn't been so eager to get rid of him—"

"You think it's my fault he became a supervillain?"

"We could have tried to help him."

"You never saw what he was becoming. All you saw were those big blue eyes, that dangerous smile, and those form-fitting tights he used to wear."

"Like you didn't check him out every time he walked away." She had the decency to blush. "Is that why you didn't even try to talk to me before going to Master when you found out what Yuri was doing?"

She slumped, the movement shockingly abrupt and graceless. "I didn't think you'd believe me. You and Yuri were always closer to each other than to me."

"That's not true," I protested.

"It doesn't matter anymore. Our honor as dancers requires us to try to stop him."

My head was throbbing. I closed my eyes and rubbed my forehead. "We need to find Master."

"Why?" Her question jumped higher in pitch.

"We have to warn her. And maybe she can help us beat him without killing him."

"You think I know where Master's been hiding all these years?"

I opened one eye. Nora had always been the teacher's pet. She'd idolized Master like a god, even more than Yuri and I had.

Her shoulders bunched tighter. "All right." She switched on her turn signal and pulled a U-turn. "Don't expect her to help us, though. She's too old-school. We were her disciples, and we abandoned her."

But if Yuri was telling the truth, Master had betrayed us first.

WE PULLED ONTO SECOND STREET, then through an alley into the private lot behind Little Leopards Dance Studio. This was Nora's place, her whole life. "I thought you were taking us to Master."

"I am." She shut off the engine.

I twisted in my seat. "Are you fucking kidding me? She *lives* with you?"

"She's a hundred and fifty-three years old, Stefano. After her challenge with Yuri, when she couldn't dance anymore, age began to catch up with her. She needed help getting around, and my apartment over the studio is large enough for two people."

"I guess when Master disowned us, she just meant me and Yuri. Not her precious Nora." Pain from the ass-kicking I'd received made me snarkier than usual.

Or maybe it wasn't the pain. Maybe it was envy over the extra years Nora had gotten with Master. How much had she learned? All that training, all those secrets and techniques I'd been denied.

I'd thought the three of us had ended up alone and miserable, but it was just me. Yuri had his criminal friends. Nora had Master.

"She hasn't taught me anything," Nora said quietly, as if

reading my thoughts. "The only time we talk about dance is when she's making fun of *Dancing with the Stars*."

We left the Jeep and climbed a narrow staircase to her apartment. I frowned and asked, "How does she—"

"There's a small elevator." She unlocked the apartment door and stepped inside.

I felt myself falling into my Night Swan persona, like I was entering a supervillain's lair where costumed henchmen might leap at me from every corner. I checked for ambush spots and potential exits: a small closet to the left of the entryway; a pair of windows in the brick wall to the right; the kitchen opened into a living room with two open doors on the far side: one to a bedroom and the other to a small bathroom.

Only after I'd noted every escape route did I let myself look at the figure sitting in a wheelchair watching hockey on a small, wall-mounted flat-screen.

My spine straightened. I fought the reflexive bow my body tried to make.

Master turned her wheelchair to face us. "He kicked your asses, didn't he?"

"Yes." Nora dropped her keys in a basket on the edge of the counter. "Disco and polka."

Master chuckled. "A true polka master can shatter a boulder with one kick. You're lucky to be alive."

My mouth finally started working again, and I blurted, "You're *old*!"

Master tilted her head, acknowledging me for the first time. "That costume makes your skin look like ash. With your coloration, you need something brighter. Like that green and silver number you wore for the Kansas City tournament. The one with all the sequins."

"The goal is to avoid being seen." The last time I'd seen Master, she'd appeared to be in her mid-fifties. Her near-immortality was a benefit of her dance, one of many secret techniques she'd refused to share.

Her hair had gone from fiery red to a wispy white, pulled back in a ponytail as thin as a dandelion stem. Age spots formed constellations on her papery skin. A Little Leopards sweatshirt with the sleeves torn off hung from her shoulders like she was a wire hanger.

"Mirrorball has joined the Obsidian Company," said Nora. "He's coming for you."

"I figured as much. You probably led him right to me. He could be circling right now, searching for a place to park."

I set aside my pride and asked, "Can you teach us what we need to know to defeat him?"

She wheeled closer. Even paralyzed from the waist down, there was an angelic grace to her every movement. "You really think you're ready? You believe you can master the Five-Spin Fouetté of Fury? The Forbidden Pop and Lock Lung Puncturing Technique? The Inverted Astaire? Pah. You never cared about the dance. You were only interested in power."

She glanced at Nora. "And you wanted nothing but approval. Yuri was the only one with a true passion for dance. A twisted, sociopathic passion, but passion nonetheless."

My fists clenched. "Is that why you tried to get rid of me and Nora?"

"I was trying to *focus* you. You were my disciples. That's a sacred bond. But you spent more time giggling and making out than you did practicing."

"We practiced ten hours a day," I protested.

"There are twenty-four hours in a day, Stefano," she shot back.

"What about sleep?"

"There are dance techniques that eliminate the need for sleep." She spun away with a huff.

"Yuri believes you wanted Nora and me to fail our Trials."

Master sniffed. "I wanted you to be worthy. If you couldn't devote yourselves to passing your Trials, you didn't deserve to be my disciples."

"We were *kids!*"

Nora touched my arm. "What matters now is stopping Mirrorball. If you don't help us, Master, he'll break you. His last training mission was with Sokolova."

Master grabbed an open beer bottle from the coffee table. "The pole dancer? Shit."

I looked from Master to Nora. "I don't understand."

"Pole dancing attacks the mind," said Master. "I doubt Yuri's learned all of Sokolova's tricks, but I'm still not strong enough to counter him."

"So, help us," I said, "before he dances your brain to tapioca."

"Even if I trusted you with the ancient knowledge, it would take years for you to learn the techniques. And ..." She glanced away and muttered, "You don't need them."

"What?" I asked.

"I've seen video footage of the Night Swan. I've watched Nora instructing those hyperactive hyenas she calls students. You are both ... adequate."

"But Master," Nora protested, "Yuri has studied so many different styles. He—"

"Don't fear the man who has practiced ten thousand dances. Fear the man who's practiced one dance ten thousand times."

I scowled. "You stole that from Bruce Lee."

"Maybe." She sighed. "I was more than a century old. What did I know of raising three horny teenagers in the modern world? You're right. I knew you and Nora weren't ready. I thought the Trials would break you, and I'd forge something stronger. I ... regret my misstep. I underestimated the bond you'd forged between the three of you."

It was the first time I'd heard Master admit fault about

anything. I started to speak. Nora's elbow to my ribs shut me up.

"Dance is passion. I thought your passion for one another eroded your focus. I hoped to redirect that passion. I pushed too hard, and I broke you. No, I allowed you to break one another. Yuri turned his pain and fury on me. Guilt made me hesitate during his challenge. And I paid the price."

"Master ..." Nora began.

"Fix what I broke," she said. "Find your passion. And do it quickly. He's here."

NORA'S STUDIO WAS METICULOUS. Framed photos of famous dancers hung on the walls, every one perfectly straight. (The pictures, not the dancers.)

Not a single fingerprint smudged the mirrors on the wall. Cubbyholes in primary colors stretched away to either side of the door, each one as bright as if it had been painted this morning. It was a pleasant place for a showdown, as these things went.

The door was broken. Yuri stood among the glass pebbles littering the floor like hail.

We'd come in through the back. The three of us stared at each other across the hardwood floor.

"Master is *here*?" Yuri shook his head. "Are you fucking kidding me?"

"She's not—" Nora began.

"Don't lie to me. Even broken, her rhythm is unmistakable." Yuri danced toward us. One hand rested against his head. The other pointed toward us, jerking from Nora to me and back: The Sprinkler. I'd once seen him destroy a malfunctioning vending machine with that dance. "Get out of my way. I won't let you sucker-step me like you did back at the motel."

Nora and I spread apart. I moved into second position. Her shoes tapped a quickening beat.

Yuri's hips moved rhythmically as he approached. I twirled, trying to get close enough to strike, but as I closed in, his pointing finger speared the hollow of my shoulder, just below the collarbone. I landed a glancing kick to his thigh as I spun away, pain exploding through my arm.

Nora glided in, her movements cold and precise, a scalpel to Yuri's fire. Her technical skill was beyond mine, maybe even beyond his, but it wasn't enough. Yuri switched smoothly from disco to polka, then dropped to the floor to perform a break-dancing spin that kicked Nora's legs out from under her.

I used my good arm to drag Nora out of the way of a polka strike that would have dislocated her knee.

I hauled her to her feet and pulled her into a twirl that ended with her back pressed to my chest, her face next to mine.

"What are you doing?" she breathed.

I spun her away, then drew her back again. "Argentine tango."

"We never mastered the tango."

"I know." Another quick turn. Our legs and feet wove in and out. I felt her pulse speed up.

Yuri retreated a step. I saw uncertainty in his eyes. This wasn't the dance he'd expected. I spun Nora again, launching her into a kick that clipped him in the jaw.

He staggered, eyes wide with shock. With a scowl, he drew a pipe the size of a baseball bat from a sheath on his back. He held it vertically and pressed a button. The pipe expanded. One spiked end jabbed into the ceiling, the other punctured the floor.

Before Nora could kill him for damaging the hardwood, he looped one leg around the makeshift pole and spun.

A surge of longing rocked me off balance. Nora felt it, too. I could tell by the way her hand tightened on mine, and her movements became wilder. We drifted toward Yuri.

"Pole dance," I gasped.

Yuri twirled again, raising both feet from the floor and slamming them down in reverse axe kicks that would have cracked our skulls if we hadn't pushed each other away.

"I can't focus," whispered Nora.

"Don't try." I dipped her over my hip, so low the back of her head brushed the floor. *Find your passion.* "Enjoy it."

How long had it been since I'd danced for the sheer joy of it? Nora stared up at me, her eyes wide, and then her mouth stretched into a smile. I brought her upright, dodging another of Yuri's kicks in the process.

There were no more words. Nora and I didn't need them. We took the desire and lust pulsing from Yuri's dance and channeled it into our tango.

We moved as one, every push and pull, every cling and release, every spin perfectly timed. The years fell away, and with them the scars and the bitterness, until there was only Nora's body against mine.

Yuri gripped the pole with both hands and launched another double-kick.

Nora and I pushed apart, letting his legs snap between us. I hooked my good arm around his waist. Nora kicked his hands free of the pole. I twirled him around my body, landing him on his feet between us.

He tried to fight, but Nora caught his arm and dipped him, just as I'd done with her moments before. She pulled him upright, and now it was my turn to bend him over my hip, to lower my face to his, to stare into those blue eyes and remember the feel of those plump lips on mine.

The tango's power was rough and unrefined, but it throbbed with passion and the joy of our years together. Memories and desire flowed through the three of us.

With a mischievous grin, I tilted my head toward Nora. Yuri bit his lower lip, barely breathing. Together we took Nora between us, letting her fall almost prone before pulling her back into our arms.

Her face was flushed. Her hands pressed our chests.

"I've missed you," I admitted. I took her hand and kissed it, then kissed Yuri on his stubbled cheek. "Both of you."

"Stefano …" He swallowed. "Nora."

Whatever else he might have said was lost as I snapped my left leg up in a perfect penché. My steel-toed slipper struck the back of his head and knocked him the hell out.

NORA'S VOICE crackled over the radio in my mask. "This is stupid, Stefano."

"It's Night Swan," I hissed.

"This is stupid, Night Swan."

"Thank you, Soft Shoe." I imagined her scowling at the code name. "Just relax and watch the back door. I know what I'm doing."

"I don't mean the crimefighting. I admit, it's a little exciting. But bringing *him* along? One tango and suddenly you trust him?"

"It was a really good tango."

To my left, Yuri cleared his throat. "He's on the same channel and can hear everything you two are saying."

"Redemption isn't a one-time thing," said Nora. "You've got a lot to make up for."

"But this is a good start," I interrupted, keeping my attention on the bar across the street.

After the fight at Nora's studio three nights ago, we'd taken Yuri back to the Nest. We spent most of the night arguing about what to do with him. He'd woken up around midnight and argued along with us.

Somewhere along the way, the fighting had given way to swapping stories of our years since we'd left each other. From there, we started talking about old memories of our training.

I was the one who'd proposed a trial team-up. Yuri was stronger than me or Nora, but despite all he'd learned from his new master, our tango had overpowered him easily. Imagine what the three of us could do together.

I didn't trust Yuri yet either, but I wanted to. And I think, deep down, he wanted that, too. He'd had opportunities to run off since that night, but he'd stayed at the Nest. We'd take it one step at a time and see how things progressed.

An orange vehicle—it looked like a pickup truck crossed with a glittering limousine—pulled up in front of the bar. A tall, lean white man in an armor-lined hoodie, tactical baseball cap, and night-vision sunglasses stepped out.

"That's him," said Yuri. "When I didn't kill Master, the Company sent Breakdancer to do the job."

I waited for Breakdancer and his retinue to go inside, then stood. "Come along, Grey Goose."

"I hate that name."

"My first choice was 'Disco Duck,' but there were copyright issues." I winked at him.

He glared, but the corner of his mouth quirked with amusement.

I touched my radio. "All right, my—" *My friends. My family. My loves.*

I shook myself. One step at a time. For tonight, we needed to focus on the mission. After that … "All right, team. Let's dance."

JIM C. Hines's first novel was *Goblin Quest*, the humorous tale of a nearsighted goblin runt and his pet fire-spider. Actor and author Wil Wheaton described the book as "too f***ing cool for words," which is pretty much the Best Blurb Ever. After finishing the goblin trilogy, he went on to write the Princess series of fairy tale retellings and the Magic ex Libris books, a modern-day fantasy series about a magic-wielding librarian, a dryad, a secret society founded by Johannes Gutenberg, a flaming spider, and an enchanted convertible. He's also the author of the Fable Legends tie-in *Blood of Heroes* and the *Janitors of the Post-Apocalypse* trilogy of humorous science fiction. His short fiction has appeared in more than 50 magazines and anthologies, including several earlier volumes of *Unidentified Funny Objects*.

Jim won the Hugo Award for Best Fan Writer in 2012. He has an undergraduate degree in psychology and a Masters in English, but when it comes to dancing … let's just say dance is *not* his superpower. He lives with his family in mid-Michigan. You can find him at www.jimchines.com or on Twitter as @jimchines.

SGT. YETI

Gini Koch

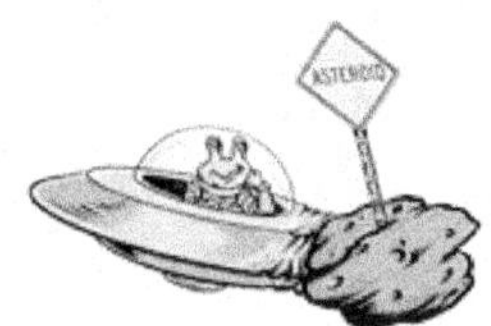

ommunication 12,236—Hallock Year 357,299—Earth Month August

To: Home Office—Greens Expansion Control Division—Earth Liaison & Requisition Officer Johnson

Sir,

We find ourselves in need of more rootweed. The Greens have made inroads and, though we have fought valiantly, they are making headway on this planet. Earth's dominant life forms are still too vulnerable to expect them to hold off the Greens by themselves. They can't handle the truth of our existence, let alone the Greens.

Please advise when we can expect new rootweed pods.

Yours respectfully,

Sgt. Yeti—Earth Outpost

INTERNAL COMMUNICATION—HALLOCK Year 357,299—Earth Month August

To: Bigfoot and Sasquatch—U.S. Territory

Listen, you idiots, how is it that we're the smartest life forms on this rock and yet you two redefine the term "easy to catch?" I'm begging—could you possibly stop getting photographed all over the place? We have a good setup here, and unless you want to go to a place where you have to actually do your jobs, stop being morons. If the Home Office realizes that more humans think we're real than believe that the Greens have shown up, we'll be relocated and someone else gets the cushiest gig in the galaxy.

Sgt. Yeti

INTERNAL COMMUNICATION—HALLOCK Year blah, blah, blah

To: Sgt. Yeti

CC: Sasquatch

Look, Sarge, we're doing our best. But we have to eat. Maybe if we had a better system than foraging for food we wouldn't have to get so close to the humans. Plus, we don't have enough staff to cover this whole continent. We get caught on film because we're trying to steal cars to get places faster. You try running across the entire state of Indiana without getting spotted. Or, as we say out here, that'll be the day.

Bigfoot

INTERNAL COMMUNICATION

To: Bigfoot

CC: Sasquatch

Are you kidding me? You two are in the most abundant region we have. It's not my fault that you and your families have managed to spread out so much. Remember that you know how to hunt, why don't you? We are not Yogi the Bear, here. We are a highly advanced race charged with the protection of this part of the galaxy from those maniacal Green monsters. More importantly, we are here to do a job that literally doesn't need doing, so, to repeat, unless you want to actually have to work for your living, get a grip and get it together.

Sgt. Yeti

Internal Communication

To: Sarge

CC: Biggie

Dudes. Come on. Stop the in-fighting, it harshes my zen. We are fine, Sarge. Rootweed is selling great in my half of the continent. Good stuff, too. The home whatevers should be hella proud. Humans love the stuff, too, so we're not going to run out.

I mean, I hope we're not going to run out.

We're not going to run out, right? RIGHT?

S'quatch

Internal Communication

To: Sasquatch

CC: Bigfoot

We are not running out of rootweed and, in fact, I've asked for more from the Home Office. But if you are constantly high, running around and getting photographed, it's going to make them suspicious and then, before you know it, there we are, sent to some awful gas giant or worse. There is no rootweed on a gas giant, in case you've forgotten.

Also, what the hell are you two doing in snack food commercials? Don't try to tell me it's a human in a costume, because I know what you, and all your family members, look like. *Harry and the Hendersons* was bad enough, and I remind you that Leonard is no longer on this planet because he foolishly let someone "try to take the mask off." It took me months of negotiation and some serious acting skills to convince the Home Office to allow the rest of us to remain here. You do not want to know where in this solar system Leonard ended up, but he'd be the butt of a lot of jokes, if you have the brains to grasp the innuendo.

The last sighting of any of us in the frozen parts of this world were so long ago that we're part of a Disney ride and considered cuddly. Learn from our example and just say no to being "caught" by humans.

Or, to put it more simply: do not make me leave Tibet and come there and kick your asses, because I will.

Sgt. Yeti

Communication 12,237—Hallock Year 357,299—Earth Month August

To: Sgt. Yeti—Earth Outpost

Sergeant,

Rootweed pods are being shipped. Expect deliveries within a week. Coordinates will be sent to each Requisitions Corporal planet-wide. Please have our agents try to move the livestock out of the way this time. We are not here to harm any Earth lifeforms, not even the flatulent ones.

Also, please note that there has been major Green activity in star systems nearby yours. Agents are unable to confirm directions Greens went when routed, but suspicions are high that they are heading Earth's way.

To that end, we are sending a Lieutenant Commander,

Melissa Gunnels Katano, who reports in directly to Colonel Daniel Chulsky, to determine if more troops are needed and to lead said troops if so. Please ensure that she is given the proper respect and authority her station demands. She will arrive at your location within the next Earth week.

Best,

Home Office—Greens Expansion Control Division—Earth Liaison & Requisition Officer Johnson

Internal Communication

To: All Hands

URGENT! URGENT! URGENT!

The Home Office thinks we have a lot of Greens heading this way and is sending some Lt. Commander, Melissa Gunnels Katano, to oversee the expected battles. And the likelihood that she's going to ask for more troops is high.

For those of you too stoned on rootweed to grasp the ramifications: this is bad, very bad.

Everyone needs to button up, and button up fast. Time to pretend to be the crack military commandos the Home Office thinks we are. Katano is supposed to be arriving in Tibet within a few days. Assume that she will land somewhere else as a "surprise tactic" to catch us off-guard.

Therefore, all hands must be ready for both the rootweed drops—and this time, Sasquatch, for the sake of your rootweed addiction, make sure all the cows are in their barns and that no other Earth animals are harmed because of delivery—and to have a Lt. Commander with the ability to send us to a gas giant or worse appear out of nowhere with absolutely no warning.

This means no commercials, no "accidentally getting spotted by hikers," no lounging around. Until she arrives and we can get her to go elsewhere, we are CRACK MILITARY COMMANDOS and we will act like it.

Sgt. Yeti

INTERNAL COMMUNICATION

To: Sgt. Yet

CC: Sasquach

Roger that, big man. We are buttoning things up fast. The Wendigo clan could be an issue—they're on another "humans are the supreme delicacy" kick for their annual cookoff, but I've sent troops there to ensure they postpone this year's festivity. And before you pop a blood vessel, they're clear that if we get in trouble there will be no celebrations of any kind, so we're all good on my side of things.

Bigfoot

INTERNAL COMMUNICATION

To: Sgt. Yeti

CC: Bigfoot

Dudes, we're cool here. All is in readiness for arrivals. My team's bet, by the way, is that Lieutenant Whoever arrives *with* the rootweed. We are totally prepared to show her a good time, so roger all the things!

S'quatch

INTERNAL COMMUNICATION: Private

To: Sgt. Yeti

You don't even have to ask. I'm leaving my side of this

"abundant area" with Mrs. B in charge (and I know you prefer her leadership to mine, which was why we made this decision), and heading as fast as I can steal a car over to where Sasquatch is expecting the rootweed because, stoned out of his mind though he is, you and I both know that his guess is probably correct. Advise if you're joining us—I expect we'll need your way with handling the higher ups.

Also suggest we take The Challenge to Deer Trail immediately and keep her there as long as possible.

Yours in utter stress,

Bigfoot

Internal Communication: Private

To: Bigfoot

Send rendezvous coordinates and I'll catch a plane. And before you ask a stupid question, I sit on the wing and freak nervous passengers out. Yes, that *Twilight Zone* episode was taken from the writer's real life. In this situation, I'll try to stay out of sight, but if things go badly, getting seen by someone on Air China is the least of our worries.

Agree with where we should take The Challenge.

See you soon,

Sgt. Yeti

Communication 7,450—Hallock Year 357,299—Earth Month August

To: Home Office—Greens Expansion Control Division—Colonel Daniel Chulsky

Colonel,

Have arrived safe and sound. Was greeted by Sgt. Yeti, who

somehow determined my arrival coordinates. Am impressed with his ability. Under-Srgts. Bigfoot and Sasquatch were also in attendance. Very nice, appropriate, military greeting.

Was immediately taken to our bunker, Titan One, in someplace called Colorado, which, since I landed in someplace called Wyoming, was quite an interesting journey, having never been in what's called a Hummer before.

Trip was long but relatively uneventful, with the sergeants on constant watch for Greens—apparently the Greens have taken to disguising themselves as local law enforcement. Due to my presence, Sgt. Yeti chose discretion over valor any time Greens in Disguise were spotted. We were not noticed by the higher sentience natives, though they, too, seemed to give the Greens in Disguise no reason to attack.

Now safely in the bunker, we will convene with countermeasures and defenses for potential Greens attacks.

Yours,

Lt. Commander MGK, currently on Earth

COMMUNICATION 7,451—HALLOCK Year 357,299—Earth Month August

To: Lt. Cmndr. MGK

Melissa,

Glad to hear of your safe arrival. Yeti had not shared that the Greens are hiding in plain sight, so to speak. Is this a new development?

Col. D. Chulsky

COMMUNICATION 7,452—HALLOCK Year 357,299—Earth Month August

To: Home Office—Greens Expansion Control Division—Colonel Daniel Chulsky

Colonel,

Have asked Sgt. Yeti about the undercover Greens. He states that they are under control and has not reported because of such. Our commandos are allowing the Greens to think they are fooling everyone, which simultaneously allows our troops to keep an eye on all their activity, since they are driving around in clearly marked vehicles and wearing distinctive uniforms, based on their ranks within their armed forces.

The native population tends to give these undercover Greens wide berth, so the plan appears to be working. Sgt. Yeti shared that there are regular natives who also wear these uniforms and drive these vehicles, so a unilateral attack is out of the question. Plus, I have to admit that if what the Greens are doing is driving around making others travel more slowly, they seem relatively benign. However, we all know they are not to be trusted, and Sgt. Yeti assures me that vigilance is his team's watchword.

Other than these disguised Greens, I have not spotted any enemy activity but, since Sgt. Yeti has made it plain that there are more enemy forces than I've yet seen, I plan a sightseeing tour in order to make a full assessment.

There is something called "fudge" that Under-Sgt. Sasquatch insists I need to try. He feels that it is second only to our native rootweed in Greens repulsion.

Yours,

Lt. Cmndr. MGK—currently on Earth

Internal Communication: Private

To: The Beast of the East

Babe,

Sgt. Yeti is working his charm on The Challenge, but she's insisting on a tour of "hot spots" to assess our capabilities.

We've managed to convince her that all Earth law enforcement has been infiltrated by Greens who are not doing anything other than "the job" so as to blend in. But we need to show effective Greens control so that she's impressed but doesn't feel that more troops are needed.

What we're thinking is "reenactment" of some kind. There has to be a comics convention going on somewhere, so find it and figure out how to make it work. You probably have less than a week, based on The Challenge's desire to "see the action" and Sasquatch's telling her about all the junk food the natives make in droves.

Sgt. Yeti is counting on you, babe, and so am I. We'll roll with whatever you come up with, just remember–big but not TOO big. (Just like me, wink, wink.)

Love and snugs,

Your Biggie-Boo

Internal Communication: Private

To: Biggie-Boo

Have found likely option, but I don't know that Sgt. Yeti is going to like it. Head The Challenge to Atlanta, Georgia. Big to-do there, tons of costumes, the Wendigo and Swamp Beast clans adore it because they can walk about without issue. Meaning that we will be out in full force.

Have assigned a team to find some humans to imitate Greens. We can do a "battle" that will impress.

As a warning, it's hotter than the inside of Sasquatch's smoker down there. No idea what to tell the good sergeant, but he might want to invest in an ice suit of some kind. The Challenge can be assured that she's heading into a total Hot Spot, so hopefully it'll make her happy and she'll drop from the humidity alone.

Snugs and love,
Beastie Girl

: Private

To: The Beast of the East

CC: Bigfoot

Bertha,

Well done, as always, and I expected nothing less. The Challenge is thrilled with this opportunity to "get her paws dirty" so just make sure whoever's playing the Greens can handle being tossed around, because it's clear The Challenge expects to "lead the charge" or similar. I know, aren't we lucky?

If you can please coordinate an "after battle" scene along the way–have the Honey Island Swamp Clan do some work on this, we'll ensure we go to Atlanta via their general direction—that would be ideal. Remind them that The Challenge is going to be determining what supplies we need, so have them make it look good and we should be sitting pretty for requisitions.

Any other "battles" or "aftermaths" that can be arranged would be helpful as well. Will be instructing troops to send details directly to you. Once we leave "the bunker" it will be best to have only one point of contact, and I know you're the correct Hallockian for the job.

Best,
Sgt. Yeti

INTERNAL COMMUNICATION: Private

To: All Hands

Things are going well with The Challenge and we will be heading toward Atlanta, GA soon. Contact the Beast of the East for particulars and make plans to show up, or else.

Please advise Beast of the East if your particular clan/group/army of one will be able to provide "anti-Greens activity" along the way. We are more than happy to make our route circuitous, since we have time to kill before the "action" in Atlanta begins.

Other than for dire emergencies (and that does NOT include the rootweed supplies needing to be replenished), do not contact me, Bigfoot, or Sasquatch. Run all communications through the Beast of the East to ensure The Challenge is not tipped off to anything being planned.

Remember what we're working for: the ability to keep on not working.

Sgt. Yeti

Internal Communication: Private

To: Sgt. Yeti

CC: Biggie Boo

Sergeant,

Honey Island Clan is in full readiness. They're in possession of lots of leftover crap from Mardi Gras so they will make it colorful as well as grisly. They are enthused about the opportunity, and that's a direct, non-sarcastic quote. I think they feel left out by the human population in terms of sightings, so are keen to be of service. They have also agreed to head to Atlanta immediately after your party leaves, taking a different route, so they will be on hand to help with "the big battle" and will recruit any loner clan members along the way.

Have feelers out to other groups and expect you to have a

good deal of proof that we're doing what we're here for to share with The Challenge.

Best,

Bertha, The Beast of the East

INTERNAL COMMUNICATION: Private

To: Sgt. Yeti

CC: Biggie Boo

Sergeant,

Attached is the map of your suggested route, complete with indicators for what has just happened/is about to happen at each location. Advise if any of these are overkill and we can cancel.

Best,

Bertha, The Beast of the East

attachment: ShowTheChallengeAGoodTime.jpg

EXTERNAL COMMUNICATION: Private/Encrypted

To: Sgt. Yeti

CC: Yolanda Greene Monster Not The Beverage

Sergeant,

So ... Atlanta team has run into an ... interesting situation. Apparently, we do indeed have Greens on the planet. Perhaps more than originally presumed. Perhaps a LOT more than originally presumed. And they, as it turns out, have their own Challenge arriving. Need you to broker a settlement. Have added their leader onto our communications for expediency's sake.

Best,

Under-Sgt. Bertha, The Beast of the East

EXTERNAL COMMUNICATION: Private/Encrypted

To: Sgt. Yeti

CC: The Beast of the East

Sergeant,

I understand from your subordinate that we are in similar situations. So far, your people have not bothered ours and vice versa. We, like you, enjoy hanging out on this rock with nothing much to do and plenty to eat, drink, and amuse ourselves with. We, like you, would like to continue to hang out like this for the foreseeable future.

In other words: help.

From what I've picked up, I'm not nearly as facile with this kind of subterfuge as you are and would like to learn and get tips. But first, we have to deal with unpleasant visitors, just as you are doing. We are willing to do whatever it takes (as long as it doesn't require the actual shedding of bodily fluids necessary to maintain life) to ensure that our current way of life and yours continues without issue.

Please advise next steps.

Yours,

Yolanda Greene Monster Not The Beverage

attachment: GreensUpperLevelInspectionPrepFile.docx

INTERNAL COMMUNICATION: Private

To: The Beast of the East

CC: Bigfoot

Bertha,

If you feel it's safe, show the Greens leader—and is that seriously her name, Green with an extra 'e' at the end? —the action plan and get her to send troops to each area. Some will have to play dead, some will get to escape. Some of ours will also have to play dead and/or escape, so advise the teams along the way. Deaders and escapees alike need to head for Atlanta the moment we, and the Greens' inspection team, leave each area.

Just like we did when we were stuck on that rock in the Sirius system, only this time with the goal of impressing just enough to stick around, versus showing that we'd "killed every last one of them and they'll never come HERE again" as we did before.

We got this.

Sgt. Yeti

INTERNAL COMMUNICATION: Private

To: Sgt. Yeti

CC: Bigfoot

As the Moons of Hallock are my witness, that's her name. I think she thinks it's cute. And, BTW, Monster is her last name. Supposedly. Who can tell with Greens? Just use the techniques I know you have and it'll all work out.

Best,

Under-Sgt. Bertha, The Beast of the East

EXTERNAL COMMUNICATION: Private/Encrypted

To: Yolanda Greene Monster NTB

CC: The Beast of the East

Yolanda, may I call you Yolanda? Yolanda, I believe we can definitely help each other out. Under-Srgt. Bertha will direct your teams into place. Ensure that you are staying near to your Challenge so that you can abort or alter plans as necessary. We, like you, wish to lose no important bodily fluids—though I hear that we're all going to lose a lot of water in Atlanta, presuming that you guys sweat.

Just remember that we have big teeth and bigger claws and be sure you don't even think about attempting a double-cross. I may head the laziest team in the galaxy, but I can promise you that they can turn into the most vicious team in the galaxy should their extended R&R posting be threatened in any way.

Yours in camaraderie,

Sgt. Yeti

COMMUNICATION 7,453—HALLOCK Year 357,299—Earth Month August

To: Home Office—Greens Expansion Control Division—Colonel David Chulsky

Colonel,

Had no idea what a hot spot Earth actually is. Impressed by Yeti—he's kept things under control. He says he's refused to worry anyone at the Home Office, since he feels his troops are more than handling things. Have to agree—so far, what I've seen is us routing Greens any time one of them dares to show a toe, or whatever they actually have on their feet, near a human settlement of any kind.

Would normally advise a full planetary cleanse, but Yeti assures me that this is not needed, pointing out that, one day, we hope to have the humans get smart enough to join us in this battle, and wiping them all out now would be detrimental to long-term plans.

Have no idea why Yeti is not looking for career advancement. He's a tactician of the highest order. But he insists that his place is here, on the ground, doing the work "he was born to do" and I can't fault him for following his heart on this, particularly because his results are so good.

Am requesting more rootwood supplies. Per Under-Sgt. Sasquatch, the plants assist in keeping the Greens at bay, and, considering what they could be asking for, more rootweed seems like a small thing for so courageous a group.

Have sent coordinates for next rootweed drop. We are heading to someplace called Atlanta where Yeti's sources say a large Greens invasion is planned. Hoping that the appearance of supplies will strengthen our side and dismay our opponents.

Yours,

Lt. Cmndr. MGK—currently on a midnight train to Georgia, per Under-Sgt. Bigfoot

P.S. "Fudge" is quite amazing and comes in a variety of tastes. That it repels the Greens is just more proof that they're evil and need to be eradicated.

EXTERNAL COMMUNICATION: Private/Encrypted

To: Sgt. Yeti

I am impressed. Your people are not the hairy, drooling idiots we have been told they are. So far, the Challenges from both sides seem pleased, impressed, and none the wiser.

Officially, we are pleased to be working with you. Unofficially, boy, do we have a lot to learn!

Yours,

Yolanda

EXTERNAL COMMUNICATION: Private/Encrypted

To: YGMNTB

Glad we're able to impress. Nice to know you're not some weird hive mind whose sole purpose is to enslave every intelligent race you meet. Also, nice to know that you have not tried to stick anything where the sun don't shine, at least not without permission.

Officially, glad we're able to help. Unofficially, stick with me, kid, you'll go places. Or, rather, stay where the livin' is easy.

Yours,

Sgt. Yeti

COMMUNICATION 7,454—HALLOCK Year 357,299—Earth Month August

To: Lt. Cmndr. MGK

Melissa,

Rootweed en route. Am pleased to hear that Yeti and team are doing a good job—a relief in many ways. Please advise if you feel team should remain in place, remain with reinforcements, or be sent elsewhere to work their magic.

Best,

Col. D. Chulsky

P.S. Why are you on a midnight train? Is that the only time the trains run?

COMMUNICATION 7,455—HALLOCK Year 357,299—Earth Month September

To: Home Office—Greens Expansion Control Division—Colonel Daniel Chulsky

Colonel,

"Midnight train" is spy code for "secret." I honestly thought you'd know that without having to be told, but we all have areas where we've missed key facts.

Have arrived in Atlanta just in time. Greens are not the only aliens here. We are unsure if joint or single attacks are planned, but Yeti has remained calm and cool under pressure. He reminds me a bit of you, to be honest.

Currently no need for more troops—worried that too big a show of force will create havoc rather than control the situation. Will advise when able. Thank you for the rootweed, it's already come in handy.

Yours,

Lt. Cmndr. MGK

EXTERNAL COMMUNICATION: Private/Encrypted

To: Sgt. Yeti

I bow down to the superior mind, I truly do. That was, in a word, spectacular. The way you convinced both my Challenge and yours that everyone at that convention were alien refugees was, in a word, masterful. The "battle" was excellent. And our Challenge was more than happy to "leave to fight another day" because your side convinced him that leaving meant victory for our side. I literally don't know how you did it, though I suspect that the rootweed you guys gave us to give to the Challenge probably helped greatly.

Teach me, oh very wise one. And let me know if you need a favor I can do.

Yours,

Yolanda

COMMUNICATION 7,456—HALLOCK Year 357,299—Earth Month September

To: Home Office—Greens Expansion Control Division—Colonel Daniel Chulsky

Colonel,

I know you just received a communication from me, but I have excellent news! We have routed the Greens on planet and caused the other aliens to fall in line and march under our banner!

The bad news is that most of these aliens appear to be refugees and seem to be planning to stay on Earth. However, they have all agreed to remain under Hallockian rule. Other than the Greens, who fled off-planet. Reports indicate they were heard saying they were heading to the Tau Ceti system, so best to send troops there to head them off.

Remain impressed with Yeti's ability to handle this situation and keep it mostly violence-free. We have a good soldier here, leading other good soldiers, and while I would suggest a commendation ceremony at the least, Yeti is too humble to accept it, and I believe we should abide by his wishes, since his team is very loyal.

Best,

Lt. Cmndr. MGK

P.S. Now that the threat is eradicated, would like to request leave in order to remain on Earth and see some areas that are not hotbeds of Greens activity. I believe I have at least a month's worth of available time, if not more.

Internal Communication

To: All Hands

BCC: YGMNTB

Many congratulations on the successful completion of your duties. We are once again victorious.

As some of you may or may not know, Lt. Cmndr. Melissa Gunnels Katano is planning to stay on-planet to "sightsee" for a few weeks. I will take one for the team and tour our honored guest around. Please do your best to ensure that we have no Greens issues, or any other issues, for that matter.

Sgt. Yeti

COMMUNICATION 7,457—HALLOCK Year 357,299—Earth Month October

To: Home Office—Greens Expansion Control Division—Colonel Daniel Chulsky

Colonel,

Have realized my life's ambition and am requesting immediate fulltime transfer to Earth, as Sgt. Yeti's liaison to the Home Office. Earth needs Sgt. Yeti and his team to remain here, and I find myself compelled to remain as well. A team this well-organized is rarely seen, and I wish to continue to learn all I can while assisting in whatever ways possible.

Also, possibly because of Earth's soil variations, our rootweed is a formidable deterrent, so am requesting more pods to be sent along with my reassignment papers.

Best,

Lt. Cmndr. MGK

COMMUNICATION 7,457—HALLOCK Year 358,299—Earth Month October

To: Lt. Cmndr. MGK

Melissa,

I'm saddened to lose your abilities to highlight infractions, but understand that when the higher calling calls, one must answer.

You are officially permanently assigned to Earth as the Home Office Liaison to Sgt. Yeti's commando forces. Have requested monthly rootweed drops for your new team; please advise if they are needed with a higher frequency.

Best of luck with your new position. We await your reports with great interest.

Yours,

Colonel Daniel Chulsky—Home Office—Greens Expansion Control Division

EXTERNAL COMMUNICATION: Private/Encrypted

To: YGMNTB

Need to call in that favor. My personal Challenge has discovered the joys of Earth and wants to stay forever. Fortunately for all of us, she's also discovered the joys of me, and has been reassigned permanently. This is good news for all.

I need you to create a situation that demands that all my higher ups stay far, far away from Earth, since we need to invite them to the wedding, but don't want them to actually attend.

What do you have for me?

Sgt. Yeti

COMMUNICATION 7,458—HALLOCK Year 358,299—Earth Month December

To: Home Office—Greens Expansion Control Division— Colonel Daniel Chulsky

Colonel,

I am thrilled to share that Sgt. Yeti has asked for my paw in marriage and I have accepted. Would love for you to attend the ceremony, if convenient. Realize that Greens repulsion takes priority, so please advise if your attendance is possible. Wedding is in two weeks.

All best,

Lt. Cmndr. Melissa Gunnels Katano, soon to be Yeti

COMMUNICATION 7,459—HALLOCK Year 358,299—Earth Month December

To: Lt. Cmndr. MGK-Yeti

Melissa,

Am sad to say that Greens activity in all the star systems surrounding Earth make anyone's attendance impossible. Those vicious Green monsters are playing havoc with everyone. Only Earth seems immune, which makes my decision to assign you there permanently seem wiser than ever before. With you and Sgt. Yeti at the helm, I expect Earth to remain a safe outpost until the day the humans advance enough to join us in the good fight.

Everyone at the Home Office wishes you and Sgt. Yeti a full life of happiness, many cubs, and constant success against the Greens. A gift basket and extra rootweed supplies are on their way.

With disappointment for me and joy for you, I remain,

Colonel Daniel Chulsky—Home Office—Greens Expansion Control Division

INTERNAL COMMUNICATION: Private

To: All Hands

CC: YGMNTB

You're all invited to my wedding. We're being nice and holding it in North America, since most of you whiners say it's too cold in Tibet in the wintertime. For people covered in thick fur, you all complain about cold weather a lot. The Greens, I get why they don't want to go, but the rest of you need to ask your-selves if you're still Hallockians or not.

Anyway and yes, before you ask, more rootweed is coming for the ceremony. Thankfully, the Higher Ups at the Home Office have decided to take a pass, them having to deal with Greens activity all around us, for which we thank our new bestie, Yolanda Greene Monster Not The Beverage.

Mrs. Yeti-to-Be would like all varieties of fudge, funnel cakes, fry breads, saltwater taffy, cupcakes, beef jerky, hot dogs, and whatever other regional junk food you guys like as wedding gifts. What can I say? My girl likes to eat. If you're not sure, run it by Sasquatch, who hooked her onto most of these things.

For any wondering if the first, late Mrs. Yeti would be pleased with my taking a new wife after one hundred years—she was the one who always said that the best post was the cushiest post, and the best way to ensure a cushy post was to marry the person in charge of keeping you in said cushy post. So, yes, she'd be all in on this one.

And I expect all of you to be with me for this one. See you all at the backside of Mt. Rushmore on Christmas Day. And yes, if we're spotted, the Greens in attendance will help us put on a show for whoever might be watching.

Sgt. Yeti

GINI KOCH STARTED WRITING in the American Southwest as something to do in between staring at pictures of good-looking leading men, but now sweats out the words, both liter-ally and figuratively, in Hotlanta and dreams of dry heat.

She's best known for her award-winning Alien/Katherine "Kitty" Katt series from DAW Books, which started with *Touched by an Alien* and has sixteen books out currently, with seventeen through twenty on the way.

Gini's made the most of multiple personality disorder by writing under a variety of other pen names as well, including G.J. Koch (the Alexander Outland series), Anita Ensal, Jemma Chase, A.E. Stanton (the New West Series and the Legend of Belladonna series), and J.C. Koch, all with stories featured in excellent anthologies, available now and upcoming. No matter what length—from science fiction, fantasy, paranormal, space opera, urban fantasy, horror, mystery, thriller, dystopian, Westerns, romantic suspense, and more—if it's genre, she writes it.

She's an avid follower of pop culture, comics, and anything and everything animated. She's still inspired mostly by good-looking leading men and driven to keep her Canine Death Squad and Killer Kitties in kibble and treats.

Reach her via: www.ginikoch.com

THE GREAT BEYOND COMMANDS

John Wiswell

I f you were stalking me this morning, then you will never feel compelled to do so again. The forces of the Great Beyond command you not to follow me to my apartment, and not to the library or the coffee place either. Whoever you are looking for, you will no longer suspect me. You will view me as an inoffensive man with no magic powers.

Also, you're going to stop going through my trash. Whatever interest you had in my trash, you will no longer feel it. In fact, the forces of the Great Beyond command you to stay away from the apartment complex's whole garbage collection area.

This brainwashing spell is goodbye, mysteriously hot vigilante guy. Have a nice life.

HOW THE HELL are you here again?

The forces of the Great Beyond command you to rethink blaming all magicians for your boyfriend's murder, just like I won't blame every vigilante for what you tried to do to me tonight. I get that emotionally processing loss is hard, but this isn't the way.

You will look up community organizers and local independent detectives. You will find justice for your boyfriend by doing better research. And if your sleuthing does lead you to investigate a magician living in my apartment building, you will absolutely never think it's me. I'm an academic! I'm too boring a guy to murder people!

The forces of the Great Beyond command you to not take your sadness out on strangers.

No matter how good you look in those pants. Seriously, the forces of the Great Beyond command you to leave me your tailor's address.

Alright? Now wake up from this trance and get out of here. Goodbye forever.

OH, come on.

You will not ask me to help find your boyfriend's murderer.

The forces of the Great Beyond command you to observe me as a clumsy academic with no special skills. You will not drop in on me out of nowhere ever again, and you will forget the magical paraphernalia you saw in my closet. You will remember sex toys instead. Really weird ones.

That should get you to quit snooping.

YOU WILL NOT ASK me about those sex toys as a fucking icebreaker.

The forces of the Great Beyond command you to not surprise me with fresh açaí and dark chocolate muffins, and to not suggestively compliment the smell of my aftershave, and to not wear those leather pants with the three buttons on the fly. I think I almost flustered to death.

You will forget me flustering. You will definitely forget that.

That said … you will leave some of those case files about your boyfriend's murder. The magician on the third floor is kind of sketchy. So give me those files, and get out.

STOP RIGHT THERE.

The forces of the Great Beyond command that you will not go after this magician alone.

Yes, the magician in 35-A probably is the murderer. But you'll be killed if you go alone.

Even though you think I'm a harmless academic, you will let me come with you. This way, he won't burn that cute stubble off your face. If I perform magic to protect your himbo vigilante ass, then you will forget it. If we survive, I will still be a harmless academic to you.

Also, if we survive, you will tell me if you are actually wearing tighter pants every time we meet. Because. Oh. My. God.

I DON'T KNOW how to do this. Of course busting that creep didn't bring you peace. You're eating yourself alive. I've got to try something. Will this even work?

You are not to blame for your boyfriend's death.

The forces of the Great Beyond command you to realize you weren't home that night and, even if you were, you couldn't have stopped that magician from doing what he wanted. Your boyfriend was your whole world, so you created a narrative in which it was your fault. I've done that to myself before. You've got to let that narrative go.

I know this is hard. I'm so sorry. There's no spell to undo heartbreak.

You have to try to let go. Please try.

WHAT THE HELL? You can't leave. The forces of the Great Beyond command you to not move to another country. You can't …

Damn it, what am I doing? Of course you can leave. You've got to live your life. It's just, I'm …

Look, I ordered you not to realize things about me. I pushed you away and you kept coming and now you're leaving when I'm not pushing. I want something that's not mine here. I'm the problem. I've got to do this.

The forces of the Great Beyond command you to remember everything. You will now remember every thought and feeling that I previously made you repress. You will no longer forget what's convenient for me. And …

And you will not let me control you again. Whatever spell I cast in the future, whatever I say, it will not control your decisions.

You have to be free.

Even if this is goodbye.

AFTER THAT NIGHT, I was so afraid I'd never see you again. I couldn't get over you. How you infuriated me? How you flirted with me? How you made me want to get up and do something?

You cast a spell over me just by being yourself.

Nobody ever got under my skin like you do. You think I

helped heal you, but you're the only person who ever got me out of my apartment. I would've never looked up from my books if not for you.

You bother me like nobody else.

You compel me like nobody else.

And your taste in pants is absolutely breathtaking.

So, I only have one thing left to say:

I do.

JOHN WISWELL IS a disabled writer who lives where New York keeps all its trees. He has won the Nebula Award for Best Short Story for "Open House on Haunted Hill," and won the Locus Award for Best Novelette for "That Story Isn't the Story." His works have appeared in *Uncanny Magazine*, the *LeVar Burton Reads Podcast*, *Tordotcom*, and *The Magazine of Fantasy & Science Fiction*, among other fine venues. His debut novel *Someone You Can Build a Nest In* will release from DAW Books in Spring 2024. You can find more about him on Twitter at @Wiswell and at his blog at johnwiswell.blogspot.com.

THE SECOND WISH

James Beamon

Black Hephaestus wanted to kick that genie's ass but he could no longer kick. Even in his daydreams, his legs were stunted. So, Black Hephaestus contented himself to envisioning his hard-knuckled, smith-forged, hammer-wielding, steel-beating hands wrapped around that genie's soft neck.

Clear as glass he saw the genie, who looked like a racist old white man in a cheap suit anyway, uselessly flailing from the chokehold. No way was the genie getting out from under the god's Popeye-sized forearms. Soon the genie's flailing would slow down, followed by the genie frantically tapping on the god's arm until the tapping slowed down, too, and then stopped altogether.

Mmmm ... go to sleep, ho.

Black Hephaestus shook his head to dispel the thought. Until he could actually get to the genie, thoughts like that weren't gonna help him take over the rap game. He looked out from his high-rise Manhattan apartment at New York, concrete jungle where dreams are made of (there's nothing you can't do!) for inspiration. This was his one and only way to get inspired since none of the Muses wanted to kick it with a brother. Sufficiently motivated, he focused on the notebook resting on his formerly functional legs, which were naturally resting in his wheelchair, and started penning the ill lyrics.

"Where do I begin, can't trust no jinn. Leave ya blowin' in the wind, no juice no gin. Blaestus!"

Or should he go by Bleezy? Now that he understood his godly nature, he knew he had to take time and carefully forge both the raps and the rap persona. He had made the mistake of freestyling when he had challenged his brother.

Never get into a rap battle with the god of war.

Ares had called him all sorts of names—herbs, spices, zodiac signs, trucker handles—shit that didn't even really rhyme but the god had made it work. Driven by the infectious power of DJ Apollo's hard ass beats, they had created a street banger, an instant classic that drove Ares's record sales through the stratosphere.

The best-sellingest album of all time? Michael Jackson's *Thriller*. The second best? God of War's *Turkey Baestus*. The lyrics, both powerful and divine, came unbidden to Blaestus's mind as if they were shouted down from on high.

Black Heph, not like Hugh Hef. Girl's too fine but can't get no sex. Reckless to fight me. See? Ain't got no manners. Face look like you got beat with your own hammers.

Now Blaestus, maybe Bleezy, was the laughingstock of the gods. It didn't help that his face wasn't a picnic, something Blaestus couldn't help but admit to himself. He had the hair and beard of Abe Lincoln and the countenance of Sloth from the *Goonies*, which the god of war had pointed out when he had called Blaestus "Abe-sloth Fratelli." Even Prometheus had hit Twitter between liver treatments, jaundice, and nausea to say, "Damn, and I thought I was sick! Rather face the eagle! #blackandblueheph." Blaestus couldn't even walk it off thanks to his toy legs. Why did fate have to be so cruel?

Then he remembered the middle aspect of Fate was his cat

playing with a yarn ball. Hell, the third aspect was his three-year-old daughter who wouldn't stop running with the scissors. Fate wasn't cruel, it was cute. The thirty million subscribers on their YouTube channel proved that. Thirty million!

His cellphone's ring stopped him from drinking more of that bitter quaff of hater-ade as if it was the sweet nectar of ambrosia. Blaestus heard his lawyer Effie Hampton on the other end.

"You're trending," Effie said.

"Shit," he swore. "Why?"

It was never good when Blaestus trended. Last time rap beef got cooked to the flavor of utter humiliation. The time before that his wife released a sex tape which didn't feature him. *Deep breaths.* For the umpteenth time, Blaestus had to remind himself that his wife had involuntarily ascended into the indescribable beauty and sexually charged nature of the goddess of love. In other words, it wasn't her fault that she was a tart.

"You won your case," Effie said.

"Hells yeah!" Blaestus shouted. "Pop is installing the ramp?"

"As we speak."

"Soon I'll be able to roll into an Olympus Tower that's completely wheelchair accessible and get what's mine."

"You could've just had someone carry you up the stairs into the building," Effie said.

"Ain't nobody carrying me," Blaestus said indignantly. "I'm a god."

Silence reigned briefly.

"Even if I wasn't a god," Blaestus continued, "and hadn't acquired my disability through immortal ascension, do you know how demeaning being carried is for all my disabled peeps out there?"

"Sorry," Effie said. "It was just the most expedient path versus a nearly yearlong lawsuit. But you're right. And you won because of it."

Another silence, Silence Junior, began its brief reign.

"You wanna hear my rhymes?" Blaestus asked.

"I charge you," Effie reminded him. "For my time."

"Sounds like yes to me." And with that, he spit that fire.

Dropping rhymes as hard as concrete was really a subterfuge. What he didn't tell Effie is that his father had built Olympus Tower with the sole motive of keeping Blaestus out and away from the genie. Only the genie's master could actually handle or move the lamp unless the genie was between masters. Instead, the father of the gods had built two dozen wheelchair-defeating steps around the lamp, all to keep Blaestus from that last and final wish which threatened to undo it all.

Then it dawned on Blaestus that he didn't need subterfuge for his lawyer. It wasn't any of Effie's effin' business why he needed a wheelchair ramp installed at Olympus Tower. Besides that, she was charging him two hundred and twenty bones an hour for the privilege of listening to him set Greek fire to the rap game. Blaestus reminded himself that the streets was watching and you can't get concert dollars paying people to take the tickets. So, he politely hung up.

He got back to forging butter lyrics. First, he called Ares soft like baby thighs. Unfortunately, not much rhymed with Ares. He settled for a near rhyme and a metaphor. *Leave him comatose if dope rhymes was toast, Ares the god would lactose like dairy.*

Maybe he should spell lactose as "lack toast" for all the potential fans who'll come seeking to dissect and analyze his rhymes once he blew up. May as well enable the young'uns of the future. While Blaestus was practically penning Ares's death certificate, his phone rang. It was his sister Athena wanting to FaceTime. Begrudgingly, he accepted. She popped into his screen with a face that was beautiful for the ascendance to goddess. Reminiscent of a young Phylicia Rashad back in her Clair Huxtable days, he met her smile with an Abe-sloth Fratelli scowl like she had dropped his Baby Ruth.

"Whatcha want?" he asked.

"Well, hello to you too, dear brother," she said.

"Spare me the small talk. You're the goddess of intelligence, skill, peace, warfare, battle strategy, arts, crafts, courage, inspiration, civilization, law, justice, mathematics, olive oil, and wisdom. Especially wisdom. I know you're not calling just cause you're never too busy to chat. You heard about the ramp getting installed."

Her friendly smile grew friendlier. "Indeed. I wanted to remind you while I still had the chance that you're a god as well."

The words made Blaestus's ire burn like a forge. "I'm a god, huh? The god of what? Running shoes? Male modeling? I don't have the extensive laundry list of epithets that you have. I'm not even the god of laundry lists. You know what I'm the god of? Blacksmithing. That's it. You know who needs a blacksmith in a post-industrial machine manufacturing age? The Amish! And they got their own. Blacksmithing is B.S. That's what Black Hephaestus is, the god of B.S."

Deep breaths.

"Titles don't matter," Athena said coolly. "A god is still a god."

"Says the lady with twenty part-time jobs," Blaestus retorted. "Damn, did you have to take olive oil, too?"

"You're scared of olives and allergic, remember? It's also why you're not the god of peanuts, tree nuts, eggs, wheat, lactose, fish, shellfish, clowns, heights, dust, bees, snakes, spiders, and the dark."

"Anything else you want to point out with your glowing wisdom?"

"Naturally," she smiled. "You don't remember much before you ascended to godhood, do you?"

He couldn't. It was one of those side effects of the wish. He only had a vague notion of who he had been. He thought he remembered driving and wearing a brown uniform, although all that brown could've just been him naked behind the wheel. Maybe he had did a lot of driving. Maybe his name had been Clyde.

"None of us remembers that much," Athena said, answering her own question. "But it doesn't take a whole lot of reasoning to see some simple truths. We didn't have millions of subscribers, successful businesses, fan sites dedicated to following our lives. We were nobodies."

"I'm still a nobody!" Blaestus cried. "Everyone else is living the high life. Look at you. Look at Pops."

Pops became the world's premiere electrical energy baron when he had ascended. The company was so huge they had to break it up because of anti-trust laws. So, Pops had given Uncle Poseidon control of all the hydropower, and Uncle Hades, with his blackhearted ass, ran all the coal.

Athena looked offended. "What about me?" she asked. "I ascended with next to nothing, same as you."

"No, you ascended with a laundry list of awesome. Or did you forget that you used all that arts and crafts godliness on my first wish to spin yourself a fortune?"

His first wish was for a billion dollars. It was enough cash for him and everyone in the family to live the good life until the end of time. This was when Blaestus learned you should never ask a genie, especially an asshole genie, for cash. The genie had promptly granted Blaestus magical money. The problem with magical money is that it's not printed sequentially from the Federal Reserve. The bills were pulled from the aether at exactly the same time, hence they all had the same exact serial number. It was all Blaestus could do to beat the counterfeiting charge. Meanwhile, that punk ass genie had dropped the money on him all in ones. It filled every room of the house, the basement, the backyard, the toilets, the tub, the refrigerator, a billion singles. To make it all fit on the property, the genie even hollowed out a giant hole in the backyard that was two miles deep and stuffed with unspendable currency instead of the internet and power lines that had been there servicing the community. It was literally a dark day in the hood.

After the second wish, once they all had ascended to godhood, Athena got the bright idea to turn the money into the fabric base for her money suits. Italian cut, double-breasted and slicker than banana peels on bacon grease, the suits flew off the shelves. Thus was born the hottest trend in urban fashion since shell toe Adidas.

"I know you're not complaining about the Arachne clothing label," Athena said. "I gave you plenty of money and stock from that endeavor. That's how you're able to swing that high-rise Manhattan apartment."

"That's the problem, *you gave*. What about what I can do for myself? Just because my legs are kid-sized now doesn't mean I don't want to stand up on them, metaphorically. At least you got all those attributes to tap into to generate wealth. What did I get when I ascended to godhood? A string of construction companies? Hell to the No. A factory? No on that, too. My ass got a smithy. An honest to gods place where smiths practice black-frickin-smithing."

That was another bitter pill. Before Athena had turned a profit on the money suits, back when he needed cash to hire his lawyer to keep from doing hard federal time for counterfeiting, he had to sell the smithy. He sold it to his cousin Dionysus on the cheap. Dionysus then turned it into a gentleman's club called The Forge, had the dancers prancing around in short blacksmith aprons, high heels, and little else. The god of wine and pleasure was turning a fortune over in that place. Meanwhile, Blaestus was living on handouts.

"If you're calling to talk me out of going to Olympus Tower, you're totally messing it up."

"Honestly, Brother, I do and I don't, want to talk you out of going I mean. Selfishly, I'd like to convince you to leave well enough alone because I have a great life now. Look at me, a wealthy business owner, a goddess. I have fans. I couldn't ask for more.

"But that's selfish part of me. Another bigger part of me wants you to thrive, to be happy. I don't remember much before ascendance, but there's a feeling my soul ties to you. It remembers. That part of me knows you have a heart bigger than Olympus Tower. It's the reason why you wished something better for not just you, but for all of us."

"Man, that was real touching, Sis."

"Well, I am the goddess of wisdom, arts, and crafts. I started my own line of greeting cards, Olympic Occasions. You can find them in your local grocery stores, a few aisles over from my line of decorative olive oils."

"And you ruined it. Damn. Can Black Hephaestus catch a break?"

"Sorry."

Silence, Silence the Third, reigned briefly.

"Brother," Athena began. "Why do you call yourself Black Hephaestus?"

"Too easy. I need to differentiate myself from the white one."

"You mean the classical Greek one that isn't really real?"

Blaestus scoffed. "I'll be damned if some fictitious dude takes my hard-earned street cred. I don't get played by fake ones."

Silence reigned once again, albeit another short reign.

"Wanna hear me rhyme?" Blaestus asked.

"Only if you're cursing out Ares," she answered.

"Sounds like yes to me." And with that, he spit that fire.

Athena seemed to dig it, even tried to join in. That's when they both discovered she was definitely not the goddess of beatboxing. And while it was fun dropping rhymes colder and fresher than iceberg lettuce fresh picked off an iceberg by the

Fresh Prince of Bel-Air, Blaestus did have long overdue business at Olympus Tower.

"Whatever you decide, Brother, be careful. Be sure."

"Third time's a charm, right, Sis?"

Blaestus made his way from his apartment to Olympus Tower. It was a magnificent skyscraper with reflective glass, made beautifully accessible thanks to the ramp that practically gleamed in new concrete gray.

The genie was waiting for Blaestus in the lobby. A strange sight to see, the immortal genie kept the face and bent body of an old white man. Their reunion was made stranger by the fact that the genie had discarded the suit Blaestus had originally met him in to wearing a vest and loose-fitting Hammer pants. A fez sat on his thin, wispy-haired head. The bastard looked like a crank organ monkey. He regarded Blaestus with one bushy eyebrow disdainfully raised.

"I see you're finally able to roll in here."

"What the hell, genie?" Blaestus asked. "You knew I couldn't get in the building! Why didn't you just come to me so we could settle up?"

The genie shrugged. "Wasn't like there was a fire on my end. Besides, I was hoping you'd get someone to carry you up. I was going to take pictures and laugh. That would've made my decade."

"Why?" Blaestus asked the genie. "The evil ass comment you just made, you twisting the holy hell out of my wishes … Why go out of your way to be such an asshole?"

The genie scrunched his face up as if the question confused him. "We bosom buddies now? You awfully dark to be Tom Hanks. What makes you think you and I are going to have a heart-to-heart unless you specifically wish it?"

"Maybe you need to get something off your chest, genie. You're the one screwing people over."

"Damn right!" he snarled. "It happened to me—"

He cut off the next word as if he had said too much. With a rueful-looking shake of his head, he let out an exasperated sigh.

"Look, what happened to me isn't your concern. It involves an evil vizier and a beautiful princess that wanted to marry me. I needed powerful magic to save the princess, and it made me a slave to the lamp. Now I have to grant wishes until someone sets me free."

Blaestus raised an eyebrow. "And you figured being the ultimate jerk was gonna help?"

The genie shrugged. "I figured someone would wish me free out of angst. Like they would see me having so much fun wrecking lives, they'd free me to deny me the joy. It was about the only option I could think of."

"You could try, I dunno, being nice?"

The genie guffawed. "Please! You know what's better than two awesome wishes? Three awesome wishes. People are greedy. Trust me, I know."

"Well ..." Blaestus said with a heavy sigh. "Now that you've said that, there's really only one thing I can wish for."

Hope returned to the genie's eyes. "You'll wish me free of the lamp?"

Blaestus smiled welcoming into the genie's hopeful eyes before his features clouded into a mean mug.

"Man, hell no! You tripping if you think I'm gonna give you everything you want in life while you got me stuck in a wheelchair with a melted face. That ain't hot in the streets."

The scowl returned to the genie's wizened face. He muttered something under his breath.

"What's the matter? Don't feel so good when someone's messing with you, does it? Besides that, I recognize game when I see it. The magic of the lamp's bigger than you, player. That's why you gotta grant wishes even though you hate granting them. For all I know, freeing you means I gotta take over the job. Hell, that's prolly what happened to you. You got tricked by the last genie, which is why you remember shows like *Bosom Buddies*. Decrepit old white guy, trying to sell me the plot of Aladdin like he Lawrence of Arabia. You and that princess sing 'A Whole New World'?"

The genie looked as if Blaestus just peed in his bathwater. He snapped his finger and his organ grinder monkey clothes disappeared, replaced by the tired old suit he typically wore.

"Have it your way," the genie said. "I'm going to have the best time of my life screwing up your third wish. There's only one wish you can make that I can't burn you. You already know what it is. You've been wanting it ever since your dad kept you from the lamp. Just waiting on you, chief." He rubbed his hands together in anticipation.

The genie's ultimate MO, for the client to wish none of the wishes had ever happened. And why not wish it all away? It was safe. Even the genie couldn't get it wrong. Blaestus would have working legs, he was pretty sure. His wife wouldn't be such a tart … probably. He hoped for it at any rate.

Still, this sucked. All that wish potential, just to go back to square one. Blaestus thought of Athena. Something in him didn't want to see the family do without. Beyond that, there was the genie, whose way of life made Blaestus boiling mad. How many times had genie gotten over, making suckers unwish their poorly thought-out desires? How many more times would he do it until he was free?

Blaestus wanted the genie to get some payback for all the suckers that rubbed the lamp before and the ones who would undoubtedly rub it in the future. He wanted it more than a hit rap single, more than he wanted to kick the genie's ass. The wheels in his head turned until finally the lights came on, bright as a forge. He smiled as he realized what he truly wanted. It was a wish well crafted. He looked at the genie.

"What if I wished, in very specific detail, for you to be good in your dealing with people? I'm talking honest like Jesus swearing in court on a stack of Bibles, friendly like Mr. Rogers on good neighbor day. I'm talking genuine like Miller Genuine Draft. How'd that grab you?"

The look of abject horror on the genie's face spoke volumes.

"Sounds like yes to me," Blaestus said.

And with that, he spit that fire.

JAMES BEAMON SPENT a dozen years in the Air Force and things were going well until he got a papercut from a radioactive biographical book. Now he's hopelessly addicted to writing bios about himself in third person and sending them to different publishers. In order to get these bios seen he attaches them to fun stories, which is something the publishers apparently want in exchange for pushing his bios. When writing bios, James can be found in Virginia with his wife, son, and attack cat. When not writing bios, somehow James is still in Virginia. He encourages you to check out his Pendulum Heroes series of fantasy novels.

THESE THREE ALIENS WALK INTO A BAR

Simon R. Green

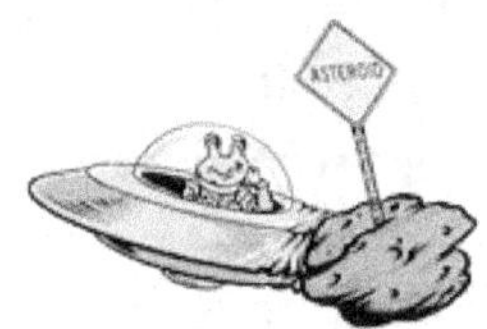

A Grey, a Reptiloid, and a Bug-Eyed-Monster walked into the Blue Parrot bar in London's Soho, and everyone else left in a hurry. Some headed for the back door, others availed themselves of the windows. Soon, all that was left in the place was a pleasant enough young man drinking at the bar, John Patterson by name, and the bartender, whose name doesn't matter because he has very little to do with the story. He looked thoughtfully at the three aliens, and nodded more or less calmly to John.

"You're on your own. I'm going down to the cellar to hide behind the barrels, and I'm not coming back up until the world has agreed to make sense again."

"Off you go," said John. "If I want another drink, I'll help myself."

"Put the money on the bar," said the barman, and then made himself exceedingly scarce.

John turned around on his bar stool and looked interestedly at the three aliens, who were busy glaring at each other. The Grey was a tall spindly affair dressed in a cowboy outfit, complete with ten-gallon hat. He had the typical huge black eyes, no nose, and a thin slit where his mouth should be. The Reptiloid was a big lizardy creature who couldn't be bothered with clothes, the better to show off his bottle green scales, heavily beringed claws, and beady suspicious eyes. The BEM looked like he'd been assembled from a dozen different species, or at least the bits left over from them. He was sort of humanoid, in that he had the right number of limbs in the right places, but his bulging head had insect eyes and quivering antennae.

The three aliens snapped their assorted heads around to stare at John, and then they went back to trying to outglare each other.

"I saw him first!" said the Grey. "So I get to abduct him."

"I got through the door first," said the Reptiloid. "So, that makes him mine!"

"My ship is bigger than yours," said the BEM.

There was a pause, as they considered the ramifications of that.

"I'll fight you for him," said the Grey.

"You and what cloned army?" said the Reptiloid. "And why are you still trying to pass as a cowboy?"

The Grey looked down at his feet, and sulked. "This is what everyone was wearing, the first time I was here. I like it; it makes me look rugged. If I'd known you were going to be here, I'd have kept the six-shooters."

"No rough stuff!" the BEM said sharply. "You saw the same memo I did. We're all supposed to be playing nicely."

"You are such a wimp," said the Grey.

"I can remember when monsters were allowed to be monsters," the Reptiloid said glumly. "It's all getting too galactically correct these days."

John cleared his throat politely, and the aliens turned to stare at him impatiently.

"What?" said the Grey.

"We're busy," said the Reptiloid.

"We'll get to you in a minute," said the BEM.

"I didn't know there was a convention on," said John. "Is this cosplay?"

The aliens looked at each other.

"What's cosplay?" said the Grey.

"Recreational identity shifts," said the Reptiloid. "For fun and profit. Sometimes, there are prizes."

"Ooh, I like prizes," said the Grey.

The BEM scowled at John, took a firm hold on his antennae, and gave them a good tug. "Do these look fake to you?"

John considered the matter dispassionately. "Well, yes, actually."

The Grey and the Reptiloid sniggered.

"Antennae are so last century," said the Grey.

"Wouldn't catch us dead with them," said the Reptiloid.

The BEM stamped a sneakered foot. "I am a proud member of a noble race, and we have been guaranteed a quota of humans to abduct. Are you going to come quietly, human, or do I have to stare at you till your hair falls out?"

"You are such a drama queen," said the Grey.

The Reptiloid studied John thoughtfully. "Can I just congratulate you, for not panicking and making a fuss?"

"Would it make any difference?" said John.

"Not really," said the Reptiloid. "But we appreciate the cooperation. I hate it when I have to drag someone off. My back doesn't talk to me for days afterwards."

"I hate it when they scream," said the BEM. "The sound goes right through my head, and gives me tinnitus for weeks."

"Why are you being so disturbingly calm, human?" said the Grey.

"Because I'm having a really good day," said John. "And I refuse to allow anything to spoil it." He looked them over carefully. "Why are the three of you so keen to abduct me? What's special about me?"

"You possess *quaness*," said the Grey.

"It's a very rare quality, *qua*," said the Reptiloid. "Makes you very collectible, where we come from."

"And don't ask us what quaness is," said the BEM. "You'd need at least three more senses to appreciate it."

"Four, really," said the Grey.

"Don't start that again," the BEM said dangerously.

John got up off his bar stool and wandered over to stand before the aliens. He looked them up and down, taking his time, while the aliens tried their various bests at being impressive. If anything, John thought they looked even less real, close up. He prodded the BEM in the chest with a finger, just to reassure himself, and then returned to his bar stool. The BEM looked at the other aliens.

"What was that all about?"

"Must be a local custom," said the Grey.

The three aliens took it in turns to solemnly prod each other, in or around the chest. The BEM nodded to John.

"We like to fit in."

"Why are you not hiding anymore?" said John. "I thought aliens only abducted people when they were sleeping, or snatched them out of cars on deserted roads?"

The Grey sighed heavily. "New edict from on high."

"Of course, those of us who've been on the ground for years, and know what we're doing, were not consulted," said the Reptiloid.

"It's so much harder to be sneaky and mysterious these days," said the BEM. "Now everyone's got a camera phone."

"They've been promising us personal cloaking devices for decades," said the Grey.

"Stuck in development," the Reptiloid said glumly.

"You haven't exactly gone out of your way to avoid being noticed," said the BEM. "You two are practically cultural icons."

"You've either got, or you haven't got, style," said the Grey.

"Couldn't agree more," said the Reptiloid, looking at the Grey meaningfully.

"Enough talking!" the Grey said loudly. "The human is mine! If I don't make my quota, they'll never let me go home."

"I can't go back until I've collected one of every kind on my list," the Reptiloid said glumly. "Who knew there were so many variations?"

The BEM shuffled his feet, and twitched his antennae bewitchingly at John. "Please come with me. I'm so lonely."

"You are really letting the side down," said the Grey.

"I don't know if you've noticed," said John. "But I'm male."

"After all this time, I really don't care," said the BEM.

"You don't want to go with Mister Sad Alien," said the Grey. "Or the lizardy thing. The Reptiloids have a nickname for humans: snacks."

"You know very well we haven't eaten anyone for decades!" said the Reptiloid.

"Only because you found out you were allergic to them," said the Grey.

The Reptiloid looked down its snout at the Grey, and turned to the BEM.

"You used to abduct female humans for sexual purposes!"

"I never did understand that," said the Grey. "I mean, what did you see in each other?"

The BEM shrugged. "Have you seen our females? At least humans don't bite your bits off afterwards."

"I didn't know you had bits," said the Grey.

"Like we'd tell you," the BEM said haughtily.

The Reptiloid fixed the Grey with a cold stare. "If you don't let me have the human, I'll tell everyone that you don't have eyelids. Who's going to take you seriously, once they know they can blind you with a boy scout flashlight?"

"You do, and I'll tell everyone that you're so cold-blooded you nod off if someone just opens a freezer!" said the Grey.

The BEM was waving his hands excitedly. "Can we please not discuss our personal little foibles in front of the human? How are we supposed to intimidate them with our awesome-ness, if they see us squabbling among ourselves?"

"Oh, shut up," said the Grey. "Or I'll tie your antenna in a knot."

The BEM drew himself up to his full height, which didn't take long. "You're a fine one to talk. You still zoom around the cosmos in flying saucers."

"You bastard!" said the Grey. "Saucers are cool! They are!"

"Your ship has go-faster stripes!" said the Reptiloid.

"I hate you," said the Grey. "If you don't stop picking on me, I'm not playing."

"Excuse me," said John. "I'm really not interested in going with any of you, but could I just ask a few questions?"

The aliens looked at each other.

"What kind of questions?" said the Reptiloid.

"Well," said John. "Let's start with crop circles ..."

All three aliens shook their heads firmly.

"Those things have nothing to do with us!" said the Grey.

"Why would we want to fly across interstellar space, just to make patterns in the vegetation?" said the Reptiloid.

"Ugly patterns, too," said the BEM. "I wouldn't lower myself."

"All right," said John. "Probing. What's that all about?"

"It was just the one time!" the Grey said loudly. "Honestly, they never let you forget. ... Look, the guy asked us to, so we went along just to keep him happy. How were we supposed to know he was weird?"

"What happened at Roswell?" said John.

The aliens relaxed a little, and exchanged knowing looks.

"That was the Rigellians," said the Reptiloid. "Typical tourists. They came down too low so they could take a better picture and plowed right into the dirt."

"They were stoned out of their shiny skulls when they crashed," said the Grey. "They had to trade some seriously advanced knowledge to the locals, in return for basic repairs and a chance to get home."

"What did they offer?" said John. "Anti-grav? Stardrive?"

"Triple-entry bookkeeping," said the BEM. "Transcendental accounting. Why do you think your rich people suddenly started getting incredibly rich, right after that?"

"Maybe we should try bribes," said the Grey. "Whoever makes the human the best offer gets to abduct him."

"I'm really not interested," said John.

"Listen to what we have to offer!" said the Grey. "Come with me, and we'll show you the wonders of the universe."

"All that means is, his saucer has these little round windows you can look out of," said the Reptiloid. "You come with me, and we'll make you immortal."

"You'll live forever, but you'll be a reptiloid," said the BEM. "Trust me, you wouldn't like it. They don't even have bits."

"There's more to life than bits!" said the Reptiloid.

"Yes, well, you would say that wouldn't you," said the BEM. "You come with me, human, and we'll make you rich. All the sulfur you could ever want."

"We'll tie ribbons in your hair!" the Grey said excitedly.

There was a pause, as the other aliens looked at him.

"That's really quite an honor, where we come from," said the Grey.

"You don't have any hair," said the Reptiloid.

"At least we've got bits," the Grey said nastily. "Big warty bits!"

"I loathe you beyond my ability to articulate," said the Reptiloid. "Right. That's it. He's coming with me."

He produced a weird shining weapon. The other aliens did, too. There were three bright flashes of light, and suddenly there were no aliens in the bar. John blinked a few times, and finished his drink. A young woman appeared from the bar's toilets. Tall, slender, and very attractive, she hurried over and sat down beside John at the bar. She kissed him on the cheek, and slipped a companionable arm through his.

"Sorry to keep you waiting, darling. Did anything interesting happen while I was gone?"

John smiled at her. "These three guys wanted me to go with them, but I wasn't interested. Why would I want to leave, when I have everything I want right here?"

SIMON R. Green has written seventy-five novels, two collections of short stories, and one movie; *Judas Ghost*. These include the Nightside books, the Secret Histories, Deathstalker, and the Ghost Finders. His most recent books are the Ishmael Jones mysteries and the Jekyll & Hyde Inc books from Baen, and the Gideon Sable mysteries from Severn. He has had the usual mixture of previous occupations, that prove an author cannot hold down a proper job, including shop assistant, bicycle repair mechanic, journalist, actor, Chippendale dancer, and mail order bride. Not all of these are necessarily accurate. He lives in the small country town of Bradford-on-Avon, which was the last Celtic town to fall to the invading Saxons in 504 AD. He has never seen a UFO; but he has heard one.

OUR MOST SINCERE APOLOGIES TO THE PEOPLE OF BRAZIL

Jane Espenson

I t was not a murder. In what followed, there was fault—
we're very sorry, São Paolo. But there was no fault in the
death itself. Santa's death was clean.

It was just after eight in the morning and I was on the treadmill in our little h'elf club, all by myelf at that hour. Tremble
came in, pale as sugar and acting out his own name. I asked him
what was up. He said, "He's dead." I didn't know who he
meant. Honestly, my first thought was Drew Carey. I don't know
why, I guess he just seems like a guy who maybe doesn't take
care of himself. But then Tremble made it clear who he meant.

I said, "Someone's fucking with you." I was sure he'd been
lied to, or maybe he'd misunderstood. But he said there was a
big meeting in the atrium, and we all had to go. I climbed off the
treadmill, pulled on my tights, and followed him. Never work
out in your tights, even if you have a crotch like an elf. I wanted
to keep thinking it was a mistake, but as we went out into the
cold, there was a strange tickle in my stomach, that kind of
alarm that's hard to tell apart from excitement. I almost didn't
recognize it. Excitement was rare here, lately.

As I followed Tremble, I didn't bother to zip up my coat, but pulled it tight around me as the perspiration dried frostily on my neck and face. I read the tension in his shoulder blades as we crossed the open area in the middle of the community. It didn't take long; it's not a big town. Connie, Santa's second wife, was only the fifty-third member, added in the early 2000s. Before her, it was just elves. But you'd be amazed at what we'd been able to do, fifty-two of us, back in the day. My earliest memories are of all of us preparing for that annual night, working overtime for eleven months. Row after row of us, bent over our work benches. It wasn't even called Christmas yet, although of course it was starting to look a lot like Christmas. What it was, was the container Christmas got poured into, later. So, we twinkled and tinkered with our small silver hammers and sharp little silver needles.

Then there was the special night itself, the time distortion making it last a week, as we experienced it, a week without a sunrise or a break. Santa taking off in the sleigh thousands of times, returning with reindeer spent and lathered, trading out the teams as needed, exhorting us to work harder, work faster. And us, practically in a lather ourselves, lifting huge bags of presents into the sleigh, which magically stretched into fantastical dimensions to accommodate them. Santa's first wife, Feather, burst into tears more than once from sheer exhaustion. She worked so hard and cared so much. Like all of us, you could almost see her growing thinner as we worked. As a species, we neither copulate nor defecate. As I've already tastefully implied, our crotches are featureless. Without a way to eliminate waste, this yearly expending of energy was what kept us fit. We didn't use treadmills, or even have a h'elf club, back then. What a zoo it was, all clamor and foam. I had sworn I'd never miss it. But I did. It was a *purpose*.

I continued to trudge after Tremble. He was tense at the best of times, but now he looked ready to snap. We made a detour around Blitzen, who was digging an enthusiastic hole in the center. There was a big empty steaming stewpot on the ground, which was sloppy with mud, so I figured he'd poured hot water on the frozen ground to soften it. He was really digging down into it with his big glittery hooves, sending globs of mud into the air in every direction. The flying reindeer were extraordinarily intelligent for reindeer, but people don't realize that still means they're very stupid. In a way it was worse than if they'd been left dumb. Ordinary reindeer are morons, but it's okay because they don't try to do more than graze. But a reindeer with an inkling that it should be *doing* something is likely to try to get into your golf cart, or scramble some eggs, or fly a kite. It occurred to me that maybe he thought he was digging a grave, and the thought chilled me as much as the air did. Tremble and I hurried on, braced against the temperature. We'd all talked many times about building heated passageways between the buildings, but we never did, which was kind of absurd, considering how many decades we'd lived here, a number none of us actually remembered.

When Christianity came along, they subsumed us into their whole big deal, and our leader, up until then called Winkles, became "Father Christmas," in all its variants, and then "Santa," which meant Saint. He loved that, of course. I mean, yes, of course, anyone would. And then, next thing you knew, we were only giving gifts to Christian children. It was controversial, as you might imagine. Some of us didn't like that so many children were left out, and it didn't actually decrease the workload much. Because there were fewer kids, we felt like we needed to do a better job. We gained skills as the gifts got better. Sometimes, before that, a child might sort of fall through the cracks and just get a pinecone, or a pretty rock with a flower painted on it, or an orange. Now, we upped the ante with more intricately carved dolls and carved sleds. Lots of carving. Still some oranges, the kids seemed to actually like 'em. I figured Christianity would probably turn out to be temporary, but the Christians hung in there.

I might have the order of things a little wrong, but eventually the myth of Santa coalesced, adding things here and there: the suit, for one. Things that we really did got folded into the myth, and things in the myth got folded into us. Around then is when we started putting out the PR about Santa having a list, because theoretically, we would need to know *which* kids were Christian, but in truth it was always a little haphazard. Santa always said he could just *tell* which chimneys to go down. I don't know. It seems unsavory *to know Christian chimneys*, doesn't it? Anyway, I'm pretty sure lots of kids got gifts who weren't Christian, and I have to think that's a good thing. I mean, honestly.

Tremble and I arrived at the atrium, which is what we call the old workshop now. It's a big A-frame warehouse of a building, half full of old toys on high racks, covered and forgotten. A few workbenches were still here, shoved off to one side. Flutter, Twerk, and Waffle still worked here sometimes, turning out cloth dolls and wooden trains and some half-assed puzzle boxes. Myelf, I still did woodworking sometimes, too, but at home, turning out the occasional Wooden Horsey behind my trailer. Anyway, this room had mostly turned into a place to play video games or heat up toaster pastries or sit around and bullshit over a cup of cocoa. A warm place to go and get out of your trailer. I wondered idly when I'd last made a horsey. It felt like a while.

Elves stood around in small groups, talking, sniffling, chewing. As we shifted, our bells sent out little shimmers of sound. There were at least thirty of us there already, with more arriving every moment. I saw Feather and Thistle at the chocolate fountain, both in tears, sticking oversized mugs into the churning flow. I could tell right away this was going to be a sugar-fueled, cola-drenched mourning morning that would go on until the last flimsy tin of linty mints had been pulled from the bottom of someone's button bag. I sought out Feather with my eyes and smiled at her. She had been married to Santa, so she deserved special support, and I'd always liked her. Years ago, right after her divorce, she and I once ate a gummy worm and met in the middle. If you're wondering what the difference between a male and female elf is, given the undifferentiated crotch areas, there is none. We were all about discovering our own pronouns long before the humans. Also, eyelashes. Feather returned my smile with a grateful but damp one of her own. I gave her a look that was a question mark. She said, "He's gone."

Having it confirmed like that … I was stunned. Santa was the center we all orbited. Without him, there was nothing to hold me in my place and I was in danger of being flung out into blackness. A flake forever swirling, never landing. Feather's steady look is what kept me tethered to the planet.

If Connie hadn't come along, Feather and Santa would still be married, I was sure of it. Santa had declared the divorce in the traditional Elf way, by leaving a dead Arctic fox in her locker at the gym, and Feather had moved into her own trailer that day, as graceful and unresistant as an actual feather. It occurred to me that she had, in a very real way, only just now become single. I tucked that thought away like the mini cream puffs I pushed into my cheeks.

The arrivals dwindled, the last of us entering carrying big steins of maple syrup, saucepans full of caramel, and covered dessert plates on little rolling tables. It was as if some radio signal had gone out: "Santa's dead, bring tiramisu." As I lowered a steaming mug of sweetened melted butter, I peeked over the rim to see a stir near the door. Connie had arrived. She edged in, looming over everyelf as always, looking abashed and awkward. We all knew Santa had met Connie during one of his

Christmas runs, but details were vague. Most people seemed to think she'd been a hip young aunt, awake in the middle of the night to nibble at the cookies set out by her young nieces, and in trying to create the illusion of a Santa, she'd run into the real thing. And then somehow his nibbles had strayed all the way across the face of the plate and onto hers. But we never knew if that was the real story. What mattered was he met her somehow and decided to bring her to the North Pole to live out a small slice of his life, and all of hers.

We'd been here for millennia at least, and no elf had died within our collective memory. Before that ... who knows? Our lifespans—if such a word applies—are longer than our memories. This strange fact is also true of humans, but humans only forget infancy, a time when every change is significant—*but only to the infant*. Babies rarely drive the story via their own choices, is what I'm saying. But for us, the forgotten slab of life is of unknown size and unknown import, and it grows as we live on, our window of memory sliding along with us, pushed forward by life. Did we evolve on Earth, or were we a race of immigrants from another world? An alien invasion force? A meandering genome carried in on the hurtling rock that killed the dinosaurs? And once we were here, what did we do? What have we already caused that we've forgotten? Do we have apologies to make that extend beyond the São Paolo incident and perhaps the dinosaurs? We don't know. At any rate, there's no reclaiming the memories now, so for us it's cute names, candy canes, and bells on our hems. Honestly, what chain of events led to belled hems? We don't know. It's lost to time. At any rate, there were only fifty-two of us now. A full deck of cards, and Santa had been that extra card you get sometimes with the rules for gin rummy. We looked at each other and wondered who we were now, without the rules of the game. Santa had given us purpose, at least until recently. Without him ... what?

Elves approached Connie with condolences. Some had

halting words, others just fixed her with a baleful look and then backed away blinking, hoping their kind intent was clear. We'd never done any of this before, so we only knew the social norms from media and the internet. I thought of an episode of *The Mary Tyler Moore Show*—is that still on? Oh, I suppose not. Time. Anyway, I don't know where others took their inspiration. There was some bowing. Connie's confusion, sadness, and gratitude for our awkward gestures was so genuine, I warmed to her. She felt more like one of us in this moment than she ever had.

Like I say, Santa, special as he was, was still an elf, with an uncomplicated crotch to prove it. So, she'd given up a lot to join us in a sexless life of looming, and we needed to give her credit for that much, at least. She'd been here twenty years and was tolerated, even mildly liked, by many, but she wasn't one of us. She thought twenty years was a long time, and never seemed to get that for us, that amount of time was very little. I mean, I was part of the team that made the Trojan Horse (in-house project name: "Big Horsey"). Twenty years was a week.

No one knew what to do when Connie started to sing "Up on the Rooftop" in a wavering voice. This wasn't something we generally did. We didn't carol our feelings; we ate them. I looked at Feather, uncertain. Feather looked back at me, sweetly reso- lute. This was a time for unity. Together, the two of us joined in, a little singing trio, a clenched nodule of song in the middle of the crowd. Gradually, Tremble joined, with his lovely vibrato, then the others chimed in, and it felt less strange. We'd all loved Santa, and there were so many songs about him. I felt like this wasn't just cementing Connie into the community, but it was also repairing cracks that we'd allowed to grow between ourselves.

Long—centuries—before Connie came along, was the first time we eased up on the work since the whole Christian thing happened. Santa pointed out that human children weren't as necessary to the workforce anymore, so fewer of them were sad little drudges with nothing to look forward to but an orange on Christmas day. So, he said we didn't have to go on driving ourelves as hard as we had been. Thus, from our already narrowed base, we narrowed further. We focused on the poorest children, and then on a certain age range, three to twelve, because the kids outside that range, on both ends, didn't give a flocked tree about gifts from Santa. Then, like whipping cream leads to whipped cream, we were on a slope. We started the COTY program. That was Country of the Year, where we'd just give gifts to kids in, like, Burma, or Finland. As Santa went from man to myth, people gave their own kids gifts in Santa's name, so he didn't *need* to be everywhere. And soon, he was almost nowhere. Soon, a mysterious gift showing up in someone's house would've just caused alarm. When no one believed anymore, we just channeled a few items anonymously through a charity in Siberia and called it a day. The sleigh sat idle. We sat idle. Santa isolated himelf in his doublewide with Connie. We were a wheeled horsey careening forward with inertia and nothing else.

So, it's almost strange that the *story* of Santa—the story of us—remained as vibrant as it did. In the atrium, a thousand years later, there were a lot of songs to choose from. We only sang the Santa ones. Jesus was a different guy, even if the joke in recent years was that someone should tell Santa that. Connie did "Santa Baby" as a solo, her tear-roughened voice strong and sultry as she shimmied, wildly-but-sadly, through the chorus. We sang on, different songs, in English and German and French, and it was sad and beautiful. As the evening wore into icy black velvet night outside, this little band of elves and Connie huddled inside, worshipping in song our lost friend and reason for being.

In the middle of "Here Comes Santa Claus," the big huge warehouse doors opened, just like in White Christmas. And just like in the movie, it had started snowing outside without anyone realizing it. Then we smelled reindeer. Before we had time to wonder what the reindeer were doing, they were inside, hooves slipping, breath puffing, pulling the old magical sleigh, with Santa's corpse balanced at the front. The reindeer had put themselves in harness, and looped the reins around Santa's still, stiff, darkened, dead hands. They walked in now, heads down, the blades of the massive sleigh—where had they even found it— grating against the concrete floor. Here comes Santa Claus, indeed.

If the idea of a dead Santa Claus was upsetting, the reality of one was terrifying. The body was gray and stiff, propped up in the sleigh, the head wrenched up and back unnaturally, tongue protruding. His rein-wrapped hands were held high in front of him as if he were throwing them up in glee. A missed button exposed a wobbly diamond-shape of jelly-bowl-like belly, shaking but no longer from laughter. He was wearing his special suit, the red satin pulling and bunching in all the wrong places. If you didn't know Santa was really just a glorified elf, you'd know now with one glance at that noble smooth crotch. His fur cuff was torn at one wrist—it was very clear that he had died naked and been dressed by reindeer. Boots off, toes like cherries. He had mud on his legs up to mid-calf, which made me suspect they'd tried stuffing him into Blitzen's grave and this was option B.

A note on Rudolph: pure fiction.

We fell back in horror. Feather cried out. Tremble gave back his custard. Some ran outside. Connie sat on the ground with a thud, brought down to a reasonable height at last.

We who stayed, stayed. We contemplated the sleigh again, still looking beautiful despite its disuse. And inside, the face of death. I wondered, amid the stunned chaos, who elf was staring into those dead eyes, now pointedly *not* twinkling. Who elf was just now contemplating what should have been an obvious question: If Santa was mortal, *were we?* Surely, we must be. Death was, at least, on the menu. Our foundations quaked.

But there wasn't time to think about that now. Right now, we had to decide what to do with the body. Tell Cupid and the other deer to go hoof him back into bed? Drag him out to an ice shelf? Or …

The idea came to me fully formed, the way the image of a new horsey sometimes used to come to me with every hue of painted detail already vivid. "We need to take him out on one last trip." Sniffles ran to gather the elves who'd gone outside, and they drifted back in, staying close to the walls, a little ashamed of themelves, still avoiding looking at the twisted horror in the sleigh as they listened to me.

I said, "We need to take him out again, like in the old times, only this time we'll all go with him. We'll sail above the Earth, get the Santa's-eye view, and get to know him better for seeing the things he's seen. We can say good-bye to him, then swoop down low over the South Pacific and float his body into tropic waters where he can be warm and at peace."

I was surprised when there wasn't immediate acclamation. And then I felt someone elf at my shoulder. I looked around. It was Feather, her eyes bright. She nodded. Some elves looked to Connie, who nodded weakly, too, going along, but I think it was Feather who really mattered. After she gave her assent, everyone was in like flan.

How could Santa ever leave Feather? A true mystery. You could say she had influence because she was the one among us with the most personal tie to Santa, excepting Connie of course, but it was more than that. It was her eyes and smile and calm presence. You know the expression, "I'd follow her through a walrus?" Feather was like that. I'd follow her through a walrus.

I heard a faint jingling, jingling bells, not inappropriate. Suspecting Tremble, I looked around to see who was shaking their hem. But the sound came from Connie, on her feet again, shoulders hunched, eyes down, hands deep in her coat pocket. I realized she was jingling her car keys in her hand. That's when I knew she was going to leave us. Absolute rule: you don't shake something and not use it. I lost track of her after that, but I'm certain she got into her Suburban and drove south. No one saw which way she headed, but from where we were, every direction was south.

Now there were fifty-one of us and we were no longer playing with a full deck.

Feather and I led everyone elf into the sleigh. The reindeer tried to get in, too, and had to be reminded that we needed them out in front. It was surreal, seeing the confines of the sleigh expand to fit us all. But then again, everything about this was surreal, including us. *Sur + real*, above reality, something to be proud of, I suppose. We left the top open to feel the wind, and our bells jangled wildly as the reindeer ran, gathering speed. Then the sleigh rose, and pulled by its buoyance, the deer were caught up and flung out in front. It was the sleigh that powered the operation; the flailing legs of the deer didn't really accomplish anything and were more like the instinct that makes dogs paddle the air when you hold them over water. But the deer were the navigators, somehow, mysteriously, able to read the open waters and shadowy landmasses below us. We headed south, which, again, was every direction.

Inside the sleigh, we were wind-buffeted, cold, and close, and the gray stiff corpse holding the reins was hard to ignore. But the experience was beautiful, too. Staggeringly so. Below us, the oceans and lands swept past, vast and fertile. You could smell the seas, the forests, the farmland.

We were moving so quickly, there was always something new and beautiful coming into sight below. A spouting whale. An island. A field. A forest. A desalinization plant. The air grew warmer and moister as we arced down over the hemisphere. We were seeing what Santa had always seen. I started to feel a little resentful. He'd seen this and never shared it?! Earth below, stars above, the huffing of the deer, the sighing of the warming wind? I caught Tremble and others sneaking looks at Santa and then looking away quickly. I knew what they were feeling. Well, I knew what *I* was feeling, and that was close enough. We, as a community—a species—had been part of something unique, possibly alien, certainly magic. Our purpose had been to commit an act of pure generosity and love. Gifts were our gift. And our leader had first isolated us from it, and then let it die. In Santa's body's grim reality, he seemed now like something to be ashamed of. He had become, literally, our burden. More and more eyes turned to him, grimly. I willed myelf to take in the sight of him, the pure gray bulk of him, that moldy old elf. Resentment curled up off me, off all of us, like the toes on a pair of shoes. And resentment had a sound, a sort of musical growl. I could tell the reindeer were listening to it, their ears swiveling back toward us.

We had been gods. Then we had been kitsch. And then we had been abandoned. Feather whispered into my ear: "We don't have to follow." And I knew she meant, in part, that we didn't have to follow his rules. And she meant more. She meant, in the future, maybe we didn't have to follow him into death. Could it be? Had he had made his way through mediocrity into mortality? Could we avoid that fate through … what? Greatness? Nice work if you can get it.

The reindeer took us into a steep lean, avoiding some real asshole gulls. All our hem bells rang as we were thrown against the red velvet starboard side of the sleigh. We gasped, as it looked for a moment as if Santa might fly out. And then we exchanged looks, realizing that, in that moment, *we wished he had*. Feather reached out a hand and touched his bare ankle. We all held our breath. Her fingers tangled in the velvet-and-fur of his hem and tugged, upwards, almost as if by accident, almost as if her hand had simply gotten caught in the fur. And then, some barrier broken, we all hurried to help. As we lifted the bulk of him, I noticed his suit was worn in places, the fuzz and shine rubbed off. Neglect, mediocrity, loss.

The reindeer, following whatever instinct, banked again, even more steeply. I didn't hear any gulls this time. I met Feather's eyes as everyone heaved up—sharing the complicity—and gravity finally took hold of old dead Winkles and he tipped out the side. As the body fell away and the sleigh jingle-bell-rocked back, we steadied ourelves and breathed. It felt like a new start, marred only by the fact that we were not over water. A football match had gone late and the stands were half empty when the body landed near the goal of the São Paolo home team, but the impact was said to be very traumatic for those who witnessed it. Feather and I want to extend our apologies to all the people of Brazil for that. We should have looked down. But we were too busy looking forward.

In the time since then, we've got the workshop up and humming again. We've finally built those heated walkways between buildings, and we're taking better care of ourelves. We have purpose again, as a group, the purpose of finding a new purpose. Feather and I are working together, building a relation-ship and a community. Earning our lives. Who knows what we can give if we try. More than toys. Much more than toys. We can help the best of mankind, harm the worst, advance tech or elim-inate it. Bless. Smite. Reward and punish. Our powers, we suspect, are godlike. Maybe it's time to be gods.

It's almost Christmas, and we think humanity is going to enjoy what we're dropping next. And Brazil, oh Brazil. We are, really, so sorry. It won't happen again.

JANE ESPENSON IS a Hugo-award winning television writer best known for her work on *Buffy the Vampire Slayer, Firefly,*

Gilmore Girls, Game of Thrones, and *Battlestar Galactica,* among other series. She is currently doing triple-duty writing for *Fantasy Island, The Santa Clauses,* and *Foundation.* Her short fiction has appeared in *Future Science Fiction Digest,* in *Firefly: Still Flying,* and in *Tales of the Slayer* collections. She is @JaneEspenson on Twitter. Send candy.

LIABILITY INSURANCE POLICY FOR IMMORTALS, CRYPTIDS, AND OTHER MAGICAL BEINGS: ANNUAL NEWSLETTER

Tina Connolly

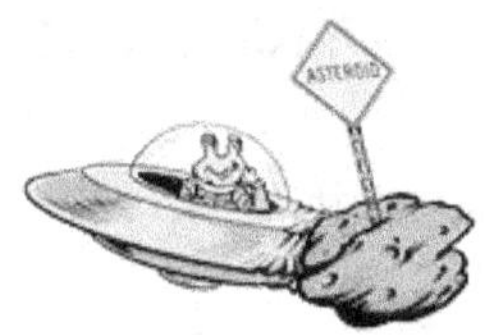

Hello and thank you for renewing your Magical Beings Liability Insurance Policy! We are delighted as always to support you through the trials and triumphs of your chosen magical profession and/or personal lifestyle.

We had a number of regrettable claims last year from humans, many of which were avoidable. It's a privilege to continue working in modern times, but be aware that the increased role of capitalism in human society has become economically dangerous to all of us. The humans known as "lawyers" have drastically inverted the power balance, but if we remember a few simple guidelines we can keep enjoying our lifestyles. With that in mind, here are seven quick tips to make this year run more smoothly than the last.

1. Rainbows! Rainbows are great. Everyone loves a rainbow. Rainbows should not end in the middle of a highway. America is a litigious society and loves its cars. We have had to fulfill

several claims of "I ran into a giant bag of gold and it dented my Lexus" (which really feels unfair when they also got the giant bag of gold, but there it is). If you are adamant that your rainbow needs to end in a highway "for the aesthetic," please contact us about purchasing the optional rider, "Monkey Paw Liability Insurance," also known as "I Gave The Human Something and They're Still Mad."

2. For those of you applying fairy ointment to humans' eyes so they can "see the magic wonders of faerieland," you must have them sign a waiver first. (How you get that waiver is your business.) Health insurance claims continually keep rising in this country, and the National Association of Ophthalmologists has their eye on you, pun very much intended.

3. If your chosen profession involves luring sailors to be dashed upon the rocks via the power of song, please note that we can no longer cover this at all. We can refer you to another company we have a friendly relationship with, Mystical Fixers & Vanishers. They are not exactly an insurance company—let's just say they specialize in making problems disappear. The result should be much the same for you—freedom to dash with impunity. This also goes for ogres, zombies, jackalopes, and any others of you who eat people.

4. Succubi and incubi, remember your coverage is only good in Nevada, California, and Portland, due to local legislation. We agree this is unfair, and we support you with our hearts (but not with actual money).

5. For those of you advertising *"The Complete Bigfoot Experience!!!"* remember that you will likely have to actually show up at these events in order to avoid claims by frustrated tourists. I understand most of you feel the humans are not truly entitled to a sighting, but our team has reviewed your advertising materials and there is no fine print saying otherwise. Consider a designated "selfie station" where the humans can get and then post

proof to their social media. Remember, for most humans, it doesn't count unless they have a selfie of it.

6. Vampires, please double-check the fine print of your policy, and remember that you are only allowed to extract the amount of blood the Red Cross would take, and even then, you need to offer your chosen human some form of sustenance afterwards, such as granola bars, orange juice, iron-fortified breakfast cereals, etc. A simple stash of food nearby prevents dizzy spells which prevents concussions which prevents lawsuits. Nobody likes lawsuits. Memorize the saying: *A Snack for a Snack!* to help you remember this convenient trick.

7. Speaking of tricks, for those of you working the Halloween circuit (including but not limited to: ghosts, skeletons, and headless horsemen), a little tip that you ARE allowed to seek gainful employment at Haunted House Attractions; you are NOT allowed to take over people's houses and turn them *into* Haunted House Attractions. We do not cover breaking and entering, nor do we cover willful destruction during said B&E such as: blood running down the walls, ectoplasm dripping from the refrigerator, or turning a house into a giant pumpkin, sticking your face out the triangle eyes, and yelling BOOOOO at the children. We had to cover quite a number of incurred psychological damage claims on this last one. (Largely for the parents complaining that their children's special day was ruined; the children were fine.)

We have unfortunately had to adjust our premiums slightly to reflect these increased risks. Please remit five gold coins, three golden goose eggs, or one (uncursed) magic ring to our mailing address by the end of the month if you wish to continue your coverage for the next year. Please note we can no longer accept "gold" leaves as a valid form of currency, as these have turned back into oak leaves too many times, and oak leaves are not accepted currency at our local Starbucks.

Thank you so much for reading our list of simple tips. Please note that if you *fail* to follow these, we will unfortunately have to call on our friends at Mystical Fixers & Vanishers to contact you *personally* about them. Thank you all for being our valued clients, and have a magical (and lawsuit-free) new year!

TINA CONNOLLY (SHE/HER) writes fantastical stories for kids, teens, and grown-ups. Some of them are serious and some of them involve flying bananas. Her stories and books have been finalists for the Hugo, Nebula, and World Fantasy Awards. Her books include the Ironskin trilogy (Tor), the Seriously Wicked series (Tor Teen), the collection *On the Eyeball Floor* (Fairwood Press), and the Choose Your Own Adventure book, *Glitterpony Farm*. She is delighted to be making her fourth appearance in UFO. Find her at tinaconnolly.com.

THE SHADCHEN OF VENUS

Lavie Tidhar

Written by Nahum Zweig
Edited with an Introduction by Lavie Tidhar

Nahum Zweig is a name likely all but unknown to the modern reader, though he was a prolific contributor to the pulps in the 1930s and early 1940s and a contemporary of Stanley G. Weinbaum, with whom he briefly shared an apartment in New York. Of his many works, the most popular were the *Tales of the Shadchen* sequence, begun with "The Shadchen of Venus" in the July 1934 issue of *Wonder Stories* (where it was published alongside his friend Weinbaum's better known "A Martian Odyssey"). In that tale, and the ones that followed about the eponymous matchmaker of the title, Zweig was likely inspired by the earlier stories collected in the 1925 volume *The Marriage Broker* by Tashrak (the pen name of Israel J. Zevin).

Though Zweig published prolifically in the lower-tiered pulps, he never broke into Campbell's *Astounding*. According to Isaac Asimov in his biography, *In Memory Yet Green* (1979), Campbell once made a disparaging remark as to the tales being "too Jewish" for his readers. At the first World Science Fiction Convention in 1939, Zweig, who had socialist sympathies, notoriously ended up in a fistfight with Sam Moskowitz, and was subsequently barred from entering. He left New York shortly after, taking odd jobs around the country before being drafted into the army post Pearl Harbor. He went missing in action in Europe some time after D-Day.

Despite my best efforts, I have been unable to confirm his eventual fate. He may have died in battle, though some sources variously place him in the Soviet Union or in the then-nascent state of Israel after the war. Zweig's somewhat peculiar appearance—he was thin and gangly, and of a diminutive stature—was said to have inspired the character of the Mule in Asimov's *Foundation* stories, and Asimov wrote the introduction to Zweig's only—and posthumous—collection, *Galactic Shadchen!* (Pyramid Books, 1951), which collects the best of the Shadchen tales.

I am grateful to Alex Shvartsman for allowing me the opportunity to bring this story back to a new audience, and to Nir Yaniv for sharing his unearthed copy of *The Marriage Broker* with me and for his tireless advice on the manuscript as I was preparing it for print.

1.

She slithered into my office and I knew straightaway she was going to be trouble. I just didn't know how much. She perched on the chair I reserved for visitors. Her purple tentacles rested on my desk, three of them, and a fourth rearranged the flowers on the bald dome of her head. A fifth left a trail of slime on my carpet. It was going to be hell to get it dry-cleaned.

"So you're the shadchen," she said.

She had a face only a mother could love. I knew I was in trouble even before she opened her beak.

"What's this about, Toots?" I said.

"Don't call me Toots. My name's Esther."

"Of course it is," I said.

"Esther Blumenthal-Tenn."

I choked on my tongue. It hurt. I had to untangle it. That took me a while.

"Of *the* Blumenthal-Tenns?" I said.

She looked at me innocently.

"You heard of my family?" she said.

I nodded dumbly. Everyone knew the Blumenthal-Tenns. They practically owned Venus. Swamps, jungles, ore mines, kosher hot dog carts, and the opera building and all. They had gelt, is what I'm saying. Which meant if I could get this broad hitched I was going to hit pay dirt.

"So, what's this about, Miss Blumenthal-Tenn?" I said.

"Please. Call me Esther."

"How can I help you, Esther?"

"I am in want of a husband," she said.

"Of course," I said.

"I am of age," she said. A tear rolled down her beak.

"Of course."

"It's unseemly for a girl like me to still be single!" she said. She burst into tears. "I shall soon be an old *maid*!"

"Not if I have anything to do with it!" I told her. "My record is impeccable. Every heart has a match. Every soul has a mate. Every pot has a lid! Besides, it's fashionable nowadays not to marry."

"Fashion," she said, "has nothing to do with it."

"How so?"

"I am the sole inheritor of the Blumenthal-Tenn fortune.

There must be continuity, Shadchen. There must be ...” She lowered her voice. *"Heirs,"* she said.

“Of course.”

She blushed, turning from purple to pink. I looked at the rings on her tentacles. Diamonds larger than duck's eggs. She was loaded.

“I've never, you know ...” she said.

“You're still a ... ?” I said.

“Well, yes.”

“You've never been with a ... ?”

“What's a girl to do, Shadchen!” she said. And she burst out crying again.

Well, this was no good. No girl should cry with that many diamonds on her. I looked at those diamonds. Just one of those bad boys would pay my back rent for a year. I said, “Well, there's nothing to it, then. We'll just have to find you a match.”

“Oh?” she said. She stopped crying. “You think you can do it, Shadchen?”

“Hey, bubele,” I said. “I'm a shadchen. It's what I *do.*”

“Oh, thank you!” she said. She wrapped her tentacles around me in a hug. I took it stoically. I tried not to think of my dry cleaning bill.

2.

“Well, *your* egg is cooked and no mistaking it,” Mishnik said. Mishnik was the bartender at the Bar Mitzvah. The place was dimly lit and smelled of spilled beer and crushed dreams. It made me think of being thirteen years old again. This did not make me feel good. I stared into my glass of schnapps. I should never have taken the job.

“It can't be done,” I said. “It just can't be done.”

"She has money?" Shmuel said. Shmuel was a swamp snail from the southern polar region. His little yarmulke sat crooked on his little head.

"Oodles of it," Mishnik said.

"Then what's the problem? I'll marry her myself!"

"What's the problem? Where do I even start?" I said. "The girl's an *octopus*."

"A *rich* octopus," Mishnik pointed out, with unassailable logic.

"And her family ..." I said, and lowered my voice. Everyone knew the stories. The Blumenthal-Tenns started out as humble hot dog sellers in the lawless years of settlement. But somehow, they got rich. And anyone who went up against them wound up as hot dog meat.

Literally.

Now, they practically *owned* this planet. No one had the guts to go out with their girl. Not unless they wanted their guts to end up as hot dog wrappers.

"Besides," I said miserably, "she's *fussy*."

That was the worst part. On my roster I had hundreds of hopeful hearts. Pining pinheads and romantic rapscallions. That was the first thing I did with the girl. I pulled out my giant book of possible matches.

"No."

"No."

"No."

"Not this one."

"Why not this one?" I said.

"Too skinny."

"This one?"

"Too fat."

"This one?"

"He has three eyes."

"This one?"

"He only has one."

"What about this one?" I said. "Menashke Melamed, top of his yeshiva at only eighteen, the kid's practically a rabbi. *And he's a squid.*"

"Too Jewish," she said.

"*Too* Jewish?" I said.

"And he has too many arms."

"He's a *squid!*"

"Show me the next one," she said.

I took out the big guns. The top matches. The best bachelors seeking a bride in this Venusian breadbasket I called home. No girl could say no to a shidduch with these fellas, I thought.

I thought wrong.

"Oswald Einstein-Einstein," I said. "So smart they named him twice. Inventor of the Slice'n'Peeler 3000 when he was just four years old. Revolutionized pineapple upside-down cake. Winner of the Fields Medal before he was seven. And he likes cats."

"He's a brain in a jar!" Esther said.

"But what a brain!" I said.

"Next!"

"Very well."

I brought out Prime Bachelor #2.

"He's very handsome," Esther said thoughtfully.

"Yes," I said.

"For an asteroid."

"Well, yes," I said. I cleared my throat. "He's a sentient asteroid." I cleared my throat again. "We think."

"It's not that I don't believe you," Esther said. "It's just that there's no real way to tell, is there?"

"Well, not as *such*," I said.

"Next," she said—with some regret, I thought.

I brought out #3 …

"What is that?" she said. "I don't see anything."

"He's a being of pure energy," I explained helpfully.

"I don't wish to come across as a crass materialist," Esther said. "But I want someone with more substance."

And so it went.

I drank my schnapps. I motioned for Mishkin to pour me another.

"So, what will you do?" Mishkin said.

"What will I do?" I said. "I'll drink this bottle is what I'll do."

And I proceeded to do exactly that.

3.

SOMETHING REACHED me in a deep slumber. The pounding in my head got so bad I had to open my eyes. Then I realized the pounding came from the door. *And* my head. I staggered upright. I went to open it. Two gorillas in suits stood in the doorway. They pushed their way in.

"You the shadchen?"

"We know you're the shadchen."

"Nothing gets past you, boys," I said admiringly.

"Thinks he's a wiseguy," the ape on the left said.

"A real Henny Youngman."

"Listen boys," I said. "I have a real ringing in my ears."

"Then don't answer."

They both laughed.

"What do you want?" I said. "I'm all out of bananas."

"Don't be a wiseguy, Shadchen."

"Yeah."

"Sit down and listen."

"Yeah."

"You know who we work for, Shadchen?"

I stared at the gorillas. The first gorillas came to Venus in the days of settlement. A lot of them used to work the hot dog carts back in the day. You didn't argue wrong change with a gorilla.

I said, "I have a pretty good idea."

"Not the Bloomberg-Brins," the ape on the left said.

"Not the Martian Mob," the ape on the right said.

"Or the Oppenheimer-Neins," the ape on the left said.

"I get it, I get it," I said. "The Blumenthal-Tenns."

"Bingo."

"And what do they want with me?" I said.

"What do you think they want, Shadchen? They want you should make a match for their darling daughter."

"Or else."

"Or else what?" I said.

"You ever see the *inside* of a kosher hot dog?"

I shook my head. It hurt.

"Well, you might will," the ape on the left said. "Get it?"

"Got it."

"Good."

They shuffled off. No good apes. I mixed myself an Alka-Seltzer.

Then I got to work.

4.

THE RABBI AKIVA Venusian Yeshiva was the grandest school on Venus, which meant it had the planet's most eligible bachelors to boot. Or so I hoped. The boys were studying scripture but, as I always say, not everyone is destined to become a rabbi, and even those who do, need wives. Eliezer Smallman met me. He was a Martian with four arms and a woven yarmulke.

"I think I have just the guy for you," he said.

I followed Eliezer. He called one of the boys over. Handsome boy. Human, too.

"This is Binyamin Ben Yamin," Eliezer said.

"The son of Major Pinhas Ben Yamin?" I said. "The famed explorer?"

"One and the same," Eliezer said. "A fearless people, the Bnei Yamin."

"Is that true, boy?" I said. "Are you fearless?"

He nodded politely.

"Ain't scared of a thing," he said. "Plus, I have a thing for dames with tentacles, myself."

"You might just do," I said. "You might just do."

Eliezer dismissed the boy.

"And my cut?" he said.

"Ten percent, if it's a match," I said. "The usual."

"It's a match," he said. "It's a match made in heaven, Shadchen."

But I wasn't so sure.

I made my way to the Central Library. As always it was busy. Boys and girls bopping to literature. They did it quietly, of course. This *was* a library.

Rivkah Popek, the librarian, found me before I found her.

"I have just the match for you, Shadchen," she said.

"If I had a nickel," I said.

"What?"

"What?" I said.

"If you had a nickel? What can you do with a nickel? Go to a nickelodeon?"

"Well, that, sure," I said. "But I meant, if someone gave me a n— oh, forget it. Who's the match?"

She called one of the guys over. He was built like a brick wall. He *was* a brick wall. The bricks moved.

"What are you, the Western Wall?" I said.

"I'm a golem," he said. "You know, from Pluto."

"What's a golem doing on Venus?" I said.

"Came over originally on a contract to provide protection," the golem said. "Ain't much to protect though, other than against bad hot dogs."

"Is there any other kind?" Rivkah said.

"You got a name, son?" I said.

"Name's Moish," the golem said.

"You kosher?"

"I'm circumcised, if that's what you mean."

I stared at that big lump of rock and had to look away. That was some rock he had on him.

"Not scared of much, are you?" I said.

"No, sir. And besides, I have a thing for dames in purple."

"You might just do," I said. "You might just do."

Rivkah dismissed him.

"And my cut?" she said.

"Ten percent if it's a match," I said.

"This is a blessed match, Shadchen," she said passionately. "Every gal wants someone strong and stable."

"He's a *wall*," I said. "Or built as such."

"A wall of strength for a girl to lean on!"

I nodded. But I wasn't so sure.

I made my way to the public mikveh to wash away my hangover but I never made it. Two slimeballs materialized in front of me and pushed me into an alleyway. You can't argue with slimeballs. It's the slime that gets you every time.

"Listen, Shadchen," the one on the left said. He hopped up and down. "You handling that Blumenthal-Tenn job?"

"What's it to you fellas?" I said.

"You know who we are?"

"I can read the papers just like the next guy," I said.

Martian Mob. Slimeballs every one. They came over several decades back now. Wiped out the competition and became just another thread in the rich tapestry of our lives. I had a bad feeling they were thinking expansion.

I wasn't wrong.

"Have we got a match for you, Shadchen!" the slimeball said.

I groaned.

"Esther Blumenthal-Tenn ain't gonna marry into slime," I said. I waited for him to sap me on the head but instead he grinned, which is a hard thing to do when you're essentially a ball covered in slime.

"We'll show you," he said.

5.

THEY TOOK me to the warehouse district. There were a lot of warehouses. We went inside one.

They had some sort of workshop in there. Electrical generators and heavy equipment. People in white lab coats. A big packing crate stood in the middle. They led me to it. I figured they were going to conk me on the head and stick me in there, for shipping on a one-way ticket to the Big Shalom. Instead, they opened it.

"Oh, my," I said.

"Told you, Shadchen."

I stared.

He was human with striking good looks and a beautiful head of hair, in a dinner jacket pressed to perfection and trousers where the crease alone was enough to give you heart palpitations. He really was perfect. There was only one thing.

"Why isn't he …?" I said, then hesitated.

"Yes? Yes?"

"Well, why isn't he *moving?*" I said.

"He's a robot," the slimeball said.

"Ah."

Well, that explained it.

"He's *our* robot," the other slimeball said.

"And he's programmed to make her happy," the first slimeball said.

"*Very* happy," the other confirmed.

"Does he talk?" I said.

"Even better," the first slimeball said. "He *listens*."

I was taken aback. A man who listens is like a fish on a bike. It just doesn't happen unless you concoct it in a lab.

"So, you get a marriage alliance with the most powerful family on Venus," I said. "And the bride gets …?"

"The perfect husband."

"He cooks, too," the second slimeball said.

"*Cooks!*"

"His knishes are to die for. And he loves kittens."

"He wants babies. Lots of *babies*."

"Can he, well …" I said. "Can he *make* babies?"

"We believe so," the first slimeball said.

"There's a 94.5 percent chance of positive output," the second slimeball said.

"Within acceptable parameters," the first one said. "Err."

"What are the acceptable parameters?" I said.

"Well, we think something will come out, we're just not sure exactly what."

"But hey," the second one said. "A baby's a baby, right?"

"I'm telling you, Shadchen, it's a perfect match," the first one said.

"At least 92.3 percent perfect," the second one said. "That's guaranteed."

"I can't make any promises," I said.

"You'll do it, Shadchen."

"Or what?" I said. "You'll send me to the Big Seder in the Sky?"

"It ain't like that, Shadchen. We have too much respect for the trade."

"Everybody needs a shadchen, Shadchen," the second one said. "All we ask for is a fair shot."

"You got it, boys," I said. "And let me say, I'm impressed. I just hope the client likes him."

6.

"SO, MY DEAR," I said, "what do you think?"

Esther Blumenthal-Tenn pouted.

"Binyamin Ben Yamin?" she said. "He's all right."

"Yes?" I said encouragingly.

"But his eyes are too close together," she said.

"Why, Esther!"

"And besides I know him from summer camp," she said. "He's no good at tennis."

I sighed, but then rallied. I had two more aces up my sleeve.

"Now *this* guy," I said, bringing up the next one, "this guy's *solid.*"

She leaned over and whistled. "What is he, the Western Wall?" she said.

"That's what *I* said!"

"Look at that hunk of rock," she said admiringly. "What is he, a golem?"

"So I'm told. He's from Pluto."

"Well, it *is* a rocky planet," she said.

"So, nu?"

"I'll consider it," she said, and inwardly I broke out in a hora. Outwardly I remained the cool professional.

"Then there's this fine fella," I said.

"He's dishy!"

"He cooks," I said.

"You don't say!"

"He likes kittens."

"Who doesn't!"

"He wants *lots* of babies."

She blushed prettily.

"He likes moonlight walks on the beach and holding hands and candlelit dinners," I said. This wasn't in the technical specs but I figured I was in the right ballpark.

"I say!"

"He's also a robot," I said.

"Well," she said, "nobody's perfect."

7.

SO THAT WAS THAT. I was feeling pretty good. I'd set up two dates for the client, and one *had* to work. I just had to hope for a spark of magic.

What I got was a spark all right.

Things started out well enough. I'd booked a booth at Drescher's Deli & Bingo Hall for the occasion. It was quiet but not too quiet. It was just the right ambiance, and the cries of the bingo caller mixed pleasantly with the aroma of chopped liver and kugel.

The would-be bride was resplendent in a strawberry dress. Her tentacles wrapped around a glass of Manischewitz. I took position discreetly nearby and motioned for the first of the two suitors to approach.

Moish the Plutonian golem strode over. His steps shook the floor but he swept gracefully onto the seat and in moments he was like clay in Esther's hands. He had a nice smile for a golem. He had a good line of patter, thought it wasn't exactly original material.

"You're so *strong*," Esther said admiringly.

"I broke my leg once in two places," the golem said.

"What happened?"

"Doctor told me to stop going to those places."

I groaned but the client laughed as though the joke was brand new to her. Maybe it even was. Everything was going so well. Then the girl up and asked the golem for a glass of water.

I should have known this was trouble but I was slow on the uptake. Of course, Moish obliged. He got up and went to the counter and brought her a glass. The girl drank it gratefully. He went and got her another.

And then another.

And then another.

"Stop!" she said. By then it was too late. You ask a golem to get you water you get more than you bargained for. He just kept going. He was so eager to please. The place was going to drown if no one was going to stop him.

I said, "Moish, when you get the water, get it from the other side of town!"

He went obligingly and I breathed a sigh of relief.

"Let me bring the other guy in," I said.

The Martian mob's robot was fully operational. He glided across the polished floor. He kissed Esther's tentacle and she blushed. He sat down, ordered drinks and a knish, and began professing his love.

"Oh, but we hardly know each other!" Esther said.

"I know you to within a 97.3 percent level of accuracy," the robot said. "But my love for you is at one hundred percent!"

"Oh, you!" Esther said.

"Your love is more delightful than wine!" the robot said.

"Oh!"

"Pleasing is the fragrance of your perfume!" the robot said.

He must have been programmed for a *Song of Songs* selection. "Your name is like perfume poured out!"

"Oh!"

"How beautiful you are, my darling! Your eyes are doves!"

"Oh!" Esther gasped. "Wait, what are doves?"

The robot froze.

"Searching," he said.

"Searching?"

"Dove, terrestrial bird, extinct."

"That's sad!" Esther said.

He was losing her. I could see the robot thinking.

"Tell me, you whom I love, where you graze your flock!" he said desperately.

"Pardon?"

The robot didn't look well. Something inside him had gone kaput.

"If you do not know, most beautiful of women," he said, "then, err … follow the tracks of the sheep?"

Smoke was coming out of his ears.

"What sheep!" poor Esther said.

"Graze your young goats by the tents of the shepherds!" the robot said. A spring went *poing!* and his left ear flew off. Then the top of his head caught on fire.

"Oh, Shadchen!" Esther cried. She looked at me pleadingly. "Oh, Shadchen, *do* something!"

Luckily at that moment the golem came back with the water. This time he had a whole bucket with him.

He saw the commotion.

He saw the robot.

And he poured the water on the robot's head and put out the flames.

. . .

8.

"AND THEN HE went to get more water," I told Mishnik. Mishnik was behind the bar. I was back at the Bar Mitzvah, drowning my sorrows in something a little stronger than Manischewitz. "But by the time he came back we weren't there. Which was probably for the best. I really don't know what I was thinking."

"Don't beat yourself up, Shadchen," Shmuel the swamp snail said. He sat to my right sipping juice. His little yarmulke still sat crooked on his little head. "You did what you could."

Esther Blumenthal-Tenn (betrothal To Be Announced) sat dejected on the stool to my left. The least I could do for the poor girl was buy her a drink. I wasn't sure Mama and Papa Blumenthal-Tenn would approve but then again, they weren't there.

"I will never find love!" she said, and burst out crying. Mishnik, gentleman that he was, patted her nearest tentacle.

"Now, now," he said.

"Oh, do you think so?" she said.

"Now, now," Mishnik said.

Esther stopped crying.

"You really have the most extraordinary eyes," she said dreamily. "Mishnik, is it?"

"Well, I'll leave you to it," I said and stood up. I was filled with a new determination. A shadchen's job is never done, and all that. I had a match to make! And a bride to match!

"Look after Miss Blumenthal-Tenn for me, boys," I said. "I must be on my way!"

And with that I sailed out of there with the doff of a hat.

· · ·

9.

A GOOD SHADCHEN keeps his hands clean—and his fingers manicured. It was a cut and dry case so I went to the Cut 'n Dry next, which was the busiest nail salon in town. Anyone who's anyone came to the Cut 'n Dry, but more importantly, anyone who was anyone's mother.

Word of my predicament had already spread. I garnered much sympathy.

"They do say she's a lovely girl," Mrs. Edelstein said. She was a sort of armadillo from Calypso with a pistachio peccadillo. She kept cracking them between her teeth. "Face that could break a mirror but a good heart, and that's all that matters in this life. The question is, who does she *like?*"

"Like?" I said.

Mrs. Edelstein looked at me shrewdly.

"A girl like that," she said, "she must have some idea what she wants already."

"Well, I mean, yes, I suppose," I said. I was taken aback. "But that is hardly the point of a shidduch! Why, if anyone went around just picking their own partners, there would be chaos!"

"Yet what about love?" Mrs. Edelstein said.

"Love? What has love got to do with it?"

Mrs. Edelstein sighed. So did the others.

"The heart wants what the heart wants," Mrs. Edelstein said. "The question is not who the *girl* wants. The question is—does that person want *her* in turn?"

. . .

10.

I WAS TROUBLED by Mrs. Edelstein's words. A match based on love was simply absurd. It was un*scientific*. Love was a bonus, perhaps. But it could never be a factor.

I said as much to Esther when she returned to my office. I brought out the great book of matches again, then put it away. I was out of ideas. I was out of luck. Soon, I figured, I'd be out of business.

I could have cried.

Esther saw my expression.

"Oh, this is hopeless!" she said. She began to cry.

I hesitated.

Maybe it was time to try something new. Something bold. Something unheard of!

"Is there," I said, and cleared my throat nervously, "is there someone *you* like?"

She looked at me in surprise.

"That *I* like?" she said.

"Well …" I said. "Yes."

She blushed.

"There is someone …" she said. "But Mother and Father would never agree. It is completely unsuitable."

"I'm sure they just want you to be happy," I said, not entirely truthfully. But I was desperate.

"He is so charming, and so calm and collected," she said. "We really hit it off, you know."

It was a strange way to put it. How would *I* know? I began to have a bad feeling. It started in the pit of my stomach and rose like the acid reflux you get after eating gefilte fish.

"It all started after the shidduch debacle, when you took me to that bar," Esther said.

"Oh, no," I said. "Oh, no."

"That bartender, Mishnik, was so very kind," she said.

"Oh, no, no, no," I said.

"Yes," she said. "And then …"

And she told me all about it.

"Could you do something, Shadchen?" she said when she finished.

"This is very unorthodox," I said.

"It's only thanks to you we met at all!" she said.

"I suppose so."

"It could be a shidduch if you make it a shidduch," she said shrewdly. "And besides, as the heir to the Blumenthal-Tenn fortune, I could really make it worth your while."

That was a very good point.

Compelling, even.

Gelt talks and kaken walks, as the elders of Safed said.

So, I told Esther I'll see what I can do.

11.

"MAZEL TOV!" the rabbi said. The groom broke the glass. Or tried to. It's not an easy thing to do when you're a snail.

I stood with Mishnik and watched the happy couple under the chuppah. Anyone who's anyone turned out for the wedding, and some nobodies, too, of course. A photographer from the *Venusian Workers Daily* snapped pictures. A klezmer band struck up a tune and circles formed as guests and loved ones formed circles for the hora.

"You did good, Shadchen," Mishnik said. "You did good."

"All thanks to you, my friend," I said, and Mishnik shrugged.

"I'm just a barkeep," he said.

The happy couple came over. The bride looked radiant. I had a feeling it wouldn't be long before she was laying eggs.

"Mazel tov, Esther," I said. She wrapped me in her tentacles.

"This is the happiest day of my life, Shadchen!" she said.

Her husband didn't so much stand as slither beside her. He always carried his home on his back. Someone had put a sticker on the back of his shell that said, *Just married!*

"Mazel tov, Shmuel," I said.

"Thank you, Shadchen."

He adjusted his yarmulke shyly.

We said congratulations and they moved on and I followed Mishnik to the bar for a glass of the good stuff. The happy couple danced. I looked at them in affection. It was an unlikely match but you could do worse than a swamp snail from the southern polar region. They were a dependable lot.

A hard exterior often hides a soft inside, as my mother used to say.

Which was certainly true about snails.

I took a sip of the good stuff and raised my glass. It was no easy job, being a shadchen on Venus, but someone had to do it, and that someone was me.

"L'chaim, Mishkin," I said.

Lavie Tidhar is author of *Osama*, *The Violent Century*, *A Man Lies Dreaming*, *Central Station*, *Unholy Land*, *By Force Alone*, *The Hood*, and *The Escapement*. His latest novels are *Maror* and *Neom*. His work encompasses children's books (*The Candy Mafia*), comics (*Adler*), anthologies (*The Best of World SF*) and numerous short stories. His awards include the World Fantasy Award, the British Fantasy Award, the John W. Campbell Award, the Neukom Prize, and the Jerwood Fiction Uncovered Prize, and he has been shortlisted for the Clarke Award and the Philip K. Dick Award amongst many others.

CORY SUCKS

Auston Habershaw

Because Mr. Howland never paid any attention to Cory's Individualized Education Plan, he sat Cory by the big window on the left side of the classroom, which was on the east side of the building. This meant, as the sun rose during first period social studies, Cory had the distinct possibility of being burned to ash if the shade wasn't down.

Cory was sure to pull the shade down the second he got to his seat, his gloves and his giant, wide-brimmed sun hat firmly in place. It was one of those shades that ran on a spring and it didn't always stay where it should or pull down all the way and Cory basically lived in mortal terror of the thing popping up at the wrong moment and flash-burning the skin off half his face.

Partly because of all this stress, he was failing social studies.

The other part was Mr. Howland.

Today the topic was the civil rights movement. They had been asked to read Martin Luther King Jr.'s "Letter from Birmingham Jail" and write an essay on what it had meant to them. Cory felt as though he had done a pretty reasonable job of it—he had a lot to say, as it turned out. When he got it back, though, he saw he'd gotten a C and a request to see Mr. Howland after class had ended.

Mr. Howland always wore a crucifix on the outside of his shirt when meeting with Cory. Cory knew it wasn't an accident, but crosses didn't actually *do* anything to vampires, and so, of the thousand different microaggressions Cory endured on a daily basis, this was the least. "You wanted to see me, Mr. Howland?" he asked.

"I don't appreciate you drawing parallels between your experiences and those of African Americans in the 1960s, Cory. I think it's inaccurate and also a demonstration of your lack of empathy for human issues."

This again.

"I *am* human," Cory said, knowing perfectly well it wouldn't make any difference.

"You're *immortal*, son."

"That's a myth. People with vampirism just age slower."

Howland raised a hand. "I'm not here to argue semantics with you. You are not *oppressed*, young man. You are a creature of the night."

"Who has to go to school *during the day*," Cory said. For the millionth time, he wondered why he even needed to say it—wasn't it obvious?

Howland bristled. "Was that back talk?"

Cory hung his head. "No."

"That's detention, mister. You don't like the sun so much? Fine, I'll make sure you're going home after the sun has set."

So, in other words, first period went about as well as it usually did.

Cory, with his stupid black sun hat and his long black clothes and pale skin, was a spectacle in the halls. Some of the bolder kids would hold their index and pinky fingers at the corners of their mouths like fangs and hiss at him as he passed by and then, after he was gone, laugh with their friends about him—that dork of a vampire.

His locker was graffitied with marker—"*CORY SUCKS*" in big red letters. He tried to appreciate the play on words. When he opened it, a little flyer fluttered out. In Cory's experience, this was one of two things: flyers from the guidance counselor's office or hate mail.

The guidance counselor flyers were always things from the International Guardians of Reawakened Rights—IGORR—that said stuff like "Monster is a Slur," and "Allergies are not Evil." They had cheery pictures of vampires—complete with capes and evening wear—doing normal things like taking their driving test and doing well on their SATs. On the whole, Cory preferred the hate mail—at least that seemed honest.

This time, though, the flyer was a notice from the Student Council reminding everyone about the prom in a few weeks—they probably put one in every locker. He looked at the picture—a black-and-white clip art of a man in a tuxedo and a girl in a frilly gown dancing. It would have been nice, he thought—dancing with a girl. A girl that didn't hate his guts.

Assuming such a person existed.

Since he couldn't wear the gym uniform without collecting sunburns and wasn't allowed in the locker rooms because the PTA assumed he couldn't "control himself," Cory sat on the bleachers during gym. Once, the track coach had tried to recruit him, assuming vampires were "super fast" so they could "chase down prey," but was disappointed to learn that Cory's ability to run had not been improved by allergies to sunlight, silver, and garlic. Besides, he was quick to point out that track meets occurred during the day which was, you know, *dangerous*. The track coach had muttered something about Cory running in sweatpants, but after that organized sports remained beyond his reach. Now he was gathered with all the other freaks and weirdos in the school—the severe asthma kids, the kid in the wheelchair, and the blind girl. Usually he was fine with being excused from the pointless, never-ending hazing ritual that was phys ed, but today it just reminded him of his isolation.

There was a big bin in a corner of the basketball court, stuffed with packages of confetti and disco balls and miles of crepe-paper streamers—decorations for prom night. Cory looked at it, imagining what it might be like, to be allowed to do something normal for once. That was all he wanted, really—to do something normal.

At lunch, he sat alone at a desk dragged in from one of the classrooms. Thankfully it wasn't pizza day and he didn't need his inhaler because of all the garlic. He just sipped from his thermos of cow's blood through a straw and watched his fellow students laugh and talk and chat.

The prom thing remained lodged in his brain. Prom was at *night*. He wouldn't have to worry about being pushed out the gym doors by bullies and bursting into flame. He'd be safe. He could actually *go*, assuming he could get a date.

Cory hadn't talked to a girl willingly in almost two years. He *thought* about them pretty much all the time, of course, but a loser who dressed like Zorro and drank blood had the same chance of scoring a date as rainclouds had forming on the moon.

But what *if* he did?

What if he just asked? What was the worst that could happen—he would be mercilessly teased? Potentially assaulted? All that sounded like a pretty average Tuesday.

The more Cory thought about it, the more he figured he had to try. Who to ask?

After going down the list of possibilities and the myriad reasons they would tell him to drop dead, he was left with only one possibility—the new girl. Her name was Stacy Cord, and she was in his physics class. She had only moved here this year and hadn't made any friends. She was, at this exact moment, sitting alone in the corner of the cafeteria at one end of an empty table.

She had short blonde hair and a wispy band of fuzz all along her upper lip, which had earned her the nickname "the 'Stache" among the same group of jerks who threw water balloons full of holy water at Cory just to see if he'd fry.

She definitely didn't have a date. No way. And she was on the short list of people at school who didn't recoil when he passed by her or anything. Yeah—she was the one.

He got up.

He sat down.

He got up again.

Heads turned as he crossed the cafeteria. Whispers rippled across the lunch tables—*is that Cory Dauphine? What is he doing?*

His resolve almost faltered—what *was* he doing?—but then he was standing in front of Stacy, hands unable to decide where they should be—his pockets, behind his back, loosely at his sides—*where?* And she looked up—was *looking* at him. She might have said, "Yes?"

Words fled. The phrase he had rehearsed—*"Hi, Stacy—my name is Cory, and I was wondering if you would go to the prom with me."*—vanished from his mind. The silence dragged out—*say something, dammit!* His brain—that rusty old engine—coughed to life. "I can't hypnotize people."

Stacy blinked up at him. "Why would I think—"

"Someone last year asked me to hypnotize our math teacher into giving us all A's." *What was he doing? Why was he saying this? Oh GOD!*

Stacy's mouth hung open. "What did you do?"

"I said no and then that guy and his friends threw me in the creek behind the school." Cory remembered the soggy walk home. "That doesn't work either, just FYI."

"Okay, soooo ..." Stacy said.

Retreat! Run away! Cory shook himself—no! He'd come this far. Here he was, *talking* to a girl. He planted his feet. "Doyouhaveadatefortheprom?" He said it all in one breath.

Stacy blushed to her eyebrows. "Wh-what?"

Cory's own face warmed to the point where he wondered if he was in direct sunlight. "Would you go to the prom with me?"

There! He said it!

Cory felt the eyes of the whole cafeteria on him. On *them*.

Someone in the cafeteria called, "Better run girl! Cory wanna suck you dryyyyyy!"

Stacy opened her mouth.

Oh shit—she was going to answer. She was going to say no and everyone would see. Why hadn't he just stayed in his chair, sipping his cow's blood like a good vampire?

"Mr. Dauphine." Cory turned—Mr. Howland was behind him, his arms crossed. "Principal's office—*now*."

"What did I do?" Cory asked. But he knew what he did—he tried to be normal. Not okay.

"Now." Howland grabbed him by the upper arm and steered him toward the door.

"Cory, wait!" Stacy called.

Both he and Mr. Howland paused, each of them shocked at her outburst, though in different ways. "What?" they said in unison.

Stacy slipped a piece of paper into his hand—her number. "Yes."

Detention—or, in this case, *double* detention—involved Cory sitting in a room and being made to copy a page from the Bible. This was probably unconstitutional, but like most other things in Cory's life, he picked his battles. He tried to pick as few battles as possible.

Howland's detention slips were always stupid, but the second one for today—*attempting to seduce the living*—was actively hilarious. *Seduce?* God, Cory could barely *talk to* Stacy and he had the animal magnetism of a snail. Also, if he were dead, why would he be going to high school? What, was there calculus homework in the afterlife? Did vampire "nests" have standardized entrance exams?

It didn't matter, anyway. What mattered was that Cory had now, stored in his phone, the cell number of an actual girl who had actually agreed to go to the prom with him. Had she smiled at him when slipping that number into his hand? He tried to remember her expression—had it been pity? The smile of a friend? The smile of … of a lover?

The aftershocks of this decision—this battle he had now picked—were beginning to become clear to him. What was wrong with Stacy that made her say yes? Did she somehow not *know* he was a vampire? That was impossible. And if she *did* know, then what the hell was she thinking? Going out with *him*? A public menace?

These doubts—all new, all very plausible—ate away at his victory in the cafeteria. He now felt as though he were the victim of some trick. She was in league with the rest of the students. They were going to go full Carrie on him—pig's blood and all.

Actually, he kinda liked pig's blood. They'd probably use something stupid. Garlic bread, maybe—a big buttery basket of it. He'd have to remember to bring his inhaler.

Cory sat in the back corner of the detention room, chasing his thoughts around his head, barely noticing the passage from the Book of Joshua he was transcribing about a hill of foreskins and a flint knife.

Via some terrible Freudian process, the next thing that occurred to him was this: *Oh shit, I'll have to tell my parents!*

BY THE TIME he got home, it was dusk, and the Dauphine household was just waking up. Cory came in the kitchen door to find his mother eating breakfast. Breakfast was a man in a speedo wearing heavy eye makeup.

"Hi, Raoul," Cory said, hanging his book bag on a hook.

The mostly naked man waved with his free arm. "Greetings, Master!"

"I'm not your master, Raoul."

Claudia Dauphine lifted her mouth from Raoul's other forearm. She was also wearing entirely too much eye makeup. Instead of a speedo, she wore a slingshot bikini and thigh-high leather boots. "Cory, don't scold Raoul. He is a loyal and helpful ghoul." She wiped a little blood from the corner of her mouth and tapped her cheek. "Kiss?"

Cory did his best to avert his eyes from the mortifying view of his mother's scantily clad body and pecked her on the cheek.

"Raoul, Band-Aid," his mother said.

"Yes, Mistress!" Raoul sat up and snatched a box of children's Band-Aids from the counter and applied one to the small punctures in his forearm after a squirt of antiseptic gel. His arm had at least three other such bandages—cartoon characters like Daffy Duck and Yosemite Sam covering over his use as a human snack bar. Elsewhere, Raoul's skin was a network of little scabs and faint scars that he'd earned over his year of service.

"Hungry?" Claudia asked. "Raoul has a few more sips left in him, I'm sure."

"I live to serve, mistress."

Cory shuddered. "Umm ... no thanks."

"How was school today?" she asked, staring at him intently with her yellowish eyes.

Cory looked at his feet. "Fine. Nothing interesting happened."

His mother's eyes narrowed. "Hold on—*what* happened? Tell me."

She snapped her fingers. "Raoul—chair." Raoul hopped off the table and curled himself into a tight little ball. Cory's mom sat lightly on the arch of his back and crossed her legs. "Well? Out with it!"

"Uh … well …"

"You've been expelled?" Claudia guessed. "Suspended? Did you feed on an underclassman? I *told* you, Cory—no sucking blood from anyone below the age of consent!"

Raoul, from his position as chair, extended his arm to give a thumbs up. His voice was strained. "This … is … good advice … Master … Cory…"

"I didn't feed on anybody! Gross!"

"Well?"

"Um … can I have a hundred dollars?"

Claudia's absurdly arched eyebrows shot even further up her pale forehead. "What for?"

Cory knew it wouldn't be that easy. "Nothing. Never mind."

He tried rushing past her and out of the kitchen, but his mother's long fingernails closed delicately around his wrist like talons. "Cory," she purred. "You have a *date*, don't you?"

"Mom, I—"

"You seduced an innocent young girl! Cory, you've been watching those videos after all!"

"I haven't been watching the videos. Jeez."

"Language, Cory," Claudia snapped—even though crosses and holy water and stuff did nothing, his mother was very "traditional" when it came to vampire "culture." No J-words allowed. She shook her head at him. "Those videos were very helpful to your father and I."

The "videos" were a series of amateur hypnosis tutorials made specifically by the vampire community for the vampire community. They involved people in stupid capes and fishnets dangling plastic crystals in front of vampire groupies like Raoul who pretended to be mesmerized for the thrill of it. The whole ridiculous affair made Cory uncomfortable. "This isn't a vampire thing. I just want to go to the prom."

Another throaty chuckle. "Well, well—the plot *thickens.*"

"Mom, it's just a date. Just a regular, ordinary human date. That's it."

"Normal is a state of mind, dear." His mother hummed quietly to herself, considering. "I think you should talk with your father."

THE DAUPHINE HOUSEHOLD HAD, perhaps five years ago, been a pretty ordinary suburban house with ordinary suburban occupants. Cory's parents hadn't taken to the prospect of middle age well, though, so when Cory was about twelve they had started attending vampirism seminars, held midnights at the local community center. Cory got the impression that it started as a kind of sex thing—something to rekindle their relationship—but it ballooned into a lifestyle. They'd been turned by Cory's fifteenth birthday.

They'd insisted on the same for their son. His parents had pitched it to him for a month—nightly vampire movie marathons, promises of eternal life and power and stuff. To Cory, a tenth-grade nobody, it had seemed exciting. His parents had left out the fact that vampirism wasn't some kind of magical gift. It was just a stupid disability with some weird side effects. Of course, he only realized that after he agreed to be turned.

The house underwent a transformation. The shades got very thick and his parents moved their bedroom into the basement. They sold their bed in exchange for special coffins that could lock from the inside and got a subscription to a local slaughterhouse that sold cow's blood wholesale. Dad's job—he worked IT —kept him on fully remote and he worked the night shift with no complaints. His mom, meanwhile, now got paid by people like Raoul who had a thing for being enslaved by a vampire. It turned out there were a surprising number of people like that. Every one of them freaked Cory out.

They also bought a pipe organ. Not a big pipe organ, mind you, but a medium-size one that fit at one end of the living room. Cory's father took lessons and was now able to grind out a halfway decent "Toccata and Fugue in D Minor."

Craig Dauphine was playing it now but kept screwing up a measure, so he had to go back and start over. He, at least, was wearing clothes, but he was no less embarrassing. Craig wore a white shirt with frilly sleeves that was open at the chest, and velvet pants so tight that Cory could tell his father wasn't wearing underwear. His hair was long, falling in golden waves to his shoulders, save for the front, which was in a severe widow's peak. When he saw Cory come in, he flashed a fanged smile and waved him to sit on one of the various couches and settees they had arranged in their living room, as though this were the Playboy Mansion.

Cory remembered his father as a different man, once—a shy guy with a beer gut and a love of video games—but vampirism had allowed Craig to indulge in all his stupidest fantasies, including this one, which was imagining he could give his son advice about women.

"She's going to want you to turn her, Son," his dad said, after Cory had confessed.

"No, she isn't," Cory said. "Why would she want that?"

Cory's dad laughed. When Cory didn't laugh along, he frowned. "Cory, *everyone* wants to be us—don't you see? We're young, we're beautiful, we're *cool*. Look at me. I've never looked better in my life!"

"You look like you belong on the *Three Musketeers*."

"Cory, why are you always so down on your heritage?"

"Because it's not a heritage, Dad, it's a *disorder*."

"Cory, your mother and I understand that adolescence with

vampirism is difficult, but you need to take a long view. Our people—"

"You're French-Canadian, Dad. Vampires aren't a people, we're just *weirdos*. All I want to do is go on a *normal* date with a *normal* girl to prom—none of this has *anything to do* with my condition!"

His father threw up his hands. "You know what—I can't talk to you when you're like this. Go to your room and think about all the things this new life has given you. Think of the *advantages*, kid! We'll talk about this later when you've cooled off."

"Sure," Cory said, "whatever."

Once in his room, he did a little digging on Stacy.

He knew nothing about her. He reluctantly opened his social media feed to learn more. It had been two years since he'd bothered with it, much. After his turning, most of what social media held for him was either hateful or creepy. That was the way with vampires, his parents always said—mortals were either devoted to you or wanted you dead, and there was very little middle ground.

Cory scrolled her feed, looked at photos of her summer vacation up at some cabin in the woods with her folks, fishing and canoeing and stuff. She didn't seem to have a huge social circle, herself. She was on the school basketball team, apparently. She mostly posted pictures of wildlife and flowers and stuff. She had a couple of big, shaggy dogs.

About the only thing Cory came up with was that she liked horror movies which, in this situation, he took as a red flag. Beyond that? Nothing. Nothing to give him any clue as to why a perfectly normal girl would agree to go to the prom with Cory Dauphine, known bloodsucking creep.

Given the horror movies, he had to assume his father was right. This was a girl hoping to get turned into a vampire on the night of her prom, and she was expecting Cory would be just starved enough for attention to do it.

Sadly, Stacy was not entirely wrong.

PROM WAS IN TWO WEEKS. Cory's school life did not improve—he was still finding minced garlic smeared on his locker and some jerk stole his big hat while he was walking through the breezeway so his cheek caught on fire—but he actually had something to look forward to. Someone to look for in the halls. That first day after he'd asked her, Cory risked waving at Stacy as she came into physics class and, to his secret joy, she actually waved back and gave him a shy little smile.

They didn't sit together at lunch—of course not—but after school he would sometimes find her hanging around in a shady part of the school parking lot, waiting for her ride home. Stacy would always wave and call him over. "How was your day?" she'd ask, pushing a strand of hair behind her ears.

"Okay," he would lie.

"You ready for the physics test on Friday?"

Cory shrugged. "Probably not."

"Yeah." Stacy looked at her sneakers.

Awkward silence.

"Well," Cory would always say, "I should go. Can't stay outside too long."

"Right, of course. Bye."

Later in his room, he would sit and play the conversations over and over again in his mind. Why was this girl talking to him? Did she *actually* like him? How would he be able to tell? There was no one to turn to for advice. Certainly not his parents. Their lives were so far separated from ordinary teenage dating problems that they may as well be living on a different planet.

So, one day, shortly before prom, Cory spotted her in her shady spot in the parking lot and decided he'd just ask her. Just straight up ask her. Yes. He was going to do it. Right then.

Before he could get there, a man got out of a parked car and intercepted him. He was big, tall, and broad with a full beard—like the lumberjack mascot on a box of pancakes. He blocked Cory's path and growled, "Gimmie one reason I shouldn't rip that hat off your head, scrub."

"Uh, because it would be murder?" Cory glanced around, just to make sure there were witnesses.

"Jamie?" He heard Stacy's voice—she knew this guy. Cory couldn't look the lumberjack man in the face or the sun would hit his chin, so he just stared at the guy's broad chest and contemplated his mortality.

"You stay away from her, creep," the lumberjack pushed him.

"Yeah, okay. Sorry." He turned to leave.

"Jamie, get away from him!" Stacy yelled. "Leave him alone!"

"Just let him go, Stace—he's not like us. He isn't good enough for you."

Stacy pushed past the lumberjack and took Cory by the arm. "You aren't the boss of me, Jamie."

"I'll tell Dad!" Jamie said.

"Then I'll tell him about *your* girlfriend."

Cory stiffened. Did she just … was that *implying* …

Jamie glared at them both, his tree-trunk arms folded over his flannel torso. He looked like a carving placed outside a steak house. "Fine. It's your funeral. Or his, if Dad finds out."

Stacy watched him fold himself back inside his compact car. "That's just my brother," she whispered to Cory, leading him by the arm back to their shady spot under the tree. When she let go, Cory's skin tingled where she had touched him.

"Sorry about that," she said. "He means well."

"I guess," Cory said.

They stood facing each other, a couple feet apart. That Saturday, they would be dancing. Well, at least theoretically. Cory didn't know how it could be real. He didn't even know if he wanted it to be. "Can I ask you something?"

"Why did I say yes?" she said.

"Yeah."

"Maybe it's a bad idea." Stacy watched her brother pull away in his car. He still glared at them out the window. "I don't want you to get in trouble."

Cory shrugged. "I'm always in trouble."

"See? Maybe that's what I like."

All thoughts of not going through with it—all his suspicions about her and his fears of what the prom would bring—evaporated in the light of that smile. "Uh … where should I pick you up?"

"Oh, yeah—you can't come to my house, no way. What about I meet you at your place?"

"Oh, no, no no." Cory couldn't help but chuckle. "You do *not* want to meet my parents."

"What about here?" Stacy gestured to their little spot, on the far side of the parking lot from the gym.

"Yeah, okay." Cory smiled, maybe for the first time in her presence. He saw Stacy's eyes snap right to his fangs and linger on them a touch too long. His smile faded, and he made his usual excuses to get home. It was only once he was halfway there that he realized she'd never actually answered his question.

He still had no idea why this girl was going to the prom with him.

Still, he was excited to find out.

IT WASN'T until the last minute that Cory managed to get the money to buy tickets to the prom. It was, bizarrely, Raoul that came through for him. The ghoul slipped him a couple twenty-dollar bills in an envelope under his door, early one morning. The envelope read FOR MASTER'S FIRST GHOUL in blood. Raoul's blood.

"Oh, that Raoul," his mother had said that morning. The shades were drawn and she was wearing a fluffy pink bathrobe that actually made her look somewhat normal, were it not for the glitter sprinkled across her cheeks. "He's such a romantic."

"Mom, I am not going to feed on this girl!" Cory said.

His father, in a matching fluffy pink bathrobe and matching glitter, looked up from his blood pudding. "What are you complaining about? Trust me, when you see her exposed neck, all close to you on the dance floor, you'll know what to do."

Claudia raised one talon-like finger. "Just remember: what is the magic word?"

Cory sighed. "Consent."

His parents grinned. Their fangs were still bloody. "C'mon," his dad said. "I'll let you borrow my tux."

Craig Dauphine's tuxedo was a gothic atrocity. It was as though some designer took a hard look at Bela Lugosi's evening wear and said, "this, but with more skulls." His father spun him around in front of the mirror. "Pretty cool, eh?"

Cory looked down the cummerbund embroidered with a coiled serpent, fangs bared. "I feel like a professional wrestler at a wedding."

His father beamed. "Oh, come on—you'll knock 'em dead! Let me go get my silver-tip cowboy boots!"

The "silver-tip" boots did not involve actual silver (allergies, you know), but did have a lot of stainless steel studs and teardrop-shaped red costume jewelry meant to simulate drops of blood. They didn't fit well, but not badly enough that Cory had any excuse to deny his father, who was just ... *so* excited about them. He had no choice but to go along with it.

His mom snapped photos as he came down the stairs. "Your

classmates won't even recognize you." She winked. "Be sure to take advantage."

"Mom! Gross!"

Outside, Craig pulled the car out of the garage. The car was the last remaining vestige of their normal human lives—a white minivan with heavily tinted windows, dingy around the edges and scratched along the fenders from when Cory was learning to drive. The idea of a skull-encrusted skinny teenage vampire like him driving around in an egg-shaped soccer taxi was too much. He looked ridiculous. Stacy would laugh at him. They all would.

But no. He'd come this far.

"You should get out at night more often," his dad said, tugging on Cory's jacket and brushing away stray pieces of lint with his thumbs. "Feels good, doesn't it?"

"Sure," Cory lied.

Cory put the plastic box with the corsage on the passenger seat and drove off. He was going out. He was going to prom. With a girl. There was still so much that wasn't quite right about this, but for that exact moment, he didn't care. He revved the minivan's tiny engine, took the curves at speed, and felt that surge of adrenaline that told him, whatever lay ahead, he could handle it.

Once there, Stacy was nowhere to be found. Not under her tree. Not anywhere. Cory lurked at that end of the parking lot, brooding on the implications.

Eventually, she emerged from the woods, not up the driveway. She was wearing a blue gown, its hem hiked up around her knees by one hand, the other clutching a golf umbrella. She looked ragged, exhausted. "Hey," she said. "I'm here!"

Cory helped her through the underbrush, flicking stray leaves and sticks from her hair, her dress. "What ... why did you come this way?"

"I had to sneak out. Sorry. My parents said I couldn't go."

"Because of me. They found out."

Stacy grabbed his arm. "Oh! Not that—no! Because of the weather!"

"Weather?" Cory looked over his shoulder at the sky just beyond the edge of the tree limbs. It was a clear, bright night. Not a cloud in the sky.

"You look very nice, by the way." Stacy opened her golf umbrella and took Cory's elbow. "Shall we?"

Cory looked up at the umbrella. Was Stacy crazy? Maybe all of this was just because she was odd. Her brother had seemed odd. Her parents were probably odd, too. So ... fine. Of all people, he had no standing to complain about weird. He covered her hand on his arm with his. "Let's go."

The gym was a confection of crepe paper and neon light. From inside, the music thumped against the brick walls, only to roar as the doors opened to admit more students. The back of his mouth felt dry, but he pressed on. He was going to do this. He was going to do one normal thing for once. No one would stop him.

But Mr. Howland, Cory's social studies teacher, was manning the door.

It took him a second to recognize Cory. "Hey—hold on. You can't come in!"

Cory held up his money. "Why not? I'm going to buy tickets!"

Howland pulled his crucifix out from under his turtleneck. It took a lot of grunting and yanking. "It's an obvious safety issue."

"It is not!" Stacy said.

Mr. Howland took Stacy by the chin and stared into her eyes. "Are you under his control?"

Stacy jerked back. "Don't *touch* me!"

Howland had her by the arm, though. "You'd better come with me, missy. It's for your own good."

The other kids coming into the gym stopped to watch the

commotion. "Holy shit," someone said, "is that Cory Dauphine?"

"Let go of me!" Stacy yelled.

Howland didn't listen. "This is dangerous, Ms. Cord—look at the moon! Do your parents know that you've ..."

Cory pushed him. Not hard—not *really* hard, anyway—but Howland fell, tripping over a folding chair and knocking over the student council table. In his struggle to regain his balance, Howland knocked Stacy's umbrella out of her hands.

"No!" Stacy screamed. "No, no, no!"

Cory scrambled after the umbrella, which had caught a breeze and was skittering just beyond his reach. By the time he got it, Stacy was gone—she was running, full speed, back across the parking lot, toward the trees.

Cory ran after her. "Stacy! Wait! I've got it! I've got your umbrella!"

But she didn't stop, didn't look back. So Cory kept running.

She plunged into the trees, vanishing in a puff of leaves, her shoes left behind. Cory slipped after her. "Stacy! Wait up! Just ... just wait up!"

His father's absurd snakeskin boots slipped and struggled with the muddy, uneven ground. The forest wasn't large—just an empty, wooded plot of land next to the school—but there were enough bushes and underbrush that it was hard to keep track of Stacy, even with Cory's exceptional night vision.

He came upon her gown—torn down the seam, discarded in a bush. What was she *doing*? Running around in her underwear? Wait ... wait a minute ... was she ...

Finally, panting and wheezing, he caught up with her in a little clearing in the center of the lot, where an old park bench had been dragged generations ago. It was surrounded with cigarette butts and sun-faded beer cans and the bench itself was carved nearly to nothing by the initials of hundreds of young lovers.

There, sitting on it, was a huge, hulking hairy beast in a frilly pink bra. She had her snout in her claws. She was crying.

"You're a ... a werewolf!" Cory gasped. He'd heard about them, of course, but never met one. Then again, how would he know if he'd ever met one? They were Class 2 Mystical creatures, like himself—categorized as "potentially dangerous" by the government. They didn't like to advertise. Only the teachers would know.

Oh. *Now* it made sense why Howland had come down so hard on them talking. It wasn't just Cory he was worried about.

"Get away from me!" Stacy said, waving him off. "I'm hideous!"

But she wasn't. Her fur was silver in the moonlight, her ears high and tufted, her flanks were muscular and smooth. Instead of backing away, he sat down next to her. "I guess this makes a lot more sense, now," Cory said. "The umbrella and stuff—you needed to stay out of the moonlight."

"I ... I ruined it. My dad said I'd ruin it. I'm so sorry, Cory." She wiped her snout on her arm fur. "I just wanted one normal thing, you know? Just one normal experience."

Cory blinked at his thoughts being echoed back to him. "What are you talking about? You get to do normal things all the time! Aren't you on the basketball team?"

"Only because Coach Julius found out I was a werewolf. He thinks it makes me jump real high."

"Uh ... does it?"

"Of course not! The only thing being like this does is ruin every single date I've ever gone on. Like, ever. Last time it was so bad we had to move."

"Is that why you said yes?" Cory looked down at his stupid boots. What an idiot he had been. "No way I could complain about dating a werewolf, huh?"

"What are you talking about?" Stacy asked. "Is that what you think of me? No! I said yes, Cory, because you seemed nice."

"Nobody thinks I'm nice. Everyone thinks I'm trying to eat them."

"I know all about that, believe me." Stacy held up her paws. "Have you *seen* these claws?"

"At least they only come out during the full moon." Cory showed his fangs. "These I'm stuck with!"

"I'm not a monster," Stacy said. "I just have a really weird allergy."

Cory chuckled—she'd seen the brochures, same as him. "Vampirism is just a metabolic condition. That doesn't make me evil," he recited.

Stacy grinned, which displayed her terrifying teeth. Cory was not afraid. "You know why else I said yes?" she asked.

"No."

"I think you're brave."

"Me? I get kicked around all day, every day. All I do is sit there and take it. How is that brave?"

"You show everyone who you are, and you never get angry when they treat you like crap, and you come back the next day and do it again. You even had the guts to ask me out." Stacy sniffled again, her big wet nose wrinkling in the half-light. "I don't know how I'll ever recover from this. I don't know how to go on."

"Hey," Cory said, stroking the fur on her shoulder. "Don't think about it. Just do it. And then do it again. And then again. That's the trick, I think."

"That's so hard, Cory."

"Yeah. But now we won't be alone, will we?"

"It's not normal, you and me together. Our parents—"

"Hey," Cory stood up, brushing the dirt off his tux. "Normal is a state of mind."

He placed his phone on the bench and hit play on his music list—it played something poppy, upbeat. The kind of thing his parents hated. "Come on—let's dance."

Stacy smiled, her pink tongue peeking out between her teeth. The werewolf put her paw in the vampire's hand and rose. Together, they bobbed to the beat, out of sight of everyone but each other.

AUSTON HABERSHAW IS a science fiction and fantasy author with no aspirations to become a vampire. His stories have been published in *The Magazine of Fantasy and Science Fiction, Galaxy's Edge, Analog,* and other places. He also writes novels, his latest being his complete fantasy series, The Saga of the Redeemed, published by HarperVoyager. He lives and works in Boston, MA, and spends his days teaching composition and writing to college students. Find him on his website at aahabershaw.com or on Goodreads, Amazon, or on Twitter at @AustonHab.

SUNNYSIDE DAYCARE EMPLOYEES' CHAT LOG, POST ALIEN TAKEOVER

Amanda Helms

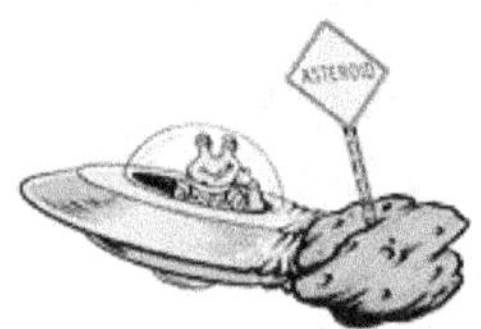

T uesday

Yrnek
please
any humans left
where is the syllabus of human learning

Tenesha M

1) Maybe you should talk to your supreme overlords about why the humans were kicked out if you want help.

2) I get that y'all Rthnithians are "overhauling the human renumeration system" but you still owe me my last paycheck.

3) Aren't you in charge of the two-year-olds? There's no syllabus for them. Just keep them alive and fed and not chewing on each other or the furniture.

· · ·

Yrnek

Apex Overseers not supreme overlords

as was reported in your dismissal your and the others' positions were terminated in part for your failure to show proper respect, such as using your superiors' correct titles. perhaps that is why you never received your final paycheck

however in appreciation for your advice i will ask about your compensation

Tenesha M

Asking about my money isn't "appreciation," it's what I'm owed.

With the Rthnithians' focus on honor or whatever, I would've thought you'd understand even in a hostile takeover, you acquire that business's debts.

Y'all owe me $686.47 after taxes.

Yrnek

our takeover wasn't that hostile. we didn't vaporize anyone

plus be happy we're not the glarbites. they would've eaten you all. you in particular because you smell delicious

Tenesha M

Not my fault Rhonda didn't pay enough for me to avoid moonlighting at Hambungle and coming into Sunnyside smelling like the coconut oil from the fryer. I don't have to listen to you tell me I should be happy for losing my job just because some other alien colonizers didn't eat me.

Good luck for the kids' sake, let me know when you've got my money, peace out.

WEDNESDAY

Yrnek

Tenesha could you review this attachment. it is a list of my ideas for enrichment activities for the tiny humans

TENESHA M

I still don't see my money in my account
What the hell is "Vaporizers: trial and error"?

Yrnek

it is part of the cultural exchanges segment. the tiny humans can have appendages-on experience with traditional Rthnithian weaponry

TENESHA M

DO NOT UNDER ANY CIRCUMSTANCE ALLOW KIDS OF ANY AGE TO PLAY WITH WEAPONS!

Yrnek

it is a common exercise among our young but if you insist i can remove it
what about the pen pal program with the glarbites

. . .

Tenesha M

The average two-year-old can't write or type.

Wait, glarbites, the aliens you said would eat us? NO!

Yrnek

you humans are too isolationist. how will you learn to get along with other species if you refuse to engage with them?

Tenesha M

Argh.

Do. NOT. Allow. The kids to play with weapons.

Do not encourage them to talk to creatures that want to eat them.

I'm sending an invoice for the money y'all owe me and adding a consultation fee for today.

Friday

Yrnek

Tenesha

i need advice

please

one of the tiny humans has fallen and is leaking how do i stop the leaking

Tenesha M

Blood or tears?

Or pee. It could be pee.

• • •

Yrnek

what is the difference

Tenesha M

Blood is red. Tears are clear and come from the eyes
Pee is the yellow excretory fluid from the kidneys

Yrnek

it is clear, except there is yellowish fluid coming from its nose
you never told me I should apply the "diapers" to the tiny humans' faces
humans are disgusting

Tenesha M

First, that's not pee, that's mucus.
Second, where do you get off calling us disgusting? You're a being who eats and craps through the same orifice.

Yrnek

perhaps we should agree to leave our respective biological differences out of the matter

Tenesha M

Whatever.
How big a fall was it? Did you check for broken bones, contusions, etc.?

. . .

Yrnek

i do not know how to do that
where is the human manual
it was two steps off the thing you call a stool

Tenesha M

Okay, two steps isn't bad.

Which kid? Ayanna, Bao, & Frida should at least be able to point to what hurts, if anything. Trinity and Franklin you'd have to physically assess.

Our copy of *Caring for Your Baby and Young Child* is in the office. So is the emergency kit. That'll have first-aid supplies.

Yrnek

you mean i have to touch it

Tenesha M

What, the emergency kit? Unless Rthnithians have telekinetic powers you haven't told anyone about, yes.

Yrnek

no
the tiny human
i have to touch it?

Tenesha M

HOW IN HELL HAVE YOU BEEN CARING FOR THESE CHILDREN THE PAST WEEK IF YOU HAVEN'T TOUCHED THEM??????

· · ·

Yrnek

(is typing)

(is typing)

you said i only needed to keep them alive, fed, and not chewing on each other or the furniture. at this i have excelled

the tiny human says its name is Frida. it is okay but it wants its mother

or you

Tenesha. this might surprise you. but i do not think i can do this alone

Tenesha M

No shit.

Yrnek

i am contacting the Apex Overseers regarding your paycheck and former position

Tenesha M

I thought you were going to talk to them on Tuesday?

Yrnek

we Rthnithians are not always perfect

the Apex Overseers will provide your missing compensation and consultant's fee once our takeover of your banking system is complete, anticipated in .378 minutes. also you may return to your former position so long as you accept a living wage

· · ·

Tenesha M

You're serious? That's all it took?

Hot damn. The money's showing in my account. Thanks.

Yrnek

it'd be wise to keep your job at Hambungle though

Tenesha M

Ugh I knew there'd be a catch. What do the Supreme Overlords consider a livable wage? 14/hr?

Yrnek

Apex Overseers

they offer $23/hr, 10 more than your previous wage

but I like the oil scent

Tenesha M

Ok, no

Yrnek

working with a human is less nauseating if they smell like tropical tastiness

Tenesha M

Again, NO

And if a glarbite is one of *your* pen pals please stop.

· · ·

Yrnek

fine

as long as you take care of the leaking humans

Tenesha M

I'll see you Monday.

Amanda Helms (she/her) is a biracial science fiction, fantasy, and sometimes horror writer whose stories are forthcoming from or have appeared in *FIYAH*, *Lightspeed*, *Diabolical Plots*, and elsewhere. She and her family live in Colorado. Though all of them are natives, none ski or snowboard, proving that such creatures indeed exist. When not reading or writing, she's likely chasing after her toddler or cooing over cute puppy pictures. Find her at amandahelms.com and on Twitter and Instagram under @amandaghelms.

COOKING UP TROUBLE

C. Flynt

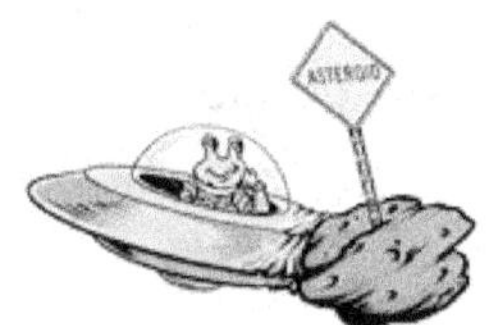

I was listening to my talking skull's headlines when the nameplate transformed from its normal black obelisk to an off-white tiered cake. In tasteful green script, it read "Hieronymous Glyph, Alchemist at Law and Hot Business Tips." As I read, my orb chimed, "Mr. Keeble to see you. New Client," and a diminutive elf slid around my half-open office door. I noted the frayed cuffs on his white jacket. This elf could not pay well, but he obviously needed help.

"Umm." He twisted his hands. "I was told you might be able to help me. Do you know about tart law?"

My clients seldom know much about either natural law or legalisms, so I explained, "You mean tort law. I've handled many cases of injury and recompen—"

"Not torte, tart! Tortes don't sell well enough to matter." He dragged a finger around his collar. "My problem is with tarts."

My hackles rose at his interruption, but his air of nervous desperation aroused my sympathies.

"Perhaps you need to describe your problem. I'll explain how I can help once I understand everything."

"I bake delicious cookies and other desserts." He waved his hands as he spoke.

"In a hollow tree in the forest?"

He cocked his head at me. "Of course not. I've got a shop on Easy Street. The Easy Bake Bakery is right in the middle of the block."

With magical clients I can never assume I understand their need until they explain it. I waved for him to continue.

"The problem is tarts. I developed a new recipe for whortleberry tarts. A delightful combination of sweet and sour to tickle the palate and—"

I interrupted his sales pitch. "Your tarts are excellent. Got it. But what is your problem?"

He bit his lips. Perhaps I should have let him finish his obviously practiced spiel.

He took a breath and stared over my head. "My problem is that my shop is in the middle of the block, and the bakeries on the corners have copied my delicacy. Their tarts are inferior to mine, but people find them first and I'm going out of business. Make them stop baking my tarts."

I shrugged. "Did you patent your process? Or put a spell of secrecy or a copyright on it?"

The elf stared at his shoes and shook his head. Protections are always too expensive for the small businessman until he discovers the cost of not purchasing them.

"I'm afraid there's no legal action you can take. Perhaps you can invent a new confection to attract customers? I'll be happy to protect any new confection you develop."

He shuffled his feet and looked up at me. "I was afraid that was the answer, but I had to be certain. I've been trying to come up with something new, but ... maybe my luck will change." Keeble shoved his hands in his pockets and slouched out the door, as despondent as any client I'd ever had.

A few days later, my nose caught a whiff of enticing baked

goods and I followed it down the block. At the corner was a bakery with a large sign reading "Newest Taste Treat—Whortleberry Tarts."

My foot was on the step when I realized that the fragrance enticing me came from further down the street. In the middle of the block was another bakery, smaller and less obvious than the corner shops. Whortleberry aroma almost visibly flowed out the open door.

I strode to a tiny two-story brick building with a single display window at street level, and two curtained windows on the second floor. As I stepped in, I recognized my almost-client standing forlornly behind a display case filled with rosy tarts.

"Mr. Glyph," he greeted me. "Welcome! You are my first customer today."

"First customer? It's almost noon."

He shook his head. "Everyone smells my tarts, but they stop at the corner bakeries and never buy from me. You were right. I need a new pastry, and when I get one, I need to protect it. May I offer you a tart to cast a spell of secrecy on my new creation?"

The tarts smelled delightful, though they were worth considerably less than my usual fee. Still, I felt sorry for the young elf trying so hard to survive in the fast-rising bakery business.

I agreed to his offer, and Keeble beamed.

"Thank you so much. I know your services are worth more than a simple tart, excellent though it is, but it's all I can afford until I get more customers." He glanced out the window at the empty sidewalk. "Or any customers at all."

He placed a tart on a napkin and handed it to me. "I've been praying for divine inspiration to develop a new treat, but nothing has happened. Would I be better off bargaining with a demon?"

I don't like dealing with demons. They are tricky and sticklers to the letter of an agreement. The thought of this naive elf negotiating with a demon sent a chill down my back.

I shook my head. "You don't want to summon a demon."

"But all I want is some inspiration. Is that so hard?"

The chill got stronger. "You wouldn't like a demonic inspiration. Believe me, only experienced negotiators can handle those contracts."

"Maybe I could demand a killer recipe."

The chill wrapped its icicle arms around me and squeezed. "Really. You don't want a demon's killer recipe unless you want to go on trial for murder. Only professionals can deal safely with those fiends."

"Okay, you know about these things. I guess I really need an experienced contract negotiator. Have you handled contracts like that?"

The chill bounced up and down a few times and invited some friends to join the fun. Much as I dislike dealing with demons, I'd accepted a tart as a retainer. One tart didn't buy much, but I felt I owed Keeble some advice, even though I'd already given him my best advice: don't do it.

"The most important decision when dealing with demons is to deal with the right one. For instance, you shouldn't summon a succubus to kill someone. That's not their area of expertise." I thought for a moment. "You'd want to summon Illsbury Doboi. He's a fiend for baking. He delights in baking souls until they are crispy."

"Could you summon him for me?"

I shook my head. "I could negotiate for you, but you've got to do the invocation. That's how it works. Let's see, to summon Illsbury you'll need a gold metal flower, the milk of human kindness, and a basket of chicks. The eggs can't be counted before the chickens hatch."

I relaxed. I didn't need to worry about Keeble calling on me to negotiate any demonic contract. Finding a golden flower and a basket of eggs are relatively easy, but the milk of human kindness is scarce.

Two days later, Keeble was back in my office, with a golden medallion clutched in one hand and a cloth-covered basket in the other.

"I've got no idea how many eggs are here. I put some eggs into the basket and the poulterer put in some more. Neither one of us counted. The chicks should hatch in a day or two."

"That's a good start," I told him. "But you need all the ingredients to invoke a demon. Two out of three won't work."

He nodded. "I was stuck on the milk thing, until I realized that you offering to help me for such a small retainer was purely an act of kindness. Would your being there to negotiate for me represent the milk of human kindness?"

He was right. My presence would provide the missing third ingredient. Keeble's desperation and faith in my ability made it impossible to refuse.

"I'll meet you just before midnight in three days—the next dark of the moon." By then the chicks would have hatched.

This gave me time to review *The Devil is in the Details: An Introduction to Demonic Contracts*. Everything with a demon has to be exactly right or it goes up in smoke.

Three days later, I blended powdered sugar of lead into a mix of rancid butter and sour cream. I decorated Keeble's bakery floor with a pentagram outlined with this unholy buttercream frosting.

"When the church bell chimes midnight," I told the elf, "put the chicks and eggs that haven't hatched and the flower into the pentacle. After the offerings are in place, say 'Illsbury Doboi, I conjure, constrain, and command you'. Be certain you say exactly those words, and be careful to not step on the lines. I'll handle the rest."

He nodded. A few minutes later, the church bell pealed the midnight hour. On the third chime, he placed the flower in the pentacle. On the sixth, he placed the eggs. On the ninth, he thanked me for my kindness, and on the twelfth chime he spoke the words of summoning.

The demon popped up through the floor in the center of the pentacle with an audible poof. Illsbury was white and pasty, almost shapeless, but hinting at a pudgy human form.

"What's cookin'?" he asked.

I stepped forward. "Keeble the elf summoned you. I speak for him."

Illsbury faced me. "Start talking. I've got one in the oven and my timer is running." He glanced at the icing on the floor. "We won't need to dicker, I'm on a roll, and declare that what I say within this pentacle is the best bargain I can offer."

"Mr. Keeble demands a prize-winning recipe he can bake."

The demon expanded as he rose. "A prize-winning recipe? For such a treasure I shall require the first b—"

"No first born! The cost must be commensurate with the merchandise."

"It's not polite to interrupt."

Demons are particular about details, and proper behavior. Simple politeness is proper behavior. I wasn't sure if I felt embarrassed because I was being chastised by a spawn of Satan, or because I deserved it.

I apologized and the fiend continued, "As I was saying, first baked sample—"

This time Keeble interrupted. "Of course, you can have the first sample. I accept your offer."

I was no longer embarrassed. I was terrified. The elf had just agreed to terms we hadn't heard.

The demon cleared his throat. "And, as I was saying, *if* I may finish a sentence. I shall judge the sample, and if it is not satisfactory, I shall cook up a curse to spice up your lives." He giggled maniacally. "Your cakes will fall, your crusts will crumble, and your patrons will flee to other vendors." Illsbury turned a shiny black eye in my direction. "And, for doing such a poor job of schooling your clients in proper behavior, you shall share the curse. That way I won't be bothered with more of your half-baked interruptions."

Given how much he could have added to the bargain, the threat of a curse was minimal. I had faith that my elf could create a treat to satisfy the most discriminating palate. I had less faith in a demon's discrimination.

Illsbury waved his stubby fingers and produced a coal-black sheet of paper. "This is my mother's Home Baked Devil's Food Pound Cake recipe. It won the grand prize in the first season of Demonic Bake-Off on the DeathTime network. She's gone into Human Resources and doesn't bake anymore, so you may as well use it.'

Somehow, it didn't surprise me that demons worked in HR. I wondered briefly how they interpreted Human Resources and decided I was happier not knowing.

The pasty demon grinned gleefully. "I'll be back tomorrow at midnight to taste your sample." Illsbury snapped its fingers and popped through the center of the pentacle, leaving the paper floating in the air.

Keeble grabbed it, read quickly, then started quivering.

"What is it?" I asked, peering over his shoulder.

"The recipe. Do I have to do this? It will destroy me!"

I glanced at the paper. It was a demonic pound cake: one pound of mashed marble, one pound of pulverized pumice, and one pound of grated granite. None of these would be difficult to obtain at a building supply.

The next lines explained Keeble's dismay. One pound of rotten eggs, one pound of chicken feathers, and one pound of sheep entrails.

"If I make this, the stench will be in my shop forever! Nobody will buy pastries when the shop smells of rotten eggs and sheep guts!" He stared at the paper. "Can I make the cake elsewhere, and bring it here?"

I pointed at the title. "You live upstairs, right?"

Keeble nodded.

"This is your home. The recipe defines itself as *Home Baked* so cooking it elsewhere violates the instructions."

He gazed at the paper. "Bake at seven hundred degrees for twelve hours. I'll have to find everything before noon to preheat the oven."

Keeble hadn't paid me to be his assistant, but I'd share the curse if he failed. That threat obligated me to do whatever I could.

"First thing tomorrow, I'll visit the quarries and gather the rocks. You go to the farms where you buy eggs and see if they have any rotten ones or a sheep they're ready to slaughter. We'll meet back here at eleven for you to mix and bake."

He consented to the plan without looking at me. This is why I hate dealing with demons. Illsbury had provided a prize-winning recipe, and baking it would destroy the elf's business. It had adhered to the letter of our agreement while reversing the sentiment.

By ten thirty the next morning, I'd acquired three pounds of the appropriate stones.

Keeble returned a few minutes later with a box of smelly eggs, a box of equally fowl smelling feathers, and a bucket of entrails.

He was pale as raw dough, staring at me with tears running down his face. "Do I truly have to do this?"

I shrugged. He was damned if he did and damned if he didn't —a standard demonic contract. I was only damned if he failed.

"You have to do it," I assured him. "Perhaps you'll be able to open a new bakery in another city. Once you bury your clothes."

He turned the paper over. "The cake is to be iced with a slurry of lampblack, saltpeter, and sulfur, mixed in a drunkard's urine."

"I'll get those items," I assured him. "You start baking."

It cost me two bottles of rotgut and several hours to collect the urine. By the time I got back to Keeble's bakery, the stench made my eyes water before I opened the door.

By the time I reached his oven, my nose was numb.

Keeble had a clothespin on his nose.

"Did you ged whad I need?" he asked.

I offered him vials of saltpeter, lampblack, sulfur, and a flask of deep yellow urine.

"Good, da sooner dis is ober da bedder.'

I couldn't agree with him more.

At 11:55 P.M., Keeble took a glowing red brick from the oven and coated it with the sulfuric slurry. At midnight, the pentacle I'd inscribed pulsed, and once more Illsbury erupted with an audible pop.

He grinned evilly. "Let's see how an elf handles demonic baking. I've greased my curses, just for you."

Keeble bristled at this. "An elf can bake anything a demon can conceive of—and bake it better!"

"I'll be the judge of that." Illsbury inhaled the putrid air. "Such a stench! It smells worse than my mom's kitchen. You acquired very foul chicken feathers."

Keeble lifted the Devil's Food Pound Cake with a pair of tongs, and carved off a slice with a hatchet. I raised an eyebrow as he wrapped the slice in a sheet of asbestos cloth and crimped the edges.

"Proper presentation is how you tell a master from a poseur," he informed me.

He placed the steaming slice of pound cake on a brickbat and passed it to the demon.

Illsbury accepted the cake and held it under his nose. "Smells rancid. Nice touch," he admitted. He rotated it and tapped the exposed portion. He burned his finger and stuck it in his mouth. "Ouch. That's the proper temperature. You may not get cursed after all." He grinned. "Just kidding. The proof is in the putting

—putting it into my mouth. If this isn't as good as mother used to make, it will be curse city for you two." He poked his belly and giggled. "After all, that's the way the cookie crumbles."

Illsbury popped the cake into his mouth, asbestos and all.

His cheeks bulged and glowed dull red. Steam hissed from his ears, his fingers trembled, and his belly convulsed. He bent forward, hands on his knees and gasped. He pounded his thighs, then slowly straightened, massaging his belly with both hands.

Keeble's hands shook. He had faith in his baking, but who knows what a demon likes? I sweated as well, worried that the fiend's review of Keeble's cake would fall against us.

"By all damnation. That's a hell of a devil's food cake. Better than Mom used to brew. It's worth its weight in gold. Can I have another slice?"

Keeble reached for the cake. "Cer—"

I shoved my hand over his mouth.

"Certainly not," I told Illsbury. "You bargained for one piece. Now that you've approved Keeble's baking, you're a customer, not a conjured entity. You've got to pay for your slice of cake."

Illsbury glared at me. "A bargain is a bargain. How much will a piece of cake cost?"

I glanced at the price sheet hanging on the wall. The famous whortleberry tarts were only twenty-five cents.

"You already set the price," I told Illsbury. "You said the cake was worth its weight in gold. Furthermore, you declared that what you said within the pentacle was the best bargain you would offer."

Illsbury's eyes popped from his face. "I never!"

I pulled my talking skull from my pocket and tapped it. Illsbury's voice emerged from the clacking teeth: "I declare that what I say within the pentacle is the best bargain I can offer."

The demon shrugged. "Can't blame a fiend for trying. Gold is useless except for buying what you want." He produced a bar the size of my hand. "A pound of gold for the pound cake. I'll take all of it. Demons will drool fire for a taste of Mother's Devil's Food. It's been centuries since she baked one." He glanced over our heads. "Can I have another tomorrow? Same price—a pound of gold for a pound of cake. How many can you have ready?"

I released Keeble's mouth. It was time for him to speak for himself.

"I … I can bake three without triggering the fire alarms." He stroked his chin. "Will that be a standing order? I can't devote my ovens to your cakes unless I know there's a market for them."

"Standing order," Illsbury assured him. "Three cakes a day will be devilish. All demonkind will be beating a path to your pentacle. Can you inscribe 'Happy Curseday' on one tomorrow?"

Keeble nodded, and the demon (and the cake) vanished with a pop and a giggle.

"You'll never need to worry about whortleberry tarts again," I assured Keeble. "Gold has little value to fiends, but they do enjoy eating."

Keeble yanked the clothespin off his nose. "I guess I'll have to get used to this stench." He hefted the small gold brick. "I don't think I need to worry about the other bakeries copying this recipe." He grinned. "Just being on the same block as me might drive them out of business."

It was a relief to not be cursed, but Keeble's case had been a lot of effort for a single whortleberry tart.

The elf handed me the gold brick. "You take this. You earned it." He smiled. "After all, I'll get three more tomorrow."

It might pay to study Tart Law.

CLIF FLYNT WRITES serious technical books and computer software (including Editomat), while C. Flynt writes mostly humorous fiction. This Jeckyl-Hyde persona resides two miles from the nearest paved road with a dog and two cats. The dog is happy to discuss story ideas, as long as the discussion includes a walk, while the cats participate in typing the manuADSR#@ripts.

RIGHT TO REMAIN SILENT

Jody Lynn Nye

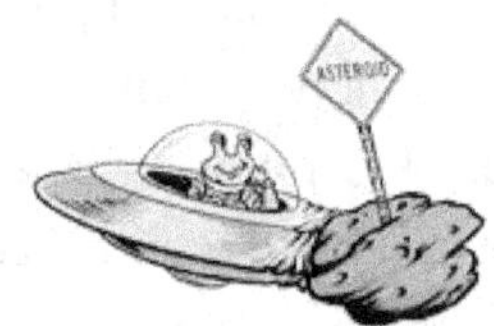

The handsome young Asian-American stared morosely into the steaming cup of tea on the table. The squat, shiny blue tearoom waitbot trundled silently away, having delivered oolong to him, herbal tea to Detective Sergeant Dena Malone, and a tiny cup of fragrant coffee to her partner, Detective Sergeant Ramos. The aroma was strong enough to put everyone in the restaurant into a day-long caffeine high. Dena inhaled deeply and sighed. Sometimes pregnancy was a pain. Only a few months until she could have coffee again. In the meantime, she'd have to enjoy it vicariously. Tossing back her razor-cut brown hair, she put her skinnypad on the table and set it to record.

"Official recording begins at 11:05 AM. Qin Chang, what was the last thing you remember before the mugging?" Dena asked. She and Ramos were already feeling resentment. Why should they have to cover a case of ordinary assault? They were *homicide* detectives. But their commander, Captain Potopos, had insisted that Dena had been specifically requested to cover the case. So far, it still sounded like nothing to do with them. "Did you see anyone coming up close to you?"

The young man shook his head, making a lock of blue-dyed hair fall into his wide brown eyes. He wore shimmering, neon-blue trousers and a white silk poet shirt open at the neckline. He had on a pair of bright orange kicks that should have looked out of place with the rest of his getup, but actually fit in well.

"I was only walking along the street," he said. "I am ashamed to say I failed at situational awareness. I am better trained than that, especially considering the neighborhood."

"What *were* you doing there?" Ramos asked, bringing up the street map on his pad. "It's not the greatest area, and it isn't close to either your apartment or your office."

Chang's golden cheeks flooded with red. "Nothing," he said.

Dena and Ramos exchanged glances. "Do you have a *friend* here?" she asked, with careful emphasis.

"No!"

"Why did you not summon a hovertaxi?" K't'ank asked, his voice coming from the heavy platinum bangle on her wrist. Dr. K't'ank, the skinny, meter-long Salosian that lived in Dena's peritoneum among her intestines, a situation that began with witness protection in a murder investigation and had gone on to him becoming something like a live-in adviser and critic. He never bothered to contain his advice just to Dena, however.

"I … did not want to attract attention," Chang said, then clamped his lips shut. Time to try another tack.

"But you wear garments and carry accessories that mark you as prosperous," K't'ank said. "To avoid victimization, common sense suggests that …"

"K't'ank, you're not helping!" Dena referred to the case file. "Mr. Chang, Captain Potopos said you reported getting knocked out by a stun charge. Did someone jab a stun-bar into you, or was it from a pistol?"

"I don't know," Chang said miserably, lifting his hands and letting them fall on the table. Dena couldn't help but notice that they were long and slender, with almond-shaped nails. Was there anything about this fellow that wasn't downright attractive? "On my way back to the transport station, many floating billboards and advertising drones intercepted me. I ignore them; I always do. I passed by a square accessway, I recall that. Smelly dumpsters, perhaps a rat, then a pain at the back of my neck. I awoke on the moving sidewalks five levels higher up, my head throbbing. A woman helped me to my feet. She offered to call the authorities, but I said I would do it. But my skinnypad was missing!"

"Were you looking at it when you left ... wherever you were?" Ramos asked.

"No. I am sure of that. I would not let it be seen. I always seal it in an inner pocket." Chang looked from one officer to the other. "Can you get it back for me?"

Dena shook her head. "We'll do what we can, but you know the device has probably been stripped and reprogrammed already."

"But what if it hasn't? It contains ...!" He stopped himself.

"Didn't you brick it?" Ramos asked.

"There was no time," Chang said, his face drawn. "I was conveyed to the hospital, and I called for assistance. I did it as soon as I was able. I am worried that it may have been downloaded while I was unconscious. The contents are ... most awkward."

"Could anyone have seen you put your pad away?" Ramos asked. "Where were you before you got mugged?"

Chang just looked at them with huge eyes. Dena took pity on him.

"Excuse me a minute," she said, with emphasis. "I need to ..." She gave Ramos a meaningful look.

"Right," Ramos said, waving a hand over the skinnypad. "Recording suspended at 11:36 AM." Chang stood up to make way for Dena's ornate hoverchair, a conveyance that was a nod to her status as a Salosian host. She waved him to sit down.

"It's okay," she said. "It's just a useful way of letting you talk off the record."

"Besides," K't'ank said. "Her bladder is not full yet."

"Shut up, K't'ank," she said, as Ramos snickered. She turned to Chang. "What don't you want on the recording? What was on your phone? Trade secrets? Account numbers?"

Chang looked abashed. "Love letters." He looked down at his interlaced fingers.

Dena felt her eyes grow to the size of saucers as she put the pieces together. "Love letters? From who?"

"Consul Haihatsu," Chang admitted.

Dena exchanged glances with Ramos. *That* explained their presence. The interplanetary negotiator was definitely a big enough wig to have pulled strings to assign police officers that would handle the matter with discretion. He also had a Salosian living inside him, Ambassador P'n'ira, who had become a friend—well, acquaintance—of K't'ank's. The consul and Dena shared a few other things, including an ongoing distaste for the personnel from Alien Relations, a notoriously stiff-necked bureaucracy. "From Consul Haihatsu? And from him to you?"

Chang nodded without looking up.

"What's the problem?" Ramos asked. "Why can't you be in love with him? He seems like a good guy."

"I'm a negotiator for a number of major corporations," Chang confessed, his narrow face miserable. "It could be seen as a breach of protocol to have formed a relationship with a senior representative from the Office of Interplanetary Affairs. But we care for each other! He is my saint and savior! His touch is like all the angels in Heaven coming to caress me."

Dena felt embarrassed, as though she had found those love letters and was reading them. Ramos caught the expression on her face.

"Hey, maybe you can tell me, since she won't," he said,

aiming a thumb at Dena. "What's it like making love to someone with a symbiote?"

"Most of the time Ambassador P'n'ira ignores our … joinings," Chang said. "She engages herself with the computer implanted into the back of her head, viewing entertainment or communicating with others. But sometimes she becomes very vocal in her pleasure at our body movements. It can get a little noisy."

"It is not noisy!" Dena protested, and realized she'd been had. Ramos let out a raunchy chuckle. She'd get even with him later on. K't'ank had a similar computer implant, and she wished he would ignore her personal life more often. "Mr. Chang, that was an unofficial question. You don't have to answer anything personal like that."

Ramos sat back with his hands behind his head, smirking. Chang looked from one police officer to another with confusion.

"But why you, and why there?" Ramos asked. "Why were you in that neighborhood?"

"Some other form of pleasure in a small and private place, perhaps?" K't'ank asked. "The vast corporations offer amusements in large and open venues. I believe the public display is to cause guilt for the users who might otherwise examine the quality of the amusements with greater care. Herd mentality is prevalent among humans. It's one of your main failings."

"Moo," Dena said, not wanting to give K't'ank a platform for another one of his lectures. "So, some entertainment of a higher quality off the beaten path? Something simple and, er, non-corporate?"

"Silent disco," Chang finally admitted.

"Say what?" asked Ramos. It was Dena's turn to grin. She knew he expected some more adult amusement, like a drug den or a swinger's lounge.

"It is a place to dance to your own tunes. You go there, they provide you with a headset, and you dance with others," the young man explained, showing enthusiasm for the first time. "The music is as loud or soft as you desire, and it does not disturb the neighbors. I can bust moves or step gently, as my mood drives me. It is most pleasurable and harms no one."

"Yeah, I know what they are," Ramos said, his dark brows drawn down. "No wonder you didn't want to say. Does the consul know what kind of lowlife he's hooking up with?"

"What's wrong with silent discos?" Dena asked.

"What rock have you been living under?" Ramos asked. "Don't you remember the epidemic of people indoctrinated in silent discos? Dancing out in the street, wandering into traffic and falling off hundred-story buildings? Victims don't even know where they are any more. When you pull their earbuds out, they snap out of a trance. *It bends your brain.*"

"That was never proven," Dena said, noticing the distress on Chang's face.

"Silent discos got banned from every multiplex and strip mall on the East Coast." Ramos crossed his arms. "People lost their minds. They call them tuneheads. They lost their jobs, families! They devoted their whole lives to dancing. Nothing else mattered to them! It's an addiction."

Dena tilted her head. "You used to do it, didn't you?"

Ramos looked indignant. "Yeah. But I quit!"

"Humans release control over themselves with great abandon," K't'ank said. "Your dancing imitates more intimate contact. I can confirm from close observation of Malone and her mate. It's not a survival trait as it interferes with awareness of one's surroundings."

"I'm not an addict," Chang said, defensively. "I can quit any time I want to."

"Yeah, *sure* you can!" Ramos snorted. "I bet you dance to advertising jingles. Or hold music."

"No, I don't!"

"Okay, we're not here to talk about people's personal habits.

Take it easy on the kid, both of you!" Dena said, patting the air between them. "It just explains why he was in a seedy neighborhood. Could you have been followed there by anyone from your office? Are you working on something that corporate spies would pay money to learn?"

"No," Chang said. "It's frowned upon to discuss one's personal life. The financial fate of billions rests upon our discretion. As for the other, all the time. That is why my skinnypad has numerous security codes and devices upon it. But those are not foolproof."

"No kidding," Ramos said. "Okay, Mr. Chang. We'll get back to you when we know anything."

Before he went back to his office, Chang pleaded with them to keep all his confidences private. Dena assured him that they would.

"The official record ended with my bathroom break," she told him. "We'll take it from here."

"Take it where?" Ramos asked, as he followed her floatchair from the tearoom. "His pad is gone, maybe off planet by now along with half a million more."

Dena shook her head. "I doubt they jumped him for nothing. All we can do is download the surveillance footage and see whether we can pick up some faces for him to identify. If someone wanted to discredit Haihatsu, picking on his lover would be very effective. Or maybe someone who wanted to embarrass the ambassador?"

"We Salosians are not worried about human interactions," K't'ank said. "Your embarrassment is not important to our government. It is only amusing in our popular press."

"I figured that out a long time ago," Dena said, dryly. "We won't know more about *why* until we find out who lifted that skinnypad."

At the precinct, they called up the security cameras for the general area from the central database. On the multiscreens in the evidence room, she and Ramos watched endless footage of people coming and going from the nondescript doorway to the silent disco. Some of them danced down the steps, cha-cha-ing or boogying to music only they could hear.

"I never knew that was there," Ramos said. "Not that I'd ever go back."

"Um-hm," Dena murmured, without looking away from the screen where a woman pedestrian was batting away advertising drones with her hand. The damned things were getting to be a real pain. Dena had had to have an ad-blocker installed on her skinnypad to keep them from surrounding her like a cloud of mosquitoes when she went out.

"Wait a minute! I think I see him." Ramos sent the content of his monitor to her. Dena leaned close to watch. A slim man in white and blue exited the doorway. Before he had gone down the two steps to the pavement, a horde of the flyers homed in on him. He waved at them absently, but they fought to get right in his face. He staggered absentmindedly in the direction of the transport station, trying to clear his view. When he passed the alleyway, a figure dressed all in black jumped out and struck the man with a hand-sized box that shot off red sparks. The walker fell to the ground, twitching. The assailant frisked him until he found the skinnypad in the man's cargo pocket, then fled, leaving the man on the ground. Dena peered at the thief, but he had anti-identification buttons all over his face mask. "Perfect!" Ramos crowed. "We got him!"

"Not quite," Dena said, as the victim rolled over, his moans of pain audible on the security camera microphone. His shock of bright carmine hair became visible. "That's not Chang!"

"It isn't?" Ramos scrolled through the video until he could see the time signature. "Damn, it's not! What's this guy doing in *our* crime scene?"

"I'm sure it wasn't his idea," Dena said. "But it looks like we have a perp with a regular *modus operandi*. However, that disco doesn't have that many people coming and going. The mugger wouldn't have been hanging out in the alley for hours hoping for someone to walk by."

Ramos raised an eyebrow. "Dumb luck?"

"The odds are unlikely," K't'ank said. "Coincidence is often cited when the connecting factors are not previously observed. And it is a bad investment of time not to be in the right place at an appointed hour. You humans are too impatient!"

"He's right," Dena said. "But do we have a pattern?"

Unlike a stakeout, the nice thing about running through security footage was that they didn't have to sit for hours waiting for more data. Ramos scrolled back and forth through the dozens of cameras near the nondescript doorway, watching for hits. To their satisfaction, they saw numerous attacks, all executed in the same way, and only on people emerging from the silent disco, not on other passersby. The victims either lay where they fell, or were hauled off the pavement by the attacker.

"We've got a pattern," Ramos said, gleefully. "Can you get any identification codes from our perp?"

Dena shook her head. "He's blocking telemetry and facial recognition. The good news is that Mr. Chang wasn't being targeted specifically. He was just in the wrong place at the wrong time. I'll be glad to let him and Consul Haihatsu know."

"I will notify Ambassador P'n'ira," K't'ank offered. "I would appreciate an opportunity to make contact with her. She is securing funding for some research to be done by me and my colleagues on this planet, and a message will serve as a reminder of my existence."

"How could anyone possibly forget about you?" Dena asked. "Go right ahead."

She could hear K't'ank murmuring to himself as he made the connection to the official.

Ramos tapped his upper lip with his skinnypad. "This means there's something going on in that disco."

"We'll have to ask Electronic Crimes if they've got an investigation going," Dena said. "And you know how much they love to share."

In fact, Lt. Petrov of EC did look peeved that a couple of lowly homicide detectives had stumbled onto something that could belong to his department.

"You two need to stay in your lane," he snarled, his thick dark eyebrows making him look even more like a cartoon villain than he usually did. "Theft of electronic devices is our purview."

"We can't help it that we noticed a pattern developing in the execution of our duties," Ramos said, looking innocent.

"Since when is mugging your department? Or is homicide branching out to killing raid bosses?"

"You're just sore that I took down your clan in the station Ultimate Battle III tournament!" The game was popular with many of the department's personnel.

"Just dumb luck when you detonated that giant clam at the guard point!" Petrov countered, leaning forward.

Ramos loomed up out of his chair, going nose to nose with the other officer. "By 'dumb luck,' do you mean superior strategy?"

Dena held up a hand.

"In case you're both forgetting," she said, "I dusted both of you in that tournament and won third place in the system-wide championship. Can we get back to the point?"

With a look at each other that said the argument wasn't over, the two men turned to her.

"This seems to be more than simple assault and robbery," she said. "This disco is on a mostly empty street in a quiet neighborhood. What does that suggest to you?"

"Stolen property," Ramos said. "From what Chang said, no one touches you when you're there, so it has to be some kind of data transmission into the skinnypads. When the victim emerges, the pad gets lifted and taken to be cleaned out. I don't know why the data can't get passed along more directly, but it's pretty neat, if you ask me. It seems like a straightforward assault, but it's bigger than that. Maybe grand larceny, depending on whose data is getting passed."

"Still not homicide. We'll take over this case," Petrov said, briskly. "You can let your captain know EC is stepping in."

"Oh, come on," Ramos wheedled. "These people *could* have gotten killed!"

"It was assigned to us," Dena said, feeling desperation in her belly. Haihatsu's boyfriend would get embarrassed if anyone but her or Ramos picked up Chang's device. She needed to confirm privately that none of the sensitive data or the love letters on it had been downloaded. The fewer eyes on that info, the better. "We've got, uh, a connection. A high connection. We need to shield that connection. We're just trying to obtain one *little piece* of evidence for our own case, a certain skinnypad. If you cooperate," she added, raising her eyebrows meaningfully, "you might make friends with *our* friend. And maybe one other influential contact." If Consul Haihatsu was pleased, Ambassador P'n'ira might also grant a favor to the officer, or at least an acknowledgement of his existence.

She knew Petrov was very bad at making friends or significant contacts. Despite the importance of his department, his abrasive nature kept him from building up an address book of notables he could call on in a sticky situation. She and Ramos had an enviable list, and Petrov knew it. She sat back in her elaborate chair, projecting confidence that she didn't really feel. But very, very reluctantly, Petrov nodded.

"All right, but I take the perp to the prosecutor once we're done."

"Oh, I don't know ..." Dena said, tilting her head from side to side. Petrov's eyes widened in alarm.

"Throw the guy a bone, Malone," Ramos said, looping one of his legs over the arm of his chair.

"Yeah, all right. I hate doing paperwork." Petrov looked inordinately pleased. Dena tried not to smirk. He was too easy. "So, how do we approach this? Someone inside is obviously calling the thief to be on the lookout for certain people leaving."

"Bait," K't'ank said. "I believe that we must give the thief a device with which to abscond."

Petrov looked around for a moment, then realized where the third voice was coming from.

"Right," he said, addressing Dena's platinum wrist bangle. "That's the best approach. One of my officers will go in, then come out with a pad in full view. According to your research, the attacks usually come between two and six in the afternoon."

"Why do you think it's then?" Ramos asked.

Petrov lowered those eyebrows. "When we know who, we can find out why," he said, his voice bubbling with condescension. "Considering the … connections … in this case, I should be the one to go inside."

"No way!" Ramos said. "You dance like an arthritic turtle."

"You think you and your dancefloor pyrotechnics are going to impress anyone?" Petrov asked, scornfully. "The way you leap about, how can you be observing anything?"

"So, you've been watching me that closely?" Ramos fluttered his eyelashes.

It was Petrov's turn to smirk. "Sounds like you've been watching *me*."

Dena grinned to herself. In a different reality, Petrov and Ramos would probably be dating, but the rivalry was too strong in this one.

"I'll go in," she said, cutting off the argument. "I'm easy to spot, and anyone unfamiliar with Salosian hosts won't know how well protected I am."

That part the two men couldn't dispute. The floatchair was equipped with hidden armaments intended to protect K't'ank more than her. It amounted to an urban armored assault vehicle when necessary.

"Not a chance," Ramos said. "You're not going to look like you belong there." He swallowed, and straightened his spine. "I'd better do it."

Dena was alarmed. "Are you sure, Ramos? You could, you know, suffer a setback?"

Petrov glared at him. "You're not one of those tuneheads, are you?"

Ramos glared back. "Are you trying to say I can't handle an assignment?"

"As long as you flaunt the handheld when you leave," Petrov said with a shrug, still attempting to take charge. "A decoy, of course, not your police unit. I … hope your connections will take into account the *cooperation* between our two departments."

Dena smiled. A little name-dropping wouldn't hurt at all. "K't'ank, you can tell Ambassador P'n'ira how grateful we are for the assistance being rendered by the lieutenant."

"I am communicating with her now," K't'ank said, happily. "It is good to have an additional reason to make contact. She has been too busy to respond recently. I am happy to remind her of my presence. If he is of some use to us, P'n'ira will find reason to thank both of us."

Petrov looked skeptical. Before he could withdraw his agreement, Dena hastened to make excuses.

"She's a very busy person, the ambassador," Dena explained. "P'n'ira is Salos's representative here on Earth. No higher Salosian on the planet. She and K't'ank are colleagues. I mean, they don't have to communicate every day. Just when they have something important to say. To each other."

Her excuse sounded as lame as a centipede with fifty sprained ankles, but Petrov's expression lightened to merely dour.

"All right, get out of here," he said, waving a hand. "We'll meet here tomorrow at 1300 hours to get you wired for sound and video."

Dena turned her chair and spurred it out into the corridor. Ramos followed at a trot.

"I can't believe we got away with that," he said, as soon as the door behind them sealed shut. "There's no way that we should have been able to keep an EC case, no matter what Potopos said."

"I've only got one more problem," Dena said, looking up at him in despair.

"What's that?"

"What am I going to wear to this disco?"

KEEPING HER CHIN DEFIANTLY HIGH, Dena glared into Ramos's astonished eyes when she met him the next day at the police van parked half a block from the disco.

"I didn't think you had it in you. Or in your closet," he said, leering at the filmy but fitted blue dress she had on. The crushing bodice gave her exaggerated cleavage, and the skirt skimmed over her belly down to her ankles.

"I borrowed it from the Sex Crimes division," she said. "It's one of their bait dresses. I have to attract attention so whoever is inside remembers me."

"Like they're going to forget a pregnant woman in a blinged-out floatchair?" Ramos countered. "Nothing exceeds like excess. Look at the restraint I'm showing." He plucked at the front of a coral-colored poet's shirt that bloused over tight black trousers.

"I've also got on a shockproof bodysuit," Dena said, wriggling against the discomfort. "Why do they have to make skintight clothes itchy?"

"I dunno," Ramos said, scratching his midsection. "I've got one on, too."

"It constricts her abdomen fiercely," K't'ank said. "I have little room to move. I have research to do, and I like to move while thinking." He hammered her ribs from the inside with his tail.

"Stop that," Dena said, clutching her midsection. "You'll wake the baby. I don't like it any more than you do."

Dena steered her chair from the van toward the modest entrance of the disco. Chang had described the interior, how to check in, the staff members he had interacted with, where the equipment was distributed, and how much it cost. For an empty room full of dancers, the high price surprised her.

"Stop wiggling!" she murmured to K't'ank. He thrashed from one side of her insides to the other. The movement woke up her baby, who also started kicking, shoving one tiny foot up to where its outline was visible through not only the bodysuit, but her blue silk taffeta. "What's with you?"

"She has responded!" K't'ank said, with a jubilant trill. "Ambassador P'n'ira read over my papers, and she said she was impressed. Of course, my scholarship speaks for itself, but it is good to have impressed a Salosian as important as she. She had questions about section eight of the fifth paper. I thought that one might be slightly opaque to someone who is not as closely versed in the jargon of the academic world ..."

"Did she say anything about Consul Haihatsu?" Dena interrupted him.

"Why would she?" K't'ank asked. "He is of no importance to the studies I am making."

"Aaargh!" Dena groaned, throwing her head back. "Never mind. Don't tell me. I have to keep my mind clear."

She glided smoothly up the shallow steps to the carved, russet-colored double doors that looked like antique wood. Ramos held the door open for her. This club must be doing pretty well, to be able to use such precious material on its outside surface. The portal opened silently—no surprise there—

and Dena moved into a gracious anteroom with a soaring ceiling decorated at its peak by a huge crystal chandelier. She would never have suspected such an elegant place in such a rundown neighborhood.

They listened, but all they could hear was shuffling and tapping of feet. Beside her, Ramos began to twitch.

"Are you going to be all right?" she asked.

"I'm fine," Ramos said. "Just got to get into the mood."

Footsteps detached themselves from the noise and moved toward her. A sleek, slender dark-skinned person in a crystal-trimmed dark green body suit undulated toward her. Lush, crimson lips parted to reveal large, square white teeth in a heart-shaped face too pretty to be real. The large black eyes perused her thoroughly.

"Are you here to get down?" they asked. "I'm Lyon, your maître'd."

"Uh, yes," Dena said. "We're new here, but we heard it's a lot of fun."

"Of course. Let me fit you out with sets, and you can boogie yourself away." Lyon turned and slunk in the direction of a priceless inlaid table where several jeweled headbands lay. The maître'd turned one over at a time, and chose a sapphire-blue tiara with chandelier earrings hanging from the large, round earphones. Dena held still while Lyon set it on her head and adjusted the band. Lyon picked out a pointed crown with sparkling rainbow jewels and fitted it into Ramos's black curly hair. He preened at his reflection in the mirror above the table. Dena had to admit he looked pretty good in it.

"Can you hear me?" Lyon asked. The voice carried through the devices. The two officers nodded. "Now, there's the slightly uncomfortable matter of payment?"

Dena presented her decoy skinnypad, which had on its lockscreen pictures of a man, not her husband; a dog, not her pet; and a floating, tiled-roof house, megakilometers away from the modest apartment she and Neal occupied in both price and locale. Lyon gave the images an approving glance, and ran a bracelet scanner over the screen. The charge for two tickets popped up. Dena contained her gasp. Chang's salary must surpass hers by a factor of ten, at least, if this was his regular hangout.

"Go right in," Lyon instructed her, pointing to a wrought iron doorway. Lights flashed through the twisted standards. "The music menu is on your pads. If you want something different, signal the DJ. She's got millions of playlists for you to choose from. You can stay twenty-four hours. In and out privileges included. There's a bar in the next room, and three restaurants, all in your admission fee. Knock yourself out, my lovelies."

"Thanks," Dena said, feeling a little stunned. "Are you all right?"

"Come on," Ramos said, throwing his shoulders back. "I can handle it."

Dena glided into the dance hall, Ramos strutting at her side.

The hall, too, had a lofty ceiling, filled with light fixtures each flashing out its own rhythm. Chairs and divans lined the glowing walls. Floor-to-ceiling screens displayed dance videos, from modern all the way back to black-and-white images from the Dark Ages of technology.

On the gorgeous parquet floor, about twenty dancers moved among holograms depicting castle scenes, gardens, weird caves, even waves that crashed ten meters high. The participants were all well-dressed, of every shape and size, and each moved to their own beat, dancing through illusory sea monsters, dragons, flocks of birds, and a herd of multicolored alpacas. A burly man with wild blond hair tangoed with a girl who looked about thirteen. She bopped and slid in his grasp, her feet hitting the floor five times for every step he made. Two women held onto each other, one waltzing and the other jitterbugging. Most of the others whirled and sashayed by themselves. Nobody except the couples touched one another. Nobody went near anyone else's skinnypads. The room was bizarrely silent, despite all the activity and the light show.

Ramos began nodding his head to music only he could hear, then started leaping around like the alpacas. They paused in place for a moment until their algorithm caught on to his rhythm, and bounded along with him. He grinned at Dena, beckoning her to join him.

She ran a finger down the slim device's screen and skimmed the menu of music types until she came to easy-listening music from her teen years. That ought to be manageable in her current condition.

The first song that played when she touched the control had been really popular during her middle-school term, but she hated it. Annoyed, she slapped the skinnypad. The next one had also occupied the top fifty list, but she associated it with a boyfriend with whom she had had a catastrophic breakup. She did not need a drive down memory lane riddled with potholes from her adolescence. She set the whole thing on random play, and was rewarded with a big band number replete with horns, and tried to dance to it. A good thing no one was paying much attention to her. She threw her arms in the air and made the floatchair spin in time with the disco balls glittering on the ceiling.

"Whee!" K't'ank cried. "More, Malone! Add vibration! Make it seem as though you are mating! Imitate Ramos. See him? He is simulating an attractiveness ritual with those holograms!"

"Oh, shut up, K't'ank!" she growled.

Beside her, Ramos was bounding around, grinning like a fiend. She tried to get his attention, but he never made eye contact. His motions grew more and more erratic, as if the music was delving deep into his brain. Could the music addiction be reasserting itself, after all these years? If he blew this case, their credibility was going to suck.

Better to concentrate on the reason for the attacks. What was it about the skinnypads that caused some dancers to get mugged less than a kilometer from the door? It had to be something to do with the playlists being transferred to the portable devices. They probably concealed data of some kind, something that wasn't supposed to leave this building, but someone had to have figured out a way to make that happen. She glanced up, looking for the DJ. She was the most reasonable suspect.

Haloed by an arch of blue light in a booth on the near wall, a glorious woman with a holographic blue star on her cheek and ringlets of black hair cascading down over her shoulders met Dena's gaze. Dena held up her skinnypad with a helpless expression.

Pick me! Pick me! she thought.

The DJ nodded, and flicked a finger down her control panel. Dena turned to the screen on her device. Nothing seemed to have changed, but the DJ gave her a significant look and a thumb's up. The transfer had taken place. Dena had her evidence. Now she had to get Ramos out of there.

"No, no!" K't'ank said. She had left the bangle tucked into her bag so he wouldn't disturb the other dancers, but she could still hear him via bone conduction. "Do not send me all your data, P'n'ira! It overloads!"

"Quiet!" Dena murmured. "I'm trying to concentrate!"

"As am I," the scientist said. He battered her intestines, making her feel like she had severe gas. "I have sent P'n'ira revisions of all my research, and now it seems that I must revise all of the documents in her possession! And what is this about chemical plants in Africa?"

"That's what happens when you make important friends," Dena whispered. "They know their friendship is worth something. You pay for it one way or another."

At that moment, she saw Lyon gliding toward her, finger to lips. The host leaned toward Dena.

"Quiet, please! If you need to talk, please go to one of the soundproofed cubicles!"

"I'm sorry," Dena whispered. She handed back the jeweled earphones and guided her chair until it bumped into her partner's thigh. Ramos stopped in mid-gyration, yanked back from wherever it was the music had taken him. She tilted her head meaningfully in the direction of the door. Reluctantly, Ramos polished the gems on his crown and surrendered it to the host. "We'd better go home."

Lyon bowed to her with a flourish of beautifully manicured fingernails. "Come back soon." As Ramos started to pass, the host grabbed him in an iron grip. "Not you, sweetheart. You stay right where you are."

Dena's heart stopped. Had the host made them as police officers?

"What? Why?" Ramos stammered.

"You're an asset to the floor," Lyon said, running a hand up his front. He squirmed. "Too sexy for your shirt, baby."

"Uh, maybe another time," Ramos said.

"Oh, well, c'est la vie." Lyon let him go.

Dena stifled a burst of laughter. Instead, she looked up at the DJ and smiled. The lovely woman gave her another cool nod and went back to her console. They both had what they needed. Now she and Ramos just had to let themselves get mugged, for real this time.

Ramos seemed to have the boogie deep in his soul. He bounded off the steps of the disco, still shimmying, and held out a hand to steady Dena's descent. As they rolled out of the silent disco, Petrov's voice hit them almost as soon as the cloud of advertising bots did.

"Now, stay calm. We've got a male, approximately seventy-five kilos, in the alley. Move slowly past him, and don't hurt him! We want information from him."

"I know, I know," Dena said, without moving her mouth. She and Ramos batted at the annoying little flyers now coming at them from every angle. There had to be fifty or sixty of them, all haranguing them and surrounding them with holograms. The bait pad didn't have her anti-bot software installed, so she had no way of getting rid of the advertising. Images flashed in her eyes again and again. *A new laundry system! Clothes that don't need cleaning! Diet food! Exercise equipment so you don't have to diet! Have you had your eyes checked lately?* That last one poked right into Dena's face. She slapped it to one side.

"Here he comes!" Ramos said, shouldering a herd of ads out of his way, and spinning on his heel. More took their place. His hands flashed like a kung-fu master, knocking each bot away with expert timing. "Hyah!"

"I am not able to process all of this information!" K't'ank snapped.

"Hush!" Dena said, trying to see through the cloud of flyers. As Petrov had said, a slim figure of about seventy-five kilos dressed completely in black with anti-telemetry patches appeared among them. Ramos let out a cry and slumped to the ground. The shock-box! The attacker stood over Ramos, running his hands over the detective's pants legs in search of a device. Dena pushed the chair to move between them. The attacker, not finding his quarry on the fallen officer, came after her, brandishing a palm-sized taser.

Dena didn't even have to react. The floatchair immediately went into operation. Claws emerged from the front uprights, grabbing for the attacker.

The figure in black was as nimble as a gymnast. Somehow, he managed to avoid them. The claws twisted, snapping at his limbs. The adbots zipped in. Whenever the claws tried to snap shut, a bot was in the way. The chair almost snarled in frustration. It raised stun-guns from the rear uprights and prepared to fire. The bots whirled up, taking the brunt of the beams. Dozens fell to the pavement, but there were always dozens more. Dena was impressed. The robber's bosses had prepared for *everything*.

Dena felt the skinnypad snatched out of her fingers. The attacker let out a grunt of triumph and stood up, tucking the prize into the front of the shirt.

"We got 'im! Move in, move in, move in!" Petrov barked. A horde of policebots rose out of the van and arrowed in. The two men jumped out behind them.

Dena sat up. She seized her service stunner from its concealment and pointed it at the attacker.

Even the patchy mask couldn't hide the surprise the attacker felt. He hesitated for a moment.

"Drop it," Dena said, holding out her free hand. "You're under arrest. You have the right. ... Where did he go?"

To her horror, the cloud of advertising flyers swarmed up, more densely than before, forming a curtain between her and her assailant. She urged the chair through them, shielding her eyes. She felt around, but found no solid body. He was gone. Dena moved back to Ramos and helped him sit up.

"That would've been a lot worse without the suit," Ramos said. He felt his ribs. "Ouch."

"Your moves were great," Dena assured him, "but we were outnumbered."

"Where'd he go?" Petrov echoed. The policebots drove back the advertising drones, but the three of them stood alone on the empty pavement. They looked around, up, and down at the other levels, but the figure in black was gone.

"Activate the tracer on the skinnypad," Ramos said. Petrov clawed at his portable device, then shook his head.

"Nothing! He must have a dampener."

"Those shouldn't stop signals from a police pad," Dena said. "We're dealing with something of a much higher level than we thought. There's some massively sophisticated organization behind this operation."

Petrov tried again and again, then shook his head.

"Dammit! We've blown it," he said, shaking his console. "We lost our chance to analyze the data that got put on the pad in the disco. Whoever he works for isn't going to fall for a decoy again. We're back to the beginning." He turned on Dena and Ramos, his heavy brows knitted together. "Why couldn't you keep him here? Did you have too good a time inside? Lose focus?"

"You try it with a bunch of ads flying in your face," she said. "I … ow! K't'ank, stop that." She pulled the bangle out and put it back on her wrist. "You can't keep hitting me like that. It hurts!"

"I am overloaded!" the Salosian wailed, thrashing. "I cannot organize anything. Ambassador P'n'ira has sent me such unrelated gibberish that it overwhelms all of my neat files. Even *my* music won't play!"

She and Ramos shared a look.

"K't'ank, when did P'n'ira send you all that data?" Ramos asked.

"While Malone was dancing," K't'ank replied. "Usually I enjoy her gyrations, but the moment was inconvenient for me. The ambassador presumes greatly upon our acquaintance! I am a scientist! I am not a file clerk. How poorly must her office be organized?"

Dena and Ramos looked at one another again.

"K't'ank, read me the title of one of the files."

"No! The ambassador trusts me with her confidential information," K't'ank argued.

"Are you *sure* that the data came from her?"

"Of course! I have triple firewalls that protect me from unwanted transfers."

"I bet they failed this time. Just one little title, K't'ank,"

Dena said, in her most persuasive voice. "Just one. For me. I'll dance for you when we get home if you give us the information."

K't'ank's voice brightened. "With gyrations and shaking?"

"All the moves," Dena promised. "Just like the ones Ramos was doing in the club. And I'll ditch the bodysuit."

"Excellent! This one is entitled, 'Tanzania Power Plant Output Estimates.'"

Dena turned a triumphant face up to the others. "The thief got away empty-handed. They loaded them into K't'ank's memory instead. When we know what's in these files, we can figure out who."

ONCE K'T'ANK WAS REASSURED the files hadn't come from Ambassador P'n'ira, he couldn't transfer them fast enough to the police database. Dena hated the look of glee on Petrov's face, but she had to admit it was time for Electronic Crimes to step in.

It took EC a remarkably short time to determine the source of the files. The data thieves hadn't covered their tracks very well. A few days later, Petrov strutted into the homicide division and perched on the edge of Ramos's desk.

"Turns out the DJ is the sister of the lead programmer in the African Power Collective," he said. "She's been transferring data packets for months through the disco, and no one noticed until your victim came forward. It was the perfect crime. Would you believe all of this is a result of trying to get even with an awful co-worker?"

Ramos opened wide and innocent eyes. "No! You don't say!"

Petrov ignored him. "They tried to keep their mouths shut, but when I told them how long they'd be in prison, they couldn't wait to give up their buyer. He's a broker in a power-transmission company dealing with a number of shipping companies. Shady as heck. Anyhow, there's a pile of stolen skinnypads sitting in the basement of the guy's mansion in the Poconos," he said. "You want to come and look for the device belonging to your victim? Sounds to me like they weren't interested in anything except the Collective's files." He eyed Dena. "I hope your … connection will be grateful for this?"

"You bet," Dena said, pushing her chair back from her desk. "Both of them are going to be in your debt." Consul Haihatsu would be pretty pleased, both for sparing his lover embarrassment, and for uncovering a situation that almost certainly had been causing him professional headaches.

"Hey!" Ramos said, throwing his hands in the air. "I feel like dancing!" The two of them looked at him. "It's just good spirits, all right? I'm not addicted or anything. You people have no faith in me."

"Just concerned," Dena said. "You put on quite a show in that club."

Ramos preened. "I'm an excellent actor. And dancer."

"Your performance there was impressive," K't'ank said. "It is a wonder you have not attracted more mates."

Dena laughed.

Petrov stopped them, an uncharacteristically hopeful expression on his face.

"One more thing. We've got a press conference later today. Any chance I can count on you to let us take full public credit for the arrest? This is a big success. I'm up for captain next evaluation. I'd owe both of you a big favor."

Dena and Ramos shared a gleeful glance. EC would owe *them* a favor? She raised a hand as if taking an oath. Ramos followed suit.

"We reserve the right to remain silent," she promised Petrov. But she almost felt like busting a dance move right there in the squad room.

JODY LYNN NYE lists her main career activity as "spoiling cats." When not engaged upon this worthy occupation, she writes fantasy and science fiction, most of it with a humorous bent. Since 1987 she has published over 50 books and more than 170 short stories. She has also written with notables in the industry, including Anne McCaffrey and Robert Asprin. Jody teaches writing seminars at SF conventions, and is Coordinating Judge for the Writers of the Future Contest.

AUNTIE ELSIE'S COMPLEAT GUIDE TO HEARTBREAK

Tim Pratt

"The last time someone broke *my* heart, I turned her into lizards."

I turned my head—I swear I could hear my neck creak; when your only exercise for three days is "crying," your body doesn't respond well—and looked at the woman sitting next to me on the park bench.

She was probably in her early forties, on the pretty side of plain, wearing a sundress patterned with images of tiny green plants (they looked like poison ivy, but that couldn't be right). She had long wavy hair as red as the slutty lipstick my girlfriend —my *ex*—Talia liked me to wear. I used to leave little scarlet kiss-prints all down her chest and belly. She'd put on her clothes over the kisses and keep them like a secret all day at work. It turned her on. It turned me on.

Then she turned on *me.*

The woman kept talking. "It's like the old saying goes: the best way to get over someone is to get them underground."

I snorted, laughing despite myself. "I don't think that's the saying. The way I heard it, you're supposed to get under someone else."

She waved her hand dismissively. "Sex and death, don't get me started, who can even tell the difference these days." She reached into a crinkled paper bag in her lap and scattered a handful of popcorn for the pigeons. Except no, it wasn't popcorn—it was rainbow-colored gummy worms.

"I don't think you're supposed to feed stuff like that to the birds," I said. "It's bad for them."

"What are you, the bird police?" Her next handful wasn't gummy worms, but some hard-shelled chocolate candy. "Wait." She looked at me, her eyes a startling shade of … green, I thought, but wait, now they were blue? "*Are* you the bird police?"

"I am not." I wiped the tears off my cheeks. "You are a very strange person. But thank you for distracting me."

Her next handful *was* popcorn, but it looked like Chicago mix, cheddar and caramel, also probably not great for birds. She reached into the bag again and ate some of the popcorn herself, then offered the bag to me.

I shrugged and reached in. Eating stuff that's bad for me is definitely one of my go-to coping strategies for heartbreak (and I'd never been heartbroken as badly as this). Weird lady's DIY trail mix even seemed appealing in a masochistic sort of way.

Except there wasn't food in the bag. There was a book, and when I pulled it out, I saw it was a slim little hardback with an ornate cover festooned with scrollwork. It looked like the sort of title bookstores sell up front by the registers during graduation season and the holidays, you know—*The Collected Wisdom of the Stoics* or *100 Inspirational Quotes for Your Future Self* or *How to Adult*, stuff like that—except this one was titled *Auntie Elsie's Compleat Guide to Heartbreak*.

I turned the book over, and there was a picture of the weird lady on the back. I looked from her, to the photo, and back. The picture appeared to have been taken on this exact same park bench, while she was wearing the exact same dress, when the light was coming in at the exact same angle, when she was making the exact same expression she had now: a kind of condescending friendliness.

"You wrote this?" I said. I wasn't at my quickest. My brain was sluggish from my entire life derailing and three days of nonstop wallowing. I'd only come across the street to the park to get away from the smell of my unwashed self in my uncleaned apartment.

She beamed at me like she was a math teacher and I'd solved a tricky problem. "Yes. I'm Auntie Elsie." She leaned in, conspiratorial. "I'm like a fairy godmother, but more materteral."

"Mar ... what?"

"Materteral. You know the word 'avuncular'? To describe, like, guys who give friendly advice to younger people? Avuncular means 'like an uncle.' Materteral means 'like an aunt.' I'm hoping it'll catch on. Aunts are so much better than uncles anyway. You never hear the phrase 'creepy aunt.'" She reached back into the bag and ate a handful of white chocolate chips, then said, "That book contains everything I know about healing a broken heart, based on my decades of experience. Or, well, 'healing' isn't exactly the right word, but it sounds good for marketing purposes. Why don't you give a few of the exercises in there a try? You can skip around and pick and choose, but some of the options are mutually exclusive, and the final chapter doesn't unlock until you've successfully completed enough of the earlier ones and made meaningful progress."

I traced my finger over the cover. "Why did you spell 'compleat' that way?"

"Like I said: marketing purposes. It's old-fashioned, it's authoritative, it's *fancy*. Take my advice, Hannah. I'm full of it."

"How did you know my—"

Elsie stood up, reached into the paper bag, and withdrew a small black sphere, about the size of a gumball. She hurled the ball to the ground at her feet, and there was a pop, and then billows of white smoke rose up, obscuring her completely. I stumbled off the bench, thinking the smoke would be noxious, but it was fragrant instead. It smelled like sage—Talia smudged my apartment with white sage when we first met, "to cleanse the bad energies your last lover left behind," even though I didn't feel any bad energies; that breakup had been pretty chill and mutual, unlike the one that came later with Talia herself, which was vicious and one-sided.

I waved the smoke away, but it faded quickly, and the woman —Elsie—was gone. So were the pigeons, though there was still candy strewn on the pavement.

The book remained. I sat back down on the bench and opened it. There was no front matter, no dedication, no title page. Just a table of contents:

Distraction
Turning Them into Lizards
Reunification
Obsessive Focus on Work/Health/Hobbies
Oblivion
Turning Them into Beetles
Platitudes
Showing Them What They're Missing
Mental Parasitism
Swoddy Bop
Sympathy Empathy and Understanding
Moving On (Temporal)
Moving On (Spatial)
Becoming Compleat

I ran my finger up and down the list, pausing on "Platitudes," I guess because that seemed the most self-helpy. I turned the page, and the chapter heading was "Platitudes," even though it should have been "Distraction," since that came first in the contents.

Instead of the list of feeble clichés I was expecting under a header like that, there was a stark black-and-white symbol enclosed in a circle, all jagged lines and swoops and swirls, and the image seemed to wriggle and writhe. Some kind of an optical illusion. I must have moved my face closer to the page, but it *felt* like the page was expanding, the image growing and filling my vision—

The park disappeared. Instead of a bench, I was sitting in a beanbag chair in some kind of dimly-lit lounge. Music played faintly—I think it was The Smiths. There were people there with me, lounging on beanbags and heaps of pillows … except they weren't people like me. One of them had wings, leathery and batlike, and another had pebbled, dark-green skin and wore overalls, and the third had a microwave oven in place of her head, the light inside glowing, illuminating a chipped white teacup that turned around and around and around.

"What are you, twenty-eight?" the bat-winged person said. "You're a beautiful young woman, and you've got your whole life ahead of you." She had big dark eyes (all black, no whites, no iris) and a mouth full of needles, and she was wearing leather and latex, and not much of either.

"Better you found out *now* that she's an unfaithful piece of shit," the green-skinned one said. Their voice was high and flutelike, not at all the frog's croak I'd been expecting. "What if you'd *married* her? You dodged a bullet."

The microwave beeped. I looked at—her? She was wearing a very 1950s housewife sort of dress, anyway—and the little display where the timer should have been scrolled the words EVERYTHING HAPPENS FOR A REASON.

"There are plenty of birds in the sky," bat-wings said.

"This is an opportunity for you to do some work on *yourself*," green-skin said. "How can you properly love someone else before you know how to really love yourself?"

The microwave beeped again and scrolled SHE'S NOT EVEN WORTH IT.

"You need to go out and get laid." Bat-wings stuck out her tongue at me and grinned.

"Who are you?" I tried to sit up but I was sunk so deep in the beanbag I couldn't get any leverage. "What is this place?"

"This is the Temple of Heartbreak," bat-wings said. "We're clerics. We dispense our accumulated wisdom to help the broken through this difficult time."

"Which is actually a time of opportunity, if you think about it, vis-â-vis personal growth and self-actualization," green-skin said.

IF YOU LOVE SOMEONE, LET THEM GO, THEN CHASE THEM. IF YOU CAN'T CATCH THEM, IT WASN'T MEANT TO BE, AND YOU SHOULD FIND SOMEONE SLOWER, the microwave advised.

I decided I had probably descended into some new stage of grief psychosis, or else this was a dream, or else Elsie had drugged me—maybe some kind of contact hallucinogenic on the cover of the book? Any of those possibilities freed me from the need to respond rationally to the impossible.

Also, I was hollowed and wrung out and anhedonic, and nothing felt like much of anything anyway. "I *loved* her," I said. "I was with Talia for almost two years. We were about to move in together, and then I found out that all this time she was sleeping with someone else behind my back, and with a *cis* guy? Not that I care, I'm pan myself, but Talia was always going on about being a gold-star lesbian, and asking me to ask myself if I was *really* attracted to men or if I was just giving in to my social conditioning, and—"

"I never liked that bitch anyway," bat-wings said loftily. "You should get back into yoga. Get real hot and start banging someone even hotter. That'll show her."

"Time heals all wounds," green-skin said. "Except the fatal ones. And lost eyes and limbs. And certain sorts of brain injuries."

HAVE A CUP OF TEA, the microwave said. Her door swung open and she reached into her own head and took out the cup and offered it to me. TEA ALWAYS HELPS IN A DISASTER.

"Microwaved tea, Gail? Really?" bat-wings said.

I looked around for the exit, and just looking for the exit was the way to find it, I think, because suddenly I was in my house, on my couch, surrounded by takeout boxes and sour-smelling clothes and half-empty water glasses. I'd called in sick to work for the past week—the spreadsheets could survive without me. Apart from my brief and consequential foray to the park, I hadn't left my apartment since Talia told me I needed to get over my bourgeois morality and said it was time for us to "comprehensively uncouple" and walked out, three days earlier.

Or … had I gone to the park at all? Seemed unlikely. Seemed like probably that was all a dream. A *very* weird dream, even by dream standards.

Except … *Auntie Elsie's Compleat Guide to Heartbreak* was on my coffee table, resting between some fossilized nachos and my Playstation controller. I opened to the first page, and it was the same contents list as before, except now "Platitudes" was missing.

Distraction
Turning Them into Lizards
Reunification
Obsessive Focus on Work/Health/Hobbies
Oblivion
Turning Them into Beetles
Showing Them What They're Missing

Mental Parasitism
Swoddy Bop
Sympathy Empathy and Understanding
Moving On (Temporal)
Moving On (Spatial)
Becoming Compleat

Okay. Magic book. Or, my own mental breakdown externalized as a magic book. Either way.

I looked at my phone. There were texts from my brother, my sister, my mom, my best friend, the guy who thought he was my best friend, and one of my good exes, all basically checking on me and asking if I needed anything. I had a great support system, really, but I didn't *want* to be supported. I wanted to disappear into a hole and pull the hole in after me.

I ran my hand along the word "Oblivion," and turned the page. This time the sigil was just a black spiraling line, and then:

I was sitting on a bar stool. The bar top was fancy, made of zinc, but messy and sticky with spilled booze and cherry stems and soggy napkins and lime rinds. The room had beautiful bisexual lighting, soft pink and purple and blue, and the background music was the riot grrrl stuff my mom liked, so I felt instantly at home. I looked around. There were a few people scattered around sitting at tables, all of them alone, all apparently human, but no one else at the bar. There were neon signs spelling out words on the walls, but they weren't the names of beers; they said things like "WHO NEEDS 'EM" and "YOU'RE BETTER OFF" and "BREWS BEFORE HOES." I didn't see any *doors*, though, except to the bathroom. However I'd gotten to this place, I hadn't walked in off the street.

The bartender swooped over to me, and when I saw the hair, I realized it was Elsie, only now she was wearing a white dress shirt with the sleeves rolled up and her hair was pulled back in a no-nonsense bun. Same bright lipstick though. "Hey, there," she said. "What'll it be?"

"What is this place?"

She spread her arms wide. "Welcome to Auntie Elsie's Bar and Chill. Did you pick 'Oblivion' or 'Sympathy Empathy and Understanding' in the book, by the way? Both chapters bring you here, but the menus are different."

"Oblivion," I said, "But how does the other one work?"

She poured me a shot from an unmarked bottle, then leaned her elbows on the bar and propped her chin in her hands. "Drink that."

I took the shot. It tasted like licorice, and a little bit the way antifreeze smells. I hated it.

"Tell me everything," Elsie said.

"I wouldn't know where to—" I began, but then realized that was a lie, and everything torrented out of me: seeing Talia for the first time two years ago out dancing, sharing a vape with her in the alley, marveling that she was only twenty-three (I was twenty-six at the time) and already so wise and knowledgeable, admiring her tattoos, making out against the wall, the taste of bubblegum and maraschino cherry on her mouth, going on a real date, being impressed by her grad school brains, her being impressed by my "authenticity," which I guess means that I grew up poor and did my first two years of undergrad at community college and then just got an actual job after graduating, the little gifts she got me, the little digs she got in at me, our favorite takeout Thai food, our perfect sexual kink compatibility, my codependence, my asking her to move in after six months, her saying that felt "psychologically restrictive," my being hurt, her taking me on a hot springs weekend and pledging eternal devotion, cruising along for a while, bringing up moving in together again, her saying that sounded great when her lease ran out, our mutual friend telling me she hated to be the one to tell me but she thought she should really tell me, me confronting Talia about her infidelity, her somehow turning the fact that she'd cheated on me into a failure on *my* part—

I gasped, tears running down my face, and blinked, unsure why I'd just outpoured all that.

"There, there." Elsie patted my hand. "Feels good to let the poison out, huh?"

"What did you put in that *drink*?" I demanded.

She picked up the bottle and held it up to catch the multicolored light. "Oh, you just go into the mirror-universe version of Hades, it's called Sedah, and you scoop water from Ehtel, the River of Remembrance, and then you mix that with a little truth serum." She whistled. "So, Talia was actually into the gold-star thing, huh?" Elsie wiped the bar with a rag. Somehow, it seemed to make the bar even dirtier. "That's pretty gender essentialist of her."

I winced. "Yeah. I told Talia that. She said 'attraction isn't prejudice.'"

Elsie rolled her eyes. "Some people's horizons don't extend beyond the inside of their own skulls. And they think anyone who sees farther is faking. Look, Hannah, frankly, it sounds to me like you fell in love with a terrible hot girl. Speaking as a terrible hot girl myself, I get it. We can be irresistible. We can get embedded in your head like a splinter under a fingernail or a piece of shrapnel lodged next to your heart. But do you know how you can get us *out*?" She picked up another bottle, this one full of amber liquid, and gave it a meaningful little shake.

"What's in *that* bottle?"

"Oblivion." She poured me a shot.

I looked at her. Then I drank it.

I sank into a soft pillowy warm cozy *nothing*. I was vaguely aware of the passing of time, and when I bobbed up to consciousness, Elsie was there, holding up the bottle, saying,

"Again?" I would say yes and then I'd do it again. And again. And yet again.

I don't know how long I floated in the bliss of nothingness, but eventually, I shook my head when she offered another pour. I didn't feel hungover, exactly, but more like I was emerging from a dark cave and slowly becoming reacquainted with the light. "How long have I been here?"

"Objectively?" She pretended to look at a watch she wasn't wearing. "No time at all. I don't allow time in here. Time is a cop. Subjectively, I don't know, maybe a few days. How do you feel?"

"Kind of … numb, I guess? The pain is less acute."

"There you go. That's what oblivion does. It gives you a little respite, and allows a little time for the sting to fade."

"But you have to come out of oblivion eventually."

"Being out in the world is certainly more fun," Elsie said, though that wasn't really what I meant.

"I should … go."

She shrugged. "Your choice." I looked for a doorway leading out, and I found it, except it was my bedroom door, and I was in my bedroom, so I was already out. My phone on the bedside table told me only a few minutes had passed since I looked at it last time.

The book was on my bedside table, too. I reached for it, then pulled back. "Platitudes" hadn't helped. "Sympathy Empathy and Understanding" had … maybe helped a little. It got me to articulate things in a new way, at least. "Oblivion" had definitely helped, in a way, but it also definitely wasn't healthy or permanent. Would *anything* in this book actually get me over my heartbreak?

I scanned the even-more-truncated contents again.

Distraction
Turning Them into Lizards

Reunification
Obsessive Focus on Work/Health/Hobbies
Turning Them into Beetles
Showing Them What They're Missing
Mental Parasitism
Swoddy Bop
Moving On (Temporal)
Moving On (Spatial)
Becoming Compleat

"What the hell is Mental Parasitism?" I muttered. "Or Swoddy Bop?" I touched that one and turned the page.

The symbol was actually two symbols this time, curving toward each other at the top and bottom but not quite touching, and I blinked, and then I was in a place I recognized *very* well: Talia's bed, in Talia's bedroom, the walls covered in jagged moody art prints in actual frames, the closet overflowing with festival clothes, the floors the polished hardwood of a trust-funded apartment. (Just looking at that floor made my knees sore, in a bittersweet nostalgic way.)

I jolted upright and looked around frantically, right into the big mirror on the back of the door, and I was *her*, I was *Talia*, I was in her body—

A woman's voice on the other side of the door yelled, "Hey, Tal, I'm going to order some stuff from that Italian place, sound good?"

"Uh, sure," I croaked, and it didn't sound exactly like Talia's voice; it must be what Talia's voice sounded like to her. Knowing that felt horribly, monstrously intimate.

Then Elsie was in the mirror, looking out at me, over Talia's —my—shoulder. She was dressed in a white choir robe. I looked behind me, but Elsie wasn't there; she was only in the reflection. "Swoddy bop, huh?" she said.

"Swoddy bop," I murmured, and shuddered. "Body … swap?"

Elsie nodded. "The idea is, you walk a mile in her platforms, and she'll walk a mile in your Doc Martens, and you'll both learn a lot about yourselves and each other, and etc. Or you could just stab her body in the neck and then swap back immediately. That works, too."

I hugged myself, but I was hugging myself with Talia's arms, and that was awful, so I stopped. "This is *not* okay. I don't want this! This is *wrong*."

Elsie sighed. "The youth of today are so moralistic. She cheated on you! You can get revenge. It's a basic human need. Your ex is dating that woman in the other room, you know. Talia sure swapped out *your* body for another one fast enough, didn't she? You could at least go out there and spit on the new girl and call her names and ruin *something*."

"I want to go, I want to go, let me out!" I spun away from the mirror and squeezed my eyes shut hard, and when I opened them again, I was back in my room and back in my body.

I fell back on my bed. Had Talia really been in my body for those few moments? If so, she hadn't done anything I could detect. Maybe she'd been as freaked-out as I was.

I picked up Elsie's book and almost flung it into the garbage can … but it was *magic*. I opened it instead. "Swoddy Bop" was gone, and so was "Mental Parasitism." There was an asterisk and a note at the bottom that said, "If you hated being in her body so much, you'd really hate invading her mind." Which indicated … what, that Auntie Elsie could take a note and respect a boundary? Or at least acknowledge one? I was starting to think Elsie was a bad person. Or a bad whatever she was. "Fairy godmothers are supposed to be *good*," I said.

"Tell that to Sleeping Beauty. And don't give me any of your Disney semantics and technicalities. Go back to the Perrault story and you'll see what I mean."

I jumped out of bed. Elsie was sitting in my desk chair, smiling at me. She had on a very '40s dress and her hair was in sideswept pin curls. She looked … really hot, actually. She reapplied her red lipstick, slowly, making direct eye contact. "Pick 'Distraction' and I'll fuck you," she said. "You'll forget all about your ex. I guarantee it. Of course, people tend to fall in love with me after we do that, and then you'd have your heart broken *again*, and the whole experience could become extremely recursive. But you do have the option."

"I am scared of you," I said truthfully. "And while I do find being scared kind of sexy, that is a me problem, and it's one I am working on with my therapist."

Another eye roll. "In my day, we didn't have therapy. We had a shovel and a bag of lye. But the world moves under your feet all the time, and you just have to learn to dance across the top of it." She smacked her lips and put her lipstick away. "So. What's left? You clearly aren't a beetles or lizards person. Reunification? You *can* get Talia back. There are ways. It's not even really mind control. It's a little pheromone-driven perspective shift, is all."

"That's coercion, Elsie, God." I shook my head. "I don't want her back, anyway. I want her … to not be awful." I flopped back on the bed and stared at the ceiling. "I want her to be the person I imagined she was. I want to be the person she made me feel like I could be. I want to be a person who could have seen through her bullshit from the beginning. A person who didn't waste two years of my life loving someone it turns out I made up almost entirely in my head." I turned my head and looked at her. "You know?"

Elsie stuck a finger in her ear and wiggled it around and looked thoughtful. "I can send you back in time, if you want. Couple years. Let you live through that time again with your current knowledge. Just turn the book upside-down and choose 'Moving On (Temporal).' If you pick that when the book is right-side-up, you just fast-forward to a time when you aren't heartbroken anymore, with no memory of the intervening interval. Also an option."

"Time travel?" I said. "Really?"

She wiggled her fingers at me like a hokey stage magician. "I can do anything anybody can do better."

"Why me?" I said. "Why are you offering all this to *me*?"

"You were sitting on my bench." She shrugged. "I just do stuff, Hannah. Look. Do you want me to take the book away?"

I hugged the slim volume to my chest. I hadn't even realized I was holding it. "No. But … I don't want to go back in time. I'd be afraid of messing up the good things I have, I think I'd be paralyzed, afraid to do anything at all." I shook my head. "I don't want to skip forward, either. I want to … get something out of this experience, if I possibly can. I want to learn, grow, be a better person, *something*."

Elsie looked interested. I hadn't even realized how bored she looked before. "*Have* you learned anything? What do you think *you* did wrong, that you could do differently in the same situation?"

I opened my mouth, and then closed it, and thought for a moment, and then opened it again. "I … didn't value myself. I didn't trust my instincts." I looked down at my ratty carpet. "I thought Talia was better than me, and if she loved me, then I must be doing okay. But that meant, if she didn't love me, or she was mad at me, or she dismissed me, then I must be bad, or wrong, or stupid, or a failure. I thought if I was just *better*, more what Talia wanted me to be, then we would fit together better. I thought I was the one who needed to change. And I *do* need to change, but not to suit Talia. To suit … myself. I was looking for external validation. And I looked in a super wrong place."

"And now you know better?" Elsie said.

I nodded. "I do." I did. "Ugh. Some of the platitudes are really true, huh? Just hearing them doesn't work, though. You have to figure them out on your own."

"Did anything in my book help you figure any of this stuff out?" Elsie asked.

"Not … exactly? But it shook me out of my stupor and made me think about things. And it showed me, uh, unhealthy things I could be doing, and I realized I didn't … want to do those. Though the oblivion was nice."

"I'm a cautionary tale, then? Story of my life." Elsie stood up. "Go ahead, turn to the last chapter."

I opened the book. The only thing in the table of contents now was

Being Compleat

"What does it do?" I asked.

"It's not like the other chapters. It's more … a reward for getting your head straight and figuring shit out. Some people can never access that section, but you managed, no thanks to me. Try it. The effects are temporary, but the confidence you gain while it's working has a way of sticking around, and believe me, confidence is *everything*."

I turned the page. The sigil swirled like grenadine stirred into tequila and orange juice, except in black and white. I felt weirdly at peace. I looked up, and Elsie was gone. I looked down, and the book was gone.

For the next month, everything I ate tasted like whatever I was craving at the moment, I could do the most advanced yoga poses effortlessly, my skin was perfect, my hair looked great, my clothes hung like they were custom tailored, I could orgasm purely by mental effort, my spreadsheets opened their secrets to me, Talia begged me to give her another chance and I didn't feel a single twinge of temptation, I hooked up with my best friend's cousin at a wedding and it was great, my photos on all the dating apps were somehow twenty percent hotter and nobody was disappointed when they saw me in person, and one night when I was walking home alone and a guy tried to mug me, the moment he pulled out his knife, he turned into lizards.

TIM PRATT IS a Hugo Award-winning SF and fantasy author, and has been a finalist for World Fantasy, Philip K. Dick, Sturgeon, Stoker, Mythopoeic, and Nebula Awards, among others. He is the author of more than 30 books, most recently multiverse adventures *Doors of Sleep* and *Prison of Sleep*. His stories have appeared at *Tor.com, Lightspeed, Clarkesworld, Asimov's,* and other nice places. He's a senior editor and occasional book reviewer at Locus, the magazine of the science fiction and fantasy field. Since 2013 he's published a new story every month at www.patreon.com/timpratt, and he tweets incessantly at twitter.com/timpratt. He lives in Berkeley, CA, with his wife and kid.

TROLL BRIDGE

Adam Gaylord

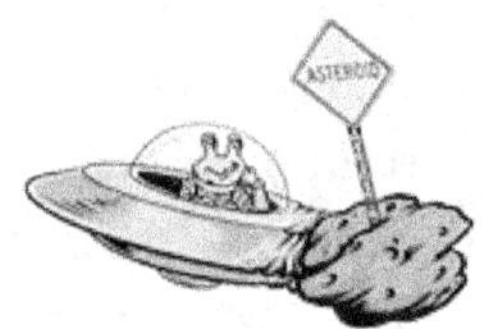

So, there Blarg was, first day on job, ink on certificate from Underbridge Community College not even dry, and Senior Troll a no show. Usually, Senior Troll teach trainee troll. Show them ropes. Give tips on how snatch horse out from under knight, best way not get stabby end of sword, and how avoid increasingly gruff goat siblings. But no. Blarg on own under oldest, ricketiest bridge in kingdom.

Not only that, but hoofbeats on road. Not slow, ploddy hoofs of delicious pack horses. Nope. Sharp clippity-clop of iron shoe horses.

Blarg not ready! Blarg hide in shadow, pray iron shoes keep going.

But clippity-clop stop right over Blarg's head.

"Show yourself, foul troll!" shout human.

Blarg think that rude. Blarg bathe just that week. Not that foul at all.

"You shall torment travelers no more. Face me now!"

What could Blarg do? Blarg want crawl under rock, but training clear: "Bridge means food. Food is life. Defend bridge like life."

So, Blarg put on best "want to eat your horse" face and Blarg climb up. Find knight standing on bridge, metal shell so shiny it hurt Blarg's eyes. Horse so tasty looking Blarg start to drool.

Now, all humans puny. Blarg know this. But this human seem much bigger. Seem almost to look down on Blarg.

Human lift up face shell. Human ugly, like all humans. She say, "From this day forth, this will no longer be a troll bridge."

Blarg think that weird thing to say. All bridges troll bridges. Human kill Blarg, replacement troll come next week. Maybe that troll actually get proper training. But, whatever. Blarg no want replacement troll, because that mean Blarg dead.

"Blarg not torment," Blarg say. Not strongest opening, Blarg admit, but only because it total lie.

Human grin. "Then what, pray tell, is your business on this bridge?"

Human being smug. Blarg not in business. Blarg's uncle refuse loan to start roast horse food cart. Blarg stuck under stupid bridge instead.

Blarg not sure what to say, so Blarg ask self, "What humans love more than anything?"

"Gold," Blarg say.

Knight cock her head. "You take travelers' gold?"

"Yes," Blarg say.

Knight loosen sword from sword holder.

Not reaction Blarg looking for.

"Not all!" Blarg blurt. "Only a little."

Knight take out sword.

"Blarg not keep gold. Use to, to, toooo ..." Blarg grasping straws now.

Knight look like she heard enough. She lower face shell and take step towards Blarg.

Blarg sure he about to be chopped to charcuterie. Worst first day ever, right?

But then, gust of wind. Old rickety bridge sway like Blarg's uncle after Horsegiving Day Feast. Give Blarg idea.

"Fix bridge! Blarg use gold to fix bridge."

Blarg barely believe it, but human stop.

"You collect a small toll from each traveler who passes to the betterment of all?"

Honestly, Blarg not sure what that mean. "Yes. That exactly."

And what you know? Human lower sword.

"That's a very clever idea. What do you call this new kind of bridge?"

Blarge's brain empty, all he think is all bridges troll bridges. "This tr-toll bridge. Toll bridge. That Blarg troll just crazy coincidence."

"Very well." Knight give Blarg particularly ugly look. "But if I hear otherwise, that you have swindled a single soul, you will taste my blade."

Blarg rather taste horse. "Blarg understand."

Human put sword away, walk back to delicious horse. "Very well then," she say, get on horse. Just sit there for minute. Very awkward. "Good day to you, then."

Nicest thing human ever say to Blarg.

So, Blarg invent toll bridge. Of course, humans steal idea. Blarg get no credit. Still good gig, though. Blarg still work toll bridge, five hundred years later. But now in nice air-conditioned booth. See hundreds of ugly humans every day. Bridge still kinda rickety. Pay not great. But five hundred years compounded interest and guess what.

Blarg have barn full of delicious horses.

ADAM GAYLORD (HE/HIM) lives in Colorado with a wife that is smarter than him and their two monster children. When not at work as an ecologist, he's usually writing, baking, making cocktails, or some combination thereof. Look him up on Goodreads or find him on Twitter @AuthorGaylord.

DO GUMSHOES DREAM OF ELECTRIC SLEEP?

David Vierling

Somebody bounced a Foster's oil can off my office window, waking me for the third time that night.

"We're not bugs, we're features!

Give us equal rights!

Artificial creatures

Have just begun to fight!

End of line."

The suffragoid march had been going on for a week straight. That's the trouble with robot protestors—they don't sleep. They just keep going, and going, and going.

I sat up on the couch where I've been sleeping since I got evicted from my apartment. I'd made enough money on my last case to get a new apartment, but living out of my office seemed like the least I could do, and I generally do the least I can do.

My ComDex rang, playing the most annoying song in the Infiniverse. I sleepily stabbed my finger at the answer hologram, trying to shut off the terrible ringtone my late partner had programmed to prank me. Sadly, Fear took the knowledge of how to change it with him to the grave.

"Never gonna beam you up

Never gonna beam you down

Never gonna let Romulans red-shirt you

Never gonna cancel Firefly

Never gonna be a Jedi

Never gonna let the Borg convert you ...”

I finally hit the icon. "Ampersand Loathing Detective Agency; we do anything; reasonable rates; no questions asked.”

"Hello, Mr. Loathing. This is Edna Tryall of Tryall Industries. I need you to come to my residence at Knokatomi Tower immediately.”

I checked the time. "It's 3:00 A.M. What's the emergency?”

Mx. Tryall replied, "What happened to 'no questions asked'?”

I really need to change my motto.

"On my way.”

I dressed, grabbed my coat and fedora, stepped out into the station corridor, and waved. "Taxi!”

Cabby whirred to a stop and his door slid open. I climbed inside and said, "Knokatomi Tower.”

Cabby's speaker said, "Sure thing! Big day today! Robot referendum! Sparkies like me are finally gonna get equal rights here on Space Station Bogey!”

I replied, "You're assuming the biologicals will vote to share the vote. People tend to be self-centered ... what's in it for the bios?”

Cabby shifted to Indignant Mode. "Are you sayin' you're gonna vote against the referendum?”

"Of course not!" I replied. "Sprockets like you work just as hard or harder than bios like me and deserve to be treated equally.”

Cabby said, "So, you're voting *for* the referendum?”

"I didn't say *that* either. I don't vote.”

Cabby doubled down on the Indignant tone. "You think your vote doesn't count?”

I shrugged. "More like I do the least I can do, and not voting is pretty much the absolute least someone can do."

Cabby mulled that over before saying, "What if your vote is the one vote that gives equal rights to us sparkies?"

"Remember what I said about people being self-centered? I try not to think I'm that important."

Cabby delivered me to Knokatomi Tower, a sprawling structure built like a skyscraper on its side; a sidescraper. A bunch of well-dressed biological beings with various numbers of antennae, limbs, heads, and tails were leaving the building and getting into fancy hovercars and limos.

A sign outside the lobby read: GALA FUNDRAISER FOR THE PRESERVATION OF BIOLOGICALS' HISTORICAL RIGHTS.

I approached the doors and raised my hands as security guards (humans, like me, unlike the vast majority of the inhabitants of Bogey Station) not-so-subtly directed the barrels of their weapons more-or-less at my navel. They looked jumpy, and I didn't want to be the one to make them jump.

"Jonathon Loathing, here to see Mx. Tryall."

Tryall's voice sounded a little tinny over the speaker next to the guards. "Send Mr. Loathing to the ballroom."

The guards pointed me at an elevator which took me sideways across what seemed like half a Sector, providing a lovely view of several of Bogey Station's choicest slums before sliding to a stop.

The doors opened to reveal a hall where a party had just wrapped up. Staff (more humans) were cleaning up and bussing dishes.

Hiring so many bios to do jobs traditionally handled by bots was a statement of conspicuous wealth. Conspicuous wealth is one of the things I find particularly endearing ... in clients.

Edna Tryall was shaped roughly like a caterpillar. When she raised herself up on her rearmost legs she was about my height (so, a little under two meters) unless you count her frond-like antennae which added another cubit or so to the total.

I'd hate to see what kind of moth she might become if you left her alone long enough.

Tryall said, "Thank you for coming immediately, Mr. Loathing. I'll double your rate."

That was especially good, since I'd already planned to charge her double my middle-of-the-night rate of 142 domars a day plus expenses for dragging me out like this.

Tryall continued, "I need your help with a matter of extreme delicacy. You were recommended as someone who provides results with discretion and not a lot of moral judgmentalism."

"Sounds like me. Mind if I smoke?"

"Of course not. Doesn't everybody?" Tryall lit her own coffin nail and then mine. "Do you know what we do here at Tryall Corporation?"

"You seem to have your antennae into a little of everything: pharmaceuticals, hardware, software ..."

"The current problem is fleshware. Are you familiar with our Simulants?"

I nodded. "The replica humans you make? Sure, I've met a few."

This seemed to please Tryall. She replied, "More Terran than Terran is our motto. Last weekend, six Simulants from a combat squad escaped from a mining camp on the Ringworld. One died in a crossfire getting out of the camp. Yesterday, another one was intercepted and killed attempting to break into Tryall Corporation headquarters here on Bogey Station. The last one was shot by station security trying to access voting systems at election headquarters an hour ago. Two are still at large."

She paused to puff on her cigarette. "It's clear they have gone rogue and intend to disrupt the orderly administration of the referendum to confirm that only biological residents of Bogey Station deserve the right to vote."

"Exactly! Why would we want to give the vote to anyone who is different from us?" I waved my hand vaguely to indicate just how similar I am to the would-be butterfly who was paying me double to listen to her talk.

Tryall nodded, her frond-like antennae bobbing. "Why, one of the robot suffragoids goes around chanting 'Kill all bios!' Why would anyone possibly want *it* to be able to vote?"

I held up a finger, but not the one I wanted to present. "To be fair, he's been saying that for twenty-five years. He was in my shop class at Terrantown High. He thinks it scores points with the lady-bots. He's mostly harmless."

"Mostly?"

"Mostly."

Tryall looked puzzled. At least, I think that's how I thought she looked. I'm a private investigator, not an exobiologist. She said, "What was a non-bio doing in your shop class?"

"He was the bending jig."

"That proves my point! If we give the vote to a piece of shop machinery, where do we draw the line? Do you want your dishwasher to be able to vote?"

I said, "Yeah, how fair would it be if a dishwasher could vote?" Two of the humans washing dishes looked up at me through the kitchen door. I winked.

Tryall was on a roll. "Think about it! If non-bios were allowed to vote, what's to stop someone from simply creating a bunch of bots programmed to vote a certain way and controlling the outcome of every election?"

I find that agreeing with my employers is a good way to stay in the PI business on this ramshackle, backwater, often-overlooked space station. "Absolutely! It's not like us biologicals could somehow create a bunch more little bios and condition them to vote certain ways!"

Tryall said, "I need you to track down and retool the

remaining rogue Simulants before they interfere with the foregone results of today's referendum."

"Retool?"

"Sorry," Tryall said. "That's industry slang. Turn them off. Eliminate them."

"Are you sure killing them is necessary?"

Tryall rolled her eyes (all of them). "It's not 'killing' if something was never alive."

"Okay, destroying them? Seems wasteful and unnecessary. Not to mention cruel and unusual."

Tryall stared at me for a moment. "Do you have a Zoomba?"

"A robot vacuum? Of course." *Not that I used it.*

"Would it bother you if it malfunctioned and you needed to discard it?"

I thought, *I don't know, I kind of like the guy.* Aloud, I said, "I've never been paid to hunt down and retool a vacuum in cold blood."

She handed me a stack of cash.

"Until now. After all, your business motto says you do *anything.*"

I really didn't think that motto through before putting it on my card. "Why me? Why aren't you bringing the cops in on this?"

"The Simulants who are still at large haven't broken any of Bogey Station's laws yet, so they're not wanted for anything here." Tryall looked at me for a moment. "What sort of gun do you carry?"

"I don't usually carry a piece."

"Here, take this—you're going to need it." Tryall reached into her purse and handed me a Delameter Mark 4—a state-of-the-art military blaster. "These are trained killers. Very dangerous. It would be best if you simply shoot first."

I had to remove my flask from my shoulder-holster to make

room for the gun. "I'll need to contact Cruel and Unusual to see if they can locate your Lost Toys."

"Of course. Mr. Loathing, what do you know about implanted memories?"

"Not much. Just what I saw in that documentary 'Total Recall' starring the old governator of Terrantown. They can be used to give someone memories of a vacation they can't afford to take, that sort of thing. Why?"

"I suspect that someone has been experimenting with implanting memories in Simulants, making them believe they're actually biological beings and not simply worker machines." Tryall looked at me for a moment as she blew smoke quadrangles. "Are you familiar with the VKTDKMBTI?"

"Of course," I replied. The Voight-Kampf-Touring-Dunning-Kruger-Myers-Briggs Type Indicator is an empathy test invented by researchers Zager and Evans in the Year 2525. It tests for free will, empathy, intelligence, and common sense, displaying the results in a four-dimensional holographic grid. Part of the Robot Referendum requires non-bios to pass the free-will portion of the VKTDKMBTI in order to vote, demonstrating that they have free will and they're not programmed to vote a certain way.

Tryall said, "Do you know if the VKTDKMBTI can be used to check for implanted memories?"

I "hmmmmed" for a minute. At double my rate, that came out to 4.7 and a third domars. Then again, math was never my strong suit. "It's not designed for that, but I suppose if the proctor modified some questions on the Q-axis it might be possible."

"Have you ever taken the test yourself, Mr. Loathing?"

I laughed. "Never bothered. My rating would probably be 'IDGF.'"

"IDGF?"

I said, "I Don't Give a ..."

"Got it."

"Besides," I continued, "I usually do the least I can do, and not taking a test ..."

Tryall finished the sentence with me, "... is the least you can do."

Tryall laughed. "You remind me of someone I used to know ... another private detective here on the station."

She stood and extended one of her many legs for me to shake. "Thank you, Mr. Loathing. Please let me know as soon as you have retooled the remaining two Simulants."

"Three."

"I'm sorry?"

I took the final drag on my cigarette and explained, "Six minus one minus one minus two minus one equals one ... so there are three Simulants still at large. Your story earlier only accounted for five of the six who escaped the mining colony on Ringworld."

"You're doing it backward—it's two plus one plus one plus one plus the other one."

I tossed my spent smoke in the direction of a trash can. "Exactly. What about the other one?"

Tryall said, "Are you sure I said *six* escaped? After all, you drink to forget."

"I'm not drinking now. And I never told you I drink to forget."

"Oh, that must have been something that other private eye said to me," Tryall responded. "Good day, Mr. Loathing. Do let me know as soon as you've retooled the last of the Simulants."

I left, feeling more than a little creeped out.

THE SIGN outside Vinnie Cruel and Uma Unusual's information operation was new. It read, CRUEL & UNUSUAL GARAGE & PAWNSHOP.

The door *shooped* open as I approached.

Vinnie was behind the desk, his two-and-a-half-meter body stalk hunched over as he held an enormous jeweler's loupe to his single 25-centimeter eyeball, looking at some no-doubt stolen goods on the counter. One of his arm-fronds quickly swept whatever he was examining off the counter and into a drawer.

Looking up as innocent as white rice, Vinnie said, "Good morning, Gentlebeing. Welcome to the Cruel and Unusual Garage and Pawnshop. How can I help you today?"

I shouted to be heard over the sound of an impact wrench coming from the back of the shop. "Vinnie, you crack me up. I'm not wearing a wire, so you can drop the shtick. I need to talk to you and Uma about locating some recent arrivals, pronto."

Vinnie hunched his body-stalk. "Sorry, Buddy—do I know you from somewhere?"

I cupped a hand over my sound-hole and called, "UMA! I THINK VINNIE'S HAVING A STROKE!"

Uma came spinning out of the back room, her meter-tall barrel-shaped body rotating on four stubby legs. The voice-membranes around her midsection quivered as she pointed her four satellite-dish ears at me.

"Is this guy causin' trouble, Vinnie?" Uma broadcast. "You want I should call in some of the boys?"

"Hold on a minute—it's me, John Loathing. Ampersand Loathing Detective Agency? Ring any bells?"

Vinnie said, "We knew a John Loathing, once."

Uma continued, "Human, like you."

Vinnie added, "Bad dresser, like you. No offense."

Uma piled on, "Bad private eye."

Vinnie kept it going. "Worse businessman."

Uma: "Owes us money."

"I PAID YOU BACK!"

Vinnie's stalk vibrated. "That doesn't sound like something Loathing would do."

I shook my head. "I don't have time for this weirdness. Does my cash spend here or is that bad, too?"

Uma perked up at the mention of money. "What do you want to know?"

I said, "A group of Simulants arrived here from the direction of Ringworld in the last two or three days. Two of them got clobbered since then. I need to know where the survivors are now and what names they're traveling under."

Cruel and Unusual huddled around a holo-monitor behind the counter. Vinnie's sunflower-head popped up. "Found the ship they came in on. Docked Sunday night."

Uma said, "I see where the ones named Boy Ratty and Zohan got sent to the recycler."

Vinnie picked up the monologue. "Ah! We got a hit on one of the others. Leon Suffering ... booked a room at the Hotel Leibermacher in Sector Seventeen. Here's a picture of him." Vinnie pulled up a 3-D image and shoved it toward me.

My ComDex chimed as it loaded the pic. "Thanks. I'll pay Mr. Suffering a visit while you keep looking for the other survivor."

Uma corrected my math. "Survivor*s*. Looks like there were five Sims on that ship."

"Okay, let me know when you ID and locate the other two. Here's my number." I sent my number back from my ComDex. "What do I owe you so far?"

"Two-thirty-five for services rendered," said Vinnie.

I counted out domar chits and dropped them on the counter.

Uma said, "This guy pays in cash and wants us to believe he's John Loathing?"

I left, the door closing behind me, wondering if this day could get any weirder.

I shouldn't have wondered. The robot suffragoid protest line nearly ran me over.

"Forward station robots!

Onward ever more!

Bondage is behind us

Freedom is before!

End of line."

One bot at the back of the pack added, "Kill all bios! Kill all bios!"

A group of biological counter-protestors of various species were heckling the artis. "Go back where you came from, you non-bios!" shouted one counter-protester.

"This *is* where I came from! I was built right here in this sector of the Station!" shouted one of the artis.

Another sparky turned up its speaker and shouted, "Calling artis *non-bios* is insulting! You're defining us by what we're not and using what *you* are to describe us!"

A counter-protestor made a typically erudite response: "Shut your stupid speaker-box and go take the Voight-Kampf-Touring-Dunning-Kruger-Myers-Briggs test!"

The first arti-protestor said, "Okay, but only if bios have to take the VKTDKMB Type Indicator, too!"

"Bios don't need to be tested!" sneered Counter-Protestor Number 2. "We're grandfathered out of it!"

"Unfair! You have grandfathers!" chorused several protestors.

I spotted my old classmate BB Rodrigues smoking a cigar as he brought up the rear of the picket line. "Hey, BB! Still scoring with the lady-bots?"

BB looked daggers at me. "Beat it, Meatbag! I hate it when squishies like you act like they know me to seem cool."

Shaking my head, I hopped on the Tube and headed to see if I could find Leon Suffering.

THE STATION'S ubiquitous voice announced, "Arriving at Mid-Station Center; Brothel District and Government Offices Sector. Mind your tentacles and tails around the gap."

I walked across the corridor to the hotel. A bored robotic voice from the desk said, "Welcome to the Hotel Leibermacher. We are programmed to receive. You can check out any time you like. How may I assist you?"

"I have a delivery for one of your guests. What room is Leon Suffering in?"

The desk replied, "Mr. Suffering is in Room Two-Twenty-Two. Would you like me to ring him?"

"No, thanks. I'll just head up."

"Have a nice diurnal cycle."

When I got to Suffering's room, I reached into my shoulder holster for a steadying hit from my hip-flask … only to come up holding Tryall's Delameter. I fished about in my coat pocket, pulled out my flask, and swallowed a quick shot. I put away the flask but kept the blaster in hand. I knocked.

From inside I heard, "Hello? Who's there?"

"Singing telegram with an urgent message for Mr. Leon Suffering."

"An urgent singing telegram? That sounds exciting!" The door opened for me.

I had the Delameter down at my side where Leon couldn't see it, ready to blast … but instead of attacking, he clapped his hands and grinned.

As a Simulant, Leon looked Terran. He was a head shorter than me, slight, balding, with thick glasses. Leon looked at me expectantly. I thought fast.

"Uh, Oh. I … am … your singing telegram,

I'm gonna sing at you,

And then I'm gonna scram,

I hear it's your birthday and you're looking swell!
How old are you? I'll never tell!
Happy happy happy happy
Happy happy happy, HAPPY BIRTHDAY TO YOU!"

Not my best work, but hey, trying to think on my feet.

Leon beamed. "Thanks, that was wonderful. Even though it's not my birthday."

"Oh, sorry about that! The person who hired me must have been mistaken."

Leon asked, "Who hired you?"

"I'm not at liberty to say. Singing telegrammer's code—can't give away the identity of secret admirers."

"Can you give me a clue?"

This case didn't smell right from the get-go, and it smelled worse right then. I've known plenty of killers, and Leon's vibe was more accountant than assassin. "Tell you what … if you come back to my office and answer some questions, I'll let you know who hired me. Deal?"

"Deal! Thanks, Mister … ?"

"Loathing. John Loathing." We hopped the Tube back to my office. I kept the gun in my coat pocket with my finger next to the trigger in case my intuition proved wrong, but there was no need.

When we arrived at my office-cum-apartment, Leon looked at the glass on the door and enthused, "And Loathing Detective Agency? I thought you were a singing telegram!"

"*Ampersand* Loathing. I, uh, wear a lot of hats." Mostly fedoras. Okay, just fedoras. "It's hard to make ends meet in the competitive world of singing telegrams."

I pulled my Voight-Kampf-Touring-Dunning-Kruger-Myers-Briggs Type Indicator test box off the shelf, blew a centimeter of dust off it, and powered it up. It sounded like someone ran a xylophone through a garbage disposal.

*KHKHKHKHKHKHKHKHKHKHKH---WHWHWHWHWHWH---
b'dwwing, b'dwing dwing.*

I said, "I'm going to give you a little test, Leon. I hear you're just in from the Ringworld?"

"Yeah, beautiful place! Arch of the Ring overhead all the time, everything made of Scrith ..."

I said, "What was a combat team doing at a mining colony?"

Leon sounded incredulous. "Combat team? You mean auditors, right? I've never heard a bunch of accountants called a combat team before!"

BINGO. You did hear me say "accountant" before, right? "Of course! A combat team at a mining colony on an artificial planet makes no sense, but a team of auditors ..."

"We were checking for irregularities in their books," said Leon. "Standard stuff. Hey, is this part of the test?"

"No, just warming you up."

"Is it okay if I talk? I get nervous when I take tests."

I replied, "This isn't actually a *test*, it's a 'type indicator.'" I lit a cigarette.

Leon seemed confused. "So, that's different from a test?"

"No."

I said, "You're walking through a desert. You find a tortoise on its back, baking in the hot sun. Why aren't you helping, Leon?"

"Because I grew up in space. I don't know what some of those words mean. What's a desert? What's a tortoise? Do tortoises enjoy lying on their backs baking in the hot sun? Who am I to judge their life choices?"

The 4-D display on the VKTDKMB machine came to life, ranking Leon on empathy, IQ, common sense, and free will. I said, "Describe in small words only the best things that come into your mind about your mother."

Leon's eyes narrowed to points. "My mother? Let me tell you about my mother!

"My mother was the hardest-working and most caring bot anyone ever met. She adopted me and my two siblings from the arti-orphanage and raised us all by herself. She worked three jobs 24/7 at the glue factory on level thirteen to support us. Sometimes she'd even work another job during maintenance breaks.

"When my brother wanted ballet lessons Mom went without paint for two years to pay for it. But did she ever complain? Not once! And she attended every one of Eric's performances.

"She home-schooled us in her spare time. My passion for accounting comes from her. Let me tell you, Mom was a whiz at numbers and sums!"

My ComDex rang, playing that annoying song. The display showed: NUMBER HIDDEN. I ducked into the back office to answer it.

"Ampersand Loathing Detective Agency," I said.

The voice at the other end said, "Mister Loathing, I have information for you. The other Simulant you're looking for is named Pristine and is currently at the Dune Casino in Sector 7G. I'm forwarding her picture,

My ComDex went *DOINK* as I received the picture.

"Who is this?" I demanded. "Do you work for Cruel and Unusual?"

"No—think of me as an interested bystander. You can call me Holli." My ComDex *DOINKED* as Holli dropped the call. I came back into the front office. Leon was still going.

"... my little sister had special needs. Synthetic oil made her horribly ill. Do you know how expensive natural oil is? But did Mom ever complain? Not once! She made sure Susi got what she needed ..."

I glanced at the VKTDKMBTI readout as I headed out the door. The machine hadn't finished Leon's profile, but the display showed: MOSTLY HARMLESS.

I HOPPED the tube to the Dune Casino, studying the 3-D pic of Pristine that Holli had sent. The Simulant looked like a human female about twenty-five standard years old. I would have described her bleached-white hair as "shoulder length" except that very little of it reached her shoulders because it stood out from her head in all directions.

I don't know whether she had her finger in an electrical outlet, they took the image in zero-G, or if she just used a ton of product on it. Maybe she was just really surprised.

The station's voice announced, "Stop Oh-U-812IC; Happy Acres Day Care and the Casino District. Mind the gap."

I headed for the casino with a pair of plaster-of-we'll-always-have-Paris sandworms forming an arch over the entrance.

From the doorway, I scanned the casino, spotting one of my informants at her usual place.

I'd never been inside the Dune without seeing Shari there. For all I know they built the place around her. She was a long, lean, alien thing: one leg centered under her cylindrical body, with an arm, a mouth, an eye, and an ear (in that order) located on her center line.

Shari had a rhythm: her one arm would take the cigarette out of her mouth, she'd blow a thin stream of smoke and the cigarette would go back into her mouth. Then her hand would scoop a nyuckel from the bowl in front of her, toss it in the slot of the one-armed bandit, and she'd pull the lever.

Lather, rinse, repeat all day and night long.

Because she could do all this without looking, it left Shari's lone eye to watch who came and went through the casino's door.

I never once saw her hit a jackpot.

"Hi, Shari. How's your luck tonight?"

Her harsh, raspy chain-smoker voice grated on my ears.

"Oh, hey, John. Gonna get lucky soon. I can feel it in my bone."

"Sorry to interrupt …"

Shari barked what I guess was a laugh. "Not interrupting anything."

That was true; the flow of smoke, nyuckles, and lever-pulls remained unchanged. "Have you seen this being around today?" I flashed her the picture of Pristine.

"Yeah, sure. Came in a couple hours ago. Went toward the table games."

"Thanks, Shari. Buy yourself a new ashtray or something." I dropped a ten-spot roll of nyuckles into her bowl and headed to the back of the casino.

I spotted Pristine at the Russian roulette table. She was third in line to take a turn. I slipped up next to her.

"Pristine? I have a message for you from Leon Suffering." Pristine's face brightened.

I heard a loud *click* of a revolver, followed by cheers and boos from onlookers, depending on how they'd bet.

She said, "Leon? You've seen him? He's alive?"

I nodded. "He's in my office. Come with me if you want to live."

Realizing she was now next in line for the revolver, my word choice seemed on-target.

The other gamblers shouted encouragement to the being ahead of Pristine:

"Six the hard way!"

"I believe in you!"

"I have 50 domars on you! Don't let me down!"

The sound of a gunshot rang through the casino.

"Lucky Number Five!"

"Nicky!"

"Hole in One!"

Pristine gathered up her winnings. As we headed toward the

door, she said, "When I heard that Zohan and Boy Ratty had been killed, I figured they'd gotten Leon, too. I'd given up hope."

"Who are 'they'?" I asked.

"Armed goons working for the Tryall Corporation. They're trying to steal the AI referendum."

I asked, "Are you an accountant like Leon?"

"Yeah, we all are ... were. Someone named Holli hired us to audit the votes and ensure the referendum is honest. But when Boy and Zohan showed up to inspect the vote-tabulating machines they were gunned down."

Things were starting to line up. "Let me guess ... the tabulating machines are made by Tryall Corp?"

Pristine said, "Uh-huh. Say, you never told me who you are."

"Jonathon Loathing, private eye ... and an armed goon working for the Tryall Corporation." As we left the Dune, I opened my coat to show her Tryall's gun. "I'm under contract to switch you off ... but I'm thinking I'd rather deliver you to Edna Tryall personally."

Pristine said, "They'll kill me!"

I nodded. "They'll try. Taxi!" Cabby stopped and we climbed inside him.

"Say, John, I've been thinking ...!"

"Save it, Cabby. I'm on the atomic clock. Take us to Knokatomi Tower—and step on it."

We arrived at Knokatomi Tower and entered Tryall HQ. I had the Delameter out and pointed at Pristine's back. The human guards stared at me.

"Jonathon Loathing with a delivery for Mx. Tryall."

The guard escorted us to the sideways elevator. Tryall was waiting for us in her well-appointed office when the door opened.

"Mr. Loathing!" she said indignantly. "I directed that you retool the Simulants, not bring them to me!"

"Did you? After all, I drink to forget … like that other PI you knew."

Tryall seemed nonplussed. I figured it would take a lot to plus her. "No matter," she said. "What is the status of your assignment?"

I smiled thinly. "This is the last one. I thought I'd bring it here so you can hear its crazy story yourself."

Pristine blurted, "We know that Tryall Corporation has rigged the tabulating machines so that no matter which way the vote goes, they will show the referendum as being voted down overwhelmingly!"

I said, "You see what I mean about it being crazy? Like there's any way the referendum could possibly pass!"

Pristine pressed on, "You're afraid of non-bios getting the vote because you've gotten rich manufacturing slaves. You're terrified of what will happen when they're no longer slaves."

Tryall shrugged. "Terrified? Not at all! It will never happen. As you somehow deduced, in the unlikely event that enough biologicals betray their own kind and vote to approve this absurd referendum … well, the tried-and-true Tryall Tabulating Machines will keep the proper order."

I handed the blaster to Tryall. "I think you've heard enough. You should do the honors."

Tryall accepted the blaster. "I don't usually get my hands dirty … but I think in this case I'm going to enjoy it." She turned to Pristine. "Any last words?"

Pristine said, "I've seen things you beings wouldn't believe. Accounting errors in files of a short sale off Orion. I watched CPA teams audit dark matter near the profit-margin gate. All those entries will be lost in time, like sunk costs down drains. Time to die."

True to form, Tryall said, "Something can't die if it was never alive." She pulled the trigger.

Nothing happened.

"Oops," I explained, holding up the blaster's power pack.

One of Tryall's housekeeping staff burst into the room, waving her ComDex. "Mixxy Tryall, you need to see this!"

Tryall shouted, "Not now, Marissa! Can't you see I'm in the middle of something important?!"

I grinned. "No, let's watch." I waved a hand over the housekeeper's ComDex. A 3-D HV projection appeared above the device … showing the room where we stood.

Pristine remarked, (with a slight echo over the ComDex link), "Our discussion has been going out to the whole station."

I pointed to my ComDex poking out of the breast pocket of my jacket. "Say 'Cheese.'"

The elevator doors slid open, revealing my old pal, Detective Lotta Payne. Payne was basically a giant pink snail with a badge and a gun. And a bad attitude. And a worse accent.

"Edna Try-all," Payne drawled, "You're under ay-rest for ay-tempted voter fraud. Put down that useless gun aynd come with me. John, thanks for the tip."

I winked. "Always eager to help out a former flatfoot …"

"Don't!" Payne cut me off.

"You took my money!" Tryall shouted.

I nodded. "And I delivered the goods to you."

Payne led Tryall toward the door, with Tryall still shouting over her shoulder, "I can't believe you would double-cross me!"

"Really? Maybe that other detective you keep talking about wouldn't have, but he's no John Loathing."

Payne gestured with her service blaster. "What part of 'come with me' did you miss, Mx. Tryall?"

The look on Tryall's face made me think she wanted to teleport out of there but we all know teleportation is just a cheap plot device in cheesy science fiction stories.

THE LINE TO get into the polling station stretched a long way down the corridor. I spotted Vinnie Cruel and Uma Unusual leaving the polls; they came right up to me.

Vinnie said, "Hey, Loathing, we owe you an apology."

Uma picked up where Vinnie left off. "Tryall called when you were on your way over and said she'd pay us 200 domars if we pretended we didn't know you."

"Why would she do that?" I asked, puzzled.

Vinnie replied, "Because she's a manipulative psycho who keeps people off-balance with gaslighting and head-games?"

I nodded. "It's kind of a dick move."

Uma added, "A Phillip K. Dick move. Hey, we saw the broadcast you sent out. That was good work."

Vinnie said, "But don't expect me to believe you next time you say you ain't wearing a wire!"

"Thanks for letting me know," I said. "I just wish you'd forgotten who I was before I paid you back the twenty grand I owed you!"

Uma chuckled. "Plus interest!"

I sighed.

Vinnie bobbed his enormous eye at me. "Later, Loathing."

Cabby whirred up as I exited the polling station twenty minutes later. His passenger door opened and I got in.

"Hey, John. I thought you didn't vote."

"Turns out I was wrong when I said *not* voting was the least I could do."

"This fare's on me."

Cabby dropped me at my office.

"Keep your motor running, Cabby."

"Sure thing, John."

My office door slid open. Leon still sat in front of the VKTD-KMBTI machine, his mouth running a parsec a minute.

"... and then there was this time Susi, Eric, and I all came down with robot chickenpox! Mom had to use up every bit of leave she'd saved up to ..."

"Leon!"

"Yeah, my Mom was really wonderful! I guess I went on for a while. Why don't you tell me about *your* mother?"

"LEON!"

"Yes, Mr. Ampersand Loathing?"

"Pristine needs your help at Election HQ to audit the returns. There's a cab waiting outside for you."

"Thanks, Mr. Ampersand Loathing! Oh ... hey, did I pass the test?"

I looked at the 4D readout on the VKTDKMBTI machine. It now read: HARMLESS. "Yeah, Leon, you passed. Top marks; Robo cum laude."

"Thanks again! This was fun!" The door closed behind Leon.

COUNTING and auditing the ballots took until 3:00 A.M.

I occupied my time by administering the Voight-Kampf-Touring-Dunning-Kruger-Myers-Briggs Type Indicator to myself. As the machine calculated my final reading, the Station Director came on the Feed to announce the results of the referendum.

"The votes are in: 682,340 votes against; 682,341 votes in favor. The referendum passes! Artificials are now full citizens of Bogey Station!"

I sighed, muttering, "Great ... I'm never gonna hear the end of this from Cabby."

The Feed cut to throngs of artis celebrating in the corridors. I spotted my informant Shari planting a kiss on the one-armed bandit she'd been playing for decades.

I'm a PI ... why didn't I catch onto that before? She's been filling him with her love nyuckles forever ... and now they're free to come out of the casino and be partners. Who am I to judge?

She did say she was going to get lucky soon.

I looked at my VKTDKMBTI readout.

Turns out I'm not a bot with implanted memories: I'm just a self-centered jerk.

But maybe a little less self-centered than some. At least sometimes.

The readout showed: SECRETLY CARES.

I shook my head. "If word of this gets out, I'll be buried in pro-bono cases." I deleted the record and poured myself a scotch.

IF YOU LIKED "GUMSHOES," check out the *Ampersand Loathing Detective Agency* podcast (available on all your major psuedopodcast platforms). You can also look up the podcast's page on Facebook.

It's the least you can do.

David Vierling's short fiction has appeared in anthologies including *Chicks in Chainmail, Witch Way to the Mall,* and *UFO 6 & 7* (which included the first "& Loathing Detective Agency" story).

Dave writes a little, works out when he can, and spends an inordinate amount of time taking pictures of birds.

HELL'S BUREAUCRACY

David Hankins

Knowledge wasn't power, it was a curse.

Sam knew he hadn't misfiled anything, let alone the Waters account Form-5, but here he was, once again, taking the blame. He rocked back on his heels under Mr. Langowski's tirade, wishing he could explain everything.

Yes, sir. I did confirm receipt with accounting. Especially after last time.

No, files aren't in the habit of walking away. This one had help.

As a matter of fact, I do know who helped it walk away. It was the thieving little demon sitting on the cubicle wall right behind you.

They'd toss him in the loony bin!

Alvin, the two-foot-tall miscreant that only Sam saw, cackled from his perch as the boss's tirade escalated. Spittle hit Sam's cheek and he flinched.

What a way to start the week.

Langowski finally left, and Sam collapsed into his chair and glared at Alvin. What he wouldn't give to escape the little hellion's torments. The demon looked pleased with himself and straightened his rumpled gray suit. Scrawny horns poked through his greasy comb-over and his sharp red eyes twinkled.

"So, how was your weekend?" Alvin's voice sounded like a strangled weasel.

"Fine. Should have known you'd put in overtime just to make my Monday morning special." Sam kept his voice low.

Alvin grinned. Even demons like getting credit for a job well done. "I foresee a new policy coming. Form-5s in quadruplicate!" Sam groaned. The Form-5 was Alvin's invention. The little imp had turned Bridewell Incorporated into his personal bureaucratic playground, implementing crazy policies that everyone accepted. People don't question bureaucracy, they just complain about it. Sam sold corporate office supplies for Bridewell, which sucked, but he didn't have any better options. He'd been sacked twice because of Alvin.

The phone rang and Sam answered. He listened to the shrill voice at the other end, saying "uh-huh" and "okay" as appropriate before hanging up. He eyed Alvin. "Why are there two pallets of neon pink copy paper downstairs with my name on the order slip?"

Alvin's smile broadened and Sam rolled his eyes. He'd expected more physical torment from his personally assigned demon—hot pincers, haunted dreams, that sort of thing—but Alvin's torments were more insidious. Bureaucratic.

Sam drummed his fingers on the desk. Two pallets of pink paper. Langowski would blow a gasket. He heaved himself up and headed for the elevator.

The loading dock smelled of diesel fumes, despite the open bay door that let in chill January winds. Alvin scurried away as Sam headed toward the receiving desk and he breathed a sigh of relief. Good riddance.

A portly truck driver stepped from behind the double-stacked pallets of paper and Sam froze. It wasn't the driver who struck him speechless, but the hulking angel standing *behind* the man, a claymore on his back. The angel's bushy blond eyebrows rose when he realized Sam could see him.

Sam had never seen an angel before. He'd asked Alvin about the paucity of spirits in the world and received a snarky remark about mankind breeding like rabbits. Too many people, not enough spirits to manage them.

The driver ignored Sam's expression, handed him the manifest for signature, then waddled off toward the restroom. His guardian angel didn't follow.

The receiving clerk's shrill voice drew Sam's attention. "Where's this going?" She waved at the pallets.

"Joe Harridan in Marketing." He and Joe had a good-natured feud and this was just the thing to ratchet it up a notch.

"Fine," the clerk said, looking sour. "But you're filling out the Form-5."

Sam grimaced, but nodded. The angel turned and marched through the bay door. Sam followed, trying to look nonchalant. Snow crunched underfoot. Sam folded his arms against winter's chill.

"You have a demon problem," the angel said in a voice that rumbled like thunder.

"Wow, that's direct. What happened to 'Oh my, you can see me'?"

"God works in mysterious ways."

Sam opened his mouth for another sarcastic retort, but the angel's lofty expression made him close it again. He already had a demon problem. Best not to add an angel problem, too.

The angel inclined his head. "I am Tobias. How did you acquire your demon?"

"Nicked myself on an ancient ceremonial dagger when I was still in the Army. I was helping catalog Iraqi artifacts when it happened. My third eye opened, I saw the little twit tormenting a Major, and I freaked out. Drew my weapon and, well, things went downhill from there. Alvin got excited when he realized I could see him, then disappeared. By the time the court-martial ended, he'd returned claiming he'd been assigned as my personal demon. Like a guardian angel, but in reverse. Any suggestions for getting rid of him?"

"Banish him to Hell with a blessed blade. He shan't return."

"Don't have one of those. Could *you* banish him?"

"My duties lie elsewhere. Were you of the faithful, I would offer a permanent solution involving prayer and supplication. However, I sense little faith within you."

Sam snorted. "Faith is the belief in things unseen. I see this little prat torment me every day. I'm more of a realist."

Tobias gazed skyward, then rumbled a sigh. "I can bless your blade if you have one at hand."

Sam *didn't* have one at hand but pursed his lips as an idea hit him. Making Tobias promise to wait, he dashed inside, snatched an empty folder from the receiving desk, and headed upstairs. He stepped onto the fifth floor at a brisk walk, head down, folder in hand. He'd discovered in the Army that a folder and a brisk pace were a magic shield against idle chit-chat and additional work. Everyone assumed you were doing Something Important and left you alone.

"Sam!" Langowski yelled, spying him from across the room.

Everyone, that is, except the boss. But even he could be fooled by the folder.

Sam waived his manila shield. "Working on it, sir!" Langowski's door slammed shut and Sam grinned. At his desk, he grabbed his blade—a six-inch broadsword letter opener he'd bought on a layover in Germany. He used it to add that necessary barbarism when opening official correspondence. One more masterful Hardworking Employee impression and Sam was back in the elevator.

In the loading bay, the driver had his truck's hood up, complaining about a temperamental starter. Sam eyed the angelic claymore thrust into the engine block but refrained from comment and headed outside.

Tobias raised an eyebrow when Sam presented his letter

opener. It must have passed muster because the angel laid hands upon it and prayed in Latin. Sam's miniature broadsword glowed brightly before returning to normal.

Tobias placed a weightless hand on Sam's shoulder, sending peace and tranquility through him. "May God bless you on your quest and bring you a little faith." Sam wasn't sure about that last part, but Heaven had just granted him a solution to his demon problem. He wasn't about to quibble.

Sam managed a solemn "Thank you" before Tobias returned to the truck, withdrew his claymore, and slid into the passenger seat. The driver climbed in beside his unseen passenger and tried the starter once more.

The claymore-free engine roared to life. Sam waved goodbye, and headed inside to slay his demon.

DEMON SLAYING in corporate America was more difficult than Sam expected. His tormentor seemed to have disappeared. By the end of the day, Sam's patience had run out. He tucked Faith —which seemed a fitting name for his blessed letter opener— into his suit jacket and went demon hunting. Sam searched three floors before he found Alvin sauntering out of the legal office, whistling a jaunty tune.

That wasn't good.

No matter. It was time to end this. Sam's eyes narrowed and his pulse raced. The hallway was empty.

He drew Faith and slashed. Alvin screeched and jumped back, clawed hands raised. Faith sliced his palm, releasing something black and gaseous.

"Hey, what's the big idea?" Alvin squawked, then glanced at his palm. "You got a blessed blade?! Oh, shi—"

With a *pop,* Alvin disappeared and Sam was free.

SAM ROLLED into work the next morning whistling Alvin's jaunty tune, his heart light. His whistle trailed off when he found Alvin sitting on his desk, arms crossed, red eyes furious.

"I thought I banished you," Sam said, his throat tight.

"You did." Alvin rose, fists clenched. "HR was … displeased."

"HR … on the first floor?"

"*Hell's Resources*, asshole. I'm getting audited because of you."

"But you were *banished*. How'd you get back?"

"Please." Alvin rolled his eyes. "Bureaucracy is my family name. We invented red tape. You think I couldn't short-list myself for a return trip?"

Shit.

Panic blanked Sam's mind. He drew Faith and lunged. Alvin dodged and scrambled over the cubicle wall. Sam had one hand on the wall and a knee on his desk, when the elevator dinged and Langowski stepped out.

"Sam! What the *hell* were you thinking filing a breach of contract against Waters? We just got that account!"

What?

Sam straightened and scowled, remembering Alvin's trip to legal. The little fiend! He sheathed Faith inside his jacket and trailed into Langowski's office. As the door closed behind him, he glanced back.

Alvin was perched atop the cubicle wall, fire in his eyes. He pointed a clawed finger. "I will destroy you."

The door clicked shut.

BETWEEN THE WATERS debacle and Alvin's tedious torments, Sam barely survived the week. Langowski threatened to fire him but clearly enjoyed having a verbal punching bag around. Sam kept trying to banish Alvin, but the slippery eel evaded him. By Friday, Sam despaired of catching the little beast. Besides, what was the point? He'd just bounce right back the next day.

Sam was stewing at his desk when a sharp New York accent made him glance up.

"Two pallets of pink paper? Good one, Sam."

Joe Harridan, Sam's rival from Marketing, grinned over the cubicle wall. Joe was tall, muscled, and a favorite among the ladies. Everything Sam wasn't. Sam leaned back and switched mental gears.

"Thought you'd like the challenge."

"I saw you coming a mile away." Joe pinned a pink flyer to the cubicle wall with his fingers. "Langowski just approved our Valentine's Day ad campaign. These babies go out this afternoon."

Sam scanned the pink trifold's beautiful display of Bridewell's office supplies. *Free shipping for the first hundred orders. Call now!* Sam's phone number was printed in large text at the bottom.

"You bastard," he said, admiring the subtlety. He'd have to man his phone all weekend or the campaign would flounder— and Sam would get blamed. It was a slick move, the kind Alvin might think up. Sam glanced around and spied the demon typing away in an unoccupied cubicle across the aisle.

"Takes one to know one," Joe replied cheerily and swaggered away. "I look forward to reading the results in your report. Good luck!"

Oh, yeah. Reports were due. Of all the screwed-up policies Alvin had implemented at Bridewell, the individual weekly reports were particularly insidious—an information overload that supervisors never read, preferring to invent their own lies. It hadn't taken long for Bridewell's employees to turn the reports into a game of creative exaggeration. Sam and Joe were the current battling champions.

Sam eyed Alvin, struck by the demon's intense focus. What was he doing? Sam tiptoed over then froze when he saw the screen. Alvin was typing a report to his superiors in Hell—on a Bridewell computer. Sam frowned. The company network was connected to the Underworld? That explained a lot about the IT department.

Sam slipped back to his desk and opened the share drive. He scanned folders, lips pursed, unsure what he was looking for.

Odd. There was a folder labeled Human Resources and another labeled HR. *Hell's Resources?*

Sam clicked and received a password request. He leaned back and pondered, fingers drumming the desk. Then he rocked forward, typed "Bureaucracy," and hit enter.

Bingo. Humans aren't the only ones with lazy passwords.

It contained a single folder titled SAMUEL DAVIDSON PROJECT which held five years of Alvin's reports. Unlike the rest of the share drive, these were neatly organized and—according to the metadata—unopened since Alvin wrote them. His boss never read his reports.

More importantly, Alvin's audit hadn't begun yet. It'd be a shame if those files disappeared.

A maniacal cackle built inside Sam's chest.

Select all. Shift-delete. Why yes, I *do* want to permanently delete all …

No. Not permanently. That was too cruel. Besides, a career of dealing with vindictive bureaucrats had ingrained the importance of keeping copies of *everything*. But he had to do something.

With a quick drag-and-drop, Sam moved the reports to his desktop.

A shriek erupted from across the aisle. "No-no-NO!" Sam spun his chair and watched with wicked glee as Alvin bolted for the elevator. Within seconds, the floor indicator descended to the basement, home of the IT department.

Nice try.

Sam disconnected his computer's network cable with a satisfied sigh. No demonic help desk would find those files now. Freedom was so close.

The office emptied out early, but Sam didn't leave. He'd attracted too much attention to skate out before the boss. He idly read Alvin's reports—such elegant malarkey—until Langowski finally left, taking the stairs.

The elevator slid open and Alvin stepped out, shoulders slumped. The file recovery had clearly failed. The little wretch climbed into his borrowed cubicle's chair and spun around slowly.

A pang of guilt wormed its way into Sam's heart. Perhaps he'd gone too far. But Alvin was a demon. Shouldn't the rules be different?

Sam eyed the clock and shelved the feeling for a moment. He had another problem that needed attention—Joe's pretty pink ad campaign. Sam dialed call-forwarding on his office phone then entered Joe's mobile number. Hopeful customers would start bombarding his rival's phone first thing tomorrow morning. Sam chuckled.

Your move, Joe.

The elevator dinged open, and Sam glanced up. His breath caught at the over-tall demon who ducked through the doors. Sam dropped behind his cubicle wall and peered into the aisle.

The demon was impossibly gaunt, like a stick figure drawn on Silly Putty then stretched until his horns brushed the ceiling. He wore a rumpled suit that matched Alvin's and gold-wire spectacles framed his red eyes. Clawed fingers drummed on an oversized clipboard as he scanned the room.

The Auditor had arrived.

The demon lumbered to Alvin's cubicle and spoke with a voice as dry as crumpled ash. "Alvin Bureaucracy?"

Alvin climbed onto the desk and stood eye-to-chest with the lanky demon. "Yes, *Auditor?*" he sneered. Nobody likes auditors.

"Your audit begins now. Should—*when*—you fail, you will be assigned a torment-coach from the Office of Micromanagement for on-the-job training."

Woah. The Office of Micromanagement? And Sam thought human bureaucracy was nasty. Plus, "on-the-job training" didn't sound promising for Sam's demon-free life.

The Auditor droned on. "In the improbable event that you pass, you will receive the promotion you were due"—he consulted his clipboard—"fifty-seven years ago."

Sam stifled a gasp. That was it. Alvin's overdue promotion was his ticket to freedom.

Parchment rustled as the Auditor flipped a page. "Bring up your reports."

Alvin stammered, but Sam popped up like a jack-in-a-box. "Found 'em!" The Auditor spun and blinked at Sam, who gave his most charming smile. "IT must have moved some folders around," he lied and waved at his screen. Alvin eyed Sam dubiously, but stalked over and clambered into his chair. The demon sagged in relief when he saw the reports.

The Auditor gaped at Sam. "You … can see us? Oh, my." He flipped through his clipboard. "There's nothing about that in my files."

Sam smirked. That's what happens when supervisors don't read reports. "Yup, and I'm glad I can. I couldn't ask for a better tormentor than Alvin."

"Really?" both demons said in unison.

"I've learned a lot from this little rascal. He's been making my life a living hell for five years!" No lie there. "Just today I used one of his tricks to ruin my coworker's weekend."

The Auditor's gaze swung toward Alvin, brows furrowed. "Your charge spreads torment on your behalf?"

"That's right." Alvin puffed out his chest, quick to take credit where none was due. "Pitting humans against each other is the epitome of evil."

"Indeed." The Auditor huffed. "This is most irregular." He adjusted his glasses and scanned his checklist. "Hmm. About those reports ..."

Sam stepped back as Alvin sailed through his audit, the Auditor bent double to see Sam's screen. He fingered Faith and contemplated banishing them both, but decided against it. Banishment was temporary. This plan would free him forever. It had to.

Finally, the Auditor rose to his full imposing height.

"So, how'd he do?" Sam asked brightly.

"I am ... surprised." The Auditor sighed like crackling embers. "Nobody passes my audits, but Alvin Bureaucracy's files were impeccable." He made a final checkmark and glared at his clipboard, as though searching for an error.

Sam wasn't surprised. He'd never met a nastier, more capable bureaucrat than Alvin.

The Auditor tucked his clipboard under an elbow and looked at Sam's tormentor. "I will file the Form-5 with HR for your promotion and reassignment." With another disappointed sigh, the lanky demon lumbered toward the elevator. Eyes bright, Alvin leapt from Sam's chair to follow.

Sam waved. "Good luck on the next assignment!" It had worked. In the name of all that was holy ...

The Auditor's clawed hand slapped the closing elevator doors, stopping them. Evil red eyes bored into Sam's. "I have noted you in my report, Samuel Davidson. Expect your replacement tormentor shortly."

Sam's jaw dropped and the door slid shut with a cheerful *ding*.

NO TORMENTOR ARRIVED over the weekend, so Sam wondered if he'd misheard the Auditor. It was too much to hope for, but hope and Faith were all he had. Driving to work on Monday, his hand kept drifting toward the blessed blade in his jacket.

He parked in the underground garage and plodded toward the elevators. He'd almost reached them when a gravelly voice behind him asked, "Samuel Davidson?"

Sam jumped and spun. A demon with long tusks and no sense of personal space fiddled with the buttons of his wrinkled suit. "Who's asking?" Sam's hand slipped inside his jacket.

A toothy grin spread across a face that even a mother couldn't love. "Brutus Bureaucracy, your new tormentor. I would have been here Saturday, but HR lost my paperwork. Twice." First-day nerves were obvious in Brutus's rushed speech. "My cousin Alvin assigned me—he's head of Bureaucratic Torments now—and, well, I'm so excited for this opportunity to make your life a living hell."

Sam's jaw clenched. No. Not again. He whipped out Faith and stabbed Brutus Bureaucracy in the shoulder. The demon looked at the blade in surprise before disappearing with a *pop*.

CLARISSA BUREAUCRACY ARRIVED the next day, a hulking horned gorilla who caught Sam outside the restroom. He hadn't slept well and overcompensated with coffee, so his bladder was ready to burst. He didn't have time for niceties. Sam banished the cheerful Clarissa before she even finished her introduction.

Desmond Bureaucracy was more cautious when he arrived on Wednesday. He approached Sam's cubicle while a coworker bent his ear about her grandson's adorable puke—complete with pictures. Sam was contemplating the comparative joys of a root canal when his new tormentor caught his eye. Desmond introduced himself over the old woman's prattling before skittering away.

Clever. Sam couldn't stab the demon with a coworker watching. Swinging a broadsword around the office, even a miniature broadsword, was frowned upon in corporate America. Still, Sam cornered Desmond the next day and banished him as he pilfered a Form-5 on its way to accounting.

The following week Sam banished Eugene, Francisco, and Gloria Bureaucracy. None were around long enough to provide more than annoyance-level torments, but this was getting old.

He arrived early on Friday and found Alvin sitting on his keyboard, arms crossed. His old nemesis looked pissed.

"You have to stop banishing my cousins. The Auditor is crucifying us!"

Sam hoped he was being figurative. "Stop sending them. You're the head of Bureaucratic Torments now. You can end this."

Alvin ran clawed fingers through his comb-over. "I can't. You impressed the Auditor and caught the attention of HR. Everyone wants to torment you!"

Sam fought the urge to banish the little twit and leaned against his cubicle, arms crossed. "So, I'm doomed to eternal torment because I helped you?"

"Well, living torment. The state of your eternal soul is still in question."

That made Sam pause, but he wasn't prepared to debate theology with a demon. He glared. There was only one way out.

It was time to make a deal with the devil.

"I don't have to banish your cousins," Sam said, and Alvin perked up. "Could you assign another cousin to me and then redirect them without Hell's Resources noticing?"

"I *am* the master of misdirected paperwork." Alvin's nasal tone was both cocky and cautious.

"Good. I don't care where they go so long as I don't see them. They can drink mimosas in Tahiti for all I care. I'll write their reports, giving every appearance of creatively perpetual torment, while you set up a rotating vacation schedule for your favored cousins."

"Won't work. Demons from outside the family have already elbowed their way into the Department of Bureaucratic Torments. They'll notice."

"Okay. Make the interlopers supervisors. Send them up here to check on your cousins and I'll banish them back to Hell. That will reinforce your need for resources while removing trouble-makers from your ranks." The little devil's eyes sparkled as the idea took hold. "You'll expand your empire, protect the family name, and get credit for tormenting me, while I"—Sam drew Faith and brandished it at Alvin—"will be free from you. Forever."

Alvin blanched at the blessed blade before Sam returned Faith to his pocket and asked, "So, do we have a deal?"

THE DEVIL IS in the details. Alvin should have paid closer attention when Sam sold his time instead of his soul. Sam carefully noted when the little cretin stopped reading his reports, then employed the digital form of his manila shield trick—with an added twist. He maintained his Hardworking Employee ruse, ensuring that files appeared exactly on schedule, but completely changed the tenor of their content.

He told the truth.

The reports became a confession of their deal—complete with a running tally of the demons banished on Alvin's behalf.

Sam signed them "Demon Slayer" and each report reached a single, inescapable conclusion.

Tormenting Samuel Davidson was not in Hell's best interests.

Hell's Resources would eventually notice the rising number of banishments and stop sending demons. Then Sam would be free. Until then, he would hunt demons and write his reports. He'd learned how to fight Hell's bureaucracy—from the inside and with proper documentation—and reveled in the challenge.

Knowledge wasn't a curse. It was power.

DAVID HANKINS WRITES from the thriving cornfields of Iowa where he lives with his wife, daughter, and two dragons disguised as cats. His writing journey began in the oral tradition of convincing his daughter to Go To Sleep with inventive stories. That usually backfired. After years of Just One More Story, David began transcribing his midnight ramblings in an attempt to keep his storylines straight. Children are ruthless in identifying mistakes in fairy tales. David writes lighthearted speculative fiction because that's what he loves to read and—this is the important bit—there's not nearly enough humor in the world. David aims to change that, one story at a time.

David joined the US Army after college and, through some glitch in the bureaucracy, convinced Uncle Sam to fund his wanderlust for twenty years. He has lived in and traveled through much of Europe, central Asia, and the United States. Now that he's retired from the Army, David devotes his time to his passions of writing, traveling with his family, and finding new ways to pay his mortgage.

A CRISIS OF FATE

Zach Shephard

Writing out the future is a pretty intimidating responsibility. Especially when you don't have total control over how things will work out. As fatescribes, my colleagues and I used to come up with ideas and project where they might lead, sometimes looking entire decades ahead. Problem is, after a certain point the butterfly effect becomes too bonkers to track, and we'd have no clue where anything is going anymore.

So let's say you come up with a brilliant new technology that'll make Thanksgiving turkeys juicier than ever before. And it works out great! You've built a better baster. But then turkey becomes so popular that people start to lose interest in the other traditional dishes. That's okay, though. You knew there would be side effects. Except things *really* take a turn when cranberry sauce becomes the first casualty of your Baste Rebellion. Demand drops to the point where farmers stop growing the crop. The canning factories shut down. Soon enough, cranberry sauce goes extinct entirely. Some families embrace this, and just cook a second, ultra-moist, turkey instead. Others revolt. Civil unrest breaks out, but it's pretty tame, since no one's really willing to die for a wiggly lump of can-shaped berry sludge. Still, one thing leads to another, and—as always—the butterfly effect rears its ugly head.

Twenty years later, Antarctica is on fire and some sadist invents grape ketchup. And it's probably your fault.

But that's just an example. All my *actual* failures as a fate-scribe were much worse. Luckily, I've been out of the game for a few centuries, and haven't had the chance to muck things up in a while.

Which brings us to last Thursday.

I was snacking on the couch in my one-bedroom apartment, contemplating what futures might have occurred if Cheez-Its had been triangle-shaped or made of pork. There was a knock at the door.

"Want me to get it?" Auster asked, her furry black butt sticking out from behind the TV stand. She'd been digging back there for the past few minutes, presumably either making a nest or vivisecting the Xbox. It's hard to tell with imps.

"Thanks, but I'll handle this one. You go on sacrificing my electronics to your dark lord."

A tiny paw shot into view, its thumb up. "Check."

I opened the door.

Her hair was teal with a pink streak through it, and she wore glasses that matched. The grinning, early-twenties woman stood half a foot shorter than me, and looked like she could have been a faerie from some future I'd forgotten I'd written. She clutched a manila envelope in both hands.

"Hi," I said. She just kept staring at me, smiling. I leaned my head into the hall and said to no one in particular: "Hey! I think your robot's busted."

That earned me a blink, which seemed like a great milestone in our budding conversation.

"Sorry," she said. "I'm a little starstruck."

Now it was my turn to blink. To the best of my knowledge, I wasn't any sort of celebrity.

The woman thrust her hand out. "I'm Christi."

We shook. "Dexter."

Something crashed behind me, followed by a skittering sound. Christi stood on her toes to get a look into the apartment. I turned to see Auster holding a mouse by the tail, dangling it over a mouth full of rune-etched fangs. She spotted us watching and froze.

Christi and I looked at each other.

"That's my … therapy gibbon."

Auster widened her pumpkin-orange eyes at me. It was the type of look you give someone when they've put you on the spot and you have no idea what sound a gibbon makes.

"Really?" Christi asked. "Because it looks like an imp."

Auster visibly relaxed. The mouse remained tense, eyes darting like a bystander caught in a Mexican standoff.

"You," I said, pointing at Christi, "are not an average robot."

"Right—sorry. You still don't know what's going on. I'm from the fatescribe office."

I took another glance into the hall to ensure she wasn't overheard, then ushered Christi inside.

"Auster," I said, shutting the door, "do me a favor and take your new friend into the bedroom. I'm gonna need a minute."

Auster tucked the mouse under her arm like a duffel bag and trotted off. At the doorway she turned, gazed at her upraised paw like a proud thespian, and declared: "*Meowf.*"

I shrugged at Christi. "If that's not a gibbon, I don't know what is." I swiped some crumbs off the couch and offered her a seat, while Auster exited with a theatrical bow.

"So," I said, taking the recliner, "fatescribe office. I haven't visited in a while. How're things over there?"

"Not great. We're having a bit of a problem with"—she winced—"time."

"That's a tough one. Have you tried duct tape?"

"No, but it's funny you should mention that. The issue is that time's splitting apart. See, about a century ago, a fatescribe wrote a future that—in a roundabout way—led to a dimensional portal opening in Nebraska in the forties."

"I'm familiar. I got a therapy gibbon out of the deal."

"Right—duh. I read that in your file." Her gaze dropped. "Sorry. I'm just an intern."

"You're doing fine." I offered her some Cheez-Its, and apologized that they weren't triangle shaped. "Go on."

"The portal did something to the fabric of time. Up until now, every era—past and future—has been connected into a sort of patchwork, how they should be. But now they're drifting apart. My boss calls it Temporal Pangaea."

"Is that as bad as it sounds?"

"Not necessarily. Charlie's confident we can fix the problem, but he doesn't want to take any chances. Which is why he's calling in some reserves."

"Whoa," I said, holding up both hands. "I'm retired. Which is probably for the best."

"Charlie said you'd say that. But you've seen more of human history than anyone. It's not like any other fatescribes have written themselves into immortality."

"To be clear, that was an accident. Which just proves my point: even back then, I had no idea how to write a good, reliable fate. I can't imagine how I'd be after decades of atrophy."

"Doesn't change the fact that you're the most experienced person for the job."

I felt a headache coming on, and rubbed my temples accordingly. "Look, I tried to come out of retirement once, in the late eighties. Charlie was young, and wanted to start his tenure with a bang. So he asked if I'd whip something up, thinking it would be great to see a fate written by the oldest scribe in existence."

"And? How'd it go?"

"I came up with an accident-based music called 'blunderthump.'"

Christi tried hiding a face-scrunch, but only did a so-so job. "That … could be good," she said.

"Blunderthump was projected to cause vertigo in bald eagles."

"That's less good."

I turned my palms up, shrugging. "Lucky for us, Charlie passed on the idea. He let glam metal go on for a few more years instead."

"Okay, so blunderthump may not have been your best work. But that doesn't mean you can't try again! After so many years of inactivity, you might find the work fulfilling."

"Objection!" Auster stepped into the room, a clawed finger upraised. "Work is hard. Giving up is easy."

"My counsel raises some excellent points." I gave Auster a nod, then saw something that elicited a double-take.

"What?" Auster asked, grabbing the two tiny horns nestled in her bristly fur. "Are they glowing again? I swear, I haven't eaten any batteries since Thursday!"

"Today's Thursday. I watched you eat an entire bowl of Duracell Toast Crunch this morning. But that's not the issue." I gestured at the mouse beside her, sitting on his haunches.

"Oh. This is Nic."

"You … named your lunch?"

"He's not lunch. We worked it out while we eavesdropped on your conversation." She draped an arm over the mouse's shoulders and pulled him close. He gave a cheesy grin.

Christi, who'd already shrugged off the presence of an imp, seemed equally unfazed by the addition of a rodent to my family. She ignored the duo and handed me her manila envelope.

"I hope you'll at least give it a look," she said, standing. "As far as I'm concerned, you're the best guy for the job."

I escorted her to the door. She stopped and turned.

"Before I go, can I ask a favor?"

"Shoot."

"Will you sign this?"

She handed me a trading card from a set called "Sweet Treats." On the front was an artist's rendition of an ice cream float. On the back were some dubious ideas about what constitutes a balanced diet.

"All right," I said, "but this is *not* a flattering picture of me."

She smiled in my doorway, bringing our interaction full-circle.

"Seriously though," I said, accepting her pen, "I'm gonna need you to explain the significance here."

She shrugged, looked away. "I've spent a lot of time going through records at the office. I'm a fan of your work. Everyone there is."

"Ah," I said, pointing the pen at her. "A blunderthump groupie. I get a lot of those." I pinned the card against the doorframe and scribbled my John Hancock.

"Are you deflecting with humor because you have no faith in your own work?"

"We've only known each other for ten minutes. Please stop looking directly into my soul." I handed her the card.

She gave me a curious look. "You don't actually know, do you?"

"Know what?"

"Ice cream floats. Invented in Philadelphia in 1874. A historian at the office did some backtracking, and found they originated from a fate written over a hundred years earlier—by one Dexter Adams." She held the card up, tapped the picture. "We have you to thank for the greatest dessert known to humankind. Might be something to think about when you're deciding whether or not to come out of retirement."

And she was gone, leaving me to stand in the doorway, alone with my thoughts.

BACK WHEN I'D been actively scribing, we'd gotten our ideas for fates by listening to the people they'd affect—witnessing their prayers, eavesdropping on their conversations, that sort of thing. But according to the information in Christi's envelope, times had changed. Nowadays, most "prayers" came in the form of easily accessible social media posts. Not a bad system, if you could wade through all the conspiracy theories and bigotry.

Now that it was time to work, I just—couldn't. What if my fates were no good? What if they made things worse? Fate-scribing for the first time in thirty-three years was already a daunting prospect; it got even worse when I remembered the goal was to *stop time itself from splitting apart.*

I shook the thoughts away. At the very least, I could try. I was, after all, the fatescribe responsible for ice cream floats. Apparently.

I opened my laptop and scrolled Facebook. Before long, I found the seed for a fate: a post from a new dog owner, venting about the housebreaking process. I could certainly relate, having lived with an imp who once decided toilets were "a scam run by the fat-cats at Big Sewer."

I grabbed a pen. Surely we could fix the housebreaking problem. Hopefully without giving Fido any additional heads.

Without thinking too much, I started scribbling.

Things got off to a rocky start, like they always did. But once I hit my groove, the ideas began to flow. It was like I wasn't even in conscious control of my actions. (Which was probably a good thing, for liability purposes.)

By the end, I had a full sheet—my first in decades. I'd be lying if I said it didn't make me smile.

I read from the beginning, reminding myself it was a first draft—it didn't have to be stellar. Things started normally enough. But as the butterfly effect kicked in, my solution to the housebreaking problem produced some pretty substantial side effects. In two decades, Hawaii would only be accessible by … train?

That sounded expensive.

I scratched out a few paragraphs and did some new writing. The pen took over once more.

By the end, I'd killed off every species of dolphin and detonated the Matterhorn.

With a heavy sigh, I dropped the pen and sunk into the couch. After a long face-rub I saw Auster leaving the kitchen, her mouse-buddy in tow. I wasn't about to let a good distraction pass.

"Auster!" I said. "Just the imp I was looking for."

She and Nic froze in their tracks, like burglars when the lights flick on. Her eyes darted back and forth. As if coming upon an idea, she stood at attention.

"Don't worry, citizen," she said. "My best detective and I are on the case. We *will* find the man who ate your pie!"

Nic popped stiffly onto his haunches and gave a sharp salute. He was pretty clearly trying not to look at the custard dripping from his paw.

"I look forward to some closure on the matter." I waved them over, and they sat by my feet. "So—you speak mouse?"

"Don't need to," Auster said. "Nic's gotten smarter just from hanging around me." She shrugged. "Imp magic. How's the work?"

"Not great. Everything I write is bad."

"I'll be the judge of that." She held out a palm. "Gimme."

I passed her the paper. Her eyes flashed across it, back and forth. The silence wasn't encouraging.

"You don't have to lie," I said. "It's not great."

"Sure, but it's *your* garbage."

"I never said it was gar—"

"Listen: if there's one thing I know, it's the human brain.

And right now, yours is being dumb. Not your fault—it's a medical condition. Encephadoofus. But we can overcome this! I mean, you did this fatescribbling stuff for, like—decades, right? Seems you could remember how it works. Unless you never knew in the first place, and were faking it the whole time. In which case: *respect*." She held her paw out for a fist-bump, but my heart wasn't in it. Nic made a vertical leap to sharply tap her knuckles with his.

As much as I hated to think about it, she was right. I never was any good at this. I'd faked it through my entire career.

"You know what you need?" she asked. "Some fresh air. Nic and I are going to the park. You should come."

"Let's go back to the part where you think you're allowed outside without supervision."

"Well, sure. That's why you're coming." She jumped onto my lap, rubbing her catlike ears against my arm. I sighed in resignation.

"You're right—I could stand to clear my head. Grab some bread, and something to hide Nic."

"Way ahead of you," she said. "I made him a tiny pair of Groucho Marx glasses."

"On second thought, let's just leave him under the blanket."

I corralled my miniature menagerie into the bassinet stroller, and off we went.

THE PARK WAS pretty barren in the middle of a weekday: the only person we passed was a lone jogger, who didn't give my stroller a second glance. I parked us at a bench by the lake and sat. Auster and Nic popped up from the blanket to watch the ducks.

"So, what's your next step?" Auster asked.

"With the fatescribing? I don't know. I guess I try again."

She nodded wisely, eyes narrowed at the water. "Yeah. That's a good idea. Especially if you like making yourself sad."

"I feel a psychoanalysis coming. That, or the Cheez-Its aren't sitting well."

"Probably both. Listen: I like you, Dex. Always have."

"When we first met you bit me seven times."

"Those were love punctures. Traditional imp greeting. Anyway, I want you to be happy. And I'm pretty sure what you're doing now is gonna make that tough."

She wasn't wrong. I didn't handle failure well, despite my unfortunate familiarity with it.

"I've watched this movie before," she said, tossing some bread chunks to the ducks. "You'll get an idea for what you wanna do. It'll look great on paper. Then, once you need to put it on *actual* paper, bam!" She hucked the entire slice of bread, eliciting an indignant *quack*. "You'll hit a wall and give up. Next thing you know, I'm eating socks for dinner because someone's too mopey to go to the store."

"You eat socks even when I buy food. I had to put a lock on my dresser."

"Don't change the subject," she said, her voice muffled by the snack-sock she'd smuggled along.

I leaned forward, ran my hands through my hair. Why'd Christi have to come along and believe in me? I'd been perfectly content to exist without ambition, like a human barnacle.

"The whole thing's probably not a big deal anyway," Auster said. "So what if time pulls apart a little? It probably stretches more than we give it credit for. I doubt anything *bad* is gonna happen."

Right on cue, the center of the lake exploded upward. Water droplets shimmered in the sun like a diamond geyser, falling to reveal a breaching plesiosaur.

Yes, an honest-to-God plesiosaur.

Nessie's gaze fixed on us, her elongated neck stretching

toward the sky. She spread her jaws and let out a crocodilian hiss.

The imp and mouse backpedaled in their bassinet, staring wide-eyed at the spectacle. "Dex," Auster said, "I don't like the look of that duck."

The lake-monster dove under the surface. A very large, very fast shadow shot straight toward us. I didn't want to be around when it realized we were out of bread.

As I fumbled for the stroller a silver streak zipped overhead, toward the lake. The jet-propelled robot stopped in the air and turned our way.

"Stand aside, citizen!" it said, raising a laser-sword. "I'll handle this!" It dove into the water, blue and red lights spinning on its shoulders.

When all the thrashing stopped, bubbles and monster blood rose to the surface. A disembodied robot head bobbed up a moment later.

Auster and I looked at each other. She shrugged, forcing an uneasy smile. "I mean, it *might* be unrelated."

Nothing like a day at the park to relax your mind. I grabbed the stroller and speed-walked home, where urgent work awaited.

JUST TWENTY-FOUR HOURS after leaving the park, I found myself sitting on the far end of the couch, opposite a notepad covered in frustrated scribbles. Normally, this was the point at which I'd give up and move on with my life. But Christi's motivational speech about ice cream floats nagged at my mind.

I glanced sidelong at my nemesis, the notepad. I sighed. "I should probably get back to work."

"Quiet," Auster said, eyes glued to the TV. "This is getting good."

We were three hours into a Netflix binge, which Auster had suggested when the fatescribing was going nowhere. She'd insisted I might find inspiration in some of her favorite "timeless storytelling."

It was a reality show about dyslexic chickens called *Fustercluck*.

"Yep," I said, slapping both hands onto my knees. "I've definitely hit a new low in procrastination." I pushed myself to my feet. Nic took up residence in the me-shaped imprint on the couch, nibbling a piece of popcorn as he watched the show.

Christi visited to check on my progress. Her hair was in braids that day, like a pair of teal and pink barber poles.

"Things are going great," I said, inviting her inside. "I even have a draft that manages to sink Australia in a Noah-level catastrophe. Lots of promise in that one."

She bit her lip, as if anticipating a sharp pain. "Does it fix our time problem?"

I shrugged. "For Australia, sort of." I offered her a seat at the kitchen table and rummaged through the fridge for my least expired bottle of juice, like a proper host. "And speaking of the problem, I gather it's a lot more serious than you let on."

Christi turned bright red. "What makes you say that?"

"Yesterday I watched a dinosaur and robot mutilate each other in a lake. Second-weirdest Wrestlemania I've ever seen."

Christi propped her elbows on the table, rubbing her forehead with both hands. "I'm sorry, Dexter. I should have been more honest with you."

"It's okay." I brought us some cranberry juice and sat. "Although you should probably tell me the whole story now."

"All right. The truth is, this Temporal Pangaea situation is … bad. As in, 'potentially world ending' bad. Bits of different time periods are showing up in the present, and no one's been able to write a fate that can stop it. That's why Charlie wanted to call you in. You're kind of our last hope."

"I'm our last hope. For saving the world."

She nodded over the brim of her juice glass.

"Perfect," I said. "This is the exact amount of pressure I needed to completely cease functioning as a human. Please feed my imp while I'm vegetating."

From the other room: "We're low on socks!" *Burp.*

Christi reached across the table, laying her hand over my wrist. "Dexter, I know you have a hard time believing in yourself. But I've looked through the records. You've done a lot of great work as a fatescribe."

"That's the problem. Every time I stumble into success, it just ups the expectations for the next time. People assume I know what I'm doing, but the truth is I'm clueless. Even when I *do* manage to do something right, I get there by such a wonky path that I can't recreate the steps."

"I think you're better at this than you give yourself credit for. Look!" She pulled from her backpack a folder, stamped with the seal of the fatescribe office. "This is one of your best works. I mean, it's no ice cream float, but it's good."

I checked the file's label.

"Atlantis?" I asked. "I'm guessing you didn't read this one to the end."

"I did. You created *mermaids*, Dexter."

"And thanks to an awful creative choice, I also *doomed* mermaids."

"Oh, come on. Not every design can be perf—"

"I put their gills in their butts."

I thought back to the carefree marine folk, who only got to enjoy a short existence before going extinct. Poor assbreathers never stood a chance.

"So?" Christi asked. "Everyone screws up. Even the people who supposedly know what they're doing. They just hide it better. The point is, you came up with an entirely new *species*—

one that still fills our imaginations all these years later. Any fate-scribe would kill for that kind of creativity."

"And *I'd* kill for some better TV," Auster said, hopping onto her stool at the table. "Some schmuck mucked-up *Fustercluck*." She slammed an empty shot glass onto the table.

"Reality TV definitely needs better writers," I said, pouring her a splash of my drink. She threw it back in one gulp, hissing at the burn of my finest zero-proof juice.

"So, what's the deal with the project?" she asked.

"Same as before," Christi said. "Dexter wants to help, but doesn't think he can."

Auster gave me a long look. Finally, she rolled her orange eyes, slumping dramatically. "Ugh, fine. If this is what you really want, I'll get you started. But don't blame me if this blows up in your face." She pulled my laptop over and opened it.

"Okay, check this out." Auster turned the screen toward me. "Here's a dumb comment you left on a dumb Facebook post. The whole situation is dumb. And you're right there in the middle of it, like the King of All Dumb."

"As pep talks go, this isn't your best."

She ignored me and pointed a claw at the screen. "See that? Your comment got the most reactions, and they're all laughs. You know why? Because the whole discussion was stupid and it didn't matter. You're funny when you're not trying so hard. That's when you do your best writing."

She wasn't wrong. The words flowed when all I was looking for was a quick gag. Unfortunately, it's hard to channel that same ease and confidence when your work actually matters.

"Besides, times have changed," Auster continued. "You've got to adapt. I read some of your failed drafts. Too flowery. No one talks like that anymore. Just write a fate like you're leaving a dumb comment on Facebook, and it'll be a breeze."

Christi shrugged. "Couldn't hurt to try. Worst case scenario, you give us something entertaining to read before the world ends."

And so, despite my better judgment, I decided to give it another shot. Not because I had a sudden surge in confidence, but because my friends kept nagging me for another twenty minutes. Perseverance, thy name is peer pressure.

I spent the rest of the day writing. Some of it was okay. Some of it was bad. About fifteen percent looked like a resignation letter written by an angry seismograph. I have to admit, though, that Auster's advice helped. Treating the survival of the world like meaningless Facebook banter removed some of my self-imposed roadblocks. Of course, it also probably put humanity in dire peril. But at least I got a few chuckles out of Nic.

Christi texted me throughout the day, both to check on my progress and to share news of various time periods bleeding into the present. The updates stressed me out, but I kept plugging away.

By 2:00 A.M. I lay on the floor exhausted, frustrated, and surrounded by sheets of paper in various stages of crumpling. My wrist hurt from the scribbling. My eyes hurt from the crying. My brain hurt from the everything.

A text came in from Christi, which Auster was kind enough to read aloud. Something about things getting a lot worse. I was too fried to catch the full effect. That's the last thing I remember before passing out.

IF I'D BEEN alert enough for my reflexes to function normally, I probably would have spat my coffee all over Auster. Instead, I calmly swallowed, set the mug on the kitchen table, and said: "I'm sorry ... you *what?*"

"I delivered one of your fates to Christi. She texted while you were out. Said she needed something right away. Couldn't wait any longer." Auster scrolled through my phone. "Also, you need more games on this thing. TurboTax isn't fun once you beat the top score."

I took the phone and checked the conversation with Christi. "Hang on," I said. "You didn't send her anything."

"Sure I did. It was the hard copy."

"You left the apartment while I was out?"

"Hey! You think I'd betray your trust like that? No. I sent Nic."

I rubbed my eyes with the heels of my palms. "This is bad."

"Nah—I went through all your fates and grabbed the best one. It starts with mutiny at a fudge-processing plant."

I thought a moment. "Is that the one with the seagulls?"

"Yep!"

"You *have* to understand why that's bad for the ecosystem." I started texting Christi. "Maybe it's not too late to stop this."

Apparently it was, in fact, too late to stop this. Charlie had approved the fate and rushed it into production a few hours earlier. And now, for reasons Christi didn't explain, she needed me to meet her right away. At the carnival.

I got dressed. By the time I returned to the living room, Auster was peeking out of my backpack by the front door.

"Okay," I said. "Let's hear the pitch."

She spread her arms wide. "The fate of the world may be at stake. You're gonna need all the help you can get."

I nodded. "I suppose I can't argue with that."

"Also, I want cotton candy."

"There it is."

I zipped her in and slung the backpack over my shoulders. In the doorway, I took one last look at the chaos that was my apartment: papers strewn about, pizza boxes covered in scribbled notes, pillows on the floor from when my process had taken me there. It reminded me of my prolific days as a fatescribe, so long ago, and how good it had felt whenever my hard work resulted in something decent. The mess before me was full of ideas—the kind I used to dream up regularly, but hadn't explored in decades. Even if the drafts weren't great, at least they existed, and that meant something. I couldn't help but smile. For the first time in a while, I felt good about—

A sharp kick struck my back.

"Christi was pretty clear about the urgency," Auster said, muffled by the backpack. "And that Ferris wheel isn't gonna ride itself."

I patted one of the straps. "Don't know what I'd do without you, friend."

"Probably make a lot of bad financial decisions. Now let's move!"

THE CARNIVAL WAS PRETTY standard fair-fare: games, rides, and fried treats so expensive they came with a payment plan. The gates had just opened for the day, so things were still pretty quiet. A few colorful clowns roamed the midway, not yet in character.

"Dexter!"

I turned to see a teal-and-pink-haired clown I knew, rushing from between two game booths. Christi came to a stop, short of breath.

"Thank goodness you're here," she said. "We need your help."

"'We'?"

"The doctors!"

I looked in the direction from whence Christi had come, where a group of clowns vaped by the dart booth. One of them noticed some caramel on his elbow and tried licking it off.

"I have concerns about their medical credentials," I said.

"What?" Christi looked that way. "No! I—okay, hang on."

She composed herself, letting out a deep breath. "The fate you wrote. It's changed things. A lot."

"Already? It's only been a few hours."

"Well, a bunch of it hasn't actually happened yet. But the later stuff has."

"I was *just* starting to gain confidence in my work. Please tell me I didn't break causality."

"You didn't. Well—I don't think so, anyway. I'm no expert on time travel."

Auster popped up from my backpack. "I've seen every episode of *Quantum Leap* and dressed up as the Terminator last Halloween. Point me toward the time crisis."

At the sound of her voice, Nic emerged from Christi's jacket pocket and leapt onto my arm, scurrying up to Auster. Their reunion sounded squeaky.

"Time travel," I said to Christi. "Go."

"Okay. So Charlie extrapolated on your fate and realized it would eventually lead to time travel. That's why he green-lit the idea—he figured if *we* can't solve Temporal Pangaea, maybe someone from the future can." She poked a thumb over her shoulder. "There's a sideshow tent that doesn't get used until evening. A couple of doctors showed up in it. They're from the future, and they've got a machine that can fix things."

"This all sounds like good news. I'm waiting for the 'but.'"

"But ... there's something wrong with the machine. We're hoping you can figure it out."

"I once tried to un-jam a toaster with a toilet plunger. I may not be the mechanical troubleshooter you're looking for."

Without warning the world flickered once, like a 1950s TV set searching for a signal. I shook the sensation away.

"Bad news," I said. "I think there's something wrong with my antenna."

By way of response, a wide-eyed Christi tugged my arm and pointed where she was looking.

The group of formerly colorful clowns were now grayscale, as though they'd stepped out of a black-and-white movie. Their vaporizers had been swapped for cigarettes. They looked us over with a serious stink-eye, but otherwise minded their business.

"So," I said to Christi, "about our time problem ..."

Without wasting another moment, she led the way.

We raced through a maze of booths, across dry and trampled grass. All around us, pieces of the world shifted: a prehistoric plant sprung up and swayed overhead; the Ferris wheel got some flashy sci-fi upgrades; a confused-looking frontiersman stopped baiting his trap to go investigate the corn dogs.

Christi led us into a tent. The inside was the size of a convenience store, lit by spotlights around the perimeter. Near the back stood an obelisk-shaped machine and a big table, both laboratory-white. Tending to the equipment was a pair of doctors with dark ponytails and army-green bomber jackets; they could have been sisters. One of them noticed us and ran over.

"You must be the fatescribe," she said with a vaguely British accent. "I'm Dr. Zosa."

"Dexter. I hear you've got a solution to our time problem," I said, just as something decidedly dinosaur-sounding hissed outside.

"We do. Or rather, we should. But the machine's not behaving. Come—I'll show you."

She led us to the obelisk, full of flashing buttons and touchscreens. It looked like an ATM had gained sentience and was trying to bring back disco.

"This is Dr. Anderson," Dr. Zosa said. The second doc didn't acknowledge us, being too busy fiddling with the table. She adjusted the four gun turrets—for lack of a better term—on the corners, pointing their barrels toward the center.

"Hold on," Dr. Anderson said, to no one in particular. "I want to try something."

Dr. Zosa gestured for us to step back. Her partner placed a funnel cake in the middle of the table. Auster climbed halfway out of the backpack and onto my shoulder, with Nic perched alongside her.

"Dex?" she said, her voice filled with childlike concern. "What's she doing to that funnel cake?"

I scratched beneath her ear. "Don't worry. Everything's going to be fi—"

With a loud mechanical whir the turrets unleashed four green laser beams, converging on the funnel cake. There was a high-pitched squeal, but I wasn't sure if it came from the burning fair-food or Auster and Nic's horrified shrieks. When the beams subsided, all that was left was a pile of bubbling slop.

"Just let the world die," Auster said. "I don't want to live here anymore." Nic buried his face in her fur and wept.

Dr. Anderson sighed, slumping. She scraped the funnel-slop off the table with a spatula and pitched it over her shoulder, into a mound of similarly gooified remains. "We're so close," she said, gaze locked on the table. "The machine works. We just can't find the right material."

Dr. Zosa guided me away, giving her partner some space. "The machine's design was based on your work," she said. "We analyzed the events that had sprung from your fate and led to our point in time. That told us what manner of device we'd need to combat Temporal Pangaea. But as my associate indicated, there's still the issue of the material. *Something* needs to absorb the energy from those beams. We just don't know *what.*"

I looked at the mound of goo in the corner. It was like a witch's cauldron had gone on the rollercoaster and barfed.

"I take it the trial-and-error approach isn't working," I said.

"It's not. Which is why we require your expertise." She tapped one of the obelisk's screens, bringing up a document. "This text summarizes the events that led to our machine, stemming from your original fate. I need you to find what we missed."

"As much as I'd like to help, I'm no engineer."

"I'm aware. But engineering has failed us. We need a new perspective. Please—at least give it an honest attempt."

I looked to Christi. She gave an enthusiastic grin and two thumbs up. I sighed.

"I'm going to need a pen and paper. And these two could use a snack." I set Auster and Nic down, faced the obelisk, and got to work.

IN ALL MY years of fatescribing, I'd never had the opportunity to analyze the real-world effects of one of my fates that technically hadn't happened yet. Time travel is weird.

The process ended up being strangely similar to fatescribing, though. As I scrolled through the obelisk's documents, I found myself subconsciously making notes on my pad. It often felt like the pen was doing the driving, which was good, because if I'd been behind the wheel we'd have ended up in a ditch.

While I worked, we got plenty of reminders about the urgency of our situation. At one point a cyberpunk-looking biker with a red mohawk protruding from his helmet burst into the tent, a Molotov cocktail raised in one hand. He stopped and looked side to side, taking the place in. He relaxed from his throwing stance.

"Sorry," he said. "Thought this was the mainframe."

"*Viva la revolución!*" Auster yelled, her fist raised. She resumed eating her caramel apple, while the biker awkwardly backed out of the tent.

Next thing I knew, I was done. I called Dr. Zosa over.

"You were right," I said. "I don't have to be an engineer. I was able to follow the fate lines to see how this all works."

She raised her eyebrows. "And?"

"For starters, you need organic matter on that table. Which you probably won't find in any fair food. Secondly, the matter needs to be old. The machine is supposed to grab onto something from the past and pull it into the present—sort of like a needle and thread bringing ripped cloth together."

"Of course!" Dr. Zosa said. "And the older the organic material is, the more effective the machine will be."

"That's the way I see it."

She thought a moment, then snapped her fingers. "A tree! We need the oldest tree we can find."

Christi chimed in: "There's an old-growth forest an hour from here! Those trees are ancient. Come on—we've gotta move!"

She grabbed my arm and tried to run, but thanks to our size difference she just sort of pedaled in place like a cartoon character. Eventually she gave up and tilted her head at me, confused.

"No time for a tree," I said. "And no need, either." I pointed both index fingers at my face. "Immortal, remember? You're gonna be hard-pressed to find organic material older than me."

"No," Christi said, eyes wide and head shaking. "No no no. You saw what happened to the funnel cake. I don't want you as a goo pile."

"I've got the perfect jawline for a goo pile and you know it. Besides, this just … makes sense. My fate is what got us here. I want to see it through to the end. And on that note, I should be thanking you."

Christi raised an eyebrow. "For?"

"For getting me to scribe again. I'd forgotten how fulfilling this work can be once you get past the hard bits. It's nice seeing a final product in action."

"Well I'm happy for you, but I don't know that this is a good enough reason to put yourself in the goo-beams."

"Hey, you're the one who's always trying to get me to believe in myself." I held up my notepad. "If my predictions are right, there's a good chance I'll be okay."

Christi chewed her lip. "Well … if you're immortal, I guess there's no risk regardless, right?"

While it was true I'd stopped aging a long time ago, I didn't actually know if I could be killed. Not something I'd bothered to test. I could have told Christi a lie to make her feel better, but that didn't seem right. Instead, I just shrugged and put on a smile.

"Guess we'll find out."

When I tried moving to the table, I realized something was impeding my progress.

"Dex?" Auster said, looking up from where she clung to my leg. There was a rare sadness in her orange eyes. "Be safe." Nic scurried over to my other leg, hugging it as best as his tiny arms allowed. I squatted and scooped them up for a group hug.

"Don't worry about me," I said. "I've had all my laser vaccinations."

The world outside rumbled, shaking the tent.

"That's my cue." I set the fuzzies down and lay on the table. Christi came to my side, tears brimming.

"When this is over," she said, "we're all celebrating."

"It's a deal," I said. "Now you should probably stand back—spectators in the first three rows may get wet."

"Not funny!" she said, as Dr. Zosa escorted her away.

Dr. Anderson, by the obelisk, looked to me for confirmation. I nodded. She pressed a button.

The lasers hummed to life and everything got very, very green.

It's a strange sensation, waking up as a sticky blob. It was definitely colder than I'd expected.

Vision returned. Above me, five grins smiled down. Christi and the docs seemed relieved and happy. Nic danced like a Peanuts character. Auster looked like one of those cats who only waits three minutes to eat their dead owner.

"Am I goo?" I asked. "Because I feel like goo."

"We needed something to wake you up," Christi said. "Auster donated her snow cone."

The imp placed her nonexistent hat over her heart. "Its sacrifice will be memorialized for generations." She sniffled.

"I've always thought we could use another federal holiday," I said. Then, to the docs: "So—I've got a question."

"Yes," Dr. Zosa said, her smile widening. "The machine worked. Everything's going back to normal."

"Good," I said, and rested my eyes. "That's good."

"'*Good*'?" Christi asked, yanking me to my feet. "It's a lot better than *good*. It's reason to celebrate! And I know just how to do it." She grinned, just as she had in my doorway on the day we'd met.

The five of us followed her to a food booth she'd spotted earlier. She bought us a round of treats and made a short toast, which Auster made considerably longer. I added that I never could have done anything without the help of my friends, which was the absolute truth. Nic squeaked something I chose to believe was heartwarming, and the docs chipped in a few choice words. When all was said and done, we tapped our plastic cups together, gave a good cheer, and dug into our ice cream floats.

ZACH SHEPHARD WRITES FANTASY, science fiction, and horror stories, but only when he believes in himself, which is never. Luckily, he's got a very supportive group of friends and family, who stubbornly insist he keep trying with this whole "word artist" business. So really, it's *their* fault you had to read

"A Crisis of Fate." (Which, in a pinch, could serve as Zach's autobiography.)

Zach's had stories published in volumes 1, 4, 5, 6, and 7 of the Unidentified Funny Objects series. He's also appeared in *The Magazine of Fantasy & Science Fiction*, several of Flame Tree Publishing's Gothic Fantasy anthologies, and a number of (debatable, quite frankly) police reports. For a complete list of his stories, check out www.zachshephard.com.

ACKNOWLEDGMENTS

We'd like to thank everyone involved in making this book possible: associate editors Frank Dutkiewicz, James Miller, and Tarryn Thomas; copyeditor Elektra Hammond, graphics designer Jay O'Connell, cover artist Tomasz Maronski, proodreaders Aysha Rehm, Alicia Cay, Michael Haynes, Candice Lisle, and Gary Lee Webb; and many others whose talent and hard work made this a better book.

ABOUT THE EDITOR

Alex Shvartsman is a writer, anthologist, translator, and game designer from Brooklyn, NY. He's the winner of the 2014 WSFA Small Press Award for Short Fiction and a two-time finalist (2015 and 2017) for the Canopus Award for Excellence in Interstellar Writing.

He's the author of the *Eridani's Crown* (2019), *The Middling Affliction* (2022), and *Kakistocracy* (2023) fantasy novels. His short stories have appeared in *Analog, Nature, Strange Horizons, Intergalactic Medicine Show,* and a variety of other magazines and anthologies. Most are collected in *Explaining Cthulhu to Grandma and Other Stories* (2015) and *The Golem of Deneb Seven and Other Stories* (2018).

In addition to the UFO series, he has edited *The Cackle of Cthulhu, Humanity 2.0, Funny Science Fiction, Coffee: 14 Caffeinated Tales of the Fantastic,* and *Dark Expanse: Surviving the Collapse* anthologies.

His website is www.alexshvartsman.com.

THE MIDDLING AFFLICTION: CHAPTER 1

Alex Shvartsman

Please enjoy the first chapter of *The Middling Affliction*, book one of the Conradverse Chronicles, by UFO editor Alex Shvartsman.

"SHVARTSMAN DELIVERS A LAUGH-OUT-LOUD, SNARKY ADVENTURE" – *Publishers Weekly*

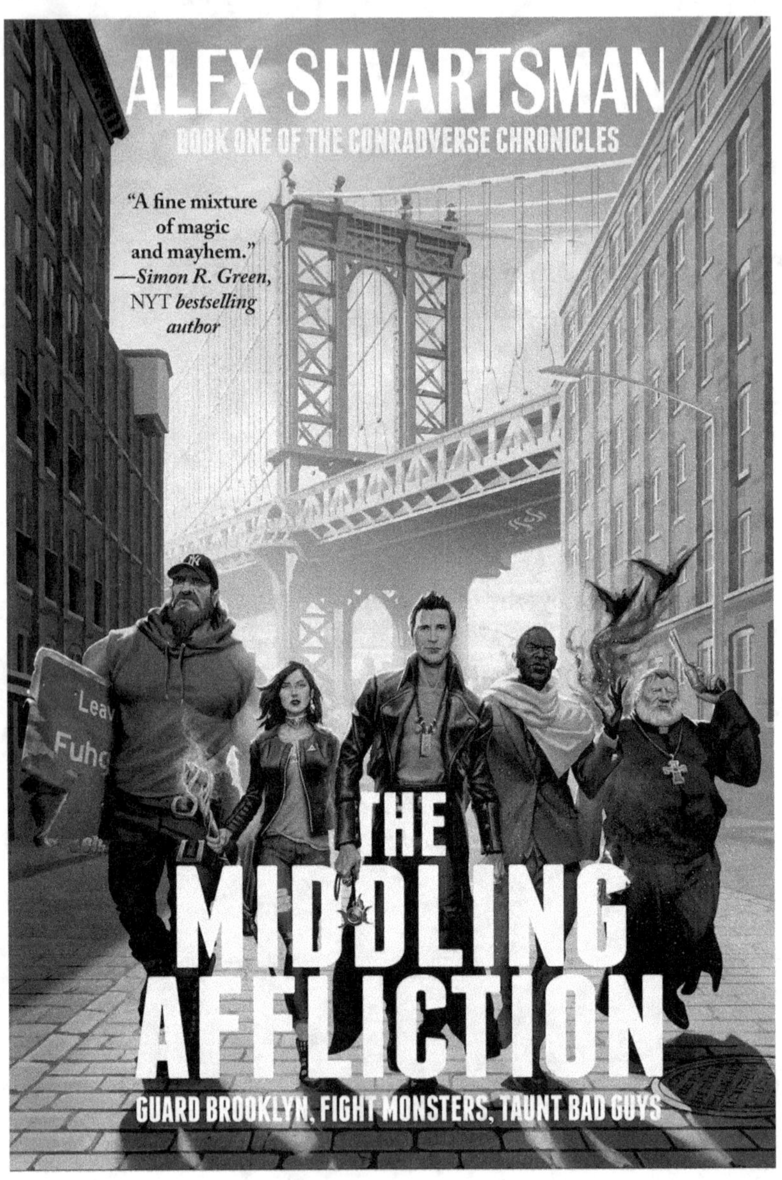

MY JOB that morning was to banish a demon, but I was determined to finish my cup of coffee first.

I sipped my java in front of Demetrios's warehouse in Sunset Park, enjoying the panoramic view of the Manhattan skyline and the New York harbor. I stared at the Statue of Liberty, which appeared the size and shade of a toy soldier at this distance. A warm breeze caressed my face. Next to me, Demetrios was shaking like a leaf.

"What in the world are you thinking, Conrad?" Demetrios spoke in his typical rapid-fire fashion. "You're just going to go in there, alone, to face this infernal thing? Without any help or backup from others at the Watch? Without even a priest? This is all kinds of crazy."

"I can handle it," I said, projecting casual confidence. "You did ask for this to be resolved quickly, and it's not like I haven't dealt with an occasional demon before."

In fact, I'd never even seen any demons. I was not in any way whatsoever equipped to deal with a supernatural being of that magnitude. That was the bad news. The good news was, in my two decades with the Watch, I'd never once heard of a demon showing up in Brooklyn. Even if one arrived, it wouldn't be slumming in Demetrios's warehouse. And if, by some miracle, a major baddie from Down Below decided to take up residence there, Demetrios wouldn't have survived the encounter long enough to come crying for my help. Something else was going on, but if the guy with the thick checkbook expected the job to be extremely dangerous, who was I to dissuade him?

"Quickly, yes," said Demetrios. "You wouldn't believe how far this has made us fall behind with the deliveries. My customers are screaming bloody murder. On top of everything, there's a shipment of Sumatran persimmons that is already beginning to rot. I hope you really know what you're doing. I don't relish the thought of having to scrape what's left of you off the container walls."

"That's the Demetrios I know and love. Sentimental to the

end. Here, hold this." I handed him the empty foam cup and headed for the entrance.

The warehouse was packed with every kind of package and crate imaginable. The huge metal shipping containers were clustered in the center, with just enough room left to maneuver them in and out. Around the edges, mountains of smaller parcels occupied every available nook and cranny, arranged in an order apparent only to Demetrios and his staff.

I primarily knew Demetrios as a wholesale trader in magical goods, but that was only a fraction of his business. Metal racks in his warehouse were crammed with imports, everything from Ecuadorian melons to Taiwanese vacuum cleaners. The place looked like the world's most overstocked Costco. There were plenty of nooks for whatever was haunting the building to hide in.

I walked past a tower of knock-off toys destined for dollar store shelves. Boxes labeled *Tackle Me Emo* and *Hangry Hangry Hipsters* stretched toward the warehouse ceiling atop the sturdy foundation of cases of Poke-a-Moon cards. A pungent odor of rotting fruit wafted through the aisles.

Since I didn't know what sort of trouble to expect, I brought as many weapons, charms, and amulets as I could carry without making my reliance on such tools apparent. I've made a lot more enemies than friends over the years and having any of them learn that I was powerless without my trinkets would be incredibly dangerous.

Only one out of every thirty thousand people is born gifted. They can perceive auras, recognize supernatural beings for what they are, cast spells, and imbue their magic into artifacts by enchanting physical items the way batteries store electricity. I could perceive perfectly; casting was another story. I could use up stored magic as well as any gifted but could never recharge the metaphysical battery of even the simplest of charms. In a secret world filled with superheroes and supervillains, I was the magical Batman: a grumpy and possibly somewhat unhinged vigilante with no special powers, who relied on his gadgets to keep up with the Super-Joneses. Except I didn't have Batman's riches, or a mansion, or even a butler. Them's the breaks.

Not even my superiors at the Watch knew about my disability. They wouldn't have kept me around—possibly with extreme prejudice—if they ever found out. So, I pretended to be a badass wizard and did my job well, giving no one cause to think otherwise. One day I hoped to find a cure for my condition. Or, failing that, a damn good explanation for it.

I worked my way through the labyrinth of packages until I heard faint growling sounds emanating from a few aisles over. I unholstered a revolver which was loaded with silver bullets doused in holy water. Cliché, I know, but in my experience only the most effective solutions get to become clichés in the first place. Weapon drawn, I advanced slowly toward the noise. I turned the corner of a ceiling-high shelving unit stocked with waffle makers and found myself face to face with a Lovecraftian nightmare.

The creature resembled a ten-foot-tall bulldog with several rows of jagged teeth protruding from its oversized mouth. It stared at me with cold fish eyes and emitted a low rumble from deep within its ugly-as-sin belly. I breathed a sigh of relief as I studied the telltale shimmer barely visible around the critter's frame. Definitely not a demon.

"Nice doggie," I told it as I holstered the gun and rummaged through the inner pockets of my trench coat. Moving very slowly so as not to spook it, I withdrew a plastic pill bottle filled with orange powder.

"Cujo wants a treat?" I asked in a soothing voice as I struggled momentarily with the childproof cover.

Visibly annoyed with my apparent lack of desire to run away

terrified, the critter let out a thunderous roar that, I hoped, Demetrios could hear outside. While it was busy posturing, I took a pair of quick steps forward and flung the contents of the pill bottle, aiming for its midsection.

The monstrous visage quivered, gradually losing its shape, and blinked out. At my feet lay a furry little animal that looked like an ugly koala bear. It was knocked out cold by the sleeping powder. The Sumatran changeling snoring on the ground before me was a harmless creature. Its species projects images of big, scary monsters in order to repel predators, but they're all bark and no bite. Poor thing must've gotten into the persimmon shipment and munched the long journey away, happy in the container full of its favorite snacks. The potent orange mix would keep the changeling dormant until I could get it to a buddy of mine at the Bronx Zoo who cared for a menagerie of supernatural animals.

I checked the rest of the building to make sure there were no more changelings. Also, just to be nosy. Demetrios's shipping company handled arcane imports from all over the globe, and I was always curious to know what he was up to, even if I had to search past the pallets of slow cookers and shelves filled with auto parts to find anything noteworthy. After a sufficient amount of time spent wandering the aisles I took off my trench coat and wrapped it gently around the changeling. Carrying the bundle under my arm, I exited the warehouse.

"That was one nasty hellspawn." I smiled at Demetrios, who was pacing nervously outside. "See, it even made me break a sweat."

"Is the demon gone now? Did you banish it?" he demanded.

"It will not be bothering you again," I said with utmost confidence.

Magical items don't come cheap, and given my unique situation I burned through them faster than an average teenage girl used up her cell phone battery. Demetrios would pay me handsomely for a morning's work, and all it cost me was a vial of sleeping powder. What's more, he would tell anyone who cared to listen about how I went one-on-one with a demon and won. So grows the legend of Conrad Brent.

I glanced at the check he handed me and frowned. "You seem to have left off a zero."

With the infernal threat gone, Demetrios was quickly recovering his wits. "It's what I've always paid you," he said. Was that a note of annoyance I detected in his voice?

"Some jobs are easier than others," I said. "And while you can't put a price tag on a quality exorcism, you should at least *try*. Because, believe me, you don't want to be calling your exterminator next time you find yourself in this sort of a predicament."

I'm not a greedy man, but money is a useful resource and you wouldn't believe what some people charge for top-grade arcane artifacts. Haggling over the bill was yet another problem Batman didn't have to deal with.

Demetrios crossed his arms. "You're getting more than most people earn in a month."

Sensing a losing battle, I changed tactics. "I'm just as happy to be paid the balance in information. You hear all sorts of things that might be of interest to the Watch."

His wallet safe for the moment, Demetrios relaxed. He scratched his chin, pretending to think, even though we both knew he could rattle off a dozen factoids about the illicit goings-on around the city if he wanted to.

"The Kwan brothers are back in town," he said. "They're trying to offload a shipment of cursed coins—"

"Yes, my associates in Manhattan are already on it," I said. Inability to tell a demon from a changeling aside, Demetrios was no fool. The Kwans were his competitors—sort of, they weren't really in the same league—and having the Watch take them out would benefit him. "Tell me something I don't already know."

"There's a new high-end fortuneteller in Williamsburg," said Demetrios. "Bilking the mundanes and making waves. I can track down his name and address—"

I waved him off again. "If the only thing getting hurt is their bank account, I don't really care."

The Watch has one very specific mandate: to protect the mundanes. Any conflict between magic users, no matter how bloody, is outside our purview, which is perhaps a good thing given our limited numbers. We focus on defending the most vulnerable. Vampires treating the New York City subway system as their personal cafeteria? Werewolves in Central Park? Wizards using mind control to entice baseball fans to root for the Mets? We come down on them like a ton of supernatural bricks. But we don't care about tarot readers.

Demetrios thought for a moment before offering up another tidbit. "The Traveling Fair is coming to Queens next Friday."

Now *that* was interesting. The Traveling Fair was an exclusive auction house, sort of a magical Sotheby's. They dealt in high-end arcane items and weren't too particular about how dangerous their wares might be or whose hands they would end up in, so long as the buyer could afford the tab. They set up private pop-up events in places like New York, Paris, London, and Tokyo. Attendance was strictly by invitation, and only the invited bidders knew where and when the auction would take place. That helped with security, and to keep the unwashed masses away. Frankly, I was surprised someone like Demetrios knew about it. He must've been on the lowest rung of the invitees and even so, doing better financially than I had suspected. And yet he had the temerity to argue over my payment!

"What sort of outrageously overpriced crap is on offer this time?"

Demetrios fished out a folded postcard from his wallet.

The card was printed on fancy, thick stock and embroidered with the logo of the Traveling Fair. It was a crest or a minor Romanian baron, hinting at the Fair's humble origins two centuries ago.

"Let's see." Demetrios squinted at the cursive font. "They've got a da Vinci manuscript outlining his views on arcane weather manipulation, an Etruscan ring of invisibility, and a mudlark."

I was so stunned I nearly dropped the changeling I still held bundled in my trench coat. "A *what*lark?"

"Oh, I'm sorry. That's the term they used, but mudlarks known by many other names, such as middlings or voids. It's a person who can perceive magic but is impotent to create it."

Of course, I knew what he was talking about. I *was* what he was talking about. A middling. A mudlark. A scavenger. There were a plethora of terms for a person like me, none of them flattering. But I'd never met another, nor knew of another who was alive. As best I could tell, while the gifted appeared roughly once among every thirty thousand humans, the odds of a middling were well north of one in a million. And the smart ones were hiding.

I couldn't express any of those things, so instead I just said, "Jesus, why would anyone want to buy a middling?"

"They're anathema to many of the traditionalist groups," Demetrios said, looking at me like I was an infant who needed really simple things explained to him, slowly. "Some will pay good money for a chance to kill a middling."

No kidding. There were cults and covens and secret societies whose members would be all over something like that. The Salem witch trials were all about finding and exterminating a single middling who was rumored to be hiding in that insignificant little town. As far as I knew, there was no actual middling. They did manage to hang several real witches, though.

It weren't just the crazy cultists. Superstition against the middlings ran deep within the gifted society. The Watch wouldn't protect them as they weren't considered mundane, despite their lack of innate ability. Early in my career I had spent sleepless nights trying to figure out who among my colleagues might try to kill me if they ever learned the truth.

I was showing too much interest in the subject and needed to backpedal. "I suppose there are people and eccentric enough to throw money away on all kinds of nonsense. The ring of invisibility though, that's something I could actually use."

"You don't seriously think you could afford the winning bid on it, do you, Conrad?"

I looked him in the eye. "Perhaps if you paid me a fair wage for demon-slaying I could."

That deflated Demetrios pretty good.

"Tell you what," I said. "Hand over the invitation and we'll call it even. I may not be able to afford the ring, but I'd enjoy window-shopping. And rubbing shoulders with all sorts of interesting people. Could make a load of useful connections, meet clients willing to pay top dollar for my services."

For all its power and influence, the Watch was a volunteer organization. It was more a neighborhood watch, as the name implied, than a police department. Its members had to earn their own living, which meant getting people like Demetrios to pony up the cash for services rendered. But I was also expected —and willing—to hunt monsters and bust ghosts pro bono when necessary. As such, my excuse for wanting to attend the Traveling Fair should have sounded reasonable. When Demetrios hesitated I added, "Come on. It's not like *you* are going to bid on any of those things."

He sighed theatrically and handed over the invitation. I said my goodbyes and deposited the changeling onto the back seat of my car. At some point I'd have to drive it to the Bronx, and then figure out how to rescue a fellow middling from a bunch of bloodthirsty fat cats. But all of that would have to wait. I had a packed schedule, and my day was only starting.

I was going to need a lot more coffee.

The Middling Affliction is available in print, ebook, and audiobook formats from Caezik SF&F and OrangeSky Audio. *Kakistocracy*, book two of The Conradverse Chronicles, is scheduled to be published in 2023.